P. F. Davids

Acknowledgments

Thank you to my proofreaders, Tim, Steven, and Matt, without who my work would still be a big mess.

Thanks to my editor, Carley Scott, for her time and patience working with a stubborn author like myself.

And thanks to my brother, JJ, for believing in me enough to make this book a possibility.

Prologue

D
emos peered around the corner. More bodies littered the room ahead, stripped bare with faces twisted in agony, signs of horrible mutilation all over. It was a disturbing sight, enough to make the veteran cringe. He breathed a guilty sigh of relief. They were heading the right way. There were no guards about. Their presence had not yet been noticed.

Outside, a battle was raging on. The torture chamber echoed with the sounds of shouting, the clashing of steel, the thunderous blasts of cannons. The desperate struggle sounded with eerie clarity, as if to remind them of what was at stake.

"I suppose this is where he entertains his company." Ottone strutted into the chamber. He looked unimpressed by the scene of depravity. "Somehow makes me glad I never got an invitation."

"Is now the time for your idiotic jests?" Colette barked. Her face was twisted in disgust as she eyed their surroundings.

Ottone smiled brightly. "As long as it bothers you, it's the perfect time."

Demos chose to ignore his companions. They were always arguing about one thing or another, but could be counted on to work together when it mattered.

"The throne room is right above us," Demos said. "But we have a few passages to go through to get there from here. Keep an eye out for patrols."

Ottone spun around and mockingly looked about the room. Only the unblinking dead looked back. "Serpentine's got everyone outside fighting. I doubt there's a single soldier left in this entire palace."

"That's the idea, anyway," Colette said. "Assuming the Church can keep this assault up long enough. If they call the retreat, we're left to die."

They all knew that everything relied on how long the forces of the Church of True Light and their allies could hold out. They had launched a desperate assault on the city, one that they could not possibly hope to win. It was a diversion, the desperate maneuver of a people out of options. They marched on the city's walls to draw out the guards so that Demos's team could move unnoticed. Through the sewers, into an old service entrance, and up to the throne room, where they could finally face off with the one responsible for all this madness.

It was a huge burden. The fate of their church, of all of Kassia, fell upon them. For anyone else it would be too much, but Demos and his companions had a reputation for achieving the impossible. They had turned the course of the Battle of Bigasti almost single-handedly by getting behind the enemy's lines and slaying their commanding officers. In North Wietrap, they brought hope to the people by clearing the barricades blocking supply routes. With each accomplishment their legends grew.

Perhaps I shouldn't have allowed my reputation to spiral so dramatically out of control. It was a thought Demos had been having frequently ever since he had received this assignment. *No going back now.*

"Ottone," Demos said, pointing to the lock on the door that barred their way forward.

"On it."

The nimble little man pulled out a small set of tools from under his cloak and went to work on the lock. Demos could see the concentration in his sharp eyes, a focus that seemed out of place compared to his perpetually disheveled appearance: wild, dirty blond hair, unkempt beard stubble, and dirt-stained cloak.

As Ottone worked, Demos could not help but take another look at the bodies spread around the torture chamber. He wondered how many of them had been friends. *How many of them did I fight side by side with just weeks ago?*

There was a low click from the door. "That should do it," Ottone declared. He cracked the door open slightly and peered inside, then made a motion that the passage in front of them was clear.

Demos went through first. He made his best effort to move carefully and quietly, but he knew he was still making a considerable ruckus. It was unavoidable dressed head to toe in mail. In a moment of caution he'd had the insignia of the Church removed from his armor and replaced with the blood-red insignia of their enemy. If he was discovered it may cause their enemy to hesitate and grant him the advantage. It would be a very brief advantage, as Demos's golden hair, light blue eyes, and fair skin were dead giveaways that he did not belong here.

There was a sound up ahead. Demos raised his hand to signal

the group to pause. Beside him, Colette had nocked an arrow and taken aim at the passageway ahead. It was near pitch black and anyone coming down the hall wouldn't be seen until they got close. Demos held his breath and silently prayed. *Please, we cannot be discovered yet.* The sound faded away. When he was sure they were clear Demos motioned for them to continue.

They continued down several twisting passages, Colette signaling which direction to take at every intersection. She had spent the last week huddled over every map of the palace and the surrounding area she could get a hold of. The libraries were a waste of time— they had been stripped of everything useful — but with Colette's talents that had hardly presented a problem. There were few among the palace guards who were loyal enough to not abandon their posts when asked for a drink with a buxom, red-headed beauty. From there it was a simple matter of putting too many drinks in them and using the right words, and the maps were hers.

"Are you sure we're going the right way?" Ottone whispered. "I swear we've passed this section of bland, dark hallway before."

Colette didn't respond. She stopped the group and pointed upwards. Demos felt along the ceiling until he felt cool air coming through from above. This was the trap door they were looking for. He swiftly pushed it open and climbed through.

They were now in a small hidden compartment behind the throne room. In old times, when the palace had first been constructed, it had served as a place for the noble family to hide during times of political turmoil. The layers of undisturbed dust were testament to how many years the room had been forgotten.

"He's right in the next room," Demos whispered.

Ottone found the lever that would move the wall aside, opening them up to the throne room where the final battle would take place. He looked at Demos and waited for the order.

This is it. Light protect me.

He nodded and Ottone pulled the lever. The wall came down all at once, much quicker than Demos had expected. He squinted as they were greeted by the light of the throne room.

Demos heard the strings of dozens of bows being pulled taut. They were completely surrounded, almost immediately. More archers than he could count filled the balcony overlooking the throne room and had taken aim, just waiting on the order to fire. Soldiers dressed in

Serpentine red lined the walls to his left and right, weapons at ready. And directly in front of him, in the center of it all, he stood.

Marcus Serpentine.

The man responsible for the war. The man whose legions had already decimated and conquered half the continent. The man responsible for untold death and suffering. The man they had come to kill stood before him, mere feet away.

"I'm impressed." Serpentine spoke in a soft but clear voice. "I honestly thought it would take you much longer. Obviously there are some holes in my home's security that I must still work out. Never mind that, I'm sure I will have little trouble tracing the path you took here."

Demos' mind went blank with confusion. *How could this have happened?*

"Bastard knew we were coming," Colette growled.

A smile grew across Serpentine's pallid face. "Of course I did. You are only here by my leave, after all."

Demos was struck with the weight of Serpentine's words. "We were set up."

"Not all the men in the Church are as righteous as you." Serpentine spoke in no hurry, relishing the moment. "You were becoming a thorn in my side, so I arranged to deal with you and the Church in one swing. The battle outside will be a great victory, but the one in this room shall be sweeter."

"I don't suppose this is the part where you offer us our lives in exchange for working for you?" Ottone asked. "Because that would probably be a pretty tempting offer right about now."

Serpentine chuckled and shook his head. "I'm afraid not. No offense intended, but you lack a certain quality that I'm looking for."

Ottone shrugged his shoulder. "It doesn't hurt to ask."

Beside him, Demos saw that Colette shaking with rage. They had worked together long enough for him to know what was going on in her mind. She was going to die here, that much was for certain, but she refused to die in vain.

In a single motion so quick that Demos's eyes could barely catch it, Colette had nocked and arrow and sent it flying at Serpentine. For a moment, Demos felt his hopes lift.

The arrow was mere inches from his body when the head deflected, the shaft cracking and shattering as if it had hit a solid wall.

Colette froze as she realized her attack had failed.

Serpentine lightly kicked the arrow's remains with the tip of his shoe. "Not a bad shot. Let's compare."

No! Demos's sword was drawn in an instant and he charged at Serpentine with all the speed he could muster. There was the sound of arrows rushing through the air followed by stabs of fresh pain all over his body. Demos dropped to one knee. Not far from him Ottone and Colette fell to the ground. Pools of blood began to form.

Demos did not know how many arrows had struck him, but the searing pain and warmth of blood told him that some had pierced his armor straight through. Still, he refused to let himself fall. With a great force of will he got back to his feet and slowly started limping towards Serpentine, sword in hand. *Just a little more. Just a few more steps and one strike. Light give me strength.* His vision blurred and every breath he drew sent fresh pain through his body like knives, but he kept his focus on Serpentine.

"You still want to fight?" Serpentine asked with an amused chuckle. "Very well."

He motioned for one of his men to hand him a sword. Walking slowly up to the mortally wounded Demos he smiled, showing just how much he was enjoying this victory. *Keep smiling. I've got strength in me yet.* Demos swung his sword at Serpentine with every ounce of strength he had left. Serpentine blocked it effortlessly. Demos swung again and again but his attacks were slow and weak, and Serpentine was able to easily parry or sidestep them. He made no effort to attack back. He merely waited for blood loss to win this fight for him.

He only waited moments. Demos was unable to keep up his assault. His head spun and the corners of his vision went dark. He coughed blood violently onto the floor, arrows making him bleed inside. Despite all his effort he couldn't force his body to stand any longer. His sword hung loose from his hand and then dropped beside him. He fell to his hand and knees, shaking.

"Is that all?" Serpentine asked. "I was just starting to enjoy our little sparring match."

"This is not the end, Marcus," Demos spoke through bloody lips. "Not for those who would stand against you."

"Is that so?"

"You will never win. Not as long as there are those who are willing to take a stand to -"

A sharp pain in the back of the neck and the floor rushing toward him were the last things Demos felt. Then the world went dark.

Marcus Serpentine pulled his sword out of the back of Demos' neck. After a few guttural whimpers the man was dead. "Quite enough of that. The dying speeches of heroic types are always the same. You hear one, you've heard them all." He tossed the sword aside and gestured at the body. "Someone get this mess cleaned up. I don't like this much blood in my throne room."

Several of his men ran by him to carry the would-be assassins away. As they left, they paused and moved aside to give a large berth to an imposing man in black platemail as he clattered into the room. Serpentine took his place on his throne before addressing the commander of his city's defenses.

"Kasimir, how does the fighting progress?"

"The battle outside goes as expected," the giant replied. His voice echoed inside his helmet. "The Church's retreat will come at any moment."

"Very good. We will follow their retreat all the way back to the Grandium and set it ablaze. Give them no quarter, no mercy. Take no prisoners, let none escape, and don't cease until every last one of them is dead."

Kasimir nodded and left to deliver the orders. Serpentine ordered his men to resume their regular duties. The room emptied of everyone, save his personal guard.

"I really wish you wouldn't take such risks," said the ugly little man pacing next to his throne. "The trap did not call for you to actually be here."

"And miss seeing Demos die with my own eyes?" Serpentine replied, shaking his head. "You know the rumors circulating about him, Ragnar. They said he was destined by the Light to kill me. If that was true, who was I to argue with divinity?"

"There are some who consider *you* a god." A smirk broke out across Ragnar's disgusting face.

The emperor couldn't help but smile with amusement. "Now, you know I've never made that claim myself. But everyone is entitled their beliefs. I certainly would not want to deny anyone their faith."

"Except followers of the Church of True Light."

"They brought this fate upon themselves."

"They moved in the wrong direction," Ragnar agreed.

Serpentine opened a hidden compartment beneath his throne and removed a bottle of fine wine and two glasses. He poured himself one and offered Ragnar the other. He would leave the rest of the battle for his officers to command. Tonight, he would drink and celebrate.

Chapter 1

'Willer' was the term given for those born with the rare ability to control the world around them through pure force of will. It manifested itself in different ways through different people: one person might have the power to push things with his mind, another might be able to produce flames from thin air. These abilities were typically minor, considered to be of little more use than a performer's trick. A very small number of people ever learned to control their ability with any proficiency.

It was the hunt for one such Willer that had brought Colonel Bialas Foreworth to this abandoned town. He had seen, and been personally responsible for, many terrible acts over the course of the war, but even he felt something of a chill when walking through this ghost town. The town of Alleways, once a bustling merchant center, was now unsettlingly silent and still. The town had been abandoned several years ago, but looked as if it had been occupied only yesterday. Signs on the doors of some shops proclaimed them open. Through the windows he could see that the homes were comfortably furnished and had a lived-in quality. In one home a table was set, as if the family living there was about to sit down for a meal. It seemed as if everyone had just vanished one day, right into thin air.

According to the information he had received in nearby settlements, the people of Alleways had to evacuate all of a sudden during the war, when it was predicted that a battle was about to take place there. They grabbed only what they could carry on their backs and fled to neighboring villages at a moment's notice. When the war shifted courses and the town was spared, the townspeople had returned to find a terrifying presence occupying it in their absence.

The Alleway Mansion, a towering behemoth at the outskirts of town, had been empty for generations. At one point in the town's history it had served both as a hospital and as a home for a prominent family of doctors. At some point, the head of the family had lost his mind and poisoned several patients, his family, and himself. Since then, the place had been abandoned and treated with distrust by the townspeople.

When the townspeople returned after the averted battle, they saw lights coming from the old mansion, and heard horrible, unexplainable sounds. It caused enough of a scare that the town was abandoned completely, the townspeople too afraid to even return for their things.

Bialas and his men were coming to the gate of this very mansion now. It was many times bigger than any of the other homes in the area and seemed out of place amongst the quaint homes around it. It appeared to be in a horrible state of disrepair. The wood was rotting, the courtyard had been taken over by weeds, and the roof no longer seemed stable. It was curious that anyone would live here. But their scouts were certain that this was where his target resided.

"The town is secure," the lieutenant informed him. The lieutenant, Nikolai, was the pasty-faced son of some merchant. He was competent enough, but always looked as if he expected a treat just for doing his job. "We've checked in all the buildings, there's no one around."

"We can see a light coming from somewhere inside," one of his soldiers added. The bald one. Rank and file soldiers were as interchangeable as grains of sand and Bialas had no intention of learning any of their names. Instead he distinguished them by physical characteristic. The bald one was a reliable scout and tracker.

Bialas allowed himself a satisfied smirk. It was always nice when things were simple. "Then it would appear our information is accurate. We can assume he lives alone. Be prepared to move in, on my order."

He didn't really know what to expect from the target. This man had reportedly been living by himself in this mansion for years. It was his presence that had kept the people of Alleways away. He was rarely seen in person, only venturing out when he made his trips to a nearby village to buy food and supplies. No one knew what it was that he did all alone in this mansion, or what caused all the strange sounds that came from it, but few were willing to find out.

Bialas pushed open the rusted gates and led his men towards the mansion. He looked down in distaste at the weeds as he crossed the courtyard. They came up to his waist in some places. He took pride in keeping his uniform in pristine condition: his black pants firmly pressed, his gray shirt free of even the tiniest stains, and the insignia of the empire — a sword floating in a blood-red ocean — looking as new as the day he got it. He was sure his pants were getting disgusting stains on them as he walked through the weeds. They would require work to get clean.

He banged on the thick wooden door. After waiting a moment and knocking again, he was satisfied that no one was coming to answer it. He reached for the handle and found the door unlocked. Letting himself in, he ordered his men to follow close. Bialas found the interior a stark contrast to the mansion's external appearance. Everything was clean and in good repair. The place was well furnished and decorated as well. If he had not seen it from the outside he would have assumed that nobility lived here.

Coming down the central stairway was a tall, slender man with dark eyes and darker hair. He was wearing black, loose-fitting clothes that looked expensive. His clothes combined with the gentle way he walked and his youthful face to make him look like some spoiled kid sprung from wealth. Only the sword sheathed at his side and the way he kept one hand on it at all times broke this illusion.

"Reis Beldaken?" Bialas asked, already fully knowing the answer.

"I am," the man responded. "And who might you be, invading my home without invitation?"

"I am Colonel Bialas Foreworth, here representing the interests of the Serpentine Empire. We've come here to offer you a chance to put your unique talents to use in the name of Marcus Serpentine."

Reis reached the bottom of the stairs and eyed the new arrivals. Bialas was sure he was sizing them up and determining his chances should this come to swords. Bialas was not concerned. Reis was outnumbered, surrounded by Lieutenant Nikolai, the bald one, the fat one, the tall one, and the one with the ridiculous beard. Nikolai had assured him that they were each skilled and capable. Even if the legends involving Reis were true, he could not possibly stand against six trained soldiers of the Empire. Maybe one or two of his men would die, but they were replaceable.

"Is it the policy of the empire to come out in force when extending a job offer?" Reis asked, coldly.

"Special circumstances."

"Why don't you explain them to me?"

Bialas could see his soldiers were getting anxious in their positions, hands at their weapons, waiting for Reis to take one aggressive step. Reis had been described as 'incredibly dangerous' and 'violent,' and was only to be approached with extreme caution. Bialas's men might be dumb as rocks, but even they were not willing to take any chances.

"We are aware that you are a Willer."

Reis's expression changed to what Bialas thought might be surprise, but it was only brief moment before returning to stony and cold.

"Did you also learn my favorite color?"

"You have quite a storied history before you went into seclusion," Bialas explained. "Drug trade, assassination, even taking on the Church. Those kind of stories don't go away just because you wish to disappear, and they tell quite a bit about you."

"All I wished for was some privacy, to be left alone. Wanting to disappear had nothing to do with it. Apparently that was too much to ask." Reis turned to walk back up the stairs. "You can tell your superiors that I declined, respectfully. My work keeps me far to busy, I have no time to be a dog of the empire."

Reis paused at the sound of swords being drawn.

"I'm afraid you don't understand." Bialas motioned to the men around him. "As I said, these are special circumstances. Orders came down right from Emperor Marcus Serpentine. All Willers are to be tracked down. They are to be given the choice to swear loyalty to the empire and come work on a special project. Those who refuse are to be killed. No exceptions."

Reis did not move a muscle. He just stood silently, facing the stairs, his back to Bialas.

"I'll give you one chance to change your mind and accept our very generous offer."

"You're making a big mistake." Reis's tone sent a chill down Bialas's spine. "And, frankly, you've wasted enough of my time. I've been more than generous in putting up with it until now. You can leave now and this will all be forgotten, or I will kill you all."

"You're hardly in any position to be making threats."

Reis turned and drew his sword.

"My patience is through."

Before Bialas even had a chance to shout an order Reis was moving. With a sudden motion he sprung to his right, sword out for the thrust. Before the fat one even had a chance to raise his sword in defense he was pierced right through, Reis's blade penetrating his armor as if it was made of paper. Reis removed his sword and blood poured from the wound. He staggered for a moment before falling to the floor.

Bialas had taken a step back from the sudden display of aggression, but his men were moving. The remaining soldiers were now closing, cautiously, on Reis, trying to flank him all on sides. Reis made no effort to avoid falling into the middle of this formation. He was remaining absolutely still and silent. The only sound coming from him was the drip of fresh blood from his blade.

The soldiers were close now, just barely out of striking range. They looked around at one another, as if to dare each other to step forward first. The lieutenant gestured forward, and in the next moment the group of them lunged at Reis with their swords.

Reis burst forward with his blade ahead of him. It clashed with the sword of the soldier directly in front of him, the bald one, and the strength behind the attack forced the soldier to scramble back just to avoid being knocked on his ass. The others found that their assault had fallen short of their target and moved in for another attack, but it was too late for the bald one. With his next strike Reis had cut him across the middle, from his right shoulder to his left hip. A bloody pile that had once been the soldier collapsed in front of him.

"Damn it! Watch his movements!" Nikolai barked. "He strikes quickly and then darts away. Keep together! And someone use your damn sword!"

Nikolai hadn't even finished the last sentence when Reis burst forward again. This time the lieutenant was his target, but Nikolai was quick and met Reis's sword with his own. Strange-beard tried to strike at Reis from behind, making use of the small window of opportunity while Reis was engaged. In that instant Reis span around, his sword slicing through the air around him as he swung. Strange-beard's hand was caught by the blade as he was in mid-swing, severing it in half. His sword fell to the ground; then, in pain and agony, he followed it as blood squirted from where his fingers had once been.

Nikolai had managed to avoid Reis's blade and came in close for his own strike. He struck high, trying to land a blow across Reis's upper body. Reis side-stepped quickly, but the attack grazed him, leaving a light trail of blood across his left side. The lieutenant struck again, but Reis deflected the blow with his own sword.

Reis and Nikolai became locked in an exchange of strikes and parries. Nikolai was able to hold his own in the confrontation, but Bialas could see that he was outclassed. Reis's attacks were coming closer and closer to landing a serious hit. Several had already scraped across his face and forearms. The lieutenant was backing up slowly, trying to get some distance between himself and Reis's blade. Soon he would be backed into a wall.

Bialas knew he should have drawn his own weapon already. He should have rushed to Nikolai's aid. But his body wouldn't respond. The way Reis moved, the way his expression didn't change as he struck and blood splattered around him, that stony countenance of his that did not break even when he was cut, it filled Bialas with an emotion he had not known since joining the Empire.

Terror.

When Bialas had been gathering information on Reis Beldaken there had been a word that had consistently been used to describe him. *Demon.* Bialas had thought it had just been the exaggerations of ignorant farmers and old men whose only pastime was to spread tales, but now he understood. Reis was no mere man.

The last standing soldier, the tall one, came at Reis from behind. Reis was forced to turn to deflect the attack and, with a swift kick to the gut, knocked the soldier backwards. He turned again to meet the lieutenant but couldn't deflect the next attack in time. It cut into his left shoulder, leaving a deep, bloody wound. Despite this, Reis didn't show any signs of slowing down. He clashed swords with Nikolai, then countered the next blow with a hard strike of his own, knocking the lieutenant off balance.

The tall one was coming at him from behind again. This time Reis was ready for it. He turned and cut the soldier across his chest.

Nikolai had regained his balance and raised his sword. Reis was already facing him, the body of the tall one crumpling behind. Reis rushed at Nikolai, swinging with powerful, wild blows. Nikolai did all he could to deflect the attacks but the strikes were hitting his own sword with such force that it was almost forced out of his grip. After a few swings Nikolai could only watch in horror as his sword was knocked aside, leaving him open to Reis's final thrust. The sword pierced him through the stomach and out his back. He stood in shock and agony for a long moment before Reis removed his sword. Nikolai fell dead to the ground.

Bialas had backed himself all the way to the door. He had watched in horror as all five of his men were slaughtered by this one man. This man who was not a man. He fought like a demon, oblivious to both pain and fear. Bialas knew he needed to get out of here. He turned around to reach for the door handle.

But it wasn't there. There was no door handle. There wasn't even a door.

In place of where the door had been just minutes before there was just blackness. A complete, utter blackness that appeared to have consumed the door and parts of the wall around it. It seemed to Bialas like he was staring into a black void.

He turned to face Reis, who was slowly approaching him. Bialas drew his sword and shakily held it in front of him.

"What have you done?" he demanded.

"What's the matter? Isn't this what you came here for?" Reis responded. "This is the form my Will takes. Command of shadows. Useful, don't you think?"

"Stay back!"

With his back to the dark void and Reis directly in front of him, Bialas had nowhere to run. He tried to steady himself and get his sword in position to defend. He was trained in swordsmanship, but he'd always been more of a leader than a fighter. He knew he stood no chance against a monster like this.

"What do you hope to accomplish by killing me?" Bialas asked, trying in vain to keep his voice steady and commanding. "If I don't report back, they will send more. A lot more. You can stand against a few of us, but what can you hope to do against the might of the whole empire?"

Reis was still approaching him, showing no sign of concern over his words.

"They won't just forget about you, you know. You're a Willer! They won't rest until you are dead or licking the emperor's boots!"

Reis was close now, raising his sword.

"I can tell them you're dead. Let me go, I can tell them you're dead. My men died, but they got you first. You will never hear from the empire again."

Reis's sword was poised for the strike.

"Please, for the love of the Light and all things holy!"

"You're in the wrong place if you seek god's help," Reis said at last. "The Light does not shine here."

A quick slash. Bialas had no chance. Reis had slit his throat. Bialas clutched his throat and felt the warm liquid flowing from it. He gurgled and spat up blood.

Demon. That was the last thought of Colonel Bialas Foreworth.

What a nuisance. Reis sighed. The officer had been right. Undoubtedly, more imperials would come knocking. *No point worrying about it now.*

Reis turned and walked back towards the stairs. As he did, he glanced over to the soldier on the floor whose hand he had severed. The soldier had been trying desperately to crawl away but the blood loss was causing him to go into shock. His body was shaking uncontrollably and he no longer seemed to have control over his extremities. Barely pausing as he walked by, Reis shoved his sword through the soldier's neck.

As the adrenaline of the fight wore off he began to feel the pain of his wounds. The gash on his shoulder was bleeding terribly. From under his shirt he pulled out a small vial of murky, red liquid. He opened it and took a small sip. Almost immediately he felt the pain start to fade. He knew the wound on his shoulder would begin to clot and heal at a rapid pace.

He gave one last look at the room filled with bodies before mounting the stairs. He would have to deal with those mess later, he decided. Right now there was work to do.

Chapter 2

Kester Belisario sat at a long table inside the sparse chamber. Seated beside him were the upper elite and commanding officers of the Church of True Light. What was left of them, anyway. Only a field-commander, Kester was the lowest ranking officer at the table. His presence there was a sign of just how deep into their ranks the Church was reaching for leadership. Still, his experience on the front-lines gave him a level of practical experience in the arts of war that many others at this table were lacking.

"There's nowhere left for our forces to run," General Andreas declared, for the third time since they sat down. "We need to go into hiding."

Delia, the High Cleric, did not seem to appreciate the suggestion any more this time. "The Light does not hide. To suggest such is blasphemy."

Andreas slammed his hand against the table. "The last of the resistance fighters have already done so! The last kings have laid down their crowns! If we are the only ones to fight in the open we will be slaughtered down to the last man."

"The Light can not be extinguished," Delia responded, unwavering. "Only dimmed."

Laid across the table was a map of eastern Kassia, covering the land from the Eastern Sea to the Marjan mountains, which split the lands of the east and west. It was to these mountains that Andreas was now motioning, tracing his finger along a route through them.

"We can go through the mountains into Allandane. They've taken refugees from other nations that fell to Serpentine, I'm sure they would be willing to take us as well."

"The difference," Kester broke in, "is that Serpentine doesn't care about those refugees. He's following us. He won't just let our forces get away."

Andreas irritably tapped the table with his fingers. "We just need to move our forces in a way he won't expect before we make a break for the mountains. Perhaps if we-"

"Serpentine has been one step ahead of us at every turn," Kester interrupted again. "What makes you think he won't see this coming?"

Andreas smashed his hand against the table, then smacked the map out of the way. The room went silent. No one went to retrieve the map; it wasn't much use anymore. Over the course of the war it had been used to track the progress of the Serpentine army across the east. When a new region fell under his control it was shaded black on the map. Now the entire map was blackened.

Kester clenched his hands on his legs to maintain his composure. *I have to show I belong here if they are ever to listen to what I am going to propose. I cannot flinch.*

Andreas got up from the table and began to pace. He was a giant of a man, tall, broad-shouldered, muscular, with the sharp features of a soldier, though now his face was drawn and lined from worry and lack of sleep. He was still a man in his youth but the stress of this war had taken years from him.

"What would you have us do, Kester?" he finally asked. "Sit and wait for our deaths?"

Kester had an idea, but was hesitant to share it until the time was right. He had earned his spot at this table for his heroics during the fall of the Grandium. It was believed that if it had not been for his leadership during the retreat, half as many men would have survived. He led a desperate retreat, a risky split of the troops. It was a sacrificial maneuver that relied on the enemy not being able to chase them in every direction. It had been effective, but his tactics were not respected by everyone. Delia had a problem with abandoning the Grandium at all and would have rather they fought to the last man defending it. Kester's position at this table was flimsy at best, and he didn't wish to jeopardize it.

Delia scoffed. "Don't look to that coward for answers. He would have us abandon our faith completely if it would mean saving his own life."

The High Cleric was seated at the far end of the table. She was, in title, the head of the Church, but in matters concerning the Church's military arm the General had final authority. She and Andreas had been at odds for a while on how the war should be run; Delia believed that the Church should face the enemy head on and allow the guidance of the Light to lead them to victory, while Andreas believed that faith alone could not guarantee victory and took a more tactical view of the war. He agreed with Kester that abandoning the Grandium, which for centuries had served as the center for their faith, was the only choice of action against such odds. It was his recommendation to have Kester join in on this meeting.

If something was not soon done, it might be their last.

Guess it's now or never.

Kester cleared his throat and mustered his courage. "I say we don't abandon Operation Behead."

Operation Behead was their failed mission to assassinate the leader of their enemy, Marcus Serpentine. Much of the empire's power structure was centered around him and there was no clear line of succession. The Empire would likely not be able to function without his leadership. 'Cut off the head of the snake and the body shall fall,' represented the central hope of the mission.

The men who embarked on the mission were killed and their bodies were put up for display outside of Serpentine's palace. Much of the Church's military had been decimated in the battle that was supposed to provide them with the distraction they needed, and shortly after Serpentine's counterattack burned the Grandium to the ground.

The General stopped pacing long enough to meet Kester's eyes. "We don't have the force to create another distraction. Even if we had someone with the ability and willingness to go after Serpentine."

"We don't need the distraction," Kester replied. "His army is currently spread thin. The majority of his forces are still all across the north, looking for where we fled after the Grandium, and he's got more in the west fighting mountain men. He's also got troops out hunting for Willers. His palace will be guarded, but not overwhelmingly so. If we plan our route into and through the palace carefully we would face minimal resistance."

"We do still have the maps Colette acquired," one of the cardinals suggested, a wizened old man with a long, gray beard.

Kester caught the High Cleric's gaze. He thought he saw approval in her eyes. Despite his best attempts at stoicism Kester felt himself go slightly flush. Delia was the youngest High Cleric ever to take the position and was a remarkable beauty. Her deep blue eyes were piercing, and now they were fixed on Kester, causing him to lose his train of thought.

"That's the first reasonable thought I've heard all day," Delia said. "Perhaps having you here wasn't such a mistake after all."

"Do you intend to volunteer for this mission yourself?" the old cardinal asked.

Kester nodded. "I would not recommend it if I did not intend such. I would not ask another to go into such danger if I would not go myself."

"I understand your desire to prove yourself," one of the lesser clerics interjected, "but you are not Demos."

Kester felt guilt and sorrow swell up within him just from the mention of his brother. His death had come as such a shock and he never really had time to deal with it properly. He had known that Demos was making a reputation for himself as a hero of the Church, but never knew where he was or what he was doing at any given time. He had always just assumed that whatever it was he was doing, no matter how dangerous, Demos would come back alive. Kester hadn't been able to imagine anything that could kill his brother. Then one day he was told his brother was dead and that his body was on display to mock the Church. It wasn't until later that he had been filled in on the details of the mission that had taken his brother's life.

"I don't pretend that I can fill my brother's shoes, but I still think this is our best chance of stopping the empire. I think I could be invaluable in the mission."

Andreas returned to the table and allowed himself to drop heavily into his seat. "Your brother was a remarkable man. The Light truly fought alongside him. But even he failed when pitted against Serpentine. Do you believe you can succeed where he did not?"

Kester knew he wasn't a physically imposing figure. In some ways he bore resemblance to his late brother; they shared the same golden hair, light blue eyes, and fair skin. However, his brother had been almost a foot taller than he was and had a muscular, imposing physique, while Kester was more slender with a more gentle appearance. Because of this he had never been taken as seriously as a soldier as his brother was.

"Not alone, no," Kester responded. "I will need to bring with me an assassin who can operate at Serpentine's level. Someone who can think like Serpentine because he *is* like him."

He drew confused glances from everyone in the room, much as he expected. Kester took a deep breath. *Best to just say it.*

"Reis Beldaken."

Those in the room who knew that name seemed stunned by the suggestion. Others looked about curiously.

"I've never heard of him," said the youngest cardinal in the room.

The wizened old cardinal scratched his beard thoughtfully. "It was before this war with Serpentine. The Church had different enemies back then, Beldaken chief among them. The man was into some dark alchemy, if my memory serves. He once created a very potent and addictive drug that would eventually suppress the will of its users. They became his slaves and he would use them for labor and protection. We burned his lab to the ground to put a stop to it, and he responded with a campaign of burning down our churches and murdering our clerics."

"And a man like this was allowed to just walk free?" the young cardinal asked.

Kester barely contained his contempt for the accusation. "He fled from the Church's grasp and disappeared. We continued to search for him, but then Serpentine began to rise in power and priorities changed."

Andreas's eyes were fixed on Kester, as if he was trying to read something written on his face. "He's recently become the subject of a lot of talk in the empire. They say he killed Colonel Foreworth."

"Foreworth was a dark man and I am grateful that he has been put down," the High Cleric said. "But what makes you think Beldaken is the man we should now turn to?"

Kester has practiced this argument a dozen times in his mind. "Killing Foreworth has proven that he's not afraid to stand up to the empire. That alone is worth mention. But more importantly, think of how he fights, his methods. Cautious but violent, and deadly effective. No sane man would have gone against the Church alone, but he did. He always knew when to strike and when he would have been walking into a trap. When it comes to facing overwhelming odds alone, I can think of none more qualified."

"He's a wicked man who basks in the darkness and abhors the Light," one of Delia's advisers objected. "He is a man they call a demon. They say when he fights the shadows shift around him and the light recedes. I've heard stories of him being cut a dozen times but never falling. A true monster if there ever was one."

"And this is the kind of man that you would seek to aid the Light?" asked the young cardinal. "A man who has been described as a demon?"

"I agree," added the General. "It sounds as if you wish us to walk one dark path in order to vanquish another."

"He is a man of a dark path, just like Serpentine," Kester agreed.

"I believe it is because of their similarities that he would actually have a chance. Beldaken would be able to think like him, fight like him, know exactly what to expect from someone like him. In this desperate hour, I don't think we have much choice but to look for aid in unorthodox places."

There was silence as the others at the table considered what he had said. Kester could feel himself sweating. He expected at any moment to be expelled from the meeting for proposing such blasphemy.

Delia broke the silence. "Fight fire with fire. It is not the usual tactic for the Church, but then again none of the usual tactics have worked. The Light must turn to whoever it can during these times to keep shining. If we can convince Beldaken to help us he would be a strong ally."

Kester was astonished to hear her say that. He thought for sure that Delia would be the hardest to convince, not the first to his side.

"You can not be serious," Andreas protested. "Beldaken is a sworn enemy of the Church, not its ally!"

"He is also the enemy of the Empire," Delia responded. "It won't be the first alliance we've made with people who would normally be at odds with us."

"But it is obviously the most dramatic withdrawal from our values!" Andreas snapped.

"It's better than anything that you've suggested!" Delia snapped back. "Which seems to be run and do nothing!"

Andreas and Delia glared at each other from across the table. The rest of the room was silent. No one was willing to get in the middle of this confrontation.

"I suppose there is no reason to stop you, Kester," Andreas conceded, "if you wish to go see Beldaken yourself."

Kester tried to think of a reply but his mind was blank. He had been certain that he would have to fight for the idea longer, and more certain that the notion would be eventually defeated. Its quick acceptance had left him speechless.

"Then I shall make ready to travel immediately," Kester managed as he rose from the table.

"That being said," Andreas continued, beckoning Kester to wait, "the Church can not provide you much in terms of support. Gold, weapons, and armor we have plenty of, but people we do not, and while your plan is worthy, the chances of success are slim. We just can't afford to send you with a full contingent."

"I'll travel faster alone, anyway, and the infiltration of the palace would do best with fewer people."

"Take Darius with you," Delia added. "He is a seasoned warrior and will do well at your side. And may the Light guide your path."

Kester nodded his appreciation. "May it guide us all."

A few hours later Kester was almost finished loading up the saddlebags on his horse. He wasn't sure how long of a journey he was going on or when he would get a chance to procure more supplies, so he packed heavy. Thankfully, his horse was a powerful young destrier and could carry quite a bit of extra weight, even accounting for Kester in full armor.

Nearby, his escort, Darius, was doing the same. Darius had not said much since receiving his orders, just a simple "Yes, sir." Kester knew that was just Darius's way: strong and silent. They had fought side-by-side before, and Darius had been a part of the unit that Kester had led from the Grandium. He was a soldier of the Light down to his very core, bearing many scars as proof of his decorated career, but he rarely spoke, preferring to let his actions do the talking.

Kester performed a final check on his armor. It had taken a few dings and scratches in recent battles. The symbol of the Church, a light shining through the clouds of a storm, had a particularly nasty scratch running down its center. He was satisfied that there was nothing that would affect its usefulness. The scratches might actually give the armor some character.

He heard someone else entering the stables. He turned and saw the High Cleric walking towards them. He and Darius both bent a knee.

"High Cleric," Kester stammered. "I did not expect you to personally see me off."

"I'd like a moment," she said, turning to Darius. "In private, if I could."

Darius nodded his understanding and quickly left the two of them alone.

"What is the matter?" Kester asked as he rose.

"What do you think your odds are?" Delia asked. "Realistically."

Kester was was silent, trying to find the words.

Delia knew what his silence meant. "This could be the end of us. Not of the Light, of course, but of our Church. We will fight to the end, but it seems inevitable that we should meet that end soon."

"That is not yet certain. We could still -"

"Please, let me finish. It is important that the ways of our Church do not die with us."

She reached into a small pouch hidden in her dress, then placed a small key in Kester's hand. Kester gave it a puzzled glance.

"There are some archives buried beneath the Grandium," she explained. "Deep underground, caged in steel. Only a few know of its existence, so I'm confident that Serpentine's men never got to it. Inside are all the records crucial to our Church, our history, our laws, our lineage. If you return from your mission alive, only to find the rest of us are no more, the task of spreading the word of the Light will fall to you."

The tiny key suddenly felt like a leaden weight in Kester's hand. "I am not worthy of such a burden. Surely there must be someone-"

Delia raised her hand for silence. "This key once belonged to your brother. He left it with me before he went on his final mission, saying that the key should fall to you if he did not return. I wasn't sure before, but now I trust completely in his judgment."

Kester was not sure what to say. His brother, who had once called him "fragile" and recommended that he take up the life of a priest if he wanted to serve the Light because he was not fit for the military life. His brother, who had personally made sure he had been stationed in the Grandium for half his career and kept him from being able to prove himself in battle. His brother, who was always performing some heroic feat or another, but telling Kester that he would only slow him down if he was brought along. That brother had entrusted him with something of such importance?

"Keep it safe," Delia said. "And yourself as well."

With that she turned and left. Kester couldn't even muster a farewell as he watched her go. His attention turned back to the key. He stared at it and became lost in thought. *Demos. What were you thinking?* Darius's strong hand on his shoulder shook him back into reality. It was time to go.

"Alright," Kester said as he pocketed the key close to his chest. "The empire isn't just going to let Beldaken get away, but if we move straight through the nights we can beat them there. Let's go."

Chapter 3

Why did his research always seem to take two steps back for every step forward?

Reis sighed and leaned back in his chair. He tried in vain to wipe the sleepiness out of his eyes with his hands. He had worked through the night, as he often did, and had been positive, as he often was, that he was on the verge of a major breakthrough.

Well, I suppose a result is a result. Now if I could just figure out what it means.

He could feel himself getting frustrated, a familiar anger rising up inside him. It would not do. Anger had its uses. It could drive you in combat, it could motivate you to press on against rough conditions and impossible odds, it could blind you to pain and sorrow. But alchemy required a cool, logical mind. Reis closed his eyes and forced himself to take a few deep breaths.

Green and red, saved from the dead. Blue and black, a life you now lack.

The annoying little rhyme played over and over again in his head. With his eyes closed he could even see the thick spectacles of his alchemy teacher staring over him as he was forced to repeat the rhyme until it was burned into his mind. Elixirs should all turn one of those four colors.

So why the hell is it purple?

Reis opened his eyes, looking again at his unusual concoction. It was not the strangest result his experiments ever yielded, but it was certainly among the most puzzling. The color told him nothing. At least when a failed experiment turned blue or black he could get an idea of what went wrong based on the shade. But purple? That was meaningless. For all he knew, the experiment was a resounding success and he had just discovered a new type of elixir.

He raised the vial up to his nose and took a deep sniff. The smell turned out to be just as useless as the color. It smelled sour at first, but then he began to notice a distinctly salty scent. None of that made sense.

Was one of my ingredients contaminated?

He had no choice but to check all his ingredients for purity. He grumbled to himself when he thought about the amount of tedious work that would require. There was no getting around it, though. Alchemy had zero room for error. Even the smallest contaminants would cause a concoction to take on unwanted properties. Any future experiments could be compromised if he did not ensure his stock was up to quality.

Reis got up slowly from his chair behind the lab desk and stretched his legs. It was good to move around again after being cramped in the lab for so long.

He stepped out into the second floor hallway. He was greeted as always by the strong smell of sulfur from one of the rooms down the hall. For all the advances he made, he had yet to come up with a solution to stench. Fragrant candles, perfumes, even scented cloths held to his nose failed to alleviate the stench. He had grown mostly used to it by now, and fortunately it saw no use in his recent elixirs, so he had no need to smell it up close.

The doctors who had built this mansion had the clever idea to do so in two layers. There was the outer layer, which encompassed the hospital and other public areas. To separate their home from the hospital they built another layer inside it, almost a house within a house. It made sense; it helped keep their personal and business life separate. Plus, in the winter it was easier to warm just the living area as opposed to the whole mansion. When Reis had found the mansion the outer layer had already fallen to disrepair, the roof rotting, the hospital leaking, the walls seemingly near collapse. The inner layer had fared much better against the elements and Reis had been able to perform some basic repairs to get it into livable condition. He also spent quite a bit of coin procuring quality furnishings, so he could continue to live the lifestyle to which he was accustomed. As Reis walked down the hall he passed several comfortable chairs, their cushions plump and ready for him should he desire a break.

It had seemed like the perfect arrangement to him. The mansion's outwards appearance of rot and disrepair discouraged visitors and enemies alike, while inside he had all the comforts he desired. At least, until the Empire decided to pay a visit.

The pushy colonel had left Reis little choice. He would have preferred not making such a powerful enemy, but he was not about to be pressed into the Empire's service either. There would undoubtedly be consequences; the Empire knew where he lived and had surely learned of the colonel's demise by now. Reis wondered how long he would have before they came marching in force towards his home.

He would have to move on before then. It would be a pity abandoning the place he had lived in so long, but Reis was not one for sentimentality. The worse part would be abandoning his massive stock of alchemical components. Even if he hired a cart to assist him, his stock was too large to take with him and many of the ingredients would become contaminated in the process. Which is why it was so crucial for him to make some progress in what time he had left.

The first store room came up on the left. The occupants before Reis had likely used this room as a child's bedroom. Now it was filled with shelves containing jars of powders, oils, plants, preserved animal parts and insects, dried leaves and grass, solid crystal fragments. All the common alchemical ingredients, as well as some that were not so common, such as blood and gemstones.

Reis checked each container in turn. He checked the seals, smelled the contents, ran the powders through his fingers. He found no signs of contamination. He checked the next store room, and the last one down the hall. In none of his inspections did he find anything that suggested contamination.

No closer to solving this mystery.

Reis was running out of options. At this rate the only way forward would be to test the elixir, and he sure wasn't going to drink it with no idea of what it would do. He was going to need to find a 'willing' test subject.

And he knew just where to find one.

There was a small village not far north of Alleways. He sent a message to it the way he always did when he needed something, by pigeon to the village's head. He did not like traveling when he could avoid it and preferred to use pigeons to keep in touch with the outside world.

The message was short and simple:

Send one man good for cleaning. -Reis

The villages around here were all terrified of him, something Reis appreciated. A lot can be accomplished when those around you either respect or fear you. He had no doubt they would send someone immediately.

Though even he was surprised when the knock on his door came just hours later. *He must have pushed his horse hard. It's nice to have such an effect on people.*

Reis took his time to answer the door. He did a quick check to make sure his clothes were unsoiled. He did not want his reputation spoiled by something as petty as a stained tunic. He also made sure to grab his sword. He doubted he would need it, but he had learned long ago that it always paid to err on the side of caution.

He answered the door and found a short but powerfully built man waiting for him. *Must be the bravest of their bunch, to agree to come here alone.* Brave or not, the man's courage seemed to be failing him now. His eyes were wide with worry and his mouth was stupidly agape. His ugly pink flesh was covered in sweat that soaked through his clothing. Overall, he reminded Reis of a farm pig, covered in its own filth, waiting for slaughter.

"Reis ... er ... Mr. Beldaken," the pig-man stammered, "I came as you asked ... I mean, I'm here to clean." He gestured to the bucket filled with water and rags he was carrying.

"You often do women's work?" Reis asked.

"Well, no," the pig-man muttered, his face impossibly turning an even brighter shade of pink, "I'm a carpenter by trade. But, well, I figure I can clean well enough. Just tell me what needs doing."

"Fair enough. Did you happen to notice the dead bodies on the lawn?" *You must be blind if you didn't.* Reis had dragged the bodies of the colonel and his men out into his mess of a yard but had decided that concealing them was a waste of time. His superiors had probably assumed the worst when he did not report back.

The pig-man nodded meekly. "I did. If that's the kind of cleaning you meant, er, that is, if you need me to bury the bodies, I'll need to go get a shovel. But I'll be back real quick, work through the night if I have to."

"That won't be necessary. They were the Empire's dogs, if the Emperor wants them buried he can come bring his own damn shovel. No, you were right to bring a bucket. Those dogs had the nerve to bleed all over my floors. I need you to scrub that mess up."

"That's it?" the pig-man asked, relief on his face.

"That's it," Reis lied.

Reis let him in and showed him where the colonel and his men met their ends. The pig-man went to work immediately, scrubbing vigorously, his pink face straining with the effort. No doubt he was eager to be finished and gone. Reis was actually slightly impressed. *This one missed his true calling when he took up carpentry.*

The work was done quickly and the pig-man was immediately on his feet and ready to go. "If that is all, Mr. Beldaken, I'll be on my way."

"Actually, I have one more thing I need from you."

The pig-man suddenly became very still. His pink face went pale and his eyes went wide.

Reis produced a vial of his purple mystery elixir. The pig-man's eyes became fixed on it. "I need you to drink this."

"What ... what is it?" the pig-man stammered, lips quivering.

"Does that matter?"

The man looked at the vial, dumbstruck. To Reis's frustration he did not move to take it. He just stood there, still and silent. *Just a pig standing before the butcher's knife.*

"Fine," Reis conceded. "It's an elixir, alright? One of my own design. It's good for your health."

"I ... well, I feel pretty well already," the pig-man said desperately. "Never felt better."

"Can never be too healthy."

"Well ... still ... it, it's mighty generous of you, really it is. But I don't think -"

"I don't care what you think!" Reis barked. His patience was expended. "This is not a request! You will drink it!"

The pig-man glared at Reis with hard eyes. *Defiance? So this one does have some courage.* Reis tapped the sword at his side a few times, just to remind his test-subject that it was there. The look of defiance quickly faded and was replaced with the fear that Reis was accustomed to. Slowly, the pig-man reached out his hand for the vial.

He held the vial in his hand for a while, staring at it disbelief. He looked to Reis pleadingly but there was no mercy to be found there. Reis just tapped his foot impatiently and willed him to get on with it. Finally, after what seemed like ages, the pig-man removed the stopper from the vial and brought it to his lips. He closed his eyes tight and muttered something that was either a prayer or a curse before tilting the vial back and swallowing the elixir.

The man took shallow, panicked breaths as he waited for something to happen to him. Reis wished he would not panic so much. If he had a heart attack right now he would not be able to tell whether it was from the elixir or nerves.

For a moment Reis began to wonder if the elixir was having any effect at all. Suddenly his test-subject lurched over and began vomiting heavily all over the freshly cleaned floors. He clutched his stomach in pain and let out several moans.

So the body is still rejecting it. I thought for sure I had figured out the adaptation.

"Am I going to die?"

"We'll know shortly. My elixirs are quite fast-acting."

A few minutes later his test-subject seemed to be recovering. He was still breathing heavily but he had stopped moaning and was standing upright again.

"Well, looks like you're not dead, in any case," Reis said. He took a closer look at his test-subject's face. The color had not yet returned, but there was something about it that seemed different. The skin seemed slightly tighter, the bags around the eyes seemed less pronounced. *He looks a bit younger, doesn't he? Perhaps I was not so far off as I thought.*

Fresh enthusiasm coursing through him, he turned away from his test-subject, eager to get back to his experiments. "Clean up the mess you made all over my floor. Afterwards, you have my permission to leave."

Reis glanced back at the pig-man. He was glaring at him, hatred lurking in his eyes. *Ungrateful bastard. I probably just added two years to your worthless life.*

Ignorant commoners would never understand the importance of his work.

Chapter 4

K ester and Darius traveled south as quickly as they could without endangering the health of their horses. They rode straight through the night more often than not. Demos had lectured Kester early on about the importance of being able to sleep in the saddle on long campaigns. Kester had taken his brother's advice to heart and had practiced until he was proficient at it. This was the first time he had to put that training into practice and he was quickly learning that a night napping in the saddle was a poor substitute for his soft bed. He was tired, so tired. His eyelids felt like they were made from lead and the world seemed blurry and out of focus.

He could just imagine his brother riding alongside him now, mocking him. *What's wrong little brother? Is your first mission too much too much for you? Why don't you just head back. I bet it's not too late for you to become a cleric.*

He shook the thought out of his head. There were enough doubts running through his head, he did not need more from the shade of his dead brother.

Fortunately it was coming time to rest the horses, which might mean a chance to get some real rest himself. Even the cold, hard ground sounded comfortable right now. They went off the road a ways until they were well out of sight of any passing patrols. The stars were hidden behind the clouds and the world was dark. They had to lead their horses carefully through the rocky terrain. It would be no good if one of them should trip and injure themselves. They came across a decent patch of flat ground and reined in their horses. Darius fed and watered them while Kester set up a meager camp site.

"I'll take first watch," Darius said. It was the most he had said to Kester in hours.

Kester wondered if Darius was anywhere near as exhausted as he was. If he was, he didn't show it. Kester wasn't even sure if Darius slept at all when they were on the road. He was always still awake when Kester was dozing off, and already up when Kester woke. Either way, Kester felt on the verge of collapse and was not going to argue if Darius wanted to take first watch.

He laid down, wishing they could start a fire but knowing the risk of it being seen from the road was too great. It was far too dark and he was a servant of the Light. He did not worry on it long before he drifted off to sleep.

It was early the next morning when they came upon an Empire patrol. Through a carefully chosen route, avoiding any major roads, they had successfully evaded the Empire for the first half of their journey. Their path ran through farmlands, ruins, and seldom used hunters' trails. The biggest dangers along those paths were bandits, but they were unlikely to bother two heavily armed and armored travelers. This far south they had decided to gamble on taking the roads to make faster time. There was very little civilization this far to the south, just scattered villages and the occasional small town. The people were quiet and scraped out meager existences, not enough wealth to be worth taxing and not enough men of fighting age to be worth keeping a guard. The Empire had little reason to spend resources patrolling down here.

And yet here was an Empire patrol, clear as day. Darius spotted them first. They were following the road up a steep hillside and had just reached the summit when Darius grunted, "Empire." Kester looked downhill and spotted them. A dozen Empire soldiers were riding along the road near the bottom of the hill, moving along at a leisurely pace. Two of them in the front wore the uniforms of officers and rode palfreys, the others were in chain mail and were atop rounceys.

The slope of the hill kept Kester and Darius out of the sight of the patrol, at least for the moment. Kester had a bad feeling about what their presence meant for the mission. *Are they after Beldaken?* He had hoped they would be well ahead of the Empire's response to Foreworth's death, but if this patrol was heading in the same direction...

And where there is one, there may be more.

Darius obviously had the same idea. He had already drawn his weapon and was ready to engage. Kester swallowed hard. He knew what had to be done, but he did not like it. The Empire soldiers outnumbered them; if they played this wrong they could quickly find themselves surrounded. They could be killed, or even worse, captured and sent into an empire prison, tortured until they broke and gave up the location of the High Cleric and all the others. *And what if they find the key that Delia entrusted me with?*

Scared, little brother? I told you that you were not cut out for combat.

Kester gritted his teeth and shook his head. "We need to question one of those officers," he said, no doubt giving voice to something Darius already knew. "We've got the element of surprise. Let's use it."

Kester spurred his horse into a full charge down the hill. Darius had volunteered to be the one to go, but this was Kester's mission and the dangerous tasks should fall to him. *Even if it feels like I might wet myself.*

He had a plan. He just had to stick with it and everything would work out fine. At least, that's what he kept telling himself.

The empire patrol was completely off-guard. They heard Kester's horse barreling towards them, but far too late. Kester had picked up speed going downhill and caught up to them too quickly. One of the soldiers began to turn around just as Kester's sword caught him on the side.

There was a wave of shouts and cursing and swords being drawn. Kester did not stop moving, not did he dare turn back to see if the soldier he struck fell. His horse was charging at full speed through the ranks of the patrol. Faces and armor and horses flashed by him a blur. He gritted his teeth and prepared himself. All it took was one of the soldiers to be quicker on the draw than the others, to get a swing at him before he was past, and it would be all over.

But no attack came. He caught up to the officers on their palfreys, surprise still in their eyes. And then he was past. Kester's horse barreled down the road, leaving the patrol behind. He heard shouted orders and horses coming after him. It was a pointless effort; Kester had too much of a head start. If he had wanted he could have disappeared around the bend in the road and never been seen again.

Of course, that was not the plan. He reared his horse. The well-trained destrier gracefully slid to a stop. Carefully, they turned about. Then he spurred his horse and charged back in the direction of the pursuing patrol.

The members of the patrol had fanned out across the road in a pursuit formation, ready for a long chase. They had not been expecting Kester to come back at them. *And why would they? What sane man would?*

Kester had only seconds to find the gaps in their formation and lead his destrier through. The palfreys the officers rode would not provide much of a threat, they were travel horses meant for comfort, not combat. The rounceys would be much more dangerous, they were quick and spry on their feet. Kester's destrier was more powerful, but a good rider on a rouncey might be able to outmaneuver him. He would have to pick his way carefully. Kester saw the opening he was looking for and commanded his horse through it.

He passed one soldier, then another. One of the officers breezed by as he struggled to get his horse to turn in time. Kester heard curses drowned out by the sounds of horses whinnying as their riders tried to close the gap. They were too late, he was almost through.

Out of the corner of his eyes he glimpsed a flash of steel. One of the riders on his left had gotten close, too close. His horned helmet glimmered in the sunlight, his sword was raised and ready to strike. Kester had just enough time to raise his left arm, to which his shield was strapped. The sword clashed hard against the shield, nearly knocking Kester out of his saddle. He righted himself quickly to find the rider coming in close for another strike. Kester tried to break free but the rouncey met his destrier stride for stride.

In front of him, an imperial rider with a long, blonde beard moved to block his path. *Shit.* He grabbed the reins of his horse and tugged. His horse broke left and nearly collided with the helmeted rider. Horned Helmet swung his sword in response, but they were too close now for him to get any power behind it and the sword bounced impotently off Kester's armor. Blonde Beard was almost right in front of him. Kester's destrier knew what to do before he even gave the command. He darted forward and to the left, just barely clearing the space before the imperial had cut him off. Horned Helmet did not make it and he collided with Blonde Beard. The two horses tumbled into the dirt, sending one rider soaring across the ground and trapping the other beneath the horses' bodies as they struggled and kicked to return to their feet.

The patrol was once again behind Kester as he headed up the hill. He could hear how close behind they were, the light frames of the rounceys giving them an advantage on the steep incline of the hill. *This is going to be close. Hope Darius is ready.*

He came to the top of the hill and fixed his attention on the road. The thin rope they had tied between two rocks on opposite sides of the road would be impossible to spot without the small marking they had left. He kicked his horses sides and the destrier gave a short leap that cleared the rope.

The riders either did not see the rope or had no time to respond. Kester heard horses crying and riders cursing as they toppled together. Kester commanded his horse to stop and looked back. Two of the riders had tripped over the rope directly. A third had run directly into the mass of flailing limbs that had once been the front two riders and joined them in the dirt. An officer who had been following close behind had gotten his palfrey to stop in time, but the scene in front of it frightened it and it reared on its hind legs, throwing the officer from the saddle. He landed hard on his back and his head twisted around in an unnatural fashion.

Snapped neck. We'll have to be careful to take the other one alive.

Only five of the imperial riders were still on their horses. Kester held his horse steady as the remaining officer commanded his men forward.

"He's making a fool of you! Go around, idiots! Around!"

That is when Darius made his appearance. He came charging into the road with his sword held high and bellowing like a wild animal. The imperial soldiers were thrown into confusion and chaos. Before any had time to react Darius cleaved his sword through the air. The head of the closest soldier was cut clean off his shoulders. The head sailed through the air before joining its body on the ground. Darius's sword came around and cut the next soldier across the arm. The cut was shallow but the impact knocked the soldier from saddle. His body flopped helplessly across the ground.

The soldiers responded to Darius with their blades. Darius parried one strike and his horse moved him out of the way of another. Kester was quickly behind the remaining soldiers. The soldiers cursed and shouted while the officer spat and demanded that Kester and Darius die. The soldiers were outmatched and they knew it. Kester's sword struck down one, Darius's the other. The officer suddenly found himself alone.

He turned his palfrey and tried to run. Darius got alongside him and reached out a long, powerful arm. He grabbed the officer by his coat and ripped him right off his horse. The palfrey continued to run without its rider.

The officer struggled and yelled and spat but Darius's grip did not loosen. Kester rode up alongside them. His heart was still hammering in his chest. He had been in more than a few battles since this war started, many of which were far more dangerous, but it seemed he never got used to it.

"Make sure he's properly bound," Kester said.

Darius bound their captor's hands and feet with rope while Kester rode around to make sure all the of the fallen soldiers were dead. He found a couple of them trying to crawl or limp away and cut them down. He could not afford one of them bringing reinforcements down on them. Once he was sure they were all dead he and Darius took the captive officer off the road to a quiet place where they could interrogate him.

The officer was a young man, couldn't have been that far into his twenties, with a sharp jaw and a handsome face. He glared at his captors with intense hostility.

"Bastard relics of a dead religion!" the officer shouted. "Serpentine will see you all rooted out. They'll hang that bitch of a High Cleric in front of the palace, burning and screaming. She'll denounce her religion and beg for mercy, just you watch!"

Darius struck him across the face. The imperial coughed and spat up blood.

"Sorry, my friend is a little protective of our High Cleric," Kester said. "I'd recommend you keep your mouth shut except to answer my questions."

"Fuck you, candle-worshiper!"

Kester ignored the outburst. "It is very rare to see an Empire patrol this far south. Keeping an eye on the farmers?"

The officer just glared at him with contempt. Kester nodded to Darius. Darius struck the officer again. This time he crushed his nose. The officer let out a moan of pain.

"Answer my questions and we don't have to harm you any further," Kester promised. "What was your unit's assignment?"

"Bastard," the officer spat.

Darius gave the officer a swift kick to the chest. He was knocked onto his back and began gasping for air. Darius grabbed him by the shoulders and forced him upright.

Kester leaned in close to their captive. "You emperor is not going to give you any rewards for your loyalty. He'll never know how much your suffered without giving in. Your resistance is pointless."

The officer looked at him with hard eyes. *A strong man, and loyal. Truly wasted on the like of Serpentine. He'll be hard to break, and we haven't the time.*

Kester needed to try a new tact. If he could not get information out of what he said, he would have to try and get information from what he would not say.

"We're after a man named Reis Beldaken," Kester said. He watched the officer's face carefully and saw a brief glimmer of recognition. *So he does know that name.* "We know that the Empire is also after this man. Was your unit a part of that?" A flash of anger. *I'll take that as a yes.*

Darius grabbed the officer by the throat and forced him to his feet. The officer gurgled and gasped for breath. "How many more did the Empire send to deal with Beldaken?" Despite the powerful hand on his throat, the officer smiled. *A lot. A whole lot.*

Kester nodded at Darius. "Finish it." At his command, Darius grabbed the officer's head and with one smooth motion snapped his neck. The body dropped limply to the ground.

"This was likely the advance scout. But there will be more. A lot more. And we have less time than we hoped."

Darius nodded his understanding and returned to his horse. Kester allowed himself one last look at the officer's body. His once handsome face had been broken and was quickly losing its color.

Light guide us.

Chapter 5

Kester and Darius arrived in the ghost town of Alleways days later. Kester tried to shake off his weariness. Reis Beldaken had a reputation for violence and Kester expected he might not be particularly welcoming to visitors. He may not be sure exactly what would happen, but he needed to be on his toes.

As they approached the decrepit mansion that Beldaken was thought to inhabit, they noticed several bodies lying among the tall weeds. They were clad in Serpentine uniforms, and were in advanced stages of decomposition.

"Beldaken is truly unafraid of making enemies of the empire," Kester said. "Good."

Darius nodded, his expression unchanging.

"Keep watch," Kester ordered. "I'll go introduce us. Be ready to come on my call if things turn to violence."

Kester walked through the tall weeds, carefully stepping over the bodies in his way. He would normally have been disgusted by the treating of the dead in such a way, but knowing the stories of the atrocities committed by Foreworth, he couldn't help but feel a sort of satisfaction.

He knocked on the door and waited. After some time, when no one had answered, he knocked again. Still no answer. He turned to Darius, who just shrugged.

Are we too late? Did the Empire beat us here?

He knocked again, loudly.

Finally, he heard some noises from inside. A few moments later the door opened and Reis Beldaken, true to every description of the man he had ever heard, appeared in the doorway.

"What is it?" Reis demanded.

Kester's etiquette training kicked in. He bowed slightly and extended his hand before introducing himself.

"My name is Kester Belisario. I come representing the Church of True Light to seek your aid in-"

"I have no coin to spare to any charities," Reis interrupted abruptly before slamming the door in his face.

Kester let out an angry sigh. All manners forgotten, he smacked on the door heavily. Reis opened the door again, this time clutching the grip of the sword at his side.

"You had best tell me what it is you are here for, and quickly. You can see for yourself what happened to the last people who thought it was a good idea to waste my time." He gestured to the bodies in the weeds. "So let's hope for your sake that what you have to say is interesting."

"I have come to ask for your help in taking down the Serpentine Empire," Kester blurted out.

Reis paused. He squinted, like he was trying to tell whether or not Kester was serious.

"Now that is interesting," Reis said. "I suppose I can spare a moment."

He stepped aside and motioned for Kester to enter. *So far so good.* Kester signaled for Darius to continue standing watch outside before he entered. He was surprised by the stark contrast of the inside of the mansion from the out. He had stepped through the doors of a worn mansion and entered into a well maintained home.

"Well?" Reis demanded. "Are you here to talk, or for a lecture in architecture?"

Kester snapped back into focus. "My apologizes. As I have said, I have come requesting your assistance in bringing down the Serpentine Empire."

"Walk and talk," Reis instructed, leading him towards the stairs. "I am quite busy so whatever you are selling, you will have to do so as we go. Though, quite honestly, I don't see what it is that you could want from me that will help to those ends. There is little love lost between me and the empire, and I would certainly enjoy a good laugh if they should meet their end, but there is little I can offer in terms of help. If you're asking for permission to use Alleways as a base of some kind, I claim no rights over the town proper, just keep your men away from the mansion. If you're asking for supplies, I don't possess much that I am not in need of. But I could guess all day, so why don't you just spit out what it is you want from me?"

They had come to the top of the stairs. In front of them was a series of long, narrow hallways. The smell of sulfur and smoke filled Kester's lungs, drifting in from behind one of the closed doors. It was a disgusting smell that almost forced Kester into a coughing fit. He wondered what kinds of strange things Reis could be working on, then decided it would probably be best if he did not know.

Kester cleared his throat. "Actually, it is your proficiency with the sword that draws me here."

Reis stopped in his tracks and turned to face Kester, a look a bemusement on his face. "You wish to hire me as a swordarm? The Church must really be scraping the bottom of the barrel if they're going door-to-door in order shore up recruits."

He turned and walked away, motioning for Kester to leave as he did so. Kester continued to follow him anyway.

"You misunderstand. This is no task for a mere swordarm. I come seeking you because of your reputation as an unstoppable fighter, your lack of fear in the face of the empire, and your experience in waging one man strikes against greater powers." *Powers like ours.* "I wish for you to accompany me in the slaying of Marcus Serpentine himself."

Reis chuckled and shook his head. "Oh, is that all? You should have opened with that line, it's the funniest part of your act."

"This is no joke," Kester said, trying his best to not let desperation show in his voice. "I admit, the Church is in desperate times, all of Kassia is. If something isn't done, Serpentine will soon have the whole world under his heel. I believe the best chance for stopping the empire lays in assassination. I also believe you may be one of the only people alive capable of succeeding in such a task."

"Perhaps," Reis said, all humor lost from his voice. "But I have absolutely no interest in doing so."

"You are afraid, then? I thought from the stories about you that the empire did not scare you."

Reis glared at Kester. "Do not confuse apathy for cowardice. There is nothing for me to gain but plenty to lose, not the least of which is my time. But if you wish to match courage, draw your sword. We will see who flees for their life first."

Kester ignored the threat, but noticed that Reis was getting antsy. His hand fidgeted in the direction of his sword, as if he was contemplating drawing it, and his eyes darted back and forth, momentarily fixing themselves on Kester before returning forward. Kester realized he needed to choose his words more carefully if he was to avoid a confrontation.

Reis stopped in front of the door at the end of the hall and reached for its handle. "I'm afraid that was all the time I can spare for this absurdity. You can show yourself out. And I wouldn't recommend returning unless you decide you have grown tired of living."

"You can't just ignore the Empire!" Kester exclaimed. "It is your enemy as well. You made sure of that when you killed one of their colonels. Do you think that's the kind of thing they will just let go? They will return."

"I know," Reis calmly replied.

"They will come in force. You are strong, but how many can you possibly think you can take on alone? Ten? A dozen? Maybe more? You can't possibly hope to stand alone against the forces the empire will send at you to get their revenge!"

"Says the man whose recommended alternative is to strike right in their capital."

"If we strike soon, we can get to the palace while I know it will be lightly guarded. I have ways to sneak through the capital undetected. I can explain details later, but know this is not some fool's plan to assault the heart of the empire head-on. It is a carefully planned mission to directly confront Marcus Serpentine himself. And it is for that confrontation that I will need you."

Reis stopped. He stared at Kester for a good time, sizing him up. Kester remained still, hoping that he had finally hit the right chord within him.

"It is an interesting proposal," Reis eventually said. "I'll give you that. And the confidence in your tone means that you're either an idiot or that this plan has some chance of success, though I'm guessing it's the former. At any rate I'd prefer to know which is which before I make any commitments. We can discuss your plan in more detail in the morning."

"The morning!" Kester objected. "There is hardly time to waste! The Empire is coming –"

"Boy," Reis said with intentional condescension. "What did you say your name was, Kester? You are the one who wishes something from me, and for some reason I am actually considering it. For now, be happy I give you the time, as opposed to complaining about one lost day. Now, excuse me, I must return to my work."

He went through the door and shut it quickly behind him, giving Kester no chance to see what was on the other side. Kester sighed and, defeated, returned down the hallway to the stairs. At the very least he had Reis's attention, so all was not lost. He and Darius would just have to camp out in the ghost town for the night.

As he descended the stairs into the entrance hall he found

Darius swiftly walking towards him.

"Darius, what is it?"

"Empire," Darius replied. "Dozens of them. Came into town from the south. I spotted torches and tinder. Probably plan to burn the mansion."

"They were so close behind?" Kester asked with disbelief. "Stay down here, come get me if they come past the gate. I'll go inform Beldaken. He may be more cooperative now that the empire is banging down his door."

He bolted up the stairs and down the hall. He banged on the door rapidly before tossing it open. Inside, Reis sat at a table covered in all manner of beakers and vials filled with liquids Kester could not hope to identify. All about the room were shelves filled with books and strange instruments Kester had never seen before.

"You've just made a terrible mistake," Reis growled as he rose.

"This place is about to overrun by Empire. They will burn the mansion to the ground, and there are far more than we can possibly hope to take on ourselves. We have to move."

Reis scowled. He dashed to one of the windows and peered behind the curtain to confirm what he was told. He let out an angry growl, like a dog that was being threatened. Then he pulled out a small vial from under his shirt and began pouring a murky red liquid from one of the beakers into it.

"What are you doing?" Kester demanded. "They'll be upon us any moment!"

"Which is exactly the reason I will be needing this," Reis responded as he sealed the vial and slipped it back under his shirt. "Alright, I suppose we should be off. There's a hidden tunnel underneath the mansion that will lead us outside the town. Follow me."

Back in the entrance hall they found two dead imperials with Darius standing over them. He motioned to the front door, which he had barricaded with various pieces of furniture from throughout the room. He then pointed to a door at the far end of the hall that was open.

"They came through there," he said. "Took them by surprise."

Reis kicked one of the bodies over with his foot. "So they found the tunnel. This could be a problem."

"Any other way out?" Kester asked.

"Not unless you want to jump out a window," Reis said, then

paused. "Actually, that's not too bad of an idea. The mansion was built in two parts: the hospital and the home. The entrance to the hospital is now blocked off, but we can go out the window upstairs onto its roof and get down on the other side."

Before he had even finished explaining he was bolting up the stairs. Kester followed behind him before realizing Darius had not yet moved. He was standing fixated on the tunnel entrance.

"Darius!" Kester called out, but he didn't move. A moment later Kester saw what had drawn his attention. Empire soldiers flooded the room from the tunnel, weapons drawn.

"Go with Beldaken," Darius said in a calm, assured voice. "I will slow them down the best I can."

Darius had taken position in front of the stairs. His sword was drawn, his face fixed in determination. No empire soldiers would be able to get through until he was slain.

Kester did not want to leave Darius behind. He clutched his sword at his side, debating internally whether he should go fight by Darius's side.

"What's the matter?" Reis called down from the top of the stairs. "Don't you Church-boys know all about the 'noble sacrifice'? You better get moving if you don't want it to be in vain."

With an angry shout Kester turned and ran up the stairs. Reis was right, even though he didn't want to admit it. Darius had made the choice to sacrifice himself in order to protect the mission. The certainty in his voice and the firm expression on his face made it clear that his mind was made up. All he could do now was escape with Reis and make sure his sacrifice was not in vain. He dashed after Reis down the top-floor hallway, the sound of swords clashing behind him.

Reis ran into a room on the left, threw open a window, and nimbly climbed through, landing on the roof of the connecting house. The maneuver was significantly more difficult for Kester, whose armor weighed him down and denied him any kind of flexibility. By the time Kester had clumsily landed on the roof, Reis had already dashed to the other end of the building and leaped off. He rolled as he hit the ground and was immediately back on his feet and sprinting away from the town. Kester's own descent was far less graceful, and he hit the ground with such a resounding 'thud' that he was sure that he had alerted the nearby soldiers. He ran in the direction he had seen Reis go moments before.

He heard shouting behind him and the sound of heavy boots running in his direction. He was being pursued. He had no way of knowing how far behind him they were, whether he had been spotted yet, or how many of them there were. He couldn't afford to turn around now to look.

He was running through the outskirts of the town now. There were very few buildings here, only isolated storehouses. He was running past one of these when a powerful hand grabbed him and dragged him inside. Reis shoved him against a wall away from the door and put a finger to his lips.

Kester listened as the footsteps came closer to the storehouse. He gauged by the shadows that there were three of them. At first they approached rapidly, then they slowed their pace the closer they got. *They know we're in here.* Reis silently drew his sword. Kester was about to draw his as well but Reis motioned for him to be still.

The figures were at the entrance to the storehouse now. Braced up against the wall closest to the door, Reis and Kester were just out of sight. Sudden as a viper, Reis struck. So fast that Kester couldn't keep up, Reis had turned the corner and run the closest figure straight through with his sword. The other two were forced back as their mortally wounded comrade was shoved into them. Before the body had even hit the ground Reis had maneuvered around it and stabbed the neck of a second soldier. Reis did not wait to see the spray of blood that confirmed his kill before charging at the remaining imperial. The soldier had just enough time to raise his sword in defense but it did him no good. Reis's attack struck him anyway, cutting him across the top of his chest.

Kester watched with wide eyes as the three bodies dropped around Reis, each hitting the ground no more than a second after the last. After taking on three imperial soldiers single-handed Reis's outfit was stained with blood, but none of it was his. He truly fought like the demon the stories had built him up to be.

Reis did not seem to give his latest casualties a second thought. He was staring up at the sky. Kester followed his gaze. Smoke was rising from somewhere not far.

"Shit!" Reis exclaimed. He ran towards the road and Kester followed after him.

"Well, hell," Reis said. The mansion was completely covered in flames now, and they could feel the heat off it even from here. "There goes my fucking house."

"May the Light guide your spirit, Darius," Kester whispered softly.

They both stood there for a few minutes and watched the flames, reflecting on what they had just lost.

Reis finally broke the silence. "So, tell me more about this plan of yours. My interest has been piqued."

Chapter 6

The Alleways Mansion burned brightly before them. Reis turned away, as if he was unable to bear the sight any longer. Then he faced it once again and cursed loudly into the sky. He rushed back to the bodies of the fallen soldiers, gave one a solid kick, then let out another yell.

"Months of progress, research, lost!" he shouted. He kicked the body a few more times until he was panting from the exhaustion. Then he suddenly pulled himself together. All that rage was immediately replaced with a calm composure. "The rest of them will be here soon. You can fill me in on the details of your plan on the road. Assuming its not too suicidal, I'm in."

Kester was kneeling on the ground, attempting to block out Reis's temper tantrum as he said a short prayer for his fallen comrade. *May the Light guide your spirit into Eternity ...*

"Hey, did you hear me?" Reis growled. "We have to move!"

"Would you not give a moment to grieve a fallen friend?" Kester asked.

"Not in the best of circumstances, and certainly not now." Reis's voice was cold but with a sharp edge to it that made Kester uneasy. "If you must grieve, do it as you move, unless you seek an early reunion."

He started to walk away without Kester. *I am sorry, Darius.* Kester let out a frustrated sigh and followed after.

They moved parallel to the road but stayed just out of sight of anyone who might be on it. As they passed the stable where Kester and Darius had tied up their horses, they dared to get closer to the road. The stable was surrounded by empire soldiers. They had found the horses and were going through the saddlebags.

"Looks like we're not riding out of here," Reis said. "But there's a village nearby where we can get replacements."

"The map of the palace is in one of those bags. We can't afford to lose them."

"Of course they are," Reis said sardonically. "Why not leave something of such importance out in the open without anyone guarding it?"

"I hadn't expected anyone to come upon it so soon."

"Well, they did. So I guess it's up to me to make up for your mistake. I'll cause a distraction and lead most of them away. You might have to contend with one or two, but unless that sword on your side is just for show I assume you can handle your own."

Before Kester had a chance to respond Reis was already rushing towards the stables. As he neared the road he put two fingers to his mouth and whistled. When the soldiers spotted him he gave them a hearty wave before dashing off in the other direction. As he predicted, the majority of the soldiers chased after him. Only one stayed with the horses.

Kester watched Reis lead the soldiers into the distance. He was impressed at the speed at which Reis was able to run. Even the quickest of the soldiers could not close half the distance between them. When they were a safe distance away Kester walked towards the horses while drawing his sword and his shield. With the noise his armor made when he moved he knew the stealthy approach was not an option. The only choice was a head-on assault.

The lone soldier was a beastly man with wild hair. He saw Kester approach and drew his sword. Kester came close, paused, and held his sword out in a threatening manner.

"Throw down your weapon and surrender and your life will be spared," Kester demanded.

His words were wasted. The imperial shouted and rushed at him, sword raised for the strike. Kester let the soldier get close before throwing his shield in between them at the last second, so the sword scraped uselessly against it. Swinging his shield to the side, Kester knocked the sword out of his way and threw his opponent off balance. A quick thrust with his sword and he pierced the enemy in his lower gut. His opponent doubled over in pain before falling to the ground to die.

Not wasting any time, he threw himself over his horse in one swift motion. Thanks to a part of his career spent in the armored cavalry, it was a maneuver he was quite familiar with. He grabbed the reins of Darius's horse and gave it the command to follow, then spurred his horse on in the direction Reis had gone.

For his part, Reis had led the soldiers on an elaborate chase. Off the road, through the shrubbery, up a hill, leaping over whatever obstacles he could find to slow his pursuers. He never showed any signs of slowing down or even breaking a sweat. He seemed quite comfortable with this kind of distance running. His pursuers, bogged down in armor and thick uniforms, were breathing heavily and exhausting themselves just to keep Reis in sight. It was likely a relief to them when the two horses bounded past them and Reis hopped on one of them. They stopped to catch their breath and watched as the two men rode off into the distance.

The two of them rode for several hours, trying to put as much distance between them and their pursuers as possible. They changed direction often, going back over their previous path in order to throw off anyone trying to track them. When they were confident that they had left the empire troops behind, Reis told Kester follow him.

They came to a small trading community on the outskirts of a farming settlement. Reis explained that this is where he periodically got supplies. Here farmers traded their spare crops to impoverished families on the countryside in exchange for whatever little they could provide in return.

"I don't see why we're coming here," Kester said as they tied up their horses. "I told you I packed plenty of supplies for our trip."

"Not the supplies I need," Reis said.

"You haven't even looked through my supplies."

"Not the supplies I need."

Kester just shook his head and decided to gave in. Reis's abilities were essential to the success of this mission, that had become all the more clear after seeing him in action. If anyone could kill Marcus Serpentine, it was him. He would just have to adjust to Reis's personality.

As Reis was about to leave the stable, Kester stopped him.. "I never got a chance to properly thank you," he said.

Reis looked confused. "Thank me for what?"

"You saved my life back there when I was being chased by those imperials. Not to mention put yourself at risk to recover the horses. My life, and this mission, are in your debt."

Kester was taken aback when Reis laughed at him. "I believe I may have given you the wrong impression. I was never in any danger. Even if you hadn't succeeded in liberating the horses, I would have eventually escaped my pursuers on foot. As for saving your life, well, as I told you before, I am interested in this plan of yours, and as you have not yet shared the details of it, it would be very inconvenient if you died. Speaking of which, any chance you see fit to share yet?"

Kester held in his resentment for being talked to in such a manner. "Not here. Never know who is listening."

Reis scoffed and walked away. Kester sighed. *Working with him will certainly be a test of my patience.* He put a hand over his heart. Under his armor, tucked safely away in an inner pocket, was the key Delia had entrusted him with. He could feel it there, weighing him down with responsibility. *Light give me strength.*

Kester watched Reis go around the various stalls from a safe distance, close enough to keep an eye on him but far enough away that they would not need to speak. To his annoyance, nothing Reis bought seemed to be related to the mission which they now faced. It was all luxury goods, such as clothing and bottles of wine. Kester did his best to keep patience and not speak up, but when this continued for over an hour he had had enough.

"All of this can not be necessary!" Kester demanded. "What possible use can you have for all of this?"

"Almost every worldly good I possessed burned to ash today," Reis reminded him. "Surely you do not expect me to travel with only one outfit and none of the conveniences to which I am accustomed, consuming only trail rations?"

Conveniences? What do you think this is? He kept his thoughts to himself. "Fine, I suppose I can make room in the saddlebags. But please try to hurry. I would feel much better if we could put some more distance between us and the soldiers who attacked your mansion."

"This won't take much longer. The traders here recognize me, so I don't need to waste time bartering."

"I did notice you getting some remarkable prices. The traders must really appreciate your business."

Reis was carrying several large bundles of his purchases but Kester had only seen a few pieces of gold change hands. Kester figured he must simply be a shrewd negotiator.

"It's quite simple," Reis explained. "My reputation preceded me. Keeping their prices low was a good way for these simple people to ensure that I didn't simply take what I wanted in a more ... aggressive fashion."

Kester stepped in front of Reis, no longer able to hide the

agitation on his face. "So you're extorting these people!"

"I suppose you can look at it that way," Reis said passively. "I prefer to think of it as the benefits of renown. My reputation comes with quite a few. It's why you sought me out, is it not? I have never had to make any physical threats to these people, they just know that being generous with me is in their best interest."

Kester shook his head in disbelief. "I will have no part of this. I will wait by the horses. Meet me when you have satisfied yourself at the expense of these poor people."

Reis shrugged, unconcerned with Kester's opinions. He continued browsing for his last few wants as Kester walked back to the stables.

Kester was steaming by the time he reached the horses. He had known when he had set out that he would be dealing with darker kind of man than he was accustomed to, and had thought he had prepared himself well for it. Nothing had prepared him for the kind of narcissism, conceit, and arrogance Reis possessed. Everything he said rang with a kind of self-satisfied coldness, a level of condescension which suggested that whoever he was talking to did not even deserve the privilege. Add to that his insults and Kester found himself struggling to maintain his calm.

He began to wonder if he had made the right decision after all coming to Reis for help. *No, I can't afford to think like that, not after Darius has already given his life for this mission.*

Kester was so absorbed in his thoughts he didn't even notice as a young boy walked into the stables. The boy tapped him lightly, bringing Kester back to reality.

"My apologies, I was lost in thought. Can I help you with something, young man?"

The boy paused as if he was unsure of himself. "Are you friends with Mister Reis?"

Kester almost laughed at the assertion. "I wouldn't exactly say that. But we are companions, yes."

He noticed the boy fidgeting nervously. He had something he wanted to say but was worried about it.

"Be at ease, young man," Kester said in his most reassuring voice. "I am a defender of the Light. If there is something which bothers you, you may tell me and I will be glad to share in its burden."

"I wasn't supposed to say anything. But I've always liked Mister

Reis. He doesn't talk much, but he's let me practice with his sword and promised that one day he would teach me how to use it."

So Reis is capable of kindness.

"Say anything about what?" Kester asked.

"Some of those empire guys came by the other day," the boy said. "They said that Mister Reis was in some kind of trouble, and there was a big reward if someone told them when he comes into the market. One of my dad's friends left as soon as you arrived to go get them."

What! Kester barely kept himself from shouting. *So much for the benefits of renown.* "Excuse me."

He rushed back to Reis and found him looking through a small selection of jewelry. The proprietor was an old woman who had likely brought what little of value she had in hopes of trading for much needed food and supplies; now she just waited nervously while Reis looked it over, hoping that he did not take anything.

Kester knocked the jewelry out of Reis's hands and start pulled him away. Reis furiously shook himself free.

"What do you think you're doing?" he demanded. "I believe there was an item or two of actual value in that collection."

"The empire is on its way. They'll be here any moment, and we must be gone before then."

"What a pain," Reis complained. Kester might as well have told him that it was going to rain.

The boy was still waiting in the stable when they returned. Reis packed his purchases into the saddlebags, callously tossing aside some of Darius's possessions in order to make room. Kester's agitation over the treatment of his fallen comrade's things was overshadowed by his curiosity towards Reis's treatment of the boy. The boy seemed genuinely excited to see him and asked Reis a flurry of questions concerning where he'd been, where he was going, and when he would be back. He even volunteered to help Reis pack. While Reis's responses were as unenthusiastic as Kester would expect, his tone lacked the coldness and condescension that Kester was becoming accustomed to. Kester had expected him to shoo the boy away, especially when the boy started asking so many questions, but instead he displayed patience in allowing the boy to help him finish packing.

As they were finishing up they heard the sounds of approaching horses. The boy ran to the entrance and looked outside.

"Those are empire horses!" he cried. "They're here already!"

"We'll never get out without them seeing us," Kester said as he mounted his horse. "Prepare for a chase."

"No, thanks," Reis said. "I'd rather go with an option that doesn't get us killed."

"What? Do you mean to fight -"

Kester saw something that left him speechless. Reis seemed to become encircled with darkness, like the light in the stables no longer could reach him. It was the strangest, and most frightening, thing he had ever seen.

The darkness spread from him and soon reached the entrance to the stables. It expanded from there until it completely covered the entryway. Only then did Reis himself become cleared of the dark aura.

"That should slow them down, at the very least," Reis said. "I'll prepare our escape."

Kester swallowed hard. It had been a long time since he had felt this kind of terror. "That was a Willer ability?" he asked. *Either that, or you are truly a demon.*

He had never seen an ability manifest itself in such force. The few Willers he had met before could barely conjure small amounts of their power through intense concentration. He had met a man who claimed to be able to command wind, then collapsed from the effort of creating a light breeze. Reis was able to summon forth enough of this dark aura to completely engulf the entrance of the stable and did so effortlessly.

Kester had not even been aware that Reis was a Willer. In the stories he had heard there had been mention of Reis becoming surrounded by darkness as he fought, but he had always thought they were merely exaggerations, a hyperbole of his vicious fighting style as told by those who had witnessed it. But it was no exaggeration. Reis was a Willer with the ability to manifest darkness.

How fitting.

"Yes, control over shadows, and when there's enough I can create voids of darkness. It's the whole reason the empire is after me," Reis explained. "Serpentine demanded all Willers be brought in for a 'special project,' and apparently ordered anyone who refused be killed. And of course I refused." He chuckled as he began fumbling for something in the saddlebags. "You came for me without even knowing that? How interesting."

The imperials had reached the stables but were unsure of how to progress. The entrance into the stables had suddenly darkened. It was as if all the lights inside had been suddenly extinguished, except no sunlight could penetrate it either. It was just before sundown and the light was cast directly at the stable, it should be well lit. Instead it was pitch black.

Lieutenant Zarik had known that going after a man who had gotten the better of Colonel Foreworth would be no easy task. But he would have never expected something like this. Around him, his men were all waiting for orders. There was a mix of nervousness and bewilderment among them. They were all waiting to follow his lead, but Zarik was stumped.

Zarik put his hand into the darkness. It passed through without resistance. He pulled it out and determined that his hand had not taken any damage.

One of the particularly brave men in his command volunteered to pass through first. He took a deep breath and walked through the entrance of the stables, disappearing into the darkness. A moment later, he walked back out. He seemed surprised.

"It was completely pitch black," he explained. "But I thought if I just walked forward I would get through it. I don't know how I got turned around."

Another attempt ended with similar results.

Zarik decided that if they couldn't get in through the normal entrance, they would just have to make a new one. Zarik ordered his soldiers to collect anything heavy they could get their hands on. They managed to collect some axes and began tearing into the side of the wooden stables. In no time they had cut a sizable hole and began pouring in. The commander walked in last and looked about.

The stable was empty. Reis, his companion, and their horses were all gone.

"How the hell?" Zarek muttered. "They can't have gotten far! Spread out and search!"

"Sir, we found something," one of his soldiers said.

The soldier handed Zarek a folded piece of paper. He unfolded it and read its short message.

"Nice try. -R. Beldaken."

Chapter 7

"This is as far as you go, Peter," Reis said. He commanded his horse to stop and waited as the boy clumsily dismounted. "Just follow the road back the way we came, it shouldn't be more than an hour's walk."

"Are you going to come back?" the boy asked.

"I've got to go topple the empire," Reis said casually, as if it was a part of his daily routine. "I'll be back when I'm done. Tell your father and his friends they have until that time to secure supplies for the rebuilding of my mansion. I'll be expecting them in exchange for this betrayal."

"I will," the boy said. "Good luck, Mister Reis."

After Kester and Reis rode off and left the boy behind, Kester finally voiced the question that had been on his mind since they escaped the stables.

"What exactly did you do?" he asked. "How did we get out of there?"

It had all been a blur to Kester. What he remembered was Reis writing something on a slip of paper, folding it up, then dropping it on the ground. He mounted his horse and had the boy get on behind him. He told Kester to have his horse charge at the entrance, into the darkness, at the same moment he did. Kester did so, and he found himself ordering the horse forward through pitch black darkness. He had no idea where he was going but heard Reis's voice urging him to press forward. Eventually he came out of the darkness and, after his eyes adjusted to the light, found that he was on the road a short distance away from the market.

"One of the more useful parts of my ability," Reis explained. "To be able to traverse the void of shadows. I had extended my shadow all the way to the road, a thin line they failed to notice because they were so fixated on the entrance. I can traverse the darkness as I please. You were able to as well, because you were following me."

It all sounded incredible to Kester. Not too long ago things made sense to him. Fighting battles alongside the men the Church, patrolling the perimeter of the Grandium, praying under the guidance of High Cleric Delia. Now he was riding alongside a monster possessing a truly frightening power.

"You've been capable of such a thing the whole time?" Kester asked. "Why didn't you use it back in the mansion, instead of allowing Darius to sacrifice himself?"

"If there had been a better alternative in our escape I would have suggested such," Reis snapped, bitingly. "Covering all mansion's possible entrances, including windows, in shadows would have required more force than I am able to exert. Then there's the matter that the stables were open and I could easily expand my shadows outside. Either way, we were out of time when my mansion was invaded. Even if I had chosen to use my ability to aid in our escape, we still would have needed a distraction to buy us some time. But no, you're right, I chose to let your friend die so that I would have one less sword at my side when I took on the empire, I was looking for an extra challenge."

"I apologize," Kester said, only half-meaning it. "I jumped to conclusions. I was just taken by surprise by your ability."

"Well if we've cleared that up, it should be noted that using my ability to the extent I just did is incredibly taxing. I'm exhausted. We're going to need to stop to rest soon."

"I'll keep an eye out for a good place to set up camp."

"Camp?" Reis scoffed. "I do not camp. I require a soft bed beneath me."

"Well I'm sorry, sacrifices need to be made," Kester snapped. "Going into a town to find a bed for the night runs the risk of running into empire, and since you are a wanted man it doesn't seem like a good idea."

"Fine, have it your way." Reis possessed all the grace of a child who had just been told to eat his vegetables. "But I don't exactly have experience setting up camp, so I suppose I'll just leave that to you."

"Of course," Kester sighed.

A couple of hours later, the sun had set. Reis and Kester found themselves sitting around a small campfire that Kester had started. They had gone off the road to a lightly wooded area that would be invisible to passing patrols. Just to be sure, they did not let the campfire grow past embers.

Kester was eating some of the rations he had packed, mostly tasteless dried meat, nuts, and hard cheese. Reis was devouring some kind of honeyed bread he had purchased in the market. He was visibly enjoying it, which Kester assumed was for his benefit.

"So, I've been meaning to ask something," Reis said, breaking the silence of their meal. "Why me? Of all the people you could have asked for help with this mission, why someone like me? Hell, why not just go yourself, with some of your buddies from the Church backing you up?"

It was something Kester had been asking himself for a while now.

"We number very few at the moment," Kester said. "Admittedly, I had my own reasons for being interested in you."

"Please, share."

I'd prefer not to. Kester thought it over in his head. *Perhaps if we bond a little his company will become more tolerable. I guess I should make the gesture.*

Kester began the tale. "Some time ago, you were involved in some shady dealings out of Mordoven. You were distributing a powerful narcotic, one so potent that just a small sample could make a man desperately addicted."

"Selling and manufacturing," Reis bragged. "It was actually a creation of mine. I was just getting started out in my research and I needed a way to fund it. My narcotic did the job very well. The addicts were also quite useful to keep around. Those idiots would fight to the death to protect my property in the exchange for a little bit of the stuff."

He chuckled as if he had just told a hilarious anecdote. Kester had to resist the urge to leap over the campfire and throttle him.

"The official position of the Church is that it is up to each individual to deal with their own earthly vices," Kester continued. "They must draw power from within themselves and from the Light in order to resist temptation and addiction. My brother, however, insisted something needed to be done, that you threatened to corrupt an entire region, maybe even build an army out of the addicts. He went out on his own, without the support of the Church, to put a stop to you."

"Belisario!" Reis suddenly declared. "I thought that name sounded familiar. Your brother, his name is Demos, isn't it?"

"Was. He died recently." He did not mention that he died attempting the same mission they were now on.

"That's a shame. Man was a hell of a scrapper. I sure wouldn't have minded having him at our side."

"I feel the same way," Kester said. In truth, he knew that if

Demos was still around, he would have never let Kester come along on this mission. It would be him and Reis around the campfire now. Maybe Darius would still be alive. "As I've heard it, your fight with him was something of a draw. He succeeded in destroying your stores of the narcotic, but you bested him in combat and forced his retreat. It really left an impression on him, and on me. He considered failing to kill you his greatest failure, and it was the only time he had ever been bested in one-on-one combat. He vowed to one day find you and end you, but then the war started and he was needed elsewhere."

"Doesn't really answer my question of why you came to me for help," Reis said. Kester had the feeling Reis was sizing him up. "Do you intend on making good on your brother's vow, slaying me once this is all over? No, that's not it. When you speak of your brother, your words are words of respect, but your tone is of resentment. So you sought me to spite your brother."

"It is true, me and my brother have not always seen eye-to-eye," Kester said. *Very rarely did, in fact.* "But it is not resentment I feel for him. It is closer to sibling rivalry. I've often found myself trying to compete with him, and the legend that grew around him. When he failed to beat you in combat, I got the idea that if I was ever able to succeed where he failed I would prove myself his better, or at the very least his equal. So I often asked around about you, sought out the stories about you, tried to learn about your fighting style. I heard that you had once slew an entire company of men single-handed. It is because of all that I learned about you, that when I thought of who could possibly take this mission and stand a chance of success, your name was first in my mind."

"A company?" Reis laughed. It seemed he did not care about Kester's reasons as long as he had a story to boast. "I believe I know of the incident of which you speak. I once hired a few mercenaries to watch after my things while I traveled in search of rare ingredients for my research. The idiots let my home get trashed in my absence, but insisted on being paid anyways. They actually wished to be paid more, if you believe it, because they were forced to fight, like that wasn't their job to begin with. Needless to say, I refused.

"Turns out those idiots were part of a larger mercenary company. When the first men they sent to collect payment never returned, the entire company came out in force to exact its revenge. I suppose they numbered as a decent military company would, but they were hardly as organized or well-trained. There were plenty of vulnerabilities to exploit, as well as fears. Truthfully, I didn't kill too many of them, just the first few who came through my doors. But I scared the piss out of the rest of them using my shadows and the severed heads of their comrades." He laughed loudly. "Eventually they broke into full retreat, scattered everywhere, and I cut down as many as I could catch. My enemies have been few and far between since that day."

"You truly are without mercy," Kester said. "To slay enemies who have shown you their backs."

"I needed to set an example," Reis said. "Does my lack of compassion towards my enemies bother you?"

"On a normal day, perhaps," Kester replied. "But I believe it will serve us well on this mission. You have a heart as dark as Serpentine's, and that allows you to think as he would. Perhaps predict his actions. Or so I believe."

"Believe?" Reis scoffed. "Starting to grow so fond of me that you're hoping there's a chance for some kind of holy redemption yet?"

Kester suddenly had an image of Reis dressed in the garbs of the Church and couldn't help but chuckle.

"I believe that might be a bit of a stretch of the imagination," he said. "But I did see how you were with that boy earlier. You showed that there's some compassion in you. You even took him with us when we fled so that the soldiers wouldn't associate him with us. It is possible that there is some good in you yet."

Reis finished his meal. He rose to stretch his legs by walking around the campsite.

"Peter interests me," he said. "I have a different attitude towards things that interest me."

"What makes him so interesting?"

"He's outspoken and fearless, despite being just a child. His parents left him in charge of their wares once, and I happened to be looking for supplies at that time. I demanded the same 'discount' that I am accustomed to, but he refused. He knew who I was, he knew my reputation, but he still stood up to me and demanded full price. That kid showed more courage than every damned man in that market put together. I've decided to take him as an apprentice once he's old enough to hold a sword."

"You really think his parents are going to be alright with that? You don't seem to have the best reputation."

"I don't intend to give them much of a choice," Reis responded matter-of-factually. "I take what I want, whether it's supplies or an apprentice."

Having learned that the one glimmer of kindness he thought he had seen in Reis truly had some ulterior motives, Kester decided he wished to learn nothing more about Reis tonight. Not if he was going to be able to stomach him tomorrow. *So much for bonding.*

"I'm calling it a night," Kester said abruptly. "You should as well soon, we set out bright and early in the morning."

Reis gave him a sarcastic smile. "Yes, Commander."

Captain Konrad Marek looked over the note left by Beldaken momentarily before crumpling it up and tossing it to the ground.

"He's mocking us," Marek said. "Who does this man think he is?"

Lieutenant Zarik fidgeted nervously as he awaited the captain's order. Marek had been sent to take over the hunt for Beldaken after he managed to slip away from them twice.

"Explain again how he managed to escape the mansion," Marek commanded. "I'm afraid I don't yet understand."

The lieutenant knew that Marek forcing him to repeat his failures over and over was just to berate him. The details were quite simple. Marek just wanted to make sure his humiliation was complete.

"I positioned men at every possible entrance, including the underground tunnel," Zarik explained for the third time. "We prepared to set fire to the mansion, and I sent some men in to ensure he had no other means of escape. We were taken by surprise that he had companions in the mansion, apparently from the Church. One of them engaged my men while Beldaken escaped through the upper levels. We lost several men in pursuit."

"A lieutenant of the empire should never be surprised," Marek said coolly.

"Yes, sir."

It was late, or early, depending on perspective. The sun would rise in only an hour or so. Zarik was exhausted from his long day. He had received word a few hours ago that an officer straight from the capital was coming and that he was to wait on his arrival, however late that would be. It made no sense to Zarik how the captain arrived in such short time.   How had someone managed to arrive at this little backwater just hours after the bird telling of his arrival? Zarik knew of the captain's reputation to always be in the right place at the right time, but was not sure how he managed it.

"Then you had the good fortune to be informed by the kind people of this settlement that Reis had made his way here," Marek continued. "And yet he managed to escape again."

"We were told that he was in the stables with his companion from the Church," the lieutenant replied.   "We had surrounded the stables when we encountered that darkness, which is the best word I can come up with to describe it. We broke into the stables as quickly as we could, but found it empty. Nothing got out past us, sir, I can't explain how he escaped."

"You allowed yourself to be surprised once again."

Zarik found the captain to be an unsettling figure. He was tall and sleek, possessing the fit build of a career soldier. He had short hair that had gone gray prematurely, contradicting the youthful features of his face.   But it was the way he spoke that caused Zarik's uneasiness. Every word was spoken lightly, just above a whisper. As he spoke he moved, pacing slowly, every movement deliberate to help emphasize his words.   And his eyes never broke contact, they remained fixed on his target like a tiger stalking its prey.

"You are a lieutenant of the empire, Zarik. Do you know what that means?"

Zarik opened his mouth to begin to speak but was immediately silenced.

"It means you represent the will of the great Marcus Serpentine. It is your job to lead our soldiers in the execution of this will. You are a tool, a weapon, that Marcus Serpentine wields in his grand struggle. You are no more than a sword, and when a sword's blade is too dull it is no longer a weapon fit for Marcus Serpentine. You are dull, Zarik."

Zarik was grabbed suddenly from behind. He tried to struggle but felt the blade of a dagger press against his throat.

"I can only hope my own blade won't dull anytime soon, captain," a voice behind him said in an amused tone.

"You are one of the sharpest in the arsenal, Lech," Marek responded. "I am fortunate you were able to respond to my summons so promptly. You will be invaluable."

"I am but a blade to be swung at the enemies of Serpentine," the man with the blade at Zarik's throat said. Zarik gulped and shuddered as he felt the dagger begin to pierce into the skin. "Just point me at them."

Chapter 8

Reis rarely ever dreamed about anything of substance. He would close his eyes and be lost to a dark void, emptiness taken form, with not a sound or a smell or any other sign that anything besides him existed there. He liked it there. It was peaceful and there was nothing to worry about. There was nothing at all.

Unfortunately, this pleasant trip through the void was rudely interrupted by a loud, obnoxious voice. "Reis, wake up, we have to get moving."

Reis groggily opened his eyes and grimaced as his senses came back to him. The sounds of birds chirping, the smells of dirt mixed with the salty scent of sweat, the first morning light glittering in the horizon. *The filthy sights and sounds of nature.*

He rose to his feet against the angry protests of his body. He stretched his limbs and tried to work the pain out of his legs. *What a disgrace. I can't believe I used to do this all the time. My, how recent years have spoiled me.*

It could be worse, he supposed. The church-boy wanted them to ride through the nights. Reis had to lie and tell him that he had no experience sleeping in the saddle. Probably only a half-lie now, it had been so long he would probably fall off his horse trying. Their compromise was a few hours of camp each night.

He rummaged through a bag to find a fresh pair of clothes. 'Fresh' being a relative term. Even with what he purchased at the market he had less clothes than days they had been on the road, and Kester would not allow them to head into any towns to buy more, or get what he had clean. Best he could do was wear whatever smelled closest to clean each day.

The church-boy was packing up their meager camp now. He had already donned his armor sometime before he had woken Reis. Reis could not help but smile every time he saw the symbol of the church. *Reis Beldaken, a demon made flesh, and a noble defender of the Light, fighting side by side against a common enemy. If there is a god, he seems to have a great sense of humor.*

It was tough, but he tried to force down what passed for breakfast on the road, an assortment of nuts and dried fruit washed down with some hardtack. The food he had purchased had not lasted long and now he had to resort to sharing in Kester's rations. There would be some dried meat later in the day, that was what he had to look forward to.

Once the camp was packed up they were on their way. Ever since that first night, Kester seemed to prefer riding in silence. Silence suited Reis just fine, though he did enjoy trying to engage him from time to time by telling tales of his exploits. The church-boy's eyes would harden and his face would grimace in disgust as Reis told him about the people he killed, cheated, backstabbed, and lied to. *Truly a paragon of the morals of his Church.* He was careful not to push too far, it would do no good if Kester decided to attack him for something he said and he was forced to kill the poor boy.

He had no such stories in mind today so they carried on in silence. The monotony of the road was finally broken when he spotted ash rising in the distance.

"Smoke up ahead," he said. "That's the ash of a ravaged town if I ever saw it. The empire's been here recently. We should take care to keep distance from it. Don't want to risk running into whoever did that."

Kester shook his head. "We must go and see if there is any assistance we can lend."

"Hold on a second! I pointed it out so we could make sure to avoid the empire, not to walk right into them!"

Kester was already commanding his horse in that direction. "The flames are already out. The empire is not in the habit of sitting on ashes. Either way, we can't just ignore the plight of a people if there's a chance we can do anything to help them."

"Of course we can," Reis said. "Are you forgetting that we have a mission to accomplish? Many more towns will burn if we don't hurry and put a stop to Serpentine."

"And if we ignore the suffering of the people we are no better than he is. Besides, the Light shines the brightest on those of us who help others through the darkness."

Is stupidity a requirement to gain entry to the Church? "Let's just make this quick, then," Reis conceded. "But keep your Light to yourself."

The town they came to bore the sign "Colby," or at least it had. Now the sign lay on the road, covered in ash. The empire had truly shown no mercy to the people of Colby. Bodies littered the street, some burned, some cut down by swords. All of the homes had been severely damaged by the fires. It was unlikely that any repairs would be possible. If the town was to be rebuilt, all the damaged buildings would need to be torn down first.

The survivors trudged through the street with their heads low and disbelief in their eyes. A woman was sobbing loudly over the body of a dead boy, probably her son. A burn victim limped down the road, trying to disguise his considerable agony. The whole scene was disgustingly morbid. The only satisfaction to be had was Kester's awestruck expression.

"What could these poor people have done to bring down such wrath?" Kester wondered out loud.

"As long as one voice of dissent remains, the empire cannot truly declare its rule supreme, can it? And where there is one dissenter, there is usually more," Reis explained. It all seemed quite simple to him.

"Are you saying you approve of their methods?" Kester asked venomously.

"I wouldn't say approve, but understand, and appreciate the efficiency of it." Kester glared at him, so Reis decided to explain further. "Look, the empire is trying to assert its dominance and put down any idea about standing against them. The only people who would dare voice any opposition at this point are the extremely righteous, or the extremely stupid. Stupid people are easy enough to deal with, its the righteous you have to worry about. They're hard to deal with because they don't fear for their own lives, they value their beliefs above themselves. But, they do fear for the lives of others. So you make it known that their actions will not only have consequences for themselves, but for those they love. Destroying an entire town when they catch wind of dissent not only ensures the death of those dissenters, it also sends a strong message discouraging anyone else from getting too righteous in the future."

"I'm going to help these people in whatever way I can," Kester snapped. Apparently he had reached his limit of Reis's philosophy for the day. *Just trying to help you see the world the way it really is, outside the walls of your church.* "You can stand around and admire the empire's handiwork all you want. I'll find you later."

"Have fun."

With Kester gone, Reis was not sure exactly what to do to keep himself occupied. He was not the kind of person who was willing to get himself all dirty picking through debris and wading through ashes to help strangers, especially if there was nothing in it for him. He was skilled in the ways of medicine, and there was certainly no shortage of injured people about, so he decided to occupy his time by looking through the town for an injury on someone who looked like they might come from some kind of wealth. Perhaps some trinkets survived the fires and they would be gracious enough for the treatment to hand them over.

Or perhaps a damsel in distress whose gratitude would be expressed in other ways.

Unfortunately, he found that Colby, even in its prime, was an impoverished area. The people were destitute, barely surviving their daily lives. The fires of the empire was just the latest installment in their lives of misery and hardship. It was the kind of place that bred desperation, and desperation breeds resilient, independent people. It helped Reis understand why the empire needed to destroy this town; it was the kind of place that would naturally grow resistance. It also meant that he was unlikely to find anyone worth helping.

Or so he thought. As he rounded a corner near the edge of the smoldering town he found a young woman sifting through a large pile of burned wood. She was the perfect model of the fragile beauty: light auburn hair, innocent eyes, and a small, petite frame. Just at the sight of her Reis felt himself burning with desire. He had lived mostly in solitude for the past few years and had not been with a woman in all that time. He decided that was about to change.

"You need a hand?" he asked as he approached.

"Thank you, yes," the woman responded without looking up. "There is a man trapped beneath all this mess somewhere. I have heard muffled cries. Please, help me find him."

Reis was not enthusiastic about getting his clothes even more dirty digging through debris, but decided it may be worth it to win favor with the young beauty. He helped her move aside the remains of what had been a two story home, once, but was now little more than charred wood and rubble. Together they moved aside a large chunk of what looked to have been part of the roof and uncovered the head of a potfaced man. He took a few deep, grateful breaths. Reis and the woman tried removing the rubble that covered his body, but discovered that he was pinned beneath underneath a large wooden beam. It was too big and heavy for just the two of them. The potfaced man struggled desperately underneath it, but could not pull himself free.

"I'll go gather some more people," Reis said. "With enough of us we should be able to lift that thing."

"No time," the woman said, shaking her head. "This man's body won't be able to hold this weight for much longer. He'll be crushed."

"Well I don't see how you intend to -"

He was stopped mid-sentence when the wood beam began to rise, apparently on its own. He looked over at the woman and saw in her face an expression of great strain and concentration. Her teeth were grit, her eyes were set in dead focus, and her brow was furrowed. As she concentrated on the beam it slowly lifted up until it was a few inches above the trapped man. As soon as he was free, Reis reached out and grabbed the man, dragging him away from the beam. Once he was clear the woman let loose a heavy sigh and the beam fell back to the ground.

"Are you alright?" she asked with what sounded to Reis like genuine concern. *Been a while since I've heard that tone.*

"Yes," the man coughed out. "I have suffered worse in the past. I am eternally in your debt."

He gave a courteous bow before leaving them. Reis turned to congratulate the woman but she had already run off to help the next person. He chased after her.

"That was quite impressive back there," he said when he had caught up, "Ms ... ?"

"Kindra Tandy."

"Reis Beldaken. It's a real pleasure to meet you."

Kindra was distracted as she helped an old man with his burns and was not paying Reis any mind. He began to get frustrated but was not nearly ready to quit.

"Let me give you a hand," he offered.

Kindra seemed surprised when Reis put his medical skills to work. He moved with the efficiency and skill of a trained doctor, from one wounded to the next. She possessed only limited supplies, but they did what they could to disinfect wounds, put ointment on burns, and bandage up the worst wounds. Reis was even successful at setting a few broken bones. He could see that Kindra was quite impressed.

"I appreciate all of your help," she said when they were finally alone for the moment.

"Anytime," Reis said in the most sympathetic voice he could fake. "I was only glad I could be of help."

"Don't do that."

"Do what?"

"Pretend. You're no good at it."

Reis frowned. *Am I that poor an actor? I should have taken more notes from the Church-boy.* "I'm afraid I don't have the faintest idea what you mean," he lied.

Kindra faced him and stared him in the eyes. She was a full head shorter than him, forcing her to arch her neck to look up him, but her gaze was intense nonetheless.

"You are a man of a dark heart and cruel intentions. It is all over your face and can be read as clearly as any book. Particularly in your eyes. Your eyes are like pools of cruelty, ready to drown anyone who has the misfortune to be caught in them. So do not mock me with false courtesy, it is far more insulting than if you just acted yourself and told me what it that you truly want from me. While I am grateful for the help, I know that there is more to your intentions."

"Fair enough," Reis said, allowing his voice to return to its usual tone. "You are very attractive, just my type. I desire you. I hope that by helping you out enough around here we will wind up in bed together. Straight forward enough for you?"

Kindra let out an exasperated sigh. "I figured as much. I'll warn you, it is an unlikely outcome. However, you do seem to possess some medical training and I will not turn down your help if you choose to continue to provide it."

"I suppose 'unlikely' is not the same as 'impossible,'" Reis said with a laugh. "I suppose I can continue to lend a hand. I don't have much else to do until Church-boy feels he done enough good deeds."

"The Church is here?"

"Just one of them," Reis said. "Actually my traveling companion for the moment, if you could believe it. We're off to be a pain in the ass of Marcus Serpentine."

"You should be careful who hears you say things like that," Kindra said softly. "Lest your home suffer the same fate as this town did."

"A little late for that. The empire made the mistake of making an enemy of me by setting my home ablaze, now I'm out for revenge. Speaking of which." Reis paused and glanced around to make sure no one was listening. "You're the one who needs to be careful. You know the imperials have standing orders to capture or kill all Willers. I'd use that ability of yours as seldom as possible if I were you."

"I am aware."

Kindra looked down at the ground, looking as if someone had just knocked the wind out of her. She quickly shook it off and regained her composure.

"I've already seen the fate of a number of Willers who refused to go with the empire. Some of them were friends. I've done my best to hide my ability to avoid detection, and I don't stay in one place for long. I don't intend to let the empire get its hands on me."

There was such determination in her voice that Reis couldn't help but be impressed. He was slowly coming to realize what he saw on the outside, the fragile beauty, was merely a disguise she wore, and that she was truly an intense and strong woman. *All the better.*

She would not be as easy to conquer as Reis had first assumed.

"Well come on, break's over," Kindra said. "There's still plenty of people to help, let's get moving."

"And we return those who have passed to the Light. May the Light guide them now as it did in life and illuminate their path into eternity. Though we are left behind, let us too turn to the Light, now more than ever. Only it will illuminate these dark times and give them meaning. And though we mourn the losses we have suffered today, take solace in knowing that our loved ones will always be with us, watching us from eternity, and acting as keepers of the Light shining on all of us. For as long as the Light continues to shine upon us, we are still connected to our kin."

Kester had performed far too many burial rites in the past few months. Up until now they had been mostly for fallen soldiers in his command. This was the first time he had performed it for civilians. The surviving townspeople had gathered most of their dead into a mass grave and were relieved when Kester showed up. They had been worried that the spirits of their friends and family would not be able to rest easy without someone to perform the rites. Kester was glad to provide whatever small amount of solace to these poor people that he possibly could.

"May the Light shine forever brightly, and may it shine brightest on those who have lost their lives to the darkness so they may never know darkness in eternity. To these we now bid our final farewell."

He finished the rites by dropping a candle on the ground of the grave site. One of the survivors near him began to weep more loudly. It was tragedy, that so many should lose their homes and loved ones in the same day. They would have no time to properly mourn, not if they intended to survive themselves. They would need to move on soon. The elder man who had organized the grave gave Kester a courteous bow, which he returned.

"You must have truly been guided here by the Light to appear just when we needed you the most," the elder said.

"The Light guides us all," Kester replied. "And right now, it guides me to provide any help I can to ease the suffering of your people. Is there anything else I can do to ease your burden?"

"I believe there just might be."

"You're not serious, are you?" Reis asked with growing frustration. "We really don't have time for this."

Kester would not listen. "It will only set us back a day, and it will go a great way to helping these people."

"But our horses?"

Reis could hardly believe what he was hearing. Kester had just found him, which Reis took to mean he was done playing hero and they could be on their way. Apparently, Kester had just stopped by to let Reis know that he had volunteered their horses in aiding the survivors. They were all moving to a nearby settlement and needed the horses to carry injured people and move personal possessions. It would stall them at least a day, time which they did not have.

"A sellsword happened by and I've paid him to procure wagons and horses. He should be back midday tomorrow with them. We can reclaim our own horses then."

"You know," Kindra said in a voice thick with faux seduction, "Women find men willing to make personal sacrifices very attractive."

"That line might work better if you hadn't already used it three times to get me to dig into my personal medical supplies," Reis responded. "I'm almost out of bandages. If I am wounded now I'm going to bleed all over my clothes."

"This isn't your choice," Kester said with a surprisingly commanding voice. "These are my horses and this is my mission. I'm making the decision to help these good people out, and you'll just have to wait until I say it's time to go."

So the church-boy does have some stones. But he chose a damn stupid topic to assert himself over.

He glared at Kester, felt the rage building within him. *Maybe I should show him what happens to people who try and give me orders.* His fingers brushed against the hilt of his sword. *Though I guess it is mostly my fault. I knew what I was getting into when I agreed to work with the Church. This kind of thing is inevitable. Self-righteousness over practicality.*

Kindra's eyes were on him. As much as he wanted to give Kester a lesson, he figured that doing so might hurt his already poor chances. He was still pissed off, though, and knew he would not be able to just sit on his ass all day waiting for the carriages to arrive.

"The sellsword you hired," Reis muttered as calmly as he could manage. "Where is he?"

"I believe he just left by the eastern road," Kester said. "Why?"

"I have no intention of sticking around and sitting on my hands for an entire day. Besides, with time such an important factor, someone should be watching him to make sure he doesn't dawdle."

"Fine, if that's what you want," Kester said, the authority in his voice drained. "His name is Alvis, if I remember correctly. If you leave right away you should be able to catch up to him. Just make sure not to draw any attention to yourself, alright? This is supposed to be a simple job, but you're a wanted man, so don't complicate things by getting noticed by the empire."

"I'm not stupid. Enjoy your smoldering ruins until I return." He turned his attention to the not-so-delicate beauty. "Kindra, this isn't over between us, just so you know."

"There isn't anything between us," Kindra said, passively.

"So you claim. But you know you shall not be able to resist me forever."

"Charming."

"Watch my woman while I'm gone, Church-boy, and if you lay a hand on her I will run you through when I return."

"Your woman?" Kester and Kindra replied almost

simultaneously.

Reis turned and hurried away.   He could hear them talking behind him.

"You have a strange choice in bedfellows for a man of the Church," Kindra said.

"Desperate times," Kester replied.

Desperate times, Reis agreed.

Chapter 9

Reis rushed down the road in pursuit of the sellsword. He had no idea what the man looked like, but had met plenty of his kind. There was only one kind of mercenary in Reis's experience: large, hairy, and dumb as a brick. The sellsword should not have had too much of a head start, and with Reis's speed, he should catch up to him quickly.

After a short time he came across a lone man walking down the path, a pack across his shoulder and a sword at his side. He assumed that this man could not be the sellsword he was looking for, he was far too thin and scrawny to be a mercenary. Just to be certain he approached the man.

"Hm?" the man grunted when he heard Reis's approach.

"Alvis?" Reis asked.

The man nodded. "Yes, that's me."

"Alvis, the sellsword who is currently on a job for the people of Colby?"

"That's right."

Reis was surprised that this man could make a living as a sellsword. He was small and gentle looking. His body lacked the muscular tone of the typical mercenary, and his face was soft and boyishly smooth. Every mercenary Reis had ever met had been gruff and ungroomed, their grimy appearances serving to help sell themselves as tough, hardy warriors. Alvis was well-groomed, wore clean clothes, and smelled strongly of soap. He was the opposite of what Reis was expecting.

"Look, if you've come to cancel the job, I don't return advances, so you can just tell that man from the Church that I'm not giving him back his coin," Alvis said.

And just how much coin did Kester pay for this?

"I'm more here to watch our investment," Reis said.

"If you wish," Alvis said with a shrug. "Seemed like a pretty simple task to me, I'm just to secure some horses and carriages. But I won't turn down the company and conversation, I suppose."

"I'd prefer if we walked in silence," Reis said. He had no intention of being friendly with a lowly mercenary.

"Whatever you prefer, my master," Alvis said with an

exaggerated bow. "I am but a humble sellsword here in your employ. If you wish it, I could also provide the master with a foot-rub to ease his aching feet."

Reis didn't respond, he just let out a low growl.

No one watching here. It would be easy to just kill him and return with the horses myself.

He decided the unpleasant argument with Kester would not be worth the satisfaction he would momentarily gain for cutting this mercenary down and decided against it. He instead motioned for Alvis to lead the way and followed far enough behind to discourage conversation.

Reis watched the sellsword carefully as they walked, trying to get a read on him. Mercenaries might be dumb as dogs but they were not without a certain low cunning. An instinct for survival they had to pick up early on or die. Reis had met sellswords who could take his gold with one hand and try to stab him in the back with the other, and the more clever of them had come close to succeeding.

The key was the ability to mask any sign of emotion. A stone-cold face and a closed mouth. These were the signs of an experienced mercenary. One that never let anyone know what they were thinking.

Alvis, on the other hand, never seemed to have a thought he did not vocalize. Despite Reis's absolute silence, or perhaps encouraged by it, Alvis decided to announce everything he was seeing. He described the trees, the road, the rocks, the fucking sky. He even stopped to talk to the animals. "Hello, Mr. Bunny. Do you want to be my friend? No one else seems to want to talk to me."

That easy smile, the constant jabbering, the exaggerated movements of his arms as he made his proclamations about the world all made for a very difficult read. *He's either incredibly stupid or incredibly dangerous. Possibly both.*

After a few hours Alvis slowed down to let Reis catch up to him.

"I'm still not interested in conversation," Reis said. "Sorry if my silence gave you the wrong impression."

"Worry not, your charm has not been lost on me," Alvis said in a hushed voice. "I only wished to let you know that you've picked up a secret admirer."

He motioned subtly behind Reis. Reis did not need to turn around to catch his meaning. They were being followed.

"How long?" he asked.

"I noticed him a few miles ago. He's a sneaky sort, always sticking to the trees, so it may have been longer. I think he's following you, I don't have any enemies besides a few angry husbands, and they're typically more 'blind fury' and less 'patient stalker.'"

"Empire?"

"Possibly. He's not wearing any kind of distinguishing marks I could see, but I've only caught glimpses of him."

They continued walking, trying to make their conversation seem casual. Reis felt himself gripping the sword at his side. He tried to relax, he didn't want to let his stalker know that they were on to him prematurely.

"We can probably lose him," Alvis said. "But I have a feeling you're the confrontational kind."

"I do lean a little bit on that side. Just give me one minute, I'll have this fool's throat slit and we can be on our way."

"I'd advise against a straight-on attack. The moment he senses danger he's going to disappear."

Reis frowned. The sellsword was right, of course. "Then what you suggest?"

"Just follow my lead."

Lech watched his target from his concealed spot within the foliage. The assassin steadied his crossbow, ready to take his shot the moment the opportunity arose. Reis Beldaken was now talking with that other man; it seemed he was right in his assumption that the two of them were traveling companions. It certainly complicated things. Both men were armed and Beldaken was known to be an incredibly dangerous opponent alone. He would only get one shot with his crossbow, in the time it would take him to reload he would already be set upon. And with the winds as strong as they were, there was no guarantee his shot would be fatal.

He would have to wait until the two of them were separated to make his move. Nature had to call for one of them eventually. Fortunately, Lech was nothing if not patient. He fondly remembered tracking a priest, one who had the ill-idea to preach that open resistance to Serpentine was the work of the Light, for months before finally getting the opportunity to strike. The priest had had the good sense to surround himself with adoring crowds at all hours of the day. Finally he saw the moment, when the priest's devotion failed him against the advances of an attractive young fan and the two sought some privacy. He was able to sneak in, slit both of their throats, and sneak out without anyone seeing him. Patience had its rewards.

Tracking Beldaken had been simple enough. He was seen traveling north from Alleways with some blond in Church armor. They avoided towns and major roads, but their path was not hard to follow. The remains of recent campsites had allowed Lech to stay right behind them. He tracked them to the recently fire-ravaged town of Colby, where he learned Beldaken had left by the eastern road just a few hours before. The idiot in the Church armor was still in Colby, but he was not Lech's target.

Beldaken and his companion stopped and faced each other. They seemed to be arguing about something, loudly. Money, from the sounds of it. Suddenly Beldaken had his sword in his hand and his companion was on the ground.

It seemed he may get his shot. Beldaken stopped and knelt over his collapsed companion. Checking him for something, maybe. He was completely immobile and defenseless, and his companion seemed to be in no position to do anything about it. Lech couldn't have asked for a better opportunity.

He took his time and carefully lined up for his shot. At the first lull in the wind, he would fire.

"You're a decent actor," Reis said.

"It's useful for getting into ladies' beds," Alvis said from his position on the ground. He had dropped so hard that Reis himself almost believed he had really stabbed him. "You should see my wealthy nobleman act."

"You see him?" Reis asked.

Reis had bent over and was pretending to search Alvis's pockets. In truth he was knelt down so that the Alvis could see over his shoulder.

"Third tree from your left when you turn around. He's got a crossbow fixed on you, if I'm not mistaken, so we have to move fast. You ready?"

"Better be as quick as you claim," Reis growled.

Lech had his perfect shot lined up and was about to fire when Beldaken grabbed a bag from the fallen man and spun around. In reflex Lech pulled the trigger. Beldaken held the bag in front of him and the bolt pierced it.

Damn, he sees me!

Beldaken bolted off to his right. Lech tried to follow his movements, but his attention was needed elsewhere as Beldaken's companion leaped to his feet and started barreling towards him. He ducked out of his position and tried to disappear into the high grass, where he would crawl away. Beldaken's companion was too fast and there was no way for him to disappear in time. He was only a few strides away now.

Lech dropped his crossbow and pulled a dagger from one of his many hidden holsters. With a reflexive flick of the wrist he tossed it at the charging man. In a single motion the man drew his sword, a rapier, and deflected the dagger mid-flight. Lech backstepped, drawing another dagger in each hand and sending them flying. Without slowing down the man spun around, allowing the daggers to pass by him harmlessly.

Lech realized that this was no amateur combatant he was dealing with. He would have to be careful. He drew another dagger as the man stepped towards him.

"I would drop that if I was you," the man said, his sword in a readied position.

"Don't underestimate me, I've killed more men with these daggers than you can count," Lech said. "Your sword won't get close."

"Not me you should be worried about, but him," the man replied, pointing behind him.

Lech turned just in time to take the blunt end of a sword to the face. The world went white and for a moment he was weightless. He could feel the blood running down his face. His nose felt like it was broken.

As the world came back into focus he realized that he was on the ground. He looked up and saw Reis Beldaken standing over him.

"We should talk," Beldaken said.

"Told you it'd work," Alvis said triumphantly. "The old 'feint fight.' I've used it before to escape a few jilted lovers. Admittedly, this is the first time I've used it to take down an assassin."

"We're all very proud of you," Reis said sarcastically. "How are you with interrogations?"

Alvis smiled his easy smile. "Afraid I'm a little sensitive for anything too serious."

"You might want to turn away then. Things are going to get serious."

The assassin watched the conversation from his back. Reis looked to see if there was any fear in his eyes over the talk of the impending 'interrogation,' but he saw none. Instead his eyes were fierce with determination. He would be a hard man to break, and dangerous. He was like a wolf backed into a corner and could strike at any moment. Reis was not taking any chances. He held his sword at ready.

"Let's start with something simple," Reis said, "Are you from the empire?"

"You already know that I am," the assassin responded. "The empire will never stop chasing you. Your days are short, Beldaken. You should have let my bolt hit you, your death would have been far more merciful than what the next one will do to you."

"I'll take my chances. Imperials don't travel alone. How many others are around? Where are they camped?"

"That's two questions."

"Pick one," Reis shortly replied.

"What were the options again?" the assassin said as he smiled through his bloody face.

Reis delivered a sharp kick to his gut. The assassin coughed and wheezed from the impact, his breath taken.

"How many are there?" Reis repeated.

"Enough," the assassin answered.

Reis delivered another powerful kick, this one to the assassin's ribcage. He yelled out in pain and clutched his chest.

"How did you find me?" Reis asked. "I didn't exactly advertise this little side trip."

"The empire sees all," the assassin groaned. "Nothing escapes the eyes of Marcus Serpentine. No matter where you run, where you hide, he will always find you."

"I wish he would," Reis said. "Would save me the trouble of going all the way to the palace to kill him. Instead I've got to waste my time on lackeys."

The assassin was arrogant. Reis knew that with people like that, when physical intimidation fails, revealing some information yourself could cause them to let something slip. *Not that he'll live long enough to use anything I tell him.*

"Do you honestly intend to tell me you intend to go after Marcus Serpentine himself?" The assassin laughed before breaking into a cough. "Is that the point of this little trip of yours? Here we thought you were just running away. Just wait until Marek hears about this!"

And there it is.

"Who is Marek?"

The assassin chuckled. "A good man. You'll meet him soon enough, I'm sure."

Reis put his foot on the assassin's chest to hold him still and held his sword at his throat.

"If you don't start answering my questions, this conversation is going to be very short."

"You have no idea."

The assassin's next move happened so suddenly that Reis did not even realize it was happening until it was too late. With a lightning quick flick of the wrist a dagger shot out from under the assassin's sleeve and struck Reis in the back of the hand. It pierced straight through his hand until the blade stuck out of his palm. The injury forced Reis to drop his sword and loosen the force on the assassin's chest. The assassin rolled out from under him and jumped to his feet, another dagger already in hand.

Alvis rushed back and drew his sword. Reis pulled the dagger from his hand with a pained shout and tossed it to the ground. He looked to his sword and prepared to make a grab for it.

"You're a dead man now!" Reis shouted.

"Such anger," the assassin said. His attention was focused on Alvis, who was trying to flank him with his sword lowered and ready. "You'll be calm soon enough."

Reis dove and made a grab for his sword. His hand gripped the handle and he sprang back to his feet. To his surprise, the assassin did not even try to stop him. His attention remained fixed on Alvis. A second later Reis realized why. He began to get dizzy, very dizzy, and incredibly tired. Soon he no longer had the energy to stand and he dropped to one knee.

"What did you-" Reis started but couldn't muster enough will to finish.

"My daggers are laced with a fast-acting poison. You should appreciate it, I am given to understand you are a man of chemicals yourself. I created it myself. I find that other poisons just don't have that immediate effect."

Reis could barely think straight. The world seemed to be spinning around him. The assassin's words echoed hollowly. His eyes were heavy. He struggled to stand but couldn't. He lost his balance and dropped to his side. It was all he could do to try and keep his focus on the assassin.

The assassin drew another dagger so that now he wielded one in either hand. He poised to strike, he and Alvis slowly dancing around one another, waiting to see who made the first move.

"All it'll take is one little cut with either of these, and that's the end for you," the assassin threatened.

"I'll have to be careful not to be cut then," Alvis replied.

Alvis lunged and the assassin deflected it with one blade while attempting to strike with the other. Alvis brought his sword around fast enough to parry. The two became locked in rapid struggle of blocks and parries, one false move meaning death. Alvis's swordsmanship had style, suggesting formal training in swordplay as a sport as opposed to a tool of war. His movements were fluid, his footwork was flawless, and he was able to keep up with the blades of his ambidextrous opponent. The assassin's movements were rapid and relentless, a furious flurry of strikes that showed no signs of slowing from fatigue or his injuries.

The fight faded out of Reis's vision. He was quickly losing consciousness. He struggled just to stay awake. With great effort he was able to move his hand and take the small vial of murky red elixir from inside his shirt. After a few clumsy attempts to remove the cork, he finally succeeded and hastily swallowed its contents.

His vision slowly cleared. He tilted his head. Alvis and the assassin were still locked in a struggle. Alvis was gaining ground, forcing the assassin backwards, his strikes getting closer to landing. One strike cut the collar on the assassin's shirt. Another cut him across the forearm.

Reis forced himself to his feet. He was groggy, dizzy, nauseous, but he forced himself to focus. Slowly, quietly, he approached the assassin.

One of the assassin's jabs found its mark. A small trickle of blood, the assassin's dagger had managed to sneak under the rapier's hand-guard and nicked Alvis's hand. It would hardly qualify as a wound if it weren't for the blade's poison. Both of them stepped back, withdrawing from the combat.

Alvis tried to stop the poison from spreading. He cut the wounded area and tried to let it bleed out. The assassin laughed.

"You underestimate just how quick this poison spreads," he said. "You're already a dead -"

Reis came up from behind him. The assassin heard him coming too late. Reis lunged. The assassin flinched out of the way just enough to avoid being run through, instead taking a nasty cut across his side. Blood poured out of the wound in sheets. The assassin staggered away from Reis, his daggers barely raised to defend himself.

The blow took the last of Reis' energy out of him. He dropped back to his knees, leaning on his sword for support. Alvis had already fallen to the ground as the poison took hold. Both were defenseless and could be easily finished off. Reis braced himself for the impending strike.

The assassin staggered and clutched at his wound, trying to stem the flow of blood. He gave Reis one last look before turning and staggering away, leaving a trail of blood behind him.

Reis was slowly regaining his strength, but did not have enough yet to chase the assassin. He just cursed after him and slowly brought himself back to his feet. He unsteadily walked over towards Alvis, who was lying weakly on the ground.

"Hey," Reis said. "You still alive?"

"Barely," Alvis said weakly.

Reis pulled out his vial. There was only a small amount of the elixir left. If he wasted it on the sellsword, there would be none left for him if he was wounded again. After giving away so much of his medical supplies in Colby, he was not sure that he could afford to leave himself so vulnerable.

Not unless he could use it improve his chances, anyway. The sellsword's personality was grating, but he had proven to be a decent fighter.

Plus, it might not hurt to have a buffer between me and the Church-boy. Might keep us from killing one another.

"Sellsword, I will save your life," Reis said. "Consider it payment for a job I am about to offer you, one you will have no choice but to accept."

Alvis nodded his agreement. Reis put the vial to his lips and let Alvis drink the remainder of the elixir. A few minutes later, strength had returned to both of them.

"That was some effective medicine," Alvis remarked as he examined his hand. "I've never seen anything like it."

"My own concoction," Reis commented. "And that was the last of it, which is why I expect you to accept this job without question."

"Guess there's no point in arguing that now. So what epic quest have I just signed up for? Saving a princess? Slaying a dragon?"

"Assassinating an emperor."

"Oh, of course." Alvis sighed. "I thought you were just bluffing when you said that during the interrogation. I couldn't imagine you were serious."

"Marcus Serpentine has crossed me. I don't care who he is or how much power he wields, if someone crosses me they will die."

"Somehow I doubt that Serpentine will be the one doing the dying."

Reis glared at the sellsword. "This matter isn't up for debate. I saved your life because I was moderately impressed by your skill and could use an extra sword at my side. Otherwise I could have just let you die and kept the elixir for myself."

"Of course, my life would not have been in danger if not for you in the first place," Alvis pointed out. "That assassin was obviously after you."

"Details that do not concern me. You already agreed to accept the job when I gave you the elixir. Is a sellsword's word not his bond?"

Alvis smiled. "Today started out with such a simple job. I was hardly expecting any royal assassinations in my near future. But I suppose I am so obligated. Very well, to our deaths we go. But first, we have another task to complete."

Lech had managed to staunch the bleeding and take cover in some high grass while he waited for the pain to subside, and his strength to return. He had lost a lot of blood, but he was fairly sure he managed to stop the bleeding in time to keep from dying. His biggest concern now was the easily tracked trail of blood he'd left behind. Both men were poisoned, dying, but Beldaken's sudden recovery left Lech unsure of just how fatal his poison was to him. Just to be safe, Lech had run another half a mile after treating the wound.

Now he was exhausted and in a great deal of pain. He was going over and over in his head where he went wrong. He had allowed himself to be spotted, that much was certain. He fell for their deception. He underestimated Beldaken and took his eyes off him just because he was poisoned. All unforgivable mistakes.

The more he thought back to Beldaken's sudden recovery the more convinced he was that he was still alive. The poison had failed to kill him for some reason. Perhaps he had an immunity.

He had failed.

But at least something good would come of it. Lech now knew where Beldaken was heading and what he was planning. Captain Marek would certainly find this information interesting.

For now, though, he needed to rest and recover. He would need his strength.

Chapter 10

A full day had gone and past since Reis had set out after the sellsword, Alvis. They should be returning any hour now, assuming they ran into no problems along the road. With the Empire after him, Kester wondered whether letting Reis go had been a good idea. *Not as if I could have talked him out of it if I wanted.*

Kester had been working side-by-side with Kindra, helping as many of the survivors of Colby as they possibly could. Many more succumbed to their injuries in the night, and Kester performed more burial rights. It was a heart-wrenching ordeal, even for someone with Kester's training. He could see Kindra struggling to maintain her composure.

They had done everything they could. Only time would tell the fates of the rest of the survivors. All they could do now was wait to move on.

"You should get some rest," Kester said. "You barely slept last night. Don't let your own health deteriorate."

Kindra shook her head. "I'll be fine. I am used to the late nights."

She was a remarkable woman, strong and resilient in character. Despite their grim surroundings, he couldn't help but notice she was a remarkable beauty, soft and shapely. He felt an uncharacteristic twinge of jealousy at Reis.

Kester found himself thinking of how she reminded him of the High Cleric, Delia. He thought of their last encounter, when she handed him the key that held the future of the Church. He wondered how she was doing now. Was the Church still fighting? How many more were dead? Was Delia still protected? He remembered how worried she had seemed, how certain she was that these were the last days of the Church as they knew it. It was like she had been predicting her own demise. Kester's heart sank thinking about it.

"Empire soldiers, coming in from the north!" someone shouted, snapping Kester back to reality.

"What in Light's name could they want now?" Kindra exclaimed. "They've already taken everything from these people. Surely they could not be coming back to finish what they started?"

"That seems cruel, even for them," Kester said.

They may have tracked Reis here. Kester felt a pang of guilt. *We may have led them here.*

"Tell everyone to hide the best they can," Kester shouted. He began working to loosen the straps on his armor. "I will see what they want, and if needed, do what I can to draw them away."

He did not need to ask twice. Kindra led the survivors into the one building still standing nearby. Kester stood alone in the middle of the ruins. He could hear the sounds of at least a dozen horses approaching, far more soldiers than he could hope to take on alone. Fleeing wasn't an option. Too many of the survivors were in no condition to run and he could not just abandon them. His only hope was diplomacy. Reis was not here. They could search if they wanted. Hopefully he would not return until after they had gone.

The imperials' horses stepped carefully through the wreckage towards him. Kester laid his sword and shield on the ground, next to his chestpiece, to show that he was not looking for a fight. The horses stopped in front of him and the soldiers dismounted. The one with the most polished armor, whom it was clear led this rabble, approached Kester first.

"I am Lieutenant-Colonel Bartam Ramsay," he introduced himself. He was short and stocky, not exactly what you would expect of a soldier. He eyed the insignia on the shield. "We are here in search of Willers, not to combat the Church, that's not my mission." He tilted his head to speak to his men. "Never do more work than you have to, right, boys?" His men chuckled politely.

"I do not wish a confrontation," Kester said. "Just merely the chance to state the facts. There are no Willers here, just myself and a handful of survivors, none of whom have shown any sign of such an ability."

"Some are able to hide it well," Ramsay said. "Very well, as a matter of fact, to be able to hide it from me."

"What do you mean?" Kester asked.

"The Emperor has ordered all Willers report for a special assignment. I was dispatched to this town because it was reported that they were harboring one. After they refused to turn him over when I asked nicely, I set the town ablaze. I assumed whoever it was died in the fire, but apparently I showed too much mercy. I've been informed there is still a Willer who has managed to survive. It seems I should have left none alive, just to be safe. Now I have to waste my time coming back to finish the job I started instead of returning home and relaxing after an exhaustive trip. Mercy always comes back to sting you, doesn't it?"

"I don't know whom you speak of," Kester said. He honestly didn't.

"Perhaps you don't," Ramsay said, sounding unconcerned. "Perhaps it would be simpler just to kill everyone to ensure the Willer is killed." He looked over to the building that the survivors were hiding in. "That's where they all are, isn't it? This can be solved quite simply. Men!"

Kester looked at his sword and shield on the ground. He could grab them before the soldiers had time to react. But then what? He would be cut down in a matter of seconds and the survivors would all be killed. He had no options. No action he could think of taking that had any chance of helping those survivors.

Before he could act, Kindra appeared from the building, her hands raised in surrender.

"I am the Willer you seek," she said. "Please don't harm any of the others."

"Kindra!" Kester exclaimed. He had no idea.

They burned down the town because of her. Of course she would hide it.

Ramsay looked at the young woman with surprise and pleasure. He held up his hand to signal his men to stay back.

"I think we can avoid the unpleasantness of having to slaughter all the rest of your folk," Ramsay said. "Seeing as you've given yourself up so willingly. If you wish to ensure their continued safety, you will come with us and continue to be so cooperative."

Kindra nodded and solemnly gave herself up. Kester stood silent, stunned, as she was bound and thrown over the back of Ramsay's horse.

"What do you intend to do with her?" he finally managed to asked.

"She's a Willer who refused to provide her service as was demanded by the great Marcus Serpentine. As he has ordered, she will be killed." He smiled wickedly. "After I'm through with her, anyway."

Kester swelled up with righteous anger. How any man could could be so callous was beyond him. He once again found himself eyeing his sword on the ground. He wondered if there would be enough time before he was killed to get one good attack on the colonel, one that would sever his manhood and leave him incapable of carrying out his intentions.

Ramsay must have seen where Kester's eye fell. He moved over to the weapon and laid a foot over it.

"Go on," Ramsay taunted. "Pick it up."

He gave it a light kick to knock it closer to Kester. It came to rest at Kester's feet.

"Come on," he continued. "Are all men of the Church so indecisive, so cowardly? You want to pick it up, don't you? You want to take that sword and silence me. But you're afraid. As you should be, of course. If you picked that sword up you know I would not only kill you, I would slaughter everyone just because you dared to stand up to me. And I would still have my way with the woman, nothing there would change. But yet you eye the sword, contemplate picking it up, taking that chance, because you are a man of justice, isn't that right? So which wins out in the end, hm? Your righteousness or your good sense? Your anger or your cowardice? Come on, what will it be?"

He walked up to Kester til he was only inches away from his face. Kester glared at him, his hands shaking in fury. The other soldiers were close by, laughing and enjoying their colonel's bravado. Kester had never felt so powerless in his life. He wanted nothing more than to grab his sword and, at the very least, die with glory and honor.

But he knew he couldn't. He could feel the key on him, weighing him down and staying his hand. He still had his mission to accomplish, one that needed to be done to prevent more innocent people from dying at the hands of the Empire. He still needed to face Marcus Serpentine. The best he could do now was not provoke the colonel into killing the rest of the survivors.

Even if it means allowing an innocent woman to be sacrificed. He felt disgusted with himself.

"I thought so," Ramsay said with a self-satisfied smile.

He kneed Kester in the gut before delivering a mighty punch to his face. Kester was knocked to the ground. He clutched his stomach and spat out blood. Ramsay laughed as his men cheered him on. He kicked Kester in the back repeatedly, the blows sending shards of pain down Kester's spine and causing him to scream out. Finally he let up. Kester struggled to catch his breath.

"This is what the Church has been reduced to," Ramsay laughed. "Pathetic." He signaled to his men. "Alright, we're done here.

Let's move out. You two, ride back to the camp and let them know of our success, tell them we move to Ivor and we should meet there. You, I'm tasking you with dealing with our little 'debt.' You can catch up to us at the next camp afterward. The rest of you, you ride with me on to Ivor."

There was grunts of acknowledgment of their orders and they all rode off in their respective directions. Kester got one last glance of Kindra before she disappeared from sight on the back of Ramsay's horse. He cursed aloud and punched the ground.

This all needs to be worth it in the end, he pleaded with himself. *Please, it has to be.*

Reis and Alvis were not far from Colby when they spotted two horses riding away from it. Reis immediately recognized the imperial colors.

Somehow I doubt they're here to welcome us back.

"They're coming right our way," Alvis said. "What should we do?"

"Isn't it obvious?" Reis said. "We kill them."

"We don't even know if they're here for us."

"Do you want to take that chance?"

They were each riding at the front of a wagon being pulled by two horses. Kester had only given Alvis enough money to rent two wagons, pulled by older cart-horses that were accustomed to travel, not war. Reis hesitated only a moment.

Got to make do with what you have.

He leaped from the driver's seat of the wagon onto the back of one of the horses. Drawing his sword he cut the harness that was connecting the horse to the wagon.

"You coming?" he asked Alvis.

"Nice to see someone so excited about what they do," Alvis jested.

Reis commanded his horse forward. The old cart-horse proved to actually have some speed in its bones. The imperials were taken by surprise by this horseman who was charging at them with sword drawn. They reached for their own weapons but by the time they drew Reis had already rode past them, his sword swinging at his side and catching one of the imperial rounceys. The horse let out a pained scream as the sword cut a deep wound along its side. It collapsed, sending its rider flying helplessly. He hit the ground in a mess of flailing limbs, bending in unnatural directions.

The remaining soldier let out an angry shout. He turned his horse around and was soon in pursuit of Reis. There was no way his cart-horse was going to be able to outmaneuver or outrun a trained war horse. He commanded it to stop suddenly. Its hooves dug into the dirt road and it skidded forward clumsily to come to a stop, almost throwing Reis from its back. The confused soldier rode right past him, taking a desperate swing with his sword too late to come even close to connecting. The soldier cursed and tried to get his horse to turn about.

Reis waited as Alvis finally caught up to him. He was looking uncomfortable atop another of the cart-horses.

"Take left, I'll take right," Reis commanded.

"I suppose this is a bad time to mention I don't have much experience fighting on horseback?"

The soldier was bearing down on them now, his sword ready to strike. Alvis and Reis commanded their horses to either side of the soldier as he passed. The soldier swung at Reis, who deflected the attack with his own sword, and left Alvis free to strike with his rapier. Alvis struck high and cut deep into the soldier's face. The lifeless body continued to ride on the horse for a few moments before collapsing to the ground.

"Those soldiers came from Colby." Reis said. "Meaning there might be more where that came from. Kester might have gotten himself into some kind of trouble, or worse, gotten our maps into trouble. We need to hurry and see what's happening."

"What about the wagons?" Alvis asked.

"We can send the townspeople back for them. We have to worry about our own problems first."

Reis kicked his horse's sides and commanded it towards Colby with all the speed it could muster. He just hoped that Kester hadn't got himself in too much trouble in his absence.

They left the horses just outside the town so they could move quieter. The ruins were empty and silent, with no sign of Kester or the survivors. If everything had been alright, Kester should have been there to get the wagons and help get the survivors on their way. Something was definitely wrong.

While searching the streets of the ruined town, Reis heard what sounded like a raised voice. They moved closer to the sound's source and could clearly make out an argument between two people.

"This is not the amount we agreed upon!" one man yelled.

"You should be grateful to receive any payment at all," the other man calmly replied. "Just the knowledge that you've done a service for the Empire should be payment enough."

Reis spotted the pair. One was an empire soldier. He recognized the other man from somewhere. After a moment, he realized it was the man that he had helped Kindra pull from the wreckage just a day before. He was shaking a small bag of coins angrily at the soldier.

"But you found the Willer, right? The woman?" the man asked. "I turned in a Willer in hiding. I want the reward the Empire promised!"

"You're an ungrateful sort," the soldier responded. "And you should really watch your tone."

Kindra. Kindra had been sold out to the Empire by a man who owed his very life to her. Without thinking, he drew his sword and started sprinting towards the two of them.

They saw Reis charging at them like a furious beast. The man yelled out and tried to flee. Fear in his eyes, the soldier drew his sword and raised it futilely. Reis cut him down without a moment's pause and went after Kindra's betrayer. He caught him with ease and tossed him to the ground. The man flailed around on the ground and desperately tried to escape. Reis kicked him onto his back and pressed his foot against his throat.

"You sold out Kindra to the empire, didn't you?" Reis growled. "Well, answer me!"

"We have nothing left," the man choked out. "Because she hid here, everything we had in this world is gone! The coin I got for turning her in is desperately needed. It's the least she owes us!"

"You bastard," Reis barked. "After she saved your life! She should have just let you die!"

"Please!" the man desperately pleaded. "Please! Spare me! I'll give you everything he gave me!"

"I don't want you coin, you bastard!" Reis yelled. "What I wanted, you took from me!"

With that, he pushed his foot down harder on the man's throat, until he crushed his windpipe. The man struggled and gasped for breath desperately. Reis continued pressing down and watched coldly as the man's face changed colors. Eventually he stopped struggling, and his body went still. Only then did Reis remove his foot.

"You feel better now?" Alvis asked as he cautiously approached Reis.

"I'm going to find Kester," Reis said. "He better be either dead or have a damn good explanation for letting the Empire get their hands on her."

Kester was still cleaning the blood from his face when someone spotted Reis's return. Reis and the sellsword were walking back alongside one another. Kester was not looking forward to telling Reis what happened to Kindra.

"Where are the wagons and horses?" Kester asked as they approached.

"Where's Kindra?" Reis asked in return.

Kester saw on him an expression of furious anger that reminded him of a rabid dog. Something told Kester that Reis already knew the answer to that question.

"The Empire came for her," Kester said, as calmly as he could. "They would have killed all the survivors but she gave herself up instead."

"You can't even protect a single woman," Reis growled. "You're useless."

Reis's words stung deeper than Kester expected they would. He was already feeling unbearable guilt over Kindra's capture. He had only known her for a day, but could tell she was a good, honest person. That was made clear when she willingly gave herself up to protect the rest of the survivors. What good was he, a soldier of the Light, if he could not protect those few truly good people who were out there?

"They took her alive," Kester surprised himself by saying. "My hand was stayed before because of the risk fighting would have presented to the survivors. But now that the risk to them has passed, a rescue may not be impossible."

Reis's anger seemed to suddenly subside and was replaced with a look of bemusement. "I want her, but I'm not about to die for her. I'm assuming they came in some force, I don't think charging into the middle of the enemy camp would accomplish anything more than our deaths."

"I'm not suggesting we take them head on," Kester said. "If you knew anything of tactics, you would know there are other options. I know quite a bit about pulling off rescues, deep in the enemy line." *Or, at the very least, I've heard the tales of how my brother did such.* "Typically not against these kind of odds, but it is possible."

Kester paced around a bit as he imagined the possible rescue scenarios, weighing them against the mission they would be abandoning if they failed.

"I'll leave it up to you, Reis. You know what we set out to accomplish and how much time we have to do so. You know that any rescue plans are going to carry considerable risk with them. If you think it is too much of a risk, puts our mission in too much danger, we will move on and try to put this behind us. But if you want to take that risk, I will support that decision and put the mission on hold to help make the attempt."

"I've done crazier things for a good woman," the sellsword chimed in.

If Reis was weighing over the options in his mind, his face did not show it. It remained cold and expressionless, his steely focus directly on Kester. Reis remained completely silent for what felt like an eternity.

"We're going after her," Reis said. "The Empire will not get away with taking what's rightfully mine."

"Very well. We'll get ready to go after her right away. But first." He turned his attention to the sellsword. "What of the supplies you were to fetch?"

"We encountered a few imperials just outside of town," Alvis explained. "We left two of the horses tied up on the outskirts and the rest of it is just a small ways down the road."

"Alright, good work." Kester pulled out a few coins. "Here is the rest of your payment, thanks for your help."

"Actually, it turns out you won't be getting rid of me quite so easily." The sellsword had a mischievous grin.

"I've extended his contract with us," Reis explained. "I'll explain later."

Kester fixed his attention on the sellsword. *What is Reis thinking?* He knew better than to try to argue with Reis's logic.

"As you wish," Kester said.

Chapter 11

I t's too early for this. The pounding on his door grew louder and Kasimir groggily pulled himself out of bed. "What do you want?" Kasimir barked.

"I am sorry," a trembling voice called out. "Emperor Serpentine has asked for you. He says it is urgent."

Isn't it always. "Tell him I'll be right there."

Through his windows the first light of morning was barely visible. Kasimir remembered the days of his youth when he would just be getting into bed around now, after a night of drinking and chasing women along with his friends.

Back when he had friends. Back before he earned the name 'Kasimir the Black.'

He quickly washed up and began the arduous process of putting on his armor. Most people who wore heavier armor, particularly plate armor, had assistance putting it on. Without assistance, it could be a very lengthy, difficult process. Unfortunately, part of Kasimir's ever important reputation was that nobody ever saw what he really looked like. After all, who would be so frightened of him if they knew that under all that armor was just an old man with gray hair, and wrinkles under his eyes? So he struggled into one piece and then other. It was a routine he had gone through every day for more years than he cared to count, and yet it never seemed to get any easier.

Process completed, he stood in front of his full-length mirror to inspect himself. A terrifying figure stared back at him, wearing solid black platemail that covered him from neck to toe, and a helm with points on the top like demon horns. It was elaborately designed to give him an imposing appearance: the red tip of the gauntlets that gave the illusion of his hands dripping blood, the sabatons that added a couple of inches to his height, the overextended pauldrons that added width to his shoulders, the light indentations on the chest that subtly hinted at the fangs of some great beast. The helm had no visor, just a narrow slit for the eyes. It was all part of Serpentine's desire that he maintain a reputation as something not human. He couldn't even wear the Empire's symbol because the emperor felt it broke the illusion.

Satisfied that he was appropriately terrifying, he set out for his meeting with the emperor. Lesser men might be humbled to be called on personally by Serpentine, maybe get little nervous or excited. But this was all part of Kasimir's daily routine. He did not think any more of it than if he was going to meet a member of his own family.

He made his way from the barracks where his room was and into the palace proper. All around him people scrambled to get out of his way as he walked by. Officers, soldiers, servants, bureaucrats, self-important officials, they all made every effort to give Kasimir a wide berth, bracing themselves against the walls in narrower hallways and darting their eyes back and forth, trying to avoid looking directly at him. Staring at Kasimir the Black was akin to staring at death.

He climbed the steps to the throne room while watched by two of the indistinguishable members of Serpentine's personal guard. To their credit, they did not flinch or try to inch away from him. They just gazed down at him with the same stony expressions the always had. He walked past them and through the large, gilded double doors into the throne room.

Serpentine was seated in his throne, leaning back in a position that was somewhere between comfortably relaxed and lost in thought. His ugly, hunched little lapdog, Ragnar, was pacing back and forth just in front of him.

Emperor Serpentine looked as splendid as he always did. He was dressed in fine silks in the black and red colors of the Empire, trimmed with gold lace and a fine fur cloak. His blond hair was long and straight, flowing down his back and shoulders like golden silk. His face was hard yet handsome, with a strong jaw and prominent cheekbones. Most striking of all, his eyes were a dim red, and when they caught the light the right way, they looked to be the color of blood.

"Kasimir, good, we have much to discuss," the emperor said. It was as close to a greeting he ever got.

"As my emperor commands."

"There was an attack in Laraque last night," Ragnar said in his hurried voice. "Twelve of our men dead. Several more injured. The city nearly broke into riots, we had to send a whole contingent to quell them."

"It was that same damn group of insurgents again," Serpentine said. His words were harsh but his voice was calm, almost jovial. "The Resistance, they call themselves. I thought they had been dealt with."

So did I. These bastards are as persistent as a bad rash. And just as irritating.

"My men discovered and raided one of their bases just last week," Kasimir replied. His voice was muffled by the helm. "During interrogation several of the prisoners we took confessed to being the leaders. We had assumed that if any part of the group had gotten away they would fall apart without leadership."

"It is dangerous to assume," Ragnar blurted. "You stopped moving, Kasimir. Never stop moving."

Never stop moving. That phrase he repeats over and over like a religious chant. And like most religious things, there is no meaning to it.

"I am not military, Ragnar," Kasimir said, trying to sound threatening. "I just do as I am told. I was told to track down the Resistance base and I did. I was told to interrogate the prisoners and I did. I have not received any further orders in regards to this group."

"Of course, Kasimir, no one is blaming you," Serpentine said with a dismissive wave of the hand. "But I do value your opinion."

"My opinion is that rebels are like ants. You can crush one anthill, but there will still be a hundred more. Best you can do is try to keep them out of your garden. For all we know, this may not even be the same group. 'The Resistance' is not a terribly original or creative name."

"Their methods are the same," Ragnar said, the speed at which he paced increasing. "Late at night or early in the morning, close to the time the guards would be changing shifts. The guards are tired and distracted by the thoughts of what they'll do once they are relieved. Then there is an attack. They come from the rooftops, from the shadows, from the windows of empty homes. They strike quickly, ferociously, killing as many guardsmen as they can while they have the advantage of surprise. Once the guards have recovered from the shock and are ready to fight back they suddenly disappear just as quickly, cowards that they are. Never a straight engagement, just cowardly strikes from the shadows. Murder. Who knows what they hope to accomplish by it."

"It's pretty clear to me," Serpentine said. A servant came in to refill his cup. He waited for the servant to leave before he continued. "Every time they strike they come closer and closer to Marjan. Closer and closer to my capital, and this palace. They want to prove they can strike right in the heart of my territory and live to tell about it. Make me seem weak to anyone else who might harbor ill-will towards me and my empire. Perhaps even sow discontent right here, in Marjan."

"Marjan is a large city, emperor," Kasimir said. "Whenever you get this many people in one place, there will naturally be some dissenters among them."

"The emperor can not afford dissenters in his own capital!" Ragnar exclaimed.

"Now, now, Ragnar, calm yourself," Serpentine said lightly. "I assume that Kasimir here is doing everything possible to see all our dissenters quieted. Surely he has not left any stone unturned."

So this is what this meeting is really about. He knows I've cut the amount of patrols to the poor areas of the city.

"My guards patrol as much of the city as they can," Kasimir said. "Some of my men have been sent east, to Rochest. It leaves us slightly undermanned here."

"Why does Rochest need the extra protection?" Ragnar asked.

What kind of idiot question is that? "Much of the trade that comes into the capital flows through Rochest. Keeping the roads between here and Rochest safe for traders is a high priority. Recently those roads have been plagued by bandits, come down from the north."

Ragnar nodded. "We have crushed the armies of many former nations. Those soldiers we didn't capture or turn were bound turn to banditry as a way to make a living with their skills. I saw it often enough in the west."

"Rebels, bandits, dissenters." Serpentine let out a sigh. "No one said ruling half the world would be easy." His eyes fixed on Kasimir. "But if we ever intend to conquer the other half we must first get our own house in order. As Ragnar has said, we can not tolerate dissent right here in the capital."

"More men would allow me to increase the patrols," Kasimir said. "I know a bulk of our forces are still engaged with the remnants of the Church, but maybe we could pull men from somewhere else. Perhaps we could recall some of the units who are currently occupied with tracking down Willers -"

"No!" Serpentine barked. His eyes fixed on Kasimir in anger and his mouth twisted into a snarl. Kasimir was suddenly happy his helmet hid his expression, lest his emperor see him cower.

Serpentine blinked hard, as if he himself was disturbed by his sudden outburst. He leaned back in his seat and relaxed, his passive demeanor returning. "No. I'm sorry, but Ludwig's work with the

Willers is vital to the future of the Empire. I would not expend such forces if it was not so. No, you'll just have to find a way to keep the citizenry under control with the manpower at hand."

Kasimir inclined his head. "Of course, emperor."

"Good. I expect this time next week I'll have a report telling me that the citizenry is well in line."

"I shall see to it, emperor." *Perhaps you would like me to conjure a dragon to eat your enemies while I'm accomplishing the impossible.*

"Very good, Kasimir. You are free to go."

"Never stop moving, Kasimir," Ragnar chimed in. *Freak.*

Kasimir walked away from the throne room, his head swimming with the task ahead of him. *Silence all dissent in Marjan? With a limited guard? Oh, well. No sense crying about it.*

Failure was not an option. Not unless he wanted to end up like the last man to wear this armor.

Not unless he wanted to end up like the last man to take the name Kasimir the Black.

A long time ago, before he was named Kasimir, he used to dream about being able to draw a crowd the size of which was now before him. In his dreams, the crowd was cheering for him, celebrating a great victory or a heroic accomplishment of some importance. He had never imagined that the crowds he drew would be quite like this.

Marjan's central plaza was packed tightly with excited citizenry. They struggled and squeezed and pushed up against one another to get closer to the podium. *They smell blood.*

It was a fine day for an execution. The sun shone brightly through the clouds and lit up the platform, so even those far in the back would be able to see. The air was still and quiet so Kasamir's voice would carry far, as hopefully would the prisoner's final cries.

The prisoner was brought up the steps to the platform. He was naked except for the black sack covering his head, the shackles on his wrists, and a simple loincloth to preserve his modesty. *After all, there are children in the crowd. It's fine for them to see a man die, but gods forbid they be exposed to a grown man's dick.*

The crowd booed and heckled the prisoner as he was brought up to the podium.

"Traitor!"

"Justice!"

"For the emperor!"

Kasimir saw that for every person in the crowd cheering for the prisoner's death, there was just as many stony faced and quietly observant. *Those that are less sure of their feelings toward the rebels.* These were the people who needed convincing.

If Serpentine was not going to give him the men needed to properly patrol the city, then best he could do was quell those thoughts of dissent with fear. For that he would need to put on one hell of a performance.

"Citizens of Marjan!" he bellowed. His voice echoed in his helmet. The crowd fell silent. "Before you stands Martin Sprier, citizen of the Empire, and rebel. Mr. Sprier betrayed the emperor and his fellow citizens by conspiring to murder members of his emperor's military and undermine the rule of Marcus Serpentine. Emperor Serpentine's rule has brought nothing but wealth and prosperity to the people of Marjan. He made the city his home, and a center for enterprise and commerce, and the city has thrived. And yet there are still those who would try to take this all away. We all know the emperor is generous to those loyal to him, but he is unforgiving to his enemies."

Kasimir grabbed the prisoner roughly by the shoulders and dragged him to the front of the podium, then dramatically pulled the sack off his head.

"Witness the fate of all rebels!"

There was a collective gasp from the crowd, followed by cries and quiet murmuring. The sight of what remained of Martin Sprier was shocking indeed. His face was a twisted mockery: his eyes sunk deep into purple sockets, his nose smashed almost flat into his face, his top lip missing, his jaw stuck open and revealing a set of shattered teeth. His body was not much better, badly bruised and scratched and missing large chunks of flesh. *A man who has been through this much pain probably looks forward to his death.*

"Martin Sprier, as per your own confession, you are guilty of treason and murder. Your sentence is immediate execution!"

Kasimir gestured to the two closest guardsmen. The guardsmen knocked the prisoner to his knees and held his head forward.

One of his guardsmen struggled to drag the impractically large executioner ax up to the podium. Kasimir let him struggle a few more steps before walking over and grabbing the ax himself. It was far too heavy for any normal man to lift, much less swing.

Kasimir was no normal man. He hefted the ax over his shoulder with the ease one might lift a small child, then returned to the waiting traitor.

He raised the axe high. The crowd went completely silent. He swore he saw Martin Sprier smile. Then he brought the ax down. It cut cleanly through the prisoner's neck. His head rolled across the platform. The guardsmen holding up his body let it fall to ground.

The crowd burst into applause. Applause for justice or applause for blood, Kasimir could not say.

"Get this mess cleaned up," Kasimir barked at the guardsmen.

He dropped the ax, its weight causing the podium to shake on impact, then skulked away from the crowd.

And so the legend of Kasimir the Black grows.

Chapter 12

Captain Konrad Marek stood over the beaten and bloody young boy. The boy, Peter, had been caught spreading stories about how he had been with Beldaken during his escape from Empire forces. Normally stories told by children would be ignored, but Marek did not like leaving any stones unturned. At first, the boy was unwilling to talk at all about Beldaken. He possessed the kind of impertinent spirit and loyalty that might make for a good officer of the Empire someday. It took a savage beating before the boy finally opened up and told him everything.

"Commander!" shouted a young soldier as he entered Marek's tent. "A courier arrived just now with an urgent message for you."

"Always punctual with his check-ins, that Lech," Marek said. "Very well, hand me the message. And take this boy to be returned to his family. I'm done with him."

He read over Lech's recounting of his encounter with Beldaken. It disturbed him that he had been bested. Lech was one of the best assassins the Empire had to offer. The more he learned about Beldaken the more he became convinced that the legends centered on the man were more fact than fiction. He was by far the most dangerous man Marek had ever been tasked with eliminating.

Lech suggested in his message that he believed that Beldaken was heading towards Marjan, targeting Marcus Serpentine himself. This corroborated the information he'd extracted from the boy. He knew that Beldaken was traveling with a soldier from the Church. This was not the first time they had attempted such a thing. Beldaken was just the kind of arrogant to believe he could pull off such an impossible task.

He decided not to bother Serpentine with these details right now. He was a great man, and had bigger things to concern himself with right now. If Beldaken got close enough to the capital to actually be a threat, it would mean that Marek had completely failed at his job, and Marek never failed.

There were many roads Beldaken and his companions could take to reach Marjan. But no matter which way they went Marek would be right on their tail. He had eyes everywhere and a thousand blades ready to strike.

He began to feel excitement rise up within him at the thought of taking down such a worthy opponent. He forced himself to quell those feelings right away. It was unprofessional to feel such pleasure. It was just another job, and Reis Beldaken was just another enemy of the Empire.

And like all enemies of the empire, his time was short. Marek would make sure of that.

The world rushed around Marek in a blur of light and images. Trees appeared and then vanished in a fraction of a second, the outlines of thousands of strange faces blinked by him. Road was underneath him, then grass, then stone pavement. After a few seconds the images stopped and the world came back into focus. He was standing down the road from the ruins that had once been the town of Colby.

Marek was a Willer, one with an unique ability that made him the Empire's most valuable fugitive hunter. He could focus on a location, anywhere in the world, and if he could picture it vividly enough, chart the geography in his mind, and concentrate hard enough on that image, he would suddenly be transported to that location. It was something he kept a secret from all but of a few. Using it earned him a reputation of always being in the right place at the right time.

The fact that he wound up so close to Colby was a bit of good luck. Typically he found his ability far less accurate. A few times he'd found himself in a lake or river, and once atop a tall tree in a forest miles away from his destination. In large cities and important holding throughout the Empire, he had drawn up little symbols that reminded him of birds. When he pictured a specific symbol within his target area he could be accurate to within a few feet. He had no symbols down here, though.

After a short walk, Marek was strolling down the ash-covered streets and surveying the remains of the town. *Whoever did this was certainly thorough. I almost feel bad for the people who lived here. Almost.*

There was no sign of life. Lech's report told of a handful of stragglers still amongst the ruins. They must have moved on already.

He had hoped that he would have arrived in time to find Reis's companion from the Church. The report had said that Beldaken had continued on with another, unknown man. Perhaps he meant to meet up with the soldier later, or perhaps there had been a disagreement and they had parted ways.

Many questions, too few answers. How did Beldaken survive Lech's poison? Was his companion dead, or did he somehow survive the poison as well? How did Beldaken intend to get close to Serpentine? And, most importantly, where was he now?

Marek was pleased to see an approaching group of imperial horsemen. He had sent word ahead to have an escort waiting for him in Colby, but it sometimes took time for the imbeciles in charge to respond to his summons.

"Captain Marek," the lead officer called out as he approached. "I'm Lieutenant Conners, of the Third Regiment out of Kyro. I responded as quickly as -"

"How are the roads, Lieutenant?" Marek interrupted. He had no desire to hear the young officer's life story. "Any sign of our target or his companions?"

"No, sir. Fact is, the roads down here are fairly empty these days. Those mountain men have gotten more aggressive lately."

"Still?" Marek shook his head with disappointment. "I would have thought that problem would have long been solved."

Conners shifted nervously in his saddle. "We've run many raids against them, but it's slow going. The mountain paths aren't suitable terrain for the horses. And we can't seem to find where their leaders are hiding. If such things have leaders."

"Sounds like quite a dilemma. But it's not my problem. My orders are to track this Reis Beldaken and bring him to justice. And those are your orders now too."

The young lieutenant stumbled over his words. "Uhm, yes, of course, Captain."

"He will be moving either north or west, in the direction of the capital. How many options does that give him for roads?"

"From here?" Conners scratched his face thoughtfully. "Well, there's one major road that heads towards Marjan. But there are a variety of worn paths and hunting trails, and if you keep enough distance from the mountains the land is open enough that you could ride across it with no need of a path, assuming you knew where you were going."

"In other words, no way to tell which way he went." *I could use a skilled tracker like Lech, but I haven't heard from him since his report. Guess I'm stuck with this rabble.* "There's an encampment not far from here, correct?"

"Yes, sir. Maybe a day's ride north."

"Good. We'll need more men if we're going to find him. Give me one of those horses and then lead the way. There's nothing here."

"Yes, of course. You'll have my full support in this -"

"And do me a favor, kid? Don't talk unless it's absolutely necessary."

The lieutenant's face sank. "Uhm, yes, of course, sir."

Chapter 13

It was past nightfall when Reis arrived at the outskirts of the Empire encampment. Kester and Alvis followed close behind, riding on the outskirts of the trail to watch for signs of pursuers. Reis did not want to get caught off guard by the likes of that assassin again.

Kester had overhead that the group that took Kindra was heading in the direction of Ivor, to the north. It was a solid week's journey away, so it was fairly certain that they would be stopping at the encampment for the night before moving on.

"Didn't expect the encampment to be this large," Reis said. He was feeling less confident about their rescue mission than when they set out. "These palisades are closer to true walls, and they've erected lookout towers. Looks like they're dug in and have no intention of leaving anytime soon."

"This is right on the intersection of two major roads," Kester explained. "One goes east all the way to the coast and west through the Marjan mountains into Allandane. The other goes north all the way to the Grandium." *Well, where the Grandium used to stand, anyway.* "The Empire must have decided they wanted to control the crossroads, so they've set up for the long term. Wouldn't be surprised if they've been shipping in carpenters and masons to begin constructing a proper fortress."

From their vantage point atop the hill, they could see that this encampment was composed of more than one hundred fire-pits, each surrounded by at least a dozen tents. At its capacity it could probably hold more than two thousand soldiers and officers, with accommodations for all the horses and equipment they would be bringing.

That was during war time, however. Currently the camp was less than a quarter full. Only two dozen of the fires were lit tonight, all scattered throughout the encampment. The feeling of relative safety caused the soldiers to spread out and take advantage of spacious arrangements, instead of grouping together for safety. It might be possible to move through the encampment without being noticed as long as they stayed in the shadows.

There were still some obvious risks, however. Each campsite would have the ability to raise an alarm. If they were caught they could find themselves surrounded in a matter of moments. Then there was the matter of getting into the encampment in the first place. The whole encampment was surrounded by a high wood palisades. The normal entrances would be well watched over.

Fortunately, Reis had a plan.

Jerrick watched over the the gloomy darkness of the night as he tried to fight back waves of sleepiness. This was his fourth straight day on the night-watch and it was starting to take a serious toll. He would have to be more careful when making jokes about his lieutenant in the future.

The others assigned to watching the southern road were doing their best to pass the time in whatever way they could. It was a boring shift. There was nothing for miles around that would dare come anywhere near the encampment. Even the wild animals seemed to know better than to get close.

To Jerrick's surprise, tonight he did see something moving towards them. He focused his eyes and held a torch out in front him to try and get a good look at what was on the road below. A single man came into focus as he stumbled clumsily down the road. From the way he walked it was quite obvious that he was drunk.

"Halt!" Jerrick called out. "Identify yourself."

"Identify myself?" the man drunkenly slurred. "Why don't you identify yourself? Why would you trouble me, I'm not bothering anyone."

"You're approaching an encampment of the Serpentine Empire," Jerrick shouted. "Civilians are not allowed beyond this point. If you are heading north you must go around."

The traveler gave him a befuddled look. "North? No, no, I'm going east, to Mansir."

"Well right now you're walking north," Jerrick responded with growing agitation. "You're quite off-course, the road to Mansir is a ways south of here."

"Oh that's no good." The man laughed. "I guess what my father always told me is true: 'Never travel drunk and never stay in one place sober.' Hey, any chance you fine gentlemen have a place for to sleep off this stupor?"

"I just said that there's no civilians allowed."

"You sure?" The traveler held up a flask and then motioned to the pack on his back. "I've got plenty more of the drink on me, more than enough to go around. I'd be happy to share in exchange for a warm blanket for the night."

Jerrick glanced over at his fellow guards, who looked back at him with approving glances. It seemed this night would not be as dull as they feared. He grinned widely.

"I think we can work something out."

A short time later Jerrick and his companions were enjoying fine spirits and listening with great amusement as their unexpected guest regaled them with tales of his travels. To their delight his stories were as hilarious as they were impossible, each tale prefaced with, "I may have had one too many drinks but this is how I remember it."

After a few drinks some of his fellows began falling asleep. Jerrick tried shaking them awake.

"Come on!" Jerrick demanded. "Don't tell me just a couple drinks floors you. If morning inspection comes and you're asleep the lieutenant will have your asses!"

He noticed he was beginning to feel unreasonably sleepy as well. Maybe it was the long nights mixed with the alcohol. Whatever it was, he couldn't ever remember being more tired in his life. His eyelids were heavy and he could barely think straight. Maybe a little nap would do him some good after all, just to recover his strength.

He fell asleep to the sounds of the stranger telling a story of his adventures with a savage tribe of beautiful women. It may have been his imagination, but in his last waking moments, it sounded as if the man was laughing at them.

The drug Reis had laced the drinks with should keep the guards asleep for the better part of the night, once Alvis got them to drink. He waited in the shadows alongside Kester for the signal. An hour after Alvis set off, they saw it. The light of a torch from the guard's post being waved around in a circle. He and Kester came out of the shadows to regroup with the sellsword.

"Well that was nerve wracking." Alvis said, although his smile suggested otherwise. "You're lucky I'm such a great actor."

"Indeed," Kester responded. "If the life of a mercenary ever ceases to suit you, there is a promising career in plays waiting."

Reis crossed his arms. "Empire soldiers are a bunch of idiots.

You were never in any real danger."

Alvis put his hands on his hips. "If so, how about next time you go and introduce yourself to the guards?"

"And take a role away from the great actor?" Reis said with a smirk.

The group surveyed the encampment from the guards station. Kester pointed to the largest fire-pit in the distance.

"The officer who took Kindra had a big ego on him," he said. "I imagine he would take up the largest tent, one reserved for higher ranking officers if the camp was more crowded. The command tent boasts the largest fire to help others find it at night. I'd wager we'd find Kindra there."

If she is still alive.

Kester waited while Reis forged a path through the darkness of the encampment. He was the quietest of the three of them so he would go first, scout the area, and after he determined the safest path he would motion for Kester and Alvis to follow.

He wasn't sure how he felt about relying on the sellsword to watch his back. He had hired Alvis by chance, as he had just happened to be wandering past Colby at the time. He was untested and had unknown loyalties, though he had apparently impressed Reis enough. He also was not comfortable with how well he and Reis seemed to be getting along. On the walk towards the encampment Reis had seemed to warm to Alvis's sense of humor. Of course, with Reis it was hard to tell what was real and what was an act. Either way, it left Kester outnumbered.

Avoiding the lit fires caused the path they took through the camp to be long and winding. There was real concern that they might not be able to get out before the morning came. Reis stopped them frequently to listen for passing patrols. Once, a patrol came close and they to had to duck into a nearby empty tent to wait for them to pass. Alvis reminded them more than once that it was not too late to turn back, but they had no intention of doing so.

In half an hour they finally came close to the largest fire. There the command tent stood, a dozen times the size of all the other tents in the area. The area around was empty, most likely at the orders of lieutenant-colonel to gain some privacy. Right now, it served to the group's advantage as they scoped out the area from the concealment of a nearby tent.

After watching for some time, Kester was convinced there were only two patrols who came through this area at regular intervals. If they timed things right they could avoid the patrols altogether. Other than the patrols their only worry was the two guards stationed outside the command tent and the lieutenant-colonel himself. If any one of them succeeded in sounding the alarm the command tent would be swarming with soldiers in a matter of moments. Their only chance was a coordinated strike.

He waited for the first patrol to pass by them. He estimated, based on his watching the patrols before, that they would have fifteen minutes before the second patrol passed by again. Reis and Alvis crept up to near the command tent, staying just outside the light of the fire-pit. Kester stayed just off to the side of them, ready to make his move as soon as the others acted. He took deep breaths and tried to remain calm. In order to move silently, he had left his armor behind. He hadn't realized how vulnerable he would feel without it.

Reis and Alvis waited for just their moment. The fire had to get to just the right level to conceal them for the longest time possible. After a few minutes, they got their chance when a strong breeze blew by, blowing the flame low.

They pounced on the opportunity with weapons drawn. They dashed across the gap between the fire-pit and the command tent and straight towards the two guards. By the time the guards noticed them, there was barely had a second to react. They gave out short shouts and tried to draw their weapons, but they were too slow and caught utterly unprepared. Reis cut down one and Alvis the other within moments of one another.

The bodies had just hit the ground as Kester was running past them and into the tent. The shouts of the guards had likely alerted the tent's resident that something was amiss. Kester needed to strike before he had a chance to react. Sure enough, Kester found Lieutenant-Colonel Ramsay halfway between his bed and the the chest on which he had set both his weapon and the bell he could use to raise the alarm. He was caught literally with his pants down and as he stumbled for his weapon Kester swung his sword and cut through naked flesh. Shock and pain were frozen on his face as his body fell fell to the ground.

Reis and Alvis entered the tent just behind him. They found

Kindra in Ramsay's bed, stripped bare and beaten. She was alive, but non-responsive.

"What kind of darkness can compel a man to do such things?" Kester found that he had accidentally voiced a question he had meant to ask himself.

"Bastard!" Reis exclaimed under his breath. "What did he think gave him the right!!"

Kester gathered some clothes to cover Kindra with while Reis began furiously beating Ramsay's dead body. Alvis moved the bodies of the two dead guards into the tent so they wouldn't be found by the passing patrols. With any luck they could hide in the command tent without being noticed until Kindra regained consciousness so they could escape together. It would be too difficult to move quickly and quietly while carrying her. Fortunately none of her wounds seemed too severe, at least externally, though she would have to wait till they got away from the encampment to receive proper treatment.

"How does she look?" Reis asked after he finally stopped beating the corpse. He wiped the blood from his knuckles on Ramsay's bedsheets.

Kester was not too sure himself, but thought it was best not to upset Reis any further. "I think she probably just took a blow to the head. She should be up any time now." At least, he hoped.

Reis knelt over her to get a closer look. They were all surprised when suddenly, in the distance, a horn sounded. It was a low, loud blast of noise that resonated throughout the entire encampment.

Alvis bolted upright like a startled rabbit. "Something tells me that's not a good sound. Did they catch on to us?"

Kester shook his head. "The Empire uses bells and fire as signals. I never heard of them using a horn."

"Sound like it's coming from outside the encampment," Reis said.

The horn sounded again, this time accompanied by the shouts and movements of the soldiers as they ran from the tents and desperately tried to organize themselves. There was the sounds of bells ringing all over the camp now.

"Mountain men are attacking the encampment!" a voice outside shouted. "Someone wake Ramsay!"

"Damn!" Reis exclaimed. "We need to move. Grab the girl and-"

He didn't have a chance to finish before one of the soldiers burst into the tent. The soldier looked around befuddled at the scene before him. He spotted the bodies of the dead guards and officer and quickly turned around and bolted out of the tent before anyone could stop him.

"What unfortunate timing," Alvis said.

"Alvis, you carry the girl." Reis commanded. "Kester, have your sword at ready. I doubt we're getting out of here without a fight."

Alvis carefully picked up Kindra and carried her over his shoulder. Kester drew his sword and shield and volunteered to step out first. Reis had his sword ready and would go right behind him. Kester peeked out of the tent to see if it was clear. The immediate area was empty. He motioned for everyone to follow him and stepped out.

All around them soldiers were rushing out of their tents with their armors hastily donned and weapons at their side. They were all being commanded towards the western palisade. The early sounds of battle were ringing through the night air. In all the chaos Kester's group was overlooked by many. Their luck wouldn't hold out forever as they spotted a group of soldiers heading right at them.

"There they are!" the one at the head of the group shouted. "Those are the ones who killed Ramsay!"

"On my right!" Kester shouted. Reis who responded by taking up a position a few paces behind him and to his right.

Kester was once again feeling naked without his armor. He had never fought in a battle without several inches of steel to protect him. Perhaps he should have asked Reis to take the lead. Too late now.

The imperials were confident in their superior numbers and charged at Kester without hesitation. Kester took the group head on with his shield raised and his sword poised for a strike. The first soldier to reach him went for the strike and was deflected by the shield. The moment Kester felt the impact of the blade, he slammed his shield against the assailant and knocked him to the left, sending him colliding into two others and causing them all to be thrown off balance. Kester seized the opportunity and struck with his blade against the closest one, landing a killing blow.

With both his sword and shield expended to his left, Kester had left a significant vulnerability to his right side; but Reis was there to close it. He struck to the side and sliced through the sword-arm of a soldier who had been in mid-swing. Reis followed up with a few more wild swings with no real target, trying to force the soldiers back a few steps and out of striking range.

The soldiers had become disorganized. Kester struck against the next closest target, but this blow was unable to pierce his enemy's armor. He counterattacked and met Kester's blade. Another soldier came at him from his left side. Kester raised his shield to block and then slammed it against his opponent's face. The impact sent teeth and blood flying through the air as his opponent's neck bent back at an unnatural angle. Following the momentum of this strike, he spun around with his shield at arm's length and struck another attacker with it in the side. The shield bounced off his opponent's armor but struck with enough force to knock the enemy clean off his feet.

Beside him, Reis had turned into a vicious beast, cutting down one imperial after another. He ducked under one blade as he thrust forward with his own and pierced one man in the gut. A low kick knocked another off balance and allowed Reis a strike right into the vulnerable part of his neck. With one furious slash he knocked aside a sword raised in defense of its wielder and left a massive gash on the upper arm. He was as quick on his feet as his was with his blade, and he managed to dodge and sidestep many blows.

Reis and Kester kept close, watching each other's flank. Together they had killed at least a dozen of the soldiers. Their enemies collectively backed off to regroup and prepare a more organized attack. Reis and Kester stood side-by-side, ready for the next assault. The numbers of their enemies had thinned dramatically. Their biggest concern was being able to move on before reinforcements came. Fortunately, most of the camp's attention was still focused to the west.

They soon learned why. On the other side of the camp a section of the palisades exploded, sending splintering wood and several very shocked imperials flying through the air. Following immediately in the blast's wake was a large battery of of ferocious, primitive warriors riding snarling beasts who quickly set to wreaking havoc on the encampment.

The men were enormous, almost seven feet from head to toe, bulky as gorillas and just about as ugly. They sported long, unkempt beards, dark and wild hair, and faces that looked like they had been smashed in at birth and then left to heal that way. Their mounts largely resembled horses but were twice as large and had wolf-like snouts, complete with razor sharp teeth.

The imperials did what they could to try to slow the destructive plague that had been unleashed upon them, but were no match. They were trampled over, torn apart, cleaved in two by axes, and bashed by massive warhammers. And it wasn't just the men who were targeted. No part of the encampment was left standing in the wake of these savages. They trampled over tents, spread fires using logs from the encampment's own fire-pits, and slaughtered horses that were still tied up, defenseless.

The soldiers who had been attacking Kester and Reis had stopped in their tracks to watch the destruction in horror. After their impending annihilation became apparent they turned and tried to flee. They were joined by many other imperials who were making for the other side of the camp in hopes of getting away. None would get far; the savages were merciless and cut off their escape path before slaughtering the lot of them.

Amidst the chaos Kester and company had been left momentarily unmolested. Kester knew it wouldn't last long.

"Come on!" Kester shouted. "We have to find a place to hide before those barbarians come after us too."

"Where the hell do you suppose we go?" Reis snapped. "They're tearing down everything, there won't be anywhere left standing to hide in. We need to get out of here, now!"

Kester nodded in agreement. "Alvis, stay close, we can't get separated! We'll make for the south fence and try to get over it!"

They ran as quickly as they could, all effort at stealth forgotten. All around them people were yelling and dying. The air filled with the stench of smoke and blood. The shouting was closer every moment. Kester had the terrible feeling they would not make the fence in time.

"Reis, what about your ability?" Kester yelled. "You used it to help us escape the soldiers once before. Can you do that again?"

"Not enough time," Reis growled in response. "I would need to stop and concentrate. Plus, I'm not sure if there's an open area on the other side of that fence. If I'm not lucky my shadow may extend right into a tree, and our trip would result in us getting squashed like bugs"

Kester grunted in frustration. It hardly seemed fair that they might die this way, to a barbarian attack that had nothing to do with him. Was he being punished for straying off the path of his mission?

They had almost reached the fence when one of the warriors rode in front of them. He rode right by. Kester hoped that they had been ignored but they had no such luck. More of the mountain men rode by them on all sides. They found themselves being circled and completely surrounded.

Alvis sidled up close behind Kester, Kindra still in his arms. "I got to say. When I was forced to agree to a suicide mission to assassinate the leader of the Serpentine Empire, I predicted I would die. But death by barbarians? It's something of a pleasant surprise."

"You find this pleasant?" Kester asked.

"Cause it's unique," Alvis said. "Anyone can go out and get themselves killed by the Empire. But usually you have to go out of your way to be mauled by savages."

"I don't intend to die here," Reis growled. "Though I'll be honest, I don't know what's going to happen to the rest of you. If I'm going to get out of here alive I can't be concerned about any of your fates."

"Your concern is heartwarming," Alvis said. "Particularly since I'm still carrying your woman here."

Reis's face was frighteningly cold. "We all have to make sacrifices."

The barbarians were still riding circles around them. Reis had his weapon ready and was coiled to strike like a cobra. Kester had his sword and shield, but he wasn't sure how much good they would do against an enemy that so clearly outmatched him. Reis's mobility gave him some chance to avoid being trampled, but Kester was slow and couldn't stand against the might of their beasts.

But for some reason the riders didn't move in for the attack. They just kept circling and staring at them. They might have been toying with them, but based on how quickly they had cut everyone else down that didn't seem to be their style. There was no explanation for this behavior.

Finally they stopped circling and came at rest surrounding the small group. Two of them moved aside to allow a third rider to pass. This rider wore metal armor that was vastly different from the leather that the rest of the riders were wearing. He was particularly ugly, even for the mountain men. His face seemed to consist of little more than scars, scabs, and beard. By the way the others looked at him Kester got the impression that he was some kind of leader.

One of the riders spoke to the leader in a rough, harsh tongue. The leader kept his eyes focused on the group. Kester kept his sword at ready. He decided that if this came down to a fight he would see to it that this ugly bastard would be the first to die.

The leader looked at Kester and spoke, in plain language, "My men think that you're not Empire." His ability to speak stunned Kester, who had seen these men as little more than savage animals. "You don't look like Empire and you don't bear their markings. Your weapons are fresh with Empire blood." He looked directly at Reis, who had not relaxed a single muscle in his fighting stance. "You are warriors, then? Here alone?"

Kester wasn't sure how to respond. He stood in stunned silence.

The barbarian's next words came more as an order than a request. "You will tell me now who you are!"

Chapter 14

The leader of the mountain men waited impatiently for Reis's answer. Reis smirked and no doubt was about to respond to the barbarian leader with an insulting and provoking reply, but Kester managed to preempt him.

"I am Kester Belisario, a soldier in the service of the Church of True Light. My companions and I came here seeking to rescue a friend of ours who had been captured by the Empire, this woman here. We were just about to make our escape when your assault started."

"Church of True Light," the mountain man snorted. "I don't like your people. They try to give us big candles and insist that we put them in our caves. Something about the darkness harboring evil. Cowards. They wouldn't even fight us to defend their beliefs."

The Church is not popular anywhere these days.

"The Church doesn't fight except as a last resort," Kester responded. "We fight in defense and we fight against evil. We don't fight to prove ourselves."

"So you are a coward like the rest of them." The barbarians voice was full of disdain. "It would be simple enough to leave you dead with the Empire weaklings."

"There is no need for that, we-" Kester began to stammer, but Reis shoved him hard.

"You can try to kill me if you wish," Reis shouted over Kester. "But I assure you it will be a mistake. Even if one of you gets lucky and manages to strike me down, the memory of what I did to the rest of you will haunt you in your dreams. And you, whoever you are to dare to speak to me in such a manner, I will personally see that your blood is the first to spill."

"Oh great idea, Reis," Alvis muttered. "Piss off the violent barbarians who are completely surrounding you."

Kester was trying to stammer out an apology for Reis's tone, but the leader let out a loud, guttural laugh.

"So there's some warrior spirit in you after all. It would be a shame to strike down another warrior who shares a common enemy. But we cannot let you free until we are certain this is not some kind of trick. Put down your weapons and allow yourself to be captured and if the words you speak are the truth no harm will come to you."

"Yeah, I'm going to toss down my weapon!" Reis barked with heavy sarcasm.

Kester put a hand on his shoulder. "We don't have much choice here, Reis. Your pride will have to take this blow. The most important thing is for us to live to fight another day. We still have a mission to accomplish, remember?"

"Easy for someone with no pride to say," Reis spat.

Kester was afraid Reis was about to ruin their one chance to get out of this alive. Any second, Reis could raise his sword and cause all of their deaths. Kester's heart was in his throat.

To his relief, after what felt like an eternity, Reis finally tossed his sword on the ground. Kester laid down his sword and shield beside it. The leader of the mountain men barked some orders in their harsh tongue and several of the riders dismounted. They took ropes out of packs on their mounts and proceeded to tie up the group; Reis first, then Kester, followed by Alvis, and finally the still unconscious Kindra.

"Well, one thing about working for you," Alvis said as they were led away. "It certainly isn't boring."

They were tossed onto the back of one of the beasts and made to wait while the mountain men ensured that nothing remained of the encampment. With their task complete, they headed up a small path west into the hills. After about an hour, they were met by another group of the barbarians and transferred to a small, crude wagon that was dragged behind the rest of the group. The wagon was covered so they could no longer see which direction they traveled, but Reis had the strong feeling they were headed into the Talmos Mountains. When the wagon began to shake roughly his suspicions were confirmed.

The Talmos Mountains were wild and rough terrain that even the most adventurous of explorers knew to stay clear of. Between the native wild beasts, the constant threat posed by falling rocks, and the scarcity of edible vegetation, it was quite inhospitable. They ran west until it was absorbed by the grander Marjan Mountains. Reis was vaguely familiar with it, as he had had to pay handsomely for the rare herbs that grew in these parts.

They had been riding for a few hours in silence, drifting in and out of uncomfortable sleep, when Kindra finally began to stir. She slowly came into consciousness and looked around her in shock. Reis did not wish to have to explain this situation to her so he feigned being asleep.

"Good morning," Alvis said. "At least, I think it's morning. Hard to tell time back here. May be afternoon by now."

"Where am I?" she asked.

"Out of the frying pan and into the fire, I'm afraid," Alvis answered. "More specifically, we're prisoners of a horde of savage barbarians who may or may not want to eat the flesh off our bones. But your friend here can tell you more about that." He pushed himself against Reis in an attempt to wake him. "Hey, Reis, get up! Your woman is awake!"

Reis grumbled and opened his eyes. Across from him Kindra was trying to pick herself up into a seated position but her bindings made it difficult. She bumped into Kester and woke him.

Kester groggily opened his eyes, then snapped awake when he saw Kindra. "I'm glad to see you are alright. I was starting to worry that some permanent damage had been done."

"I am alright, I think," Kindra said, though she looked far from it. "But I cannot recall how I got here. Last I can remember I was in the clutches of that pig Ramsay."

"We came to save you," Alvis explained. "Almost succeeded, too. Unfortunately, there are some things that no amount of planning can prepare you for, such as an assault by savage mountain men."

"We were fortunate that they decided to take us prisoner," Kester said. "The Empire soldiers weren't quite so lucky."

Alvis rolled his eyes. "Yes, lucky. That's exactly how I'd describe us."

"You came to save me?" Kindra's eyes were wide with surprise as she looked between Kester and Reis. "But why? I barely knew either of you." She looked at Alvis. "And, I don't think I even know who you are."

"I'm Alvis. Sellsword, fighter, lover. I'm currently under Reis's employ, so where he goes, I go."

"I was merely correcting the mistake I made when I didn't act to keep you from being taken in the first place," Kester said, looking down as if the floor of the wagon had suddenly become interesting. "I am only sorry we couldn't have gotten there sooner, before ... " He trailed off. "The bastard."

"If it's any consolation, he took a sword to the gut for it," Alvis said.

Kindra nodded. "Good. He was a bastard and a coward. When he first tried to force himself on me I knocked him away with my ability. If I hadn't held back it might have killed him, but instead I tossed him and hoped that would be enough to keep him from trying again. It certainly scared him. After striking me a few times, the coward actually drugged me. I don't remember much after that point, and I'm grateful for that."

Kester's eyes were still fixed on the floor. "There are many men with such dark hearts in the ranks of the Empire."

The wagon rattled violently on the rough mountain path. For a moment there seemed to be a very real possibility that the wagon might turn over. They all waited in silence and breathed a sigh of relief when the wagon calmed down.

"You have anything to say, Reis?" Alvis asked. "This was your rescue mission."

"There's nothing to say," Reis finally said. "The situation is what it is."

"Thank you for coming for me, all of you," Kindra said. "I am eternally grateful."

"Don't thank you us yet," Reis responded. "Not until we see if our rescue does you any good or just makes matters worse."

They traveled for more than a day, tied up in the back of that wagon. Every part of Kester's body was stiff and ached from not being able to move. He remembered sleeping in the saddle on the road with Darius, how tired and sore he had been. Suddenly that felt nostalgic to him. Back here, he could barely sleep for ten minutes at a time before the wagon would jolt him back awake. It never stopped moving. These mountain men didn't seem to need a break at all.

They did not talk much. Alvis would occasionally try to break the silence with a joke or offhand comment, but eventually even he got too tired to continue. They just rode in silence and pondered what fate awaited them.

Finally, the light outside the wagon became dim and then seemed to disappear altogether. A faint musky smell filled the wagon. It didn't take Kester long to recognize they had entered into a cave.

"Looks like we've just about about reached our destination,"

Reis said.

His words were quickly confirmed as the wagon came to a stop. There was some shouting outside, followed by one of the savages opening the back of the wagon.

"Come now," the savage grunted. "Now!"

"I'd love to comply," Alvis said. "But these bindings make standing very difficult, much less walking. Perhaps a hand?"

Kester wasn't sure if the savage understood Alvis's words but he certainly took the meaning. He reached into the wagon and cut the bindings on their legs, leaving only their arms bound. Kester felt a little more confident with his mobility restored. If the mountain men tried to execute him, they would at least be met with resistance. He filed out of the wagon with the rest of his group.

They were in a cave just as Kester had expected. What Kester hadn't expected was how massive the cave was. And he certainly didn't expect the fortress that now stood in front of them, carved out of the very stone of the walls.

They must be deep in the mountain range. The cave ceiling was at least a hundred feet from the ground in some places. At others, the ceiling seemed to disappear, obscured by small beams of light that came in from cracks in the cave walls. The light spread as it came down on the expansive chamber, providing shadowy illumination. At the point where all the light came together stood the wall of the massive stone fortress.

The fortress stretched to the cave ceiling and across the breadth of the chamber. It was carved entirely from the gray stone of the cave walls. The carved stone was impressively even, covered in intricate designs of warriors in battle, beasts of the hunt, and massive figures that Kester could only assume were deities. It seemed improbable that this work of master stonemasonry had been done by these savages.

A massive, reinforced wooden gate stood in stark contrast to the rest of the fortress. It was primitive and lacked any of the subtlety of the stone walls. Kester was led towards this gate, with Reis and Alvis following close behind, and Kindra behind them. They were surrounded on all sides by the barbarians. The one they assumed to be the leader walked directly in front of them.

Another of the mountain men was waiting for them in front of the gate. This man stood a full head taller than the leader and had a considerably sleeker build than the other barbarians they had seen, although his frame was still massive. His beard was thick and dark but showed signs of basic grooming and his long hair was parted away from his face. The leather he wore was dyed blood red.

"Mankur Burdush!" he said as the leader approached him. He slapped the leader on the shoulder, a gesture which the leader returned.

"Pash!" the leader replied. The two of them exchanged words in their native language for a few minutes before the topic of conversation turned to the outsiders.

"Who are these you brought?" the one identified as Pash asked. He spoke in plain language now, which Kester assumed was for their benefit. "Prisoners?"

"That has yet to be determined," Burdush, the leader, responded. "They were in the Empire camp but claim not to be Empire. Don't seem like Empire, but we must make sure they are not working with the enemy. I leave this task to you."

"Yes, Mankur. I will discover their true intentions."

Burdush slapped him on the shoulder once again before walking into the fortress, the massive gate being cracked open before him. Pash stood in front of Reis and glared at him, sizing him up.

"You lead this group?" Pash asked.

"You could say that," Reis responded. "I'm Reis Beldaken."

"Actually-" Kester began, but was quickly silenced.

"I have dealt with your kind before, the candle-worshipers," Pash barked. "You will keep your silence here." He pointed at Reis. "This one will represent you."

"Sounds like they're not big fans of the Church," Alvis whispered. "I would do as he says. He looks big enough to eat all the meat off your bones in one sitting."

Kester didn't like the idea of Reis representing him, and the smirk Reis gave him didn't help. Still, Alvis was right. Pash showed the same disdain for the Church that his leader did. And the leader had seemed to respect Reis's aggressive attitude. For now, letting Reis speak for him was the only option.

Pash shouted something in his native tongue and one of the barbarians grabbed Kindra and began to take her away into the fortress. Reis growled and struggled against the bindings on his hands.

"What the hell do you think you are doing!" Reis yelled.

"Men will be taken for interrogation," Pash said. "Women are too soft. She will be held separately."

"If you harm her in any way I will make you pay for it," Reis snarled. He spoke with such viciousness Kester believed he meant it, bindings and all.

Pash seemed unimpressed by Reis's threats. "She will come to no harm. Unless we determine you are the enemy. Come with me."

They were escorted into the fortress through the massive gate, which closed behind them. Some of the barbarians were leading their bestial mounts into stables near the gate.

Pash must have caught Kester's gaze. "We call them Korki. They are mounts and companions to our people."

"Your people," Reis said. "It might be helpful if I knew exactly who I was dealing with here. It is obvious that there is more to you than the mindless savages that had been my first impression."

"We are, in your language, the Men of the Mountains. In our tongue, we are the Mankuri. We have lived in these mountains since we claimed them long ago."

"What mountains would those be?" Reis asked, not so subtly attempting to get some information about where they were.

"I believe your people refer to this range as the Marjan Mountains. We had settlements all along the northern mountains, stretching all the way to the frozen peaks."

The Marjan Mountains? We came this far west in such a short time? They must have taken us straight through the heart of the Talmos mountains. But that's crazy. Those mountains are damn near impassible.

The Marjan Mountains were the largest mountain range in all of Kassia, running from the frozen Northern Wastes to the ocean in the south. It effectively split the continent in half, Eastern Kassia and Western Kassia. The capital of the Empire, which shared a name with the mountain range, was located near the central stretch of the mountain range, where the mountains gave way to hills and grasslands for a short period before rising up again. Based on Pash's description, they had been taken north of their destination.

"Had?" Reis asked.

"The Empire has been raiding our mountains, killing our people, destroying our homes," Pash explained as he led them through the maze-like stone fortress. "What you see here is the last of our people. Only this place remains because the Empire has not yet found it."

"How fortunate," Reis said. "Of course, you can't expect to hide forever."

"We hide from nothing!" Pash yelled as if the very notion offended him. "Let the Empire find us! We will fight them to the last man! Such a battle is inevitably coming. For now, however, the Mankur, our leader, wants us to kill as many Empire as we can. From here, we launch our attacks on the Empire men down below. As you have witnessed yourself, we kill many."

"Didn't mean to offend," Reis halfheartedly apologized. "Obviously you take fighting very seriously."

"Fighting is who we are. We are warriors from birth, trained from the moment we are old enough to lift a weapon to fight and to kill. And we are warriors at death. There is nothing more honorable than dying a glorious death in battle. Dying old in your bed or to illness is weakness and disgrace. As long as you draw breath you can draw a weapon and die in combat. In this way, even though the Empire may kill us all, we have no regrets for we know we shall die well."

When the implication of these words sunk in Kester understood how dangerous the Mankuri really were. In normal combat, you can count on an opponent's sense of self-preservation to leave moments of weakness. A moment of fear, a moment of hesitation, a moment of doubt, it was all that Kester needed to gain the advantage. But an opponent without fear of death, one who actually embraced dying on the battlefield as an honor, would leave none of these openings. There would be no fear or hesitation, just fury. Kester knew these were not the kind of opponents he wanted to face.

"That is all I have to say about my people for now," Pash said. He had led them to a small room somewhere in the middle of the fortress. "Now it is time for me to learn about you."

Reis examined the stone room with critical eyes. It reminded him of a prison he had once spent too much time in. He tried to force the memories away. He knew if he started to go down that path he would not stop. He needed to focus now.

The room was square and plain. There were no windows and only a single door. The walls were plain stone with no distinguishing marks. The only furnishing in the room was some uncomfortable looking stools to sit down on. Reis could see no sharp edges with which to cut his bindings, nor anything he could use as a weapon. Worse case scenario, he may have to try to get his arms around Pash's thick neck and try to strangle him. Unless he could somehow maneuver his hands to draw one of his hidden daggers.

Pash barked something in his native tongue. Three of the their escorts entered the room with them while the rest waited outside. One of them approached Reis and began to frisk him. Reis barely resisted cursing aloud.

"You know, typically I only allow myself to be handled like this by the ladies," Alvis said as he resisted his own frisking. Reis thought he heard a twinge of nervousness in his voice.

"It is important to know that you are not hiding anything," Pash said. "Weapons, tools that you might use to escape, secrets that might reveal your true motives. They will be quick, but thorough. Then we will proceed."

"I don't like being manhandled any more than you do," Reis said. "But its best that we just get it over with."

Alvis let out a nervous sigh and stopped resisting. Reis wondered what it was that Alvis was hiding that he was so concerned with them finding. Reis himself was concealing two small, hidden blades on his body. Both of these were found, as well as the empty vial that once contained his healing concoction.

All that was found on Kester was a small key attached to a chain, which was handed back to him at his insistence. He was not found to be concealing any weapons. Reis wasn't surprised; he doubted the Church's principles would allow someone like to Kester to wield any weapon he didn't openly display.

Alvis's hesitation soon made sense. The Mankuri that was patting him down paused when he touched his chest. He touched it again and then grabbed it aggressively. Alvis cursed under his breath. The savage began to forcibly strip Alvis. Reis had not realized that Alvis had been wearing so many layers of clothing until it was laid on the floor before him. It quickly became apparent that the reason for this was to hide the true shape of his body.

Her body.

Underneath all those layers of clothes, Alvis had the body of a woman, with a slender waist and full hips. Cloth bindings had kept her breasts pressed down against her body but now these bindings were torn off by her captors and her breasts were laid bare.

Reis and Kester exchanged surprised looks. Reis had always

assumed Alvis was just a gentle looking man. He never even considered that the sellsword was actually a woman.

"What is the meaning of this?" Pash asked. "I said women are to be held separately. Why did you not tell me this one was a woman?"

Reis shrugged. "I'm as surprised as you are." *Probably more so.*

Pash barked some orders and the woman they knew as Alvis was taken out of the room. She didn't say anything, but as she left Reis caught a guilty look on her face.

"She will be locked up with the other woman," Pash said. "Now, it is time for you to tell me who you are."

"Captain Marek!" Conners ran up to Marek's makeshift command post. He was noticeably out of breath. "More survivors coming back through the east gate. We're reorganizing them into the new company."

Marek let out a sigh. The cowards who had abandoned the encampment during the fight, or who had found a good place to hide, had been turning up in a steady streams ever since they arrived. If it was up to him, they would each be charged with treason for their cowardice and executed. But they were short enough on men as it is. They needed to at least maintain the illusion of numbers, even if all they had was a handful.

He had come to the encampment in hopes of recruiting for his mission to hunt down Reis Beldaken. Instead, he had found an inconvenient distraction. The encampment had been totally destroyed in an attack by the mountain men, having been caught unprepared in the middle of the night. The camp's commanding officers were all dead or missing, so it fell to Marek to get things back into order. The survivors needed to be organized, the injured needed to be cared for, tents needed to be put back together, the big gap in the western palisades needed to be patched up. He sent a message to Mansir detailing his need for reinforcements, but it might be weeks before he saw any. He also sent a report on to Marjan so the emperor would be aware of the situation and could decide whether it was worth restoring the encampment or not, but a response from him could take even longer.

All the while, Reis Beldaken got further and further from his grasp. Dealing with the state of the encampment was no doubt an important job, but finishing his mission had to be a priority.

Conners was panting hard. An energetic young man, he was always eager to impress. He must have sprinted from the east gate just to give his report. Marek had met many young officers like him, whose enthusiasm and ass-kissing garnered early promotions and commendations.

Now he was smiling like he knew a secret worth another commendation.

"Is there something else?" Marek asked.

"One of the soldiers coming through had something interesting to report," Conners said with a knowing smirk. "An officer, Lieutenant Colonel Ramsay, and his retinue stopped here for the night on their way to Ivor. The Major in charge gave Ramsay the use of the command tent for the night."

"I take it he was killed in the assault?"

"Yes. But not by mountain men." His smile grew wider. "A few men were seen leaving the command tent at the time of the attack. One of the men matches the description of your wanted man, Reis Beldaken."

Marek could not contain the look of surprise on his face. "Is this for certain?"

"I interviewed several other member's of his squad. They confirmed his story, and the description."

What an unusual development. Marek's mind raced with what this could possibly mean. Was Beldaken working with the mountain men now? Had he somehow recruited them to his cause? If so, could this mean the mountain men meant to attack Marjan?

"I need to interview these men myself," Marek said. "Bring them here."

"Of course, sir. At once."

Marek was left alone, wondering excitedly if the emperor knew what caliber of enemy they were hunting.

Chapter 15

Reis was not accustomed to being captured or being held prisoner. He was typically quick and clever enough to be able to escape any confrontation that he found himself outmatched in. It had been many years since the last time he had been captured. He still remembered that incident with great clarity. After all, that was when he met Sable.

It was back in the days before he discovered his knack for alchemy. At the time, Reis followed a simple philosophy: the one who held the most coin held the most power. To fulfill his lust for power Reis would try anything to get his hands on valuable jewelry, gems, artwork, anything that traded for coin. On one occasion he had gotten the idea to try and steal jewelry from the private vault of the king of Mansir. The theft itself had gone exactly as Reis had planned it, with Reis walking away with jewelry worth a small fortune. Unfortunately, one of his buyers alerted the King's guard and Reis ended up walking right into a trap. Stealing from the king was a crime punishable by beheading. He was taken to the bottom of the royal dungeon to await execution.

The bottom level was not much more than a filthy stone chamber with cages for prisoners awaiting execution. The prisoners were kept in the dark and barely given any food or water to keep them weak so there would be no resistance at the executioner's block. Between the cramped condition of his cage and the darkness, Reis couldn't tell if the prisoners in the cages near him were even still alive. It was impossible to tell time there but he must have been in that cage for weeks. He was positive that he would soon be dead until another prisoner near him finally spoke to him.

"You still alive over there, buddy?" a voice in the dark called out to him.

"Barely," Reis muttered.

"Tomorrow's the day of the execution," the voice declared. "More like in a few hours, if it's night. I've been listening, concentrating, and they come and take prisoners once a week, from those closest to the door and moving in. Five prisoners a week. This week they will finally reach us."

"Good," Reis said, defeated. "I'm done with this damn cage."

"As am I, my friend. "But I'm not quite so ready to give up on life. How about you?"

Reis didn't respond. He knew the long period of inactivity coupled with near starvation and dehydration had left him feeling weaker than he had ever felt before. The man he was speaking to must have been in a similar condition. Even if he had come up with some brilliant escape plan, there was no way either of them were in any condition to pull it off. They would likely have to be dragged to the executioner's platform for lack of energy to stand.

"Here, take this," the voice said.

Just in front of Reis's cage, a hand appeared in the darkness holding some kind of bowl. Reis reached out and grabbed it and pulled the bowl into his cage. The bowl was half full of the small rations they were given and also contained a pouch filled with water.

"This isn't my first encounter with captivity," the voice explained. "I've learned to ration my supplies. I've also developed decent night vision. I've been watching as those in the cages around us have died and when they do I reach in and take anything that's left. You're the only one left alive close to me, whoever you are, and I need you to have some of your strength. So eat up."

Reis was suddenly filled with hope, and another feeling he wasn't accustomed to: gratitude. This man whom he didn't know, who didn't know him, was sharing what precious little he had. Of course, it wasn't a selfless gesture. He needed Reis's help as much as Reis needed him.

"I'm listening," Reis said. "What do you have mind?"

The stranger had been right. In a matter of hours, there was movement in the darkness. Reis's cage opened and he was dragged out. Every joint in his body burned as he stood and walked for the first time in weeks. His legs were so weak he could barely keep his balance. But thanks to the meal given to him by the stranger, he did feel a small amount of strength. He couldn't allow his captors to know that. He feigned being completely weak, on death's door and barely conscious. He wanted them to let their guard down around him. His captor, seeing him barely able to move, began to drag him by the arm. Reis let his body go completely limp and his captor was forced to carry him.

Suddenly there was light and Reis was blinded. He cursed himself silently for not being smart enough to close his eyes. He had been in the darkness for weeks, of course his eyes were going to need some time to adjust. He just hoped that he would regain his sight in time.

It took a few moments, but slowly his vision returned. He began to be able to make out the blurry forms around him. There were five prisoners, as predicted. They all looked weak and famished. Reis had no idea which of them was the stranger on whom he would be relying soon. They were being escorted by four guards. The guards were dragging and carrying along the prisoners who were too weak to walk on their own. Their reaction times would be slowed.

Reis watched as they were taken up several flights of stairs. They reached the ground level and were taken down a long hall. Reis looked to the left wall and began to count windows. According to the stranger, one window led to the outside on the opposite side of execution platform and far away from any guard houses. The area was hardly patrolled and with any luck they would have a decent head start on any pursuers.

When he counted the fifth window he acted. He didn't have time to check to see if the stranger he was trusting was also making his move. If he didn't, Reis was dead. If Reis was taken to the executioner's platform, he was dead. It really didn't make a difference right now. Reis reached around the side of the guard who was carrying him and pulled his sword out of its sheath. The guard was surprised and tried to grab Reis's arm but the blade was already at his throat. As his body fell Reis freed himself from his loosening grip and brought himself to his feet.

On his left another guard had just taken a blade in the gut. He assumed the prisoner with the blade and the fiery determination in his eyes was the stranger he had spoken with. They didn't stop to face the other guards who by now must have drawn their weapons. There wasn't enough time and they were too weak to survive a direct confrontation. They bolted to the window and leaped through, bounced to their feet and sprinted with as much speed as they could push their weakened bodies to give.

Their hope was that their outburst would cause the other prisoners to also attempt to flee or fight and thus distract the remaining guards. If the guards came right after them they had little hope of outrunning them. But luck was on their side, and they managed to reach the wall of the dungeon plaza. As he had been promised, a lone tree loomed over the wall, forgotten and untrimmed. They climbed the tree as quickly as they could and were soon on the other side.

After they had gotten a safe distance and found a good alley to hide in, they'd finally gotten a chance to properly introduce themselves. His new friend was Sable, an assassin for hire. He explained that in a moment of weakness he had let a particularly young and defenseless target live. This had infuriated his employer, who apparently had connections within the guard.

After they talked for a while, the two found they had a great deal in common, including a common desire for coin. Thus began Reis's longest professional partnership. Reis and Sable made a formidable duo and went on a very profitable crime spree. The two of them were successful in kidnappings, extortion, raiding trade caravans, and even some information brokering. They made more coin than they knew what to do with.

That was, up until the point Sable betrayed him and left him for dead. Reis blamed himself for that. He had grown to trust Sable and let his guard down around him. He learned that day that a companion can only be trusted so long as they have a use for you.

In this way, he liked the arrangement he had now Kester. Both knew where they stood with one another. They were not friends, they were merely working together. Kester would watch his back as long as he needed him, and as soon as they were done he would just as quickly shove his blade into it. He knew that he couldn't count on Kester in a dire situation. It was an alliance of convenience, not of trust.

Reis disliked thinking about Sable. For some reason, one memory always lead to another. Good memories, of him full and warm and fulfilled. And it always ended with him, all alone and bleeding out in the middle of nowhere.

Right now, he and Kester sat in silence in their stone prison as they waited for Pash to return. Pash had extensively interviewed Reis about who they were, why they had been in the Empire camp, and where they were going. Reis had decided to just tell him that they were out for Marcus Serpentine's head, hoping to prove they were really on the same side. Instead, Pash had become furious. He thought for sure that Reis was lying, that there was no way such a small man could have such an intention. When Reis stuck to his story Pash stormed out.

After being left alone for hours, loud footsteps outside signaled Pash's return. He slammed open the door with a weapon in either hand. One was Reis's sword, which he tossed down at Reis's feet. The other was a massive warhammer.

He pointed this at Reis. "Even our strongest warriors are slaughtered if they try to get close to that palace. If you really think you can succeed where they failed, you must be stronger than them. Come, then! Grab your weapon! Show your strength to me!"

Reis smirked and picked up his sword. This was far too good of an opportunity to pass up. He used the blade to cut the bindings on his hands. Once he was freed he held his sword at ready.

Naturally, Kester protested. "This is a bad idea. Even if you win, do you really think they'll just let you go after you killed one of them?"

Reis laughed aloud. He was in his element now. "You obviously don't understand the mind of a warrior."

Without warning he launched himself at Pash. His sword was thrust out like he intended to make a strike. At the last second he withdrew his assault and leaped to the side just in time to avoid the powerful swing of Pash's hammer. Reis had known that the size of Pash and his weapon gave him the greater reach. The hammer hit the stone floor with such force that the stone splintered and cracked. Reis attempted to use this moment of vulnerability to get in close and quickly end this fight. When his blade got close Pash grabbed Reis's hand. He had such a powerful grip that Reis's sword was stopped mid-swing. With one hand, Pash lifted Reis by the arm and tossed him across the room. Reis hit the wall on the opposite side of the room.

Pash lifted his hammer and charged furiously at Reis. Reis had seen a lot of things on his travels, but few things as frightening as this giant rushing at him with his hammer raised. Reis barely regained his balance and managed to get out of the way just as the hammer swung by him. He was surprised by how fast Pash was able to swing the massive weapon.

Reis tried to get some distance between him and Pash, but there wasn't much room to maneuver. If he was going to stand a chance he needed a more open space. He saw that Pash had left the door open and made a dash for it. Pash must have predicted this move because he maneuvered himself between Reis and the door. His hammer was raised for another blow, but this time Reis was too close to get out of the way.

Kester appeared from Pash's left as he tackled him. His shoulder landed squarely in Pash's with an impressive amount of force.

Despite the difference in size, Pash fell on his side, the wind knocked out of him. Before he could get up Reis's blade was pointed at his throat.

Reis glared down at the giant. "This would be a good moment to tell us we can go free."

The Makuri remained defiant. "You didn't beat me! And yet you take this victory as if it is your own! What kind of warrior are you!"

"The kind who is willing to do whatever it takes to win. You think the Empire will fight fair?"

Pash was silent. Kester tried to get Reis to back down but Reis refused to move his blade from Pash's throat.

Finally, Pash relented. "Fine, maybe you can kill Serpentine with dishonorable tactics. But maybe it takes a true warrior, and you are not one."

"Maybe." Reis withdrew his sword from the giant's throat.

"So you need a true warrior, in case."

"What are you suggesting?" Reis asked, already fearing he knew the answer.

"I'm coming with you," Pash declared. "Make sure you're truly an enemy of the Empire. And if you fall, I will crush Serpentine's head myself."

Reis scowled. He didn't like these Mankuri; they were an ugly, savage people. And he particularly disliked Pash. He had no desire to travel with him.

Kester extended his hand to help Pash to his feet. "We accept."

"How dare you just make that kind of decision!" Reis shouted.

The church-boy did not back down. "This is still my mission. Remember that."

Reis let out a series of angry curse words but did not argue. *Once again, he chooses a stupid topic to assert himself.*

Pash heaved his warhammer over his shoulder. "That was some hit. You have a lot of power for such a small man."

Kester beamed at the compliment. "Form counts as much as power."

"I will retrieve your things. Wait for me here till I return."

"And our companions?" Kester asked.

"The women?" Pash scratched at his beard. "They would only slow us down. The battlefield is a place for men."

"Regardless, we can't just leave them here."

The barbarian shrugged. "Fine. I will retrieve them as well."

Reis leaned against the wall and scowled at Kester. "You're going to regret this one, church-boy. Just you wait."

It was more than an hour before Pash returned. Reis had begun to worry that he changed his mind and they were going to be executed anyway. He returned carrying a large bundle of their possessions.

Kindra and the sellsword they knew as Alvis were with him. Kindra was looking stronger now. It seemed the Mankuri had been treating her well. The sellsword was back in the outfit that disguised her as a man. Reis marveled at how good the illusion was. If he hadn't seen it with his own eyes he still wouldn't have believed it.

"You were gone awhile," Kester said as he checked the straps on his shield. "Is there some problem?"

Pash was carefully watching the door. "We needed to wait for the right time. We can go out a secret way without being seen now."

Reis knew that there was going to be some kind of catch with this savage. "What are you not telling us?"

"Our leader is the Mankur, the one who has one survived the most battles and thus proved himself the most worthy to lead our people. Mankur Burdush has led us well, but his assaults against the Empire are very bold and dangerous. There is always a chance that he won't return. Our people can not be without a Mankur to lead them into battle, and I am set to take the role when Burdush falls."

Reis's eyes narrowed with skepticism. "So you're like royalty?"

Pash thumped his hand on his chest. "I am a hero of many battles. Many of our enemies have fallen dead at my feet. Mankur Burdush has declared me his worthy successor. I am bound by our custom to wait in for the day the Mankur does not return from battle and I must fulfill that role. That is why we must not be seen. I would never be allowed to leave. I would be considered a traitor for trying."

"Are you all right with this?" Kester asked, sincere concern in his voice. "Turning your back on your customs in order to accompany us?"

"The Empire killed many of my people. They are the greatest enemy we have ever known. I can not pass up such a chance for glorious battle against their leader."

Reis held up his sword for the the barbarian to see. "Just don't be disappointed if I kill him first."

Pash led them through the maze-like fortress. The winding corridors and long passageways were filled with forked paths, yet Pash did not have a moment's hesitation. Reis had the intention of memorizing the path they took, should he ever need to retrace his steps, but gave up after the tenth time they changed direction. He felt so lost that he was sure that if Pash was not leading them now he would wander these corridors for weeks without success.

Their guide remained several paces in front them so that he would be seen by any passing Mankuri first. He didn't explain what he intended to do if they were spotted and there was no explanation forthcoming. They were just to do as they were told. Fortunately, the passages seemed empty.

Reis noticed that Alvis was trailing behind the rest of them. He, or rather she, was looking downwards solemnly as she walked. This was not good. If the sellsword was not focused, then she would not be of much use to him. He slowed his pace to let her catch up with him.

"Don't fall behind," Reis said sharply, snapping Alvis back into reality. "If you get lost in here we're not going to come looking for you."

"Sorry," Alvis said softly. "I'll keep up."

It was far from the non-serious attitude Reis was used to from the mercenary. He got the sense that there was something Alvis wanted to tell him. Reis was not a personable man. He really couldn't care less what kind of personal problems his companions had. But he really needed Alvis focused on watching his back, even more so now that this barbarian would be traveling with them. He had saved Alvis's life at personal cost to have another sword at his side when he needed it. *Might as well get this over with if it will get her back to form.*

He let out an exasperated sigh. "Whatever it is you want to say, you might as well just spit it out."

The sellsword fidgeted uncomfortably. She looked she was struggling to find the right words to say. Reis scowled and wished that he had asked Kester to deal with this. This kind of thing was likely right in his comfort zone.

"Come on, out with it!" he barked.

"I'm sorry if you feel I've deceived you," she quickly burst out. "My real name is Avis. Women have a tough time being taken seriously as sellswords, but it is the only profession in which I am comfortable. I started to dress like a man and added an 'l' in my name, and suddenly I've got all the business I need. I don't mean to deceive anyone, it's just what I have had to do in order to survive. Most of the time it doesn't cause any problems. Very rarely is there ever a reason for my true gender to be exposed. But I know when it has happened issues do arise. My competence comes into question."

Reis just wished she would get to the point. "What's your point?"

"That big one, Pash, told me and Kindra. That you were bringing us along because you don't want to leave us here, but because we were women we were going to have to be protected until you find a safe place to leave us. Kindra seemed okay with this, maybe even relieved, but I'm not someone who has to be protected! I don't want to be left behind anywhere, I still have a contract with you after all!"

"Pash is a big, stupid, savage," Reis growled, not particularly caring if he was overheard. "I never said anything of the kind." He looked Avis directly in the eye so there would be no mistake. "Look, I couldn't give a damn less whether you're a man or a woman, or whether you wear a dress or choose to go around stark naked. You're good with a sword. That's all I care about. As long as you continue to be useful in a fight you can be whatever fucking gender you want to be."

Avis smiled brightly, as if Reis had just told her the secret to making a million coin, as opposed to just stating the obvious. "I suppose I should have guessed as much coming from you. Though you'll forgive me if I choose not to fight naked. Might be a tad distracting."

"Whatever you want." It seemed Reis had struck the right chord to bring the sellsword back to herself. "Glad that's all that was. I was worried you were going to try and weasel your way out of our contract."

"And miss out on your pleasant company?" She shook her head. "I take my work as a sellsword very seriously. I don't leave contracts unfulfilled. True, this contract is considerably more dangerous than what I would normally want to take on, but I accepted the terms. I'm afraid that means you won't be able to get rid of me until it is complete."

Reis was surprised by how much he found himself appreciating Avis's words. He had been worried about what kind of loyalty he could expect from the sellsword. Many mercenaries were only loyal to whatever side the coin lands, and some couldn't even be counted on for that much. It seemed that Avis would not abandon him at an inopportune time.

A thought came to him that made him smile. "There is one

thing I'm curious about. You made quite a few comments about your, let's say 'interest' in the ladies. Was that all part of your act?"

"There is no act." Avis seemed amused by the question. "I changed my look and my name, but not my personality. As for what you really want to know, I have been known to enjoy the intimate company of both men and women, but have a preference for women. It helps that they are easier to attract while dressed like this."

"Those women must be in for quite a surprise."

Avis smiled slyly. "It does complicate things. Many times I must, well, excuse myself before things progress too far. Only when my date is particularly adventurous, or particularly drunk, do I dare reveal myself."

Reis got the image in his head of a very surprised looking young woman and couldn't keep himself from laughing out loud. Avis must have found it funny as well because soon she was joining in on the laughter. The others turned around to get a look at the strange sight of the two of them laughing together.

"What do you think the two of them are finding so funny?" Kindra asked

Kester just shook his head. "Knowing Reis, we're better off not knowing."

Pash led them out of the cave and back into natural daylight. It was just about sunset and the light was fading, but Kester was glad for the few moments of light he would receive. The Mankuri fortress was far too dark for him. As a servant of the Light he never liked to be forced into darkness for long.

They were high up on the side of a mountain. Behind them was the Mankuri fortress and not far in font of them was a sheer drop. They were high enough up that Kester could see for miles around. It was a majestic view of mountains, forest, and lakes. Kester wished the circumstances would have allowed him to stop to appreciate such beauty.

"So, how do we go on from here?" Reis asked as he looked over the side of the ledge.

Pash pointed to something on the ground near the edge. Kester looked closer and noticed it was the start of a rope ladder. Looking over the side he saw that the rope ladder extended all the way down past his field of vision.

"You can't be serious," Reis demanded.

Pash grunted. "If this is too much for you then you are too weak to kill Serpentine."

Reis grumbled and muttered under his breath but ended up agreeing. Pash looked over at Kindra.

"I can carry one of the women if needed," Pash said.

"Thank you, but I am a capable climber," Kindra replied.

Avis didn't even respond. Pash looked between them and shrugged. He made sure his warhammer was securely fastened to his back before bringing his massive body over the edge.

"There's another ledge about two hour's climb down," he said. "It will be dark when we reach it so we will rest there until morning."

"Sleeping on a cold, windy ledge hundreds of feet off the ground," Reis said. "I can hardly wait."

Chapter 16

Reis was going to remember every bit of discomfort, every hunger pang, every cold night, and he would use those memories to fuel his anger when he confronted Serpentine. It was all his fault that Reis was stuck here, on a mountain ledge in the middle of nowhere.

They had very few supplies with them. When they had raided the Empire encampment they needed to travel light, so they took only the things most critical to their mission. The idea had been to reclaim their supplies with their horses or quickly resupply at the next town. They could not have predicted the recent turn of events.

Pash had taken a pack of things with him from the fortress. He distributed small chunks of hard, sour bread and a sharp cheese that was harsh on the tongue but settled easy enough in the stomach. He also had a few cloth sheets to use as blankets. That was the limit of their comforts while camped on the ledge.

The wind whipped by the ledge harshly, chilling them with bitter mountain air. Reis shuddered and muttered angrily about the conditions.

"You complain a lot," Pash grunted.

Reis bundled his sheet tighter around his shoulders. "Well, I think I've earned the right. If your people hadn't captured me I would likely be sleeping in comfort tonight with enough food and wine to satisfy me."

If Pash was cold, no part of him showed it. "Well you should have tried harder not to be captured."

"Not a terrible point," he conceded.

Across from him, Kindra was already asleep. The girl had been through a lot recently. It was not surprising she would collapse, even in these conditions. Avis had given up her sheet to Kindra to keep her warm. She sat at the edge of the ledge with one leg dangling into the empty air, embracing the chill wind as if it was an old friend.

At least Kester looked as miserable as Reis was. He was huddled over for warmth and shaking noticeably.

Everyone was being far too quiet. Reis was desperate to talk about anything get his mind off the cold. "How far is it to the next town once we actually get off this rock?"

"No towns," Pash said. "Not until after we cross the forest, five days journey."

"Five days through forest?" Kester asked. "We have few supplies. Perhaps we should find an alternate route."

"No alternate route," Pash insisted. "It is near impossible to cross to the other face of the mountain from this side. The terrain is harsh and there are few paths that could support us. If we tried to walk all the way around we lose a week. The only other option would be to go south through the mountain paths, but such a path would be foolish. There is little life and we would likely starve before we crossed. In the forest we can forage and hunt."

"At least in the forest there's not much risk of us running into the Empire," Avis added. "Reis is a wanted man, after all."

Reis shot Avis an angry glance which she did not seem to notice.

In his fingers, Kester was fidgeting with that key of his. "But we will be heading in the direction of Marjan, right? We have a limited amount of time before our opportunity fades."

Pash looked up the sky and grunted. This chain of questions was apparently wearing on the giant's nerves. "Once we cross the forest we will be near the town of Rochest."

Kester held the key between his thumb and forefinger and examined at it. "That's only a week's ride to the capital."

The mention of Rochest sparked something in Reis's mind. He tried to imagine a map of Kassia in his head, cobbling it together from the landmarks he knew from his travels. He knew something about the area around Rochest but couldn't immediately remember what it was.

He thought about where they were now, in the Marjan Mountains a short distance from a forest. If the forest was going to take them so close the capital then they must be traversing it southward.

The map took shape in his mind. A forest that ran alongside a stretch of the Marjan Mountains ending just north of Rochest. Izer Forest.

Reis leaped to his feet, his sheet falling away, the cold forgotten. "You're going to try and take us through the Izer!"

Pash kept looking at the sky, utterly unconcerned with Reis's outburst. "Yes, I believe that is what your people call it."

For the moment, Kester seemed to forget about the key. "What's the Izer?"

"The Izer Forest is the most dangerous pit in all of Kassia," Reis explained. "Some of the most potent alchemical ingredients I've ever studied come from deep within its depths, but even I'm not stupid enough to go trekking around in it. The ground is always cast in darkness because no light can penetrate the forest's canopy. It is filled with all kinds of dangerous beasts that would like nothing more than to tear you limb from limb. And that's not even considering the poisonous insects, or the overgrown vegetation that makes movement insufferable and conceals pits, hills, and all kinds of dangers. The few people who are crazy enough to go hunting for ingredients for me charge some exorbitant prices for the risk, and even they won't go that deep into it. And this idiot wants us to try to cross the damn thing."

"You complain a lot," Pash repeated.

"Is it really that dangerous?" Kester asked in a serious tone.

Pash looked around him like he could not understand the conversation. He shook his head sourly. "It is no place for the weak. But we are not the weak. And I know the forest well. When we're boys, we undergo a passage into adulthood. Become men. When a boy comes of age he is sent into the forest to hunt a beast called the hawken and return its pelt. To prepare we are taught about the forest, its dangers, how to navigate it. You will be safe as long as you follow my lead and stay close."

He spoke with enough confidence to reassure Kester, who relaxed and resumed fidgeting with his key. Avis hardly seemed to be paying attention, she just stared out into the horizon. Reis was left standing there, looking like an idiot. He was cold.

Grumbling to himself, he sat back down and wrapped the sheet around himself. "We're going to regret this."

"You complain a lot."

Pash's snores could have scared bears. The hard ground was giving him no problem. Avis was comfortably dozing in her spot not far from the ledge. Kester was tossing and turning, possibly asleep, possibly not.

Reis doubted he would get any sleep at all. Missing another night's sleep wouldn't affect him much. During his time in his lab he might go days without sleeping if he felt he was on the path to a new discovery. For now he just stared up at the clear night sky and thought back to times when he had all the comfort and luxuries he could desire.

One night always came to mind. Him and Sable had just pulled off the biggest job in their career: a royal assassination. They jumped at the chance to accept the job after they learned the target was the King of Mansir, responsible for locking them up in that dark, miserable dungeon. Their employer was the head of the king's royal guard and gave them all the information they would need, including the the king's schedule and guard details. After a few weeks of planning they pinpointed the perfect moment and struck.

It was a plan magnificently executed. After sneaking into the palace disguised as a servant and finding his way to the dining hall, Reis assaulted the guards on duty, a light guard because no one expected the king to be attacked during dinner in his own palace. He then fled and led the guards on a wild chase. It left the king all alone with one guard: Sable. As payment for the job they had been given the king's royal jewelry. Reis could hardly believe the value of what they were being given. Their employer explained that the jewelry reeked of the king's corruption and that they would be glad to see it leave the kingdom.

That night Reis and Sable celebrated like they never could before. There was a high-class tavern called The High Ale that only catered to the wealthiest patrons in the north. When he and Sable first walked in they were given harsh glances by the affluent clientele inside. Not unexpected. They were wearing their stained traveler's clothes, after all. After laying a few precious gems on the counter any objections were quickly silenced.

They treated themselves like royalty that night. They dined on the most rich foods and washed it down with the finest wines. Their beds were soft as clouds and had no lack of company. Sable had always been popular among women, with his rugged good looks and penetrating blue eyes, and when added to the new-found wealth he flaunted there was actually a line at the door to his room for a chance to be with him. Reis had his share of women interested in him, but found that without the chase it was terribly boring. Instead, he spent most of the night testing his alcohol tolerance at the bar.

It was the last good night Reis would have for a while. The very next day Sable would betray him and leave him for dead for the very wealth they had just acquired. Still, Reis felt as if he would go through it all again if he could have another night like that.

Not this cold, miserable rock on the side of mountain.

He was so lost in his memories he didn't notice Kindra until she was right beside him.

"Can't sleep?" she asked.

"Just thinking about an old friend."

Sable. He was a bastard who tried to kill him, but Reis would take him for this mission any day over a church-boy and a barbarian. They had never failed a job together.

Of course that was impossible. Sable was dead. Such is the fate of anyone who crosses Reis.

"What about you?" Reis asked. "You looked pretty comfortable."

Kindra smiled nervously. "I've never been much of a deep sleeper. A little noise, a gust of wind, and I'm back awake." She looked over at the sleeping giant snoring away. "I heard what you said, about the forest. You made it sound so dangerous. I'm not really a fighter like the rest of you. I don't know how to wield a weapon. I have my ability as a last resort, but, well, you've seen how much good it's done me so far."

"Don't worry about it. I'm going to protect you."

Kindra shook her head. "Didn't I tell you not to pretend around me?"

"Who the hell is pretending?" Reis gave her a cold stare. "I've gone through quite the hassle retrieving you from the clutches of the Empire. You are sorely mistaken if you think that I intend to let some forest beast make that all for nothing."

Kindra looked at him and smiled. "I think you really mean that. Thank you. It's comforting to know you'll be looking out for me, whatever your intentions may be."

They talked for a little longer before Kindra fell asleep curled up against him. Her warm body against his was strangely soothing, and before he knew it, Reis was drifting off to sleep with her.

Pash woke them all bright and early with loud shouting and forceful nudging. Reis awoke groggy, but thankful for the few hours of rest he got. He would need them to face the Izer. They ate a quick breakfast of hard bread before packing up and moving on. It took another hour of climbing down the rope ladder before they finally came to a path that they could walk down the rest of the way. By midday they had finally come to the base of the mountain.

They were led down a path Pash assured them the Mankuri

would take to reach the forest. Everything seemed so uniform and bland here, just rocky outcroppings and long, gently sloping fields, so they would have to take his word for it. Take the wrong path and one of those gentle slopes could lead you right onto a mountain path and cause you to lose time retracing their steps. Fortunately, Pash seemed to have an animal-like sense of direction.

Something came to Reis's mind when Pash informed them they were getting close to outer edge of the forest. "Pash, do you know if there's a cabin around here owned by a hunter who goes by the name Thomwood?"

Pash looked at Reis curiously. "Yes, I know Thom. His cabin is right at the forest's edge. Sometimes we trade with him. How do you know him?"

"Same way as you," Reis responded. "Trade. He's the only person from who I can buy rare plants from deep within the Izer. He comes to market once a year. Charges some exorbitant prices, but for what he's got that's to be expected. He told me once he lives on this side of the Izer, don't know why I didn't think of it until now. It might be useful to see if we can procure some supplies from him before heading into the forest."

Pash grunted. "If it means you will complain less, fine, I will take you there."

"It's so nice to see the two of you finally getting along," Avis chimed in.

The Izer Forest loomed in front of them. It was strange how suddenly the forest began. The tall trees that marked its edge grew almost uniformly parallel to one another, as if to form a border against the outside world. Past this boundary the grass suddenly shot up in height and became spotted with all shades of weeds, flowers, and shrubbery. It was as if some unseen force was preventing the forest from spreading and the forest was pushing up against it in turn.

Just a few yards from this border sat a small wooden cabin. On all but one side it was covered by high shrubbery. Reis imagined that this was to conceal the cabin from anything that may be looking from the forest.

"What kind of a man would want to live all the way out here by himself?" Avis asked as they approached the cabin.

"One who prefers to be left alone while he works," Reis answered quickly, a sentiment he shared. He'd often weighed the costs and benefits of living in such an unreachable area, but as his research required him to be able to reach traders on a regular basis, he always decided against it. Alleways had been a good compromise, offering solitude while not being too far from civilization. He hoped he would be able to return to that life once this was all over.

Reis made a mental shopping list of the essentials. *This is not going to be easy.* Thomwood was not known to do business on credit. "Let me do the talking. I have a long business relationship with him, I know what kind of person he is. He's a charmer, always smiling and trying to get you at case, but while you're distracted with his smile he'll be taking your coinpurse with one hand while stabbing you in the back with the other."

Kester stopped at the base of the steps. "And this is the kind of man you like to do business with?"

Ignoring Kester's hesitation, Reis climbed the few steps to the door. "I'm not left with a choice if I'm to get the plants I need. As we don't have a choice now. It's not like there's a market in the middle of the forest."

Reis banged loudly on the door to the cabin. There was no answer. He knocked again and still no answer. *Nobody home. No telling when Thomwood will be back. Perhaps we should just break in and take what we need.*

"Well, it's not very often I get visitors," a familiar voice called out.

Reis turned to see Milo Thomwood standing right behind him. Thomwood had been so silent that Reis hadn't be alerted to his presence until he spoke up. He might have been a ghost, just materializing out of thin air.

"Thomwood!" Reis exclaimed as he moved to shake his hand in their typical forced formality. His tone was suddenly friendly and jovial, which got him a few queer glances from his companions. "How have you been, you dirty forest hermit?"

"I make a living," Thomwood replied in an equally upbeat manner. "And how about you? Have your potion-stained fingers discovered the secrets to turn lead into gold?"

"If I did I wouldn't be here. We have some business to discuss."

"I figured as much. Just couldn't wait for my trip to market this year, could you? All right, come on in then. My front porch is no place to conduct business."

He walked by Reis to open to the door. He was a tall man with a slender frame, though it was built up with muscle. Light green eyes shone out like beacons from a harsh, dirty face that was covered in a light shadow of stubble and topped with wild black hair. What currently had everyone's attention was how heavily armed he was. A bow slung over his shoulder, a quiver packed full of arrows on his back; a longsword sheathed on his right side and shortsword on his left; multiple holsters on his arms, legs, and chest that held different sizes of knives; and a belt around his waist that held a dozen darts and a short tube for firing them. All of this was over heavily padded leather and covered in a dark green cloak, which assuredly concealed even more weapons.

Reis assumed this was necessary attire for someone who spent his time negotiating with the dangers of the Izer. It only served to remind him how ill-equipped they were.

It was a pleasant surprise to find the inside of the cabin was comfortably furnished. An inviting sofa sat a short distance away from a magnificent fireplace, surrounded by handcrafted wooden desks topped with golden ornaments. In the next room, a long table seated several plush and comfortable seats. Reis was reminded of his former home in Alleways, which on the outside appeared run-down and rotting but inside was furnished and decorated to meet with his desired lifestyle. He and Thomwood and had very similar tastes.

Thomwood had his guests take seats around the the table, although Pash insisted on standing. His attention was fixed on Kindra as she came into the room.

He flashed her his widest smile. "So, I see your choice in company has improved, Reis. She's a real beauty."

"You flatter me, Mr. Thomwood," Kindra said halfheartedly.

"Please, call me Thom. Everyone does."

Only the people foolish enough to trust him.

"I didn't come here to show off the woman, Thomwood," Reis said.

Thomwood had an infuriatingly innocent look on his face. "No? I thought you wanted to let me know you've moved up in the world. I remember how red in the face you were when I mocked your last female companion. You remember her? The one who followed you around like a lost puppy."

Reis was growing agitated. Every meeting with Thomwood was like this. He liked to play games so that his buyers wouldn't be focused when it came time to negotiate prices.

"Yes, just like that!" Thomwood burst out with a laugh. "Your face always gets so red when I mention her." He winked at Kindra. "Be good to this guy, huh? He's had his heart broken before."

Reis laid is head in his hands. "Can we please talk seriously for a moment?"

"Of course, of course, right to business, as always," Thomwood said passively. "So what brings you all the way down to my little cabin?"

"It's a long story. The short version is we're about to try and cross through the Izer and we need supplies. Anything you could provide to help us survive the journey would be of great assistance."

Thomwood burst into raucous laughter. "After all the time you called me the fool for risking my life in the Izer, you're going into it now?"

"The irony is not lost on me, Thomwood. So can you help us or not?"

Thomwood stopped and looked upwards as if he was lost in thought. Reis knew by now this was just a tactic he used to feign reluctance so he could ask for more coin.

"It's not the kind of business I usually conduct," he eventually said. "Any supplies I sell you will be out of my personal stores. That would come at a premium, of course."

"Of course," Reis conceded. He was not in much a position to negotiate right now. "I don't have much coin on me right now, not much anything really. Whatever I owe you, I'll pay you next time you're at market."

Thomwood tsked. "Now, Reis, you know better than that."

"I'll pay you double."

That got Thomwood's attention. He smiled wide. "Your word is as good as coin in my pocket. Come, then, let us get you supplied."

Soon they were filling packs with canisters of fresh water, dried meats, blankets, rope, and torches, among other things. They also procured a few long knives to help cut through the brush. After some negotiating and finally agreeing to pay a hefty sum, Reis was able to convince Thomwood to part with a crossbow and some bolts. He had no intention of fighting off the beasts of the Izer with just his sword.

At Kester's request, Thomwood dug through several chests of miscellaneous things he collected over the years to see if he could find some armor. He managed to find an old breastplate. It had seen better days, but after rubbing some dirt off the steel and checking the straps Kester insisted it was in good enough condition. Reis was not sure how much good armor would do him in the forest, most likely it would just slow him down. But that's the way these church-boys were, thinking that a couple of inches of steel would protect them from anything.

Pash refused any additional supplies. Such things were unnecessary for a true warrior, or something along those lines. He spent much of the time talking at length with Thomwood about paths through the forest, where animals were migrating right now, and how wide the river was at this time of year. Pash obviously had respect for Thomwood's knowledge of the Izer.

By the time they had finished it had grown dark. As they were getting ready to head out, Thomwood appeared carrying some heavy blankets.

"No point in heading out in the dark," he said with that wide smile of his. "Might as well spend the night."

That was the last thing Reis wanted to do. "It'll be dark when we get in the Izer, anyway. Doesn't really matter when we set out."

No crack appeared in Thomwood's smile. "But you'll need energy if you are going to brave its many dangers. Take it from experience, I never head into it without a full night's rest under me. Besides, I've got supper on. When was the last time you boys had a hot meal?"

"A hot meal does sound very good right now," Avis said.

"As does a warm place to sleep," Kindra added.

Kester was also eager to stay. "After all he's done for us, it would be rude to turn down his hospitality."

Reis looked at the barbarian for support. Pash just shrugged. Reis sighed and conceded. He would have to keep one eye open tonight.

For supper Thomwood was ready to impress: several types of game meat slow smoked and rubbed with exotic spices, hearty soup, thick and salty bread, and tea made from rare leaves only found within the Izer. The pleasing meal, mixed with Thomwood's charm and the comfort of their surroundings, put everyone at ease. Everyone except for Reis. He kept quiet and listened, ever alert to potential threats.

Soon the others were all sitting back, joking and laughing, and sharing stories. They listened intently to Thomwood's story of an encounter he had with a giant bird creature that had scooped him up off the ground and tried to feed him to its young. Pash shared a story in his short and to the point manner about a time he had to wrestle a rabid Korki with his bare hands. Even the supposedly modest Kester tried to impress with an encounter he and his companion Darius had with a dozen Empire horsemen.

After Avis regaled them with a tale of a time she had flirted with a woman who ended up being married to a captain of the local guard and had nearly lost her head, Thomwood said, "You're a real man's man, aren't you, Alvis?"

Pash laughed so hard little bits of bread were sprayed all over the table. When Thomwood asked what was so funny, Avis just said, "Inside joke."

Reis wished the others would be more cautious around this man. You could never trust Thomwood's hospitality. There was always a price with Thomwood, even if you couldn't see it right away.

He realized Kindra was also being silent. She must have sized Thomwood up the same way she did Reis when they first met in Colby. He couldn't help but be impressed by her ability to see right through people. *She may be even better at judging people than I am.*

"You're awfully quiet for a man who has had so many adventures." Thomwood was flashing Reis that winning smile of his. "Or is that all so far behind you that you no longer remember? Your life as an alchemist certainly seems dull by comparison."

"It's important work." Reis did not want to rise to the bait. "And I wouldn't talk down on my profession if I was you, since you rely so much on my business. How much of this place has been paid for with coin I spent for my 'dull' alchemy?" He motioned to the gold fixtures on the wall.

Thomwood laughed. "More than I would care to admit." He leaned in close. "I just cannot help but find it strange that Reis Beldaken, a man considered a demon with a blade, could find himself in such a scholarly pursuit."

Is that your game? Trying to get me to spill alchemical secrets? "The ability to wield a weapon and wield a book are not necessarily mutually exclusive."

"It's true," Avis chimed in. "I got to see the benefits of one of his potions myself. I was poisoned and on the verge of death and it cured me. Also caused the cut in my hand to heal right up. Look, it didn't even leave a scar."

Avis held out the hand that the assassin had cut for everyone to see. There was no sign that she had ever taken the injury.

"So is that the plan, then, Reis?" Thomwood asked in a cheerful tone that did not disguise his condescension. "Create medicines with your alchemy, maybe become a traveling doctor? Healing the sick? How noble."

Reis leaned back in his chair. "Don't compare my elixirs to something as mediocre as medicine. Besides, my healing elixir is only a stepping stone towards me goal."

"And what goal would that be?"

Reis paused for a moment, weighing his next words. He really had no desire to share this much information with Thomwood, but the hunter's condescending words had driven it out of him. That wasn't what was giving him pause. He would gladly tell Thomwood all about his research if it meant shutting him up. It was the church-boy he was worried about. How would he feel about the true goal of his research?

"Go on, Reis," Kindra said. It might have been the first time she spoke the entire meal. "We're all curious."

Reis could see in Kindra's eyes that she was just as eager for Thomwood to be silenced as he was. He decided he may as well just be blunt about it.

"The secret of eternal life. Immortality. I believe through alchemy it is not only possible but plausible, and my research may only be a few years away from reaching this goal."

Silence. Everyone was giving him strange looks, like they were trying to tell if he was serious or if he was just grandly delusional. At least Thomwood was now quiet.

"Only weak men fear death," Pash said, finally breaking the silence.

Reis glared at the brute. "If I feared death, I would not be here."

Kester had stopped eating, though his fork was still raised stupidly in air half way between the plate and his mouth. He regarded Reis seriously. "Then why are you so focused on it?"

Reis sat forward in his chair and folded his hands beneath his chin. It was such a ridiculous question.

"I don't understand why it is so strange. Man's desire to defeat death has always been at the forefront of innovation. When a man desired to no longer be killed by the sword, he invented armor, and since then legions of men have attempted to improve upon the design. No one would say it was for fear of death. Death came for man in the form of disease and infection, and man fought back with medicine. Like many men before me, I realized that death is just another enemy that needs to be faced."

Kester had finally set his fork down. "Is such a thing even possible? Even the best armor can be pierced, and there are dozens of illnesses for which medicine has no cure. How can one possibly defeat death for good?"

"Perhaps 'immortal' is the wrong choice of words," Reis responded. "In theory, my elixir would make me ageless, immune to any known illness or poison, and would cause any wounds to heal rapidly. But a sword through my heart or lopping off my head would still kill me well enough, I suppose."

"Reminds me of a story I once heard," Avis said. Reis hadn't noticed until now that she had also stopped eating. "A witch tricks a soldier into drinking a potion, telling him it will give him the strength to defeat any enemy on the battlefield. It does, but it also turns him into a monster, an abomination that attacks friend and foe alike. He wreaks havoc until a friend of the soldier finds the witch and demands to know how to stop his friend. It turned out the only way to stop him was to put a silver dagger through his heart." She chuckled. "Of course, in this case you're both the witch and the soldier."

Kindra, of all people, came to his defense. "There's no reason to call Reis a monster."

"I've been called worse." *Much worse.* "It doesn't bother me any. I know what I am."

Thomwood seemed amused by all of this. "So what are you, Reis?"

"More than either man or monster. Let's leave it at that."

No one seemed to know how to respond to that. The table became silent, the only sound coming from Pash's noisy chewing.

Avis attempted to lighten the mood. "Personally, I don't think I would want to be immortal. Life would become so dull after a while."

"I discovered a long time ago that wealth and power are fleeting," Reis explained. "No matter what you accomplish in this life, it is all temporary. Even if you can avoid taking a sword to the gut, or contracting some pox, one day you will get old and your body will just fail you. Even Marcus Serpentine, for all the might of the Empire he has built, will one day die. All of his efforts will have meant nothing. All life is just a futile struggle against time. My alchemy is a chance to stop the clock, give meaning to the struggles. If I die before I achieve this goal, so be it. But if I succeed, then there is nothing I can't accomplish, given unlimited time."

Pash continued to chew noisily away at his meat. The conversation seemed to be boring him. Truthfully, it was boring Reis as well. He had already said far more than he had intended, but for some reason he had felt the need to defend his research. Perhaps it was because Kindra was watching, or perhaps it was Thomwood's tone.

"Life's struggles are not meaningless!" Kester declared, far too forcefully. "We are judged in the Light so that we may find peace in Eternity -"

"And now we're on to Church bullshit," Reis spat. "The Light can judge my ass." He rose from the table. "I'm going to turn in now. Thank you for the hospitality, Thomwood."

In the next room he lay down and attempted to get some sleep on one of Thomwood's spare beds. He tossed and turned, his frustration and anger preventing him from calming down and getting comfortable. How dare they judge him like that? How dare they make fun of his research and goals?

Insinuating that he was afraid of death. That was the worst insult of all.

Kindra didn't come to talk with him that night. There was no warm body curled up next him. Thomwood's cabin was kept warm but Reis felt as chilled as if he was on that mountain's ledge.

He couldn't wait to kill Marcus Serpentine and be done with all of this. All the traveling, the cold nights away from his bed, the unbearable company he was forced to keep. When this was all over he would never have to see any of them again. Unless Kester tried to make good on his brother's debt, in which case Reis would be forced to kill him. He wouldn't be sorry to have to do it, either.

That was a problem for the future. The immediate problem was crossing that forest. Tomorrow they would be entering into what might as well be another world. A dark realm where humans are not welcome and enemies are hidden in everlasting shadows.

The Izer.

Chapter 17

Thomwood bid them farewell early the next morning. Kester triple checked the straps on the old breastplate before he was prepared to set off. It was a far cry from the protection offered by his usual armor, but having it made him feel more confident.

He, Reis, and Avis each carried a pack filled with the supplies they had obtained from Thomwood's cabin. Pash volunteered to carry Kindra's supplies for her, though he took nothing for himself. He insisted "I'll find everything I need in the forest."

Reis was being particularly quiet this morning. Kester had been uneasy all night thinking about the things Reis said over dinner. Whenever he thought he knew the limits of the darkness of Reis's heart, Reis would manage to surprise him. Kester could not help but wonder, if they succeeded in killing Serpentine, but Reis was allowed to live and continue towards his goals, would the world really be a better place? Or would they have just traded one evil for another?

"Stick close and watch your feet," Pash grunted as he led them past the forest's boundary.

They entered into a world of thick, tall trees, wild grass of various shades of green and yellow, and high shrubbery touting all manner of plump berries and colorful flowers. Kester struggled to keep up with the rest of the group. It seemed like every few steps some root was trying to trip him or the ground would cause him to nearly slip. Pash was not having any trouble with the terrain; he strode along as if the forest wasn't even there. Reis and Avis followed closely behind him, occasionally having to slow down when it came time to cross through a narrow breach in the shrubbery, but otherwise showing little sign of effort. Even Kindra seemed to be having less trouble than Kester, picking her way through the high grass and weeds a just few steps behind Avis.

The Church had a special group trained for surviving the wilderness: the Rangers. They were prepared to get along in any harsh terrain, be it rough mountains, scorching desert, or dank swamps. Kester remembered watching them train as they prepared for their duty to spread the word of the Light to the most inhospitable reaches of Kassia. He wished now that he had done more than just watch. Perhaps if he had partaken of a lesson or two, he wouldn't be struggling so much.

The further they walked, the thicker the plant-life became. After a few hours they were waist-deep in tall grass and weeds. On all sides, the trees towered over them like ancient guardians. Far over their heads a canopy formed that quickly became thicker and fuller, blocking out more and more of the sun's light above. Soon the light seemed to disappeared completely, leaving them in near absolute darkness.

Kester felt a shudder run down his spine. This was no place for a devout of the Light. This was a place where the Light held no influence and could not see or protect him. He did his best to not let his nervousness show on his face. The last thing he needed was for Reis to see him looking weak.

They brought out torches to light their way. It was only midday, but already it was as dark as night. Pash continued to lead them, a torch in one hand and a knife to cut through brush in the other. In the dark Kester was having even more trouble finding his way without stumbling. He wasn't the only one struggling now; even Reis was stumbling at times. Pash grew frustrated with the slow pace of the group and started pointing out obstacles in their path for them, grunting and adding a few select words in his native tongue that Kester could guess the meaning to.

There were no beaten paths here in the Izer. Without being able to see the sun and the sky, it was hard to tell for sure what direction they were headed. Meanwhile, their vision only extended to the end of their torches' light. If they got turned around, they might wander for hours before they even realized they were offtrack. But Pash seemed confident in his ability to navigate the forest, and no one questioned his lead. Every once in a while, he would stop and kneel. He told them he was checking for signs of what animals had been by recently and if it was something to be wary about.

Kester lost track of the time. How long had they been trekking in the darkness? Pash had said it would take five days to traverse the Izer. Surely he had not meant for them to do it without rest? What were the limit's to the Mankuri's endurance? Kester felt as if he was near collapsing.

Pash suddenly stopped in his tracks. He turned and put a finger to his lips, then pointed to his ear. Kester looked off into the darkness and tried to listen for what Pash was hearing. At first, Kester heard nothing. Then, possibly something. It was a faint sound at first, barely audible over the rustling of the leaves in the trees. Slowly it grew clearer, a high pitched sound like a whistle in the distance.

"We need to hide!" Pash whispered urgently.

Kester jumped into the undergrowth and laid flat on his stomach, allowing the tall brush to conceal him. He looked up as the high pitched noise grew louder and closer. It became so loud, he had to cover his ears. The air above them became filled with tiny flying creatures. Kester could barely make them out in darkness. They had wings like insects but the bodies and sharp beaks of birds. There were thousands of them flying in a chaotic frenzy, letting out high-pitched whistles that bore straight into Kester's brain. It was as if someone was stabbing him in the head with a knife.

"Litherbirds," Pash explained. "They travel in swarms and draw out prey with their shrieks. The prey reveals itself as it tries to flee the sound and gets swarmed upon."

As he said this, they saw an example. An animal resembling a deer, although three times as bulky, came bolting out of the foliage, shaking its head in distress against the high pitched shrieks. Almost immediately, it was set upon by the swarm and covered from end to end in the insect-like creatures. In less than a minute the swarm disbursed, leaving behind only a picked-clean skeleton.

"They can tear all the flesh off a man in less time than it takes to blink," Pash said. "We need to keep hidden until they've passed on."

The flight of the swarm was erratic at best. They didn't move with any kind of discernible pattern. It was impossible to tell how long it would be before they had moved on. As they lingered over the area, Kester became afraid they might be aware of their presence. Their shrieking continued to intensify, until it became so loud that he could hear nothing but the high pitched whistle. Kindra opened her mouth and appeared to be screaming, but if she was the sound was lost. Kester felt dizzy and nauseous. His brain pounded like was ready to explode. He wondered if a quick death by the swarm would be a merciful end right then.

But eventually the swarm did move on, and mercifully the shrieking faded. They all breathed a sigh of relief. Kester still heard a loud ringing in head. As he rose from his hiding place, he felt something familiar and warm on the side of his face. He brought his hand up to touch one of his ears, and found blood. His ears were bleeding. He snapped his fingers close to his ear. He could still hear, albeit slightly impaired, despite the ringing and the blood. Most likely his eardrums had ruptured, but there didn't seem to be any serious damage. His hearing should recover in time.

Avis was bent over and vomiting. She wiped her mouth with her sleeve as she rose. "Well, that was unpleasant."

Reis was relighting their torches. "Better unpleasant than dead. Dangers like that lurk around every corner of this damn forest."

Kester examined the blood on his fingertips. *Perhaps I should have taken Reis's warning more seriously. Our mission won't matter if this forest kills us first.*

Kindra noticed the blood and moved to try and help him. "You're hurt."

Kester waved her off. Last thing he needed was Reis to see him looking weak. "I'll be fine. It's nothing serious."

"You must learn to rely on senses other than your eyes," Pash said. He sniffed the air. "Come, we shouldn't linger here for long."

Kindra followed the strange company through the near pitch black darkness of the forest. Her legs burned from the effort already. Back when she was a child she used to hike miles through the woods near her home just for fun. It seemed city life had taken its toll on her.

She supposed she should be grateful. She should be dead right now, another corpse left to rot by the Empire. Her mind kept drifting back to Colby, how many bodies she saw, how many more were dying from their burns and from breathing in too much smoke. The people of Colby had been so kind to her, taking her in when she had nowhere to go and trying to hide her from the imperials. And because of her, most of them were dead and the rest had lost everything.

No one could hide from the Empire forever.

They made their way through the forest until they came upon a river running directly across their path. Here, the tall grasses faded away and the foliage became less dense. In its place, the riverbank was covered in strange flowers that gave off light like little lanterns. When examined closely they resembled tulips, with the light coming from stamen of the flowers. All the flowers working together gave the river a ghostly glow. It was eerily beautiful.

Pash told them to wait while he examined the course of the river. He wanted to know how fast it was flowing and if he recognized how far along it they were. Kester suggested it would be a good time to rest a little. Kindra thought she heard a twinge of desperation in his voice. He and Avis set to making a fire and warming up some of the meals they had gotten from Thomwood.

Kindra walked along the riverbank to admire the beauty of the flowers. For a moment, she forget all the terrible things that plagued her, the massacre at Colby, her treatment at the hands of the imperials, the loneliness and pointlessness of her struggle to stay out of the Empire's hands. There was nothing else but this tranquil field of luminous flowers.

She picked one and was disappointed when the light from it quickly faded.

"They're called Caden's Bloom." Reis was crouched at her side, closely examining the flowers. "Or at least, so Thomwood tells me when he's selling them to me. There's supposed to be some story to the name, about a knight named Caden who died in this forest, but I never paid much attention to it."

Kindra turned the flower in her hand carefully with her fingers. "They're beautiful. It's amazing to see something so beautiful growing in the middle of this place. It's a pity they lose their light the moment they're picked."

"You just need to have the right touch." He took a piece of cloth and soaked it in the river, then took the flower Kindra picked and wrapped the cloth around its stem. Slowly the flower came back alive with light. Kindra looked on in fascination as Reis fastened the flower to the front of her shirt.

"The water in the soil makes them glow," Reis explained. "As long as the stem is kept wet they can continue to create light for days after being picked." He finished attaching the flower to her shirt and looked up at her. "They say some of the beasts of the Izer have been in darkness for so long that they flee from the light. It might not be much, but maybe this will help keep you safe."

"Th-thank you," Kindra stammered. She was caught off-guard by Reis's sudden change in attitude. Was this a moment of genuine kindness?

Reis turned away from her and surveyed the field. "I can't believe how many of these flowers there are," Reis muttered. "Rare find my ass. I have to have a serious talk with Thomwood about what he's been charging me."

Kindra shook her head. Whatever had momentarily come over

Reis had passed now.

She wasn't sure what to make of Reis. Not as sure as she was when they first met, at least. She owed him a lot, that much was for certain. He had risked his life to save her from the clutches of that Empire dog, Ramsay, and he had vowed to protect her from the dangers of the forest. At times, some of his concern even seemed genuine.

But then there were his eyes. Her mother had taught her that the eyes were the windows to a person's soul. Reis's eyes were stone cold, pitch black voids of emptiness. They were the eyes of an unfeeling, calculating, and ruthless man. The eyes of an evil man.

He had already made his intentions clear. *He just wants to sleep with me. That is the extent of why he protects me. Isn't it?* She supposed the important thing was that he was protecting her now. In a less dire situation, she might prefer the company of a kind man, like Kester, but in the dangers of this forest she was glad to have someone like Reis looking out for her.

Kester and Avis sat around the fire, cooking up some nuts while reheating some meat. Kindra took a spot next to them as Kester set a canister of water to boil for tea. His eyes often became fixed on the flames. Sometimes he appeared to be enthralled by the fire. It was a look Kindra had seen often on the faces of men of the Church. The Church preached that men could see the will of the Light in the glow of the flames. All Kindra ever saw was fire.

"You know, before you hired me I had never met someone from the Church of Light before," Avis said. "They didn't really have a presence in Leonine, and I guess my lifestyle since leaving hasn't really lent itself to meeting many religious types."

Kester took his attention from the flames. "Leonine? That's in the Westlands, isn't it?"

Anything west of the Marjan Mountains, which split the continent of Kassia into East and West, was referred to as the Westlands by the people of Eastern Kassia. The mountain range was almost impassable. Only one road saw something close to regular use, the one that led into Allandane. Because of this the Eastern Kassians and the Westlanders had developed vastly different cultures which rarely intermingled. Even the great Church of True Light, which had for centuries been a dominant force in Eastern Kassia, was rarely seen in the Westlands.

"That's right," Avis answered. "Quite a few people would like to see me dead back there, so I'm in no hurry to return. Of course, had I known a fate like this would find me here, I may have just taken my chances."

"It wasn't something you could have predicted." Kester became thoughtful for a moment. "I apologize for getting you involved in all this. It certainly wasn't my intention when I hired you to procure a couple wagons. I suppose it's my fault for allowing Reis to follow you. He was the target of that assassin."

Avis just laughed and waved him off. "Don't think too much of it. Tell you the truth, I've found this whole experience to be quite exciting. Plus, if we pull this off, imagine the boost my reputation will get! I'll never struggle for mercenary work again. Toppling an Empire can't hurt my chances with the ladies, either."

Toppling an Empire. No one in Reis's company had yet explained to Kindra why they were heading towards Marjan, the Empire capital, but from the way they talked it seemed clear that they intended to launch some kind of attack. What they possibly thought the few of them could do against the might of the Empire's army, Kindra could only guess.

Kester smiled as he pulled the boiling water from the fire and reached into his pack to find Thomwood's tea leaves. He looked relieved.

"By the way," Avis said as she leaned in closer to Kester, "does the Church make you take vows of celibacy?"

Kester was so surprised by the sudden question that he almost poured boiling water on his lap instead of the cups. Kindra stifled a laugh.

"Well, no," Kester answered. "In the Church we all take one vow of loyalty to Light and to uphold its message. Some of the Clerics take on additional vows, such as silence or celibacy, to show their devotion, but those of us in the Church's military arm rarely do so."

Avis smiled. "So you've been with a woman, then?"

Kester's face flushed. "No. My devotion to the Church has taken much time, especially once the war started. I can't say I ever had the chance."

"So, no vow of celibacy officially, but in practice. How sad. You're missing out on so much." Avis saw how uncomfortable her teasing was making Kester and was encouraged to push it further. "Such a waste, a handsome man like you. You know, you're one of very few people who know that hidden underneath this outfit is the body of woman. If you decide you'd like to know the touch of a woman, I could show you some things."

Kester focused on the task of preparing the tea and didn't look at Avis. By now his face was bright red. "I'll keep that in mind."

Kindra had to put her hand over her mouth to keep from breaking into laughter. Who would have guessed this stoic soldier of the Light would become so easily flustered?

Pash came over and plopped himself down next to the fire. He took one of the cups of tea and swallowed the scalding hot liquid in a single gulp. He then gave Kester a serious look. "We got a problem."

Reis was summoned over to to learn what Pash had discovered. He had been picking a few of the Caden's Bloom, a useful alchemy component, and gingerly put them in his pack before joining the others standing about the fire.

"As Thom had warned me, the river is very powerful and wide right now," Pash declared. "We won't be able to cross it here. Fortunately, I know where there is a ford not far upstream. Unfortunately, accessing it might prove difficult."

He laid down in front them a pair of animal bones. The bones had been sharpened at the ends to a fine point.

"I found these floating downriver. I fear the ford may now be controlled by the natives."

Reis examined the bones curiously. They were primitive but the ends were remarkably sharp, like an arrow's point. "Natives to the forest? Thomwood has told me many stories of the Izer but has never mentioned anything about natives. He implied that the forest was inhospitable to human life."

"Calling them 'human' may not be right," said the brute whom just a few days ago Reis would have considered less than human himself. "They are as much beasts of the Izer as the Litherbirds. The fact that they may look like us doesn't change that. They're too small to be human, and have heads a size too big for their shoulders. And they have the widest eyes you've ever seen, like a cat's eyes. Lets them see in the dark. They live in the trees and feast on raw meat, the flesh of whatever they can get their hands on. Even others of their own kind."

"And they're guarding this ford in the river?" Kester asked.

"Something like that. More like hunting. They're smart enough to know that when the river gets like this, the beasts of the forest rely on the ford to cross from one side to the other. I'm positive they're there now."

Reis glanced across the breadth of the river. It was wide, but not too much. "I can cross using my shadows." Remembering that only Kester was aware of his ability he explained. "I am a Willer, surely even you Mankuri have to know what that is. My power manifests itself as control over shadows. If I have time and can concentrate, I can extend the shadows around me some distance. I can also enter into it and come out the other end, assuming my shadow took the path I expected and I don't end up crashing into a tree or some other obstacle. When I can see my destination, it is a lot easier. It should be simple enough for me to get across the river."

"And we can go with you as long as we enter the shadow right after you, right?" Kester asked.

"Yes, but I doubt I could do it in one trip. Each additional person coming with me requires more focus from me and drains me of more strength. Taking two additional people with me is about my limit before I lose control of my ability. There are four of you, so I would need to make three trips, one across with two of you, back across myself, and across with the remaining two. I would collapse after two."

"Are you too weak to push yourself?" Pash snarled. "What kind of man are you?"

Reis was about to retort but Kindra cut him off. "You don't understand what it's like!" she shouted at Pash. "Getting control of your ability, it requires so much focus and concentration. It feels like you're trying to force your eyes out of their sockets. And when you reach the point when your ability starts to manifest, the pain starts. A horrible, sharp pain that starts in your brain and then moves down your spine. The more control over your ability you try to exert, the worse the pain. And when you finally release control, the pain fades but leaves you feeling drained and empty in its place. Exert yourself too much and you black out, just fall where you stand. You couldn't understand, it's not the same as swinging some brutish hammer!"

Pash growled and took a menacing step towards her. Kester stepped between them.

"We'll just have to split into two camps for the night," Kester suggested. "Reis takes two of us over tonight and, when he's rested, the other two in the morning. Then we can continue on our way."

"Not possible," Pash barked. "These shores become hunting grounds for wild Korki at night. They are drawn to the light of the flowers and the water of the river. We need to be far from the river before then. You don't want see what happens when a pack of wild Korki think they see an easy meal."

Reis thought about the Korki, the monstrous beasts the Mankuri had ridden into battle. And those were the tame ones. He could only imagine how violent and dangerous the wild kind would be.

He frowned and weighed the options. "So, we're back to needing to ford the river again, if we want to get distance from it before nightfall." He had no idea how to tell when nightfall was in this damn forest. The beasts of the Izer must have some kind of instinctual sense of time.

"That means dealing with the natives," Kester added. The church-boy had a knack for stating the obvious.

"Dealing with the natives seems inevitable," Reis agreed. "But my ability isn't completely useless here. We can do this smart."

Kester followed close behind Pash as they made their way along the riverbank, following the river upstream. Reis and Alvis were on other side of the river and staying just out of view. Reis had brought Kindra with him through his shadows as well, so they wouldn't have to worry about protecting her while they fought their way across the ford. She should be safely concealed now and waiting for them to regroup.

Pash and Kester were the most physically intimidating members of the group. Pash said the natives would hesitate before attacking them. They would storm the ford and take advantage of this momentary hesitation. Avis and Reis would be waiting on the other side, ready to appear at the right moment to assist. Once across they would dash deeper into the forest, hoping the natives wouldn't pursue them long.

That was the plan, anyway.

Pash pointed to the ford in the river the moment it came into sight. It was a wide section of shallow water easily identified by the rocks that jutted out of it like markers. Thick, green trees grew close to water here. They concealed the almost-human beasts stalking the crossing.

They stopped just out of view of the ford. Kester strapped his shield high up on his shoulders so it would protect the back of his head and neck. They had rearranged the supplies in their packs so that one pack was empty, then filled it with wet soil. Pash carried that pack on his back. It wasn't much but it should provide a small layer protection from the natives' arrows. Kester was to follow close behind Pash to take as much of the enemy fire as he could; he doubted the primitive projectiles would be capable of piercing his shield or breastplate. Unfortunately, Pash was much larger than he was so he wouldn't be able to completely cover him.

Once they were ready they continued towards the crossing. They walked slowly at first, hoping that their approach would go unnoticed. As soon as they came close, they both broke into a sprint. The trees began to rustle and shake as they ran past. Kester looked around just enough to get a glimpse at some of the small, white figures. Perched high in a the trees were naked, wiry men half the size of a normal man. They looked like pale, misshapen children with cat-like eyes that were too big for their heads. They watched Kester and Pash with interest as they ran past.

It wasn't until they hit the water that the natives finally attacked. Kester heard the impact their primitive arrows made against his breastplate. Around him the arrows that missed splashed into the water. Pash hunched over as he ran. They ran through the river as quickly as they could, but even in the ford the water came up past their knees, to their waist at points. The current was so strong that it threatened to pull Kester off his feet.

Kester heard some loud splashing behind him. He dared to look back and saw some of the natives were leaping into the water after them. Despite the water coming up much higher on them they cut through it like knives. More frightening were the ones that avoided the water altogether, leaping from rock to rock with the agility of the cats whose eyes they bore. They carried spears, knives made of sharpened bone, and clubs bigger then their arms. Kester wasn't sure how well these primitive weapons would fare against his breastplate, but had no intention of testing it.

Several more arrows impacted against his shield. One pierced his lower left arm and caused him to wince in pain. Another arrow whizzed by his head and hit Pash's pack. It tore open and spilled soil.

The natives chasing them were getting close. One of the

jumpers leaped in the air, spear raised and on trajectory for Kester. A crossbow bolt it in its ribcage and it dropped from the air like a dead bird. Somewhere ahead of them, hidden on the other side of the river, Reis had fired off a well-aimed shot.

The others were close behind him. Kester could hear them splashing through the water. He drew his sword and held it at his side. He listened to the movement of the water, trying to block out the sounds of his panting and the splashes of the giant Pash as he moved through water. He focused his attention only on the noises behind him. One of the natives was close. He turned halfway around and slashed. He cut his pursuer across the face and it splashed back into the water.

They were almost across the river. They saw Avis come out of the cover of the foliage, ready to lead them through a route she and Reis had planned and cleared ahead of time. Avis tossed something in their direction. One of Thomwood's knives glided past Kester and buried itself into chest of a native close behind him. A crossbow bolt found its way into another jumper.

Kester felt the impact of a club against the back of his breastplate. He was prepared to turn and strike back when he saw another native trying to go around him to get to Pash. Kester lunged out and stabbed through its side. On his other side, a jumper soared past him and landed on Pash's back. It grabbed on and tried to stick its knife into Pash's throat. Pash lifted it off him with one hand and tossed it with the ease one would toss a pebble. It landed in the deeper river and was carried away by the current.

They reached the end of the river and ran ashore. Avis waved them towards her and pointed in the direction they would run into the overgrowth. Kester turned as they ran and noticed something disturbing. The natives hadn't come ashore. They remained in the river, just staring at them. Then they turned around headed back in other direction.

Pash and Avis stopped when they noticed Kester wasn't following. Reis appeared out of one of the shrubs, his crossbow loaded but lowered. They were all looking at the fleeing natives.

"Is that normal for them?" Reis asked.

"No," Pash said. "They are afraid of something, and they do not scare easy. This is bad, we have to move."

Something that would frighten even those savages. The thought chilled Kester. There was a heavy feeling in the air, a stillness.

There was no sound, not a single leaf rustling or bird chirping. It was the first time since they entered the forest that things were this quiet. There was something close by, something dangerous.

Something that was hunting.

Reis shouted, "Kindra!" He tossed the crossbow aside and dashed down the riverbank, leaving the protests of his companions behind.

Chapter 18

E verything was like a blur to Reis. He didn't know for sure at what point he had started running, or when he lost the crossbow, or when he drew his sword. He was dashing madly along the riverbank, following it downstream to where he and Avis had told Kindra to remain hidden. He wasn't sure what he would find. He didn't know what the natives had been afraid of, or even why he had suddenly felt as though Kindra was in danger. But he just knew it. She was alone and defenseless, she would be the first target of any predator.

He found the marker he had Avis had left on the riverbanks, rocks arranged in a semicircle. He was turning to run into the thick foliage of the deep forest when suddenly Kindra came stumbling into the clearing. Her face was flushed from exertion and she was panting heavily. Her clothes were torn in places and her face was scratched from running through branches and bramble. As she came upon the riverbank she collapsed into the flowers.

Reis didn't have time to check on her. Bursting out of the foliage right after was a beast larger than anything he had seen before. It stood five feet tall and more than ten in length. It had a body like a panther, covered in black and red fur like burning coals. Its head resembled that of a massive bear, with a long, protruding snout, beady eyes, and rounded ears. It was snarling fiercely as it bounded forward. The ground shook under its weight.

He couldn't even begin to imagine how to kill something like that, but he was going to try. He held his sword at ready, prepared to strike the moment it got within his reach.

But it didn't. It stopped a few feet away from him and started pacing back and forth. It was snarling angrily and looking at Reis with furious, hungry eyes. But it didn't take any more steps forward. Reis kept his weapon steady and watched the beast's every movement closely. After pacing a few more times it turned around and bolted back into the thick foliage it had appeared from.

Reis wasn't sure what had just happened. He waited for a few moments until he was convinced that it wasn't returning, then went to Kindra's side. She was collapsed in the flowers on the riverbank, their light illuminating her and making her glow like some kind of ethereal being. She was breathing heavily and her hair was matted to her face from sweat, but aside from the scratches she seemed unharmed.

"It was the light," Kindra managed to say through heavy grasps for air.

"What?"

"The light. It's afraid of it."

She unfolded her hand. In it was the Caden's Bloom that he had pinned to her shirt.

"You saved me again."

The others caught up with him shortly. Avis returned Reis's crossbow while Kester lectured him on his impulsiveness. After silencing Kester with a low growl, Reis described the beast that had been chasing Kindra. Pash shook his hand and explained that even the Mankuri hadn't encountered every beast that called the Izer home.

When she had recovered, Kindra explained what had happened to her. She had been hiding in the overgrowth as planned when this beast had suddenly come upon her. She was sprawled on the ground and the beast was over her. Then the light from the Caden's Bloom shone on its face and it pulled away. When she remembered what Reis had said about some of the forest beasts being afraid of light she took the flower in her hand and made a mad dash towards the river. The beast was always on her heels but whenever it got to close she turned around and waved the flower around and forced that forced it retreat a little. Thanks to the flower she was able to reach the river safely, where Reis himself witnessed the beast's unwillingness to follow.

It was still out there in the forest, lingering close by. They could all feel it. It was biding its time and waiting for them to leave the protection of the riverbank. No one wanted to face the beast on its home turf and, as it was now getting late, they decided the best thing to do would be to set up camp for the night. Pash told them that with the natives on one side of the river and that beast stalking the shadows on this side it was unlikely that any wild Korki would come upon their camp at night. Just to be safe they decided to sleep in shifts. Two people would watch the camp while the rest slept.

Reis and Pash drew the first shift. Reis muttered under his breath about his horrible luck. He was tired from the exertion of using his ability. And if he was going to be forced to take watch with someone, he would prefer the company of Avis. He would even settle for Kester, the Church-boy was always good for a laugh. But Pash was just an uncivilized brute who happened to speak a civilized language. What kind of conversation was there to be had with a savage?

For a long while they sat in silence. Reis's thoughts drifted frequently to the beast that lurked just out of sight. Would it still be waiting there in the morning? Or would it give up and move on?

Reis had an idea and grabbed his pack. He took out the blooms he had picked earlier as well as a number of cups and utensils. The flowers had been packed between smooth stones to flatten them.. They looked to be about ready for use. Pash watched him curiously as he carefully plucked the petals of the flowers, one by one, and set to chopping and crushing them into a powder.

"What are you doing?" Pash eventually asked him.

"Getting useable powder out of the raw ingredients. In alchemy, many ingredients are only useful as powders."

"You intend to make an elixir?"

"Something like that. It's something that should help us get by that giant bastard hiding out there."

Pash nodded his understanding. He watched Reis work quietly after that. There was something like fascination in his eyes. Reis was surprised by his interest — he thought this kind of thing would bore the warrior. But he watched with close interest. This drew Reis's curiosity.

"Do you have alchemists among the Mankuri?" he asked.

Pash shook his head. "Our craftsman make weapons and tan leather. But we have seen the effects of elixirs before, through trade with people like Thom, or as the spoils of a raid. Elixirs that can keep a warrior alive long after he should have fallen, or grant him might beyond his normal limits. We have no way of making them ourselves."

"I can show you some of the basics, if you'd like." It would be useful if the giant could assist him with some of the more trivial, repetitive tasks. "Alchemy is a tool, like any weapon. It could be useful to learn a little."

Pash agreed. In short time Reis had showed him the proper method of grinding the flower petals into powder. Pash was a quick learner and had very dexterous hands. He proved to be a very useful assistant. As they worked Reis lectured him on some of the basics of alchemy, the qualities of common plants, common solvents, how to purify ingredients. Pash listened to every word intently. Reis was surprised to find Pash was a good student.

Perhaps there is more to this savage than meets the eye.

When a few hours had passed, it was time to wake Avis and Kester for their watch. Reis packed up the ground powder and told Pash he would let him watch as he made the concoction in the morning.

Kester and Avis reluctantly awoke and took their spots. As Reis lay down he was suddenly aware of just how exhausted he really was. The Izer was no place for him. And he had at least four more days of this to go.

He wasn't able to brood on it for long because he quickly fell into a deep sleep. In his sleep he dreamed of the impending confrontation with Marcus Serpentine. The satisfaction he felt as the emperor lay bleeding before him. The comfort of being able to return home.

And then there was Kester. He was wearing the armor of his brother, Demos. With their mutual enemy gone, their temporary alliance was over. Now he was going to put an end to Reis's "dark experiments" and finish the job his brother started. Reis fought him, but the armor was too tough and his sword just bounced off. He couldn't find a weak spot on it. And then Kester ran him through, smiling as the life faded from Reis's body.

And then there was just darkness.

Chapter 19

Time for another daring nighttime strike. Lunn tried to convince himself that he was truly excited for the upcoming battle, but mostly he just felt tired. And a little bit intoxicated.

Lucas, on the other hand, seemed like he could barely contain his excitement. The kid had a broad smile plastered on his face and something close to glee sparkling in his eyes. Lunn was envious of his youthful naivety. *Perhaps after another five or six battles he will learn the reality of it all. Or perhaps not.*

They moved quietly through the dark alleys of Kresst. The noises of the city should cover the sounds of their movement, but they went as slowly and silently as they could manage. It was a tough order for Lunn, who was wearing various pieces of armor from different suits cobbled together to form a full set. If he stepped the wrong way, or so much as shrugged his shoulders too hard, his armor pieces would bang together and make a racket like a thunderstorm passing through.

Their unit reached its destination, an old church in the poorer section of the city. The church, much like others used by the Church of True Light, had been closed down by order of the emperor. A patrol passed by once a day to ensure it remained closed. That patrol was their target tonight.

A board was removed from one of the back windows. Brax carefully peered into the building. He brushed his mustache with his left hand, as he often did when he was thinking. Finally he gave the signal. Brax crawled in through the window and was followed by about half their force. Lunn waved his hand forward and the rest of the men took their positions. They sat on the side of the building, just out of the sight of the street, and waited for the signal.

"How many do you think it's going to be this time?" Lucas whispered excitedly.

"Quiet, kid," Lunn grunted.

"There was only twenty of them last time. This is a big city, it has to have big patrols, right?"

That's what we are assuming. "Be quiet and focus."

Lucas already had his weapons drawn and was drumming his fingers along their hilts. The kid had decided at some point that he would be a master of fighting with two swords, one in either hand.

Lunn had tried more than once to convince him of the foolishness of it and convince him of the benefits of focusing on a single weapon or learning how to use a shield, but Lucas was adamant.

"This sword was given to me by my father, with the promise that I would use it to uphold justice," Lucas had explained to him as he showed him the shortsword he held in his left hand. Holding up the longsword he wielded in the other, he said, "And this sword was my father's. When the Empire marched on our homeland, he had it forged and promised it would taste the blood of a hundred Empire men. Then he got killed by an arrow early in the first battle in which he wielded it, and the sword did not get a chance to spill even a drop of Empire blood. I thus became caught between fulfilling my own vow or my father's. In the end, I decided to fulfill both."

The arrogance aside, Lucas was a very capable fighter. He was only seventeen, with a boyish face and wild, sandy hair that made him appear even younger, but he had already distinguished himself as being among their best combatants. Lunn hated standing so close to him because he knew how terrible and old he must look in comparison. Truthfully, Lunn was not that old, he had not even seen his thirtieth year. Stress, alcohol, and indifferent grooming had left him looking far older than his years. He had made a habit of avoiding his reflection lately, but the last time he had seen it his hair had been going gray, his beard had become wild and unkempt, and his face had become heavily lined. He had become a shell of what he once was.

The first signal came, a bird call from one of their scouts. The patrol was coming down the road. It would not be long now. Hopefully the archers and crossbowmen were already concealed on the church's roof. He checked the strap on his shield to make sure it was tight. He had seen more than one man die after his shield had been torn from his arm. Lunn knew he was bound to die one day, but when that day came it was not going to be from stupidly losing his shield.

Gradually the sounds of the city died out and were replaced with the sounds of footsteps and men talking loudly. The patrol was passing by. Lunn felt old feelings of fear mixed with anger and self-loathing swell up inside him. He kept a flask of ale strapped to the inside of his shield for just such an occasion. Lysander told him to not drink so much before a strike, but Lysander said a lot of things. He lifted his shield so the lip of the flask reached his lips and took a deep swig. Already he could feel the alcohol dulling his emotions.

A shout from the rooftops. The second signal. It was quickly followed by shouts from the street as the first round of arrows and crossbow bolts rained down from the rooftop.

"Go!" Lunn yelled.

He drew his sword and rushed around the side of the church towards the street. Lucas had taken off sprinting before him and was already nearing the street. The rest of his men were just behind him. In the street a confused mass of Empire soldiers were struggling to draw their weapons and to identify their assailants. Several of them already lay on the ground with arrows or bolts sticking out of them and jutting into the air. Another round of arrows came down on them from the roof and more bodies joined their comrades on the ground.

Lucas reached the street first. He cut with his longsword and brought down an imperial who had been still been struggling with his sword belt. Almost casually, Lucas whipped his shortsword around and cut a long gash along the side of the next closest enemy.

Lunn barreled into the street after him. He braced his shield in front of him and put all his weight behind it. Sure enough, he crashed right into one of the imperials. The soldier was sent sprawling to the ground.

A few of the imperials near him had managed to draw their weapons. He deflected a sword with his shield and cut out to his other side. He felt his sword hit bone and quickly pulled it back. He turned his shield just in time to turn away another blow. He lowered his shield enough to stab over it. He caught an imperial in the face. The sword came free with a sickening squish.

All around him were the sounds of fighting as his comrades engaged the Empire soldiers. He lost sight of Lucas, his view blocked by a wall of imperials. He got a chance to glance down the street. It seemed like Lucas had gotten his wish: the patrol they had engaged had to have been at least fifty soldiers strong, more than twice the two dozen men that had attacked them. By now the numbers had been evened, and the imperials still struggled to put up a fight. Many of them were still in shock and trying to figure out what was happening when just twenty seconds ago, everything had been fine.

He caught the glimpse of a sword just off to his side. He tried to move his shield in front of it but was too slow. The sword caught him just above his waist. It struck armor and barely scratched the skin underneath. He swung his sword around at his attacker. The imperial stepped away from it. Lunn moved closer with his shield in front of him. The imperial swung his sword hard and the blade crashed into the shield. The force of the blow knocked Lunn back a step. The imperial tried to take advantage of lost footing and maneuvered himself around Lunn's shield. He swung again and Lunn barely had time to deflect the blade with his own.

He saw another imperial coming around him now. Soon he would be attacked on both sides. Even if he could get his shield in front of one of them, the other would be able to strike at his vulnerable side. He decided his only option was to drop any pretense of defense. He swung his sword wildly at the soldier in front of him. The soldier deflected it with his sword. Lunn went on the offensive, striking again and again. The imperial could not find an opening. After parrying three more blows his sword missed its target and Lunn's sword cut him deep across his torso.

Too late. The other imperial was already alongside him. Lunn could not react in time. He braced himself for the blade's impact.

The imperial let out a short cry. Lunn turned and saw that the soldier had been stabbed from behind. He hit the ground hard. Behind him, Lucas stood in triumph.

"Did you see that?" Lucas shouted. "I just saved your life!"

"Thanks, kid," Lunn grunted.

Most of the patrol lay dead in the street. The few survivors were running for their lives. Fortunately for them, there was no time to pursue. The battle had been taken just over a minute, though it felt much longer. Now they had to disappear just as quickly. Up on the roof of the church the archers were already retreating. Lunn waved his hands back in the direction they had come from.

And the members of The Resistance faded back into the darkness.

As the first light of dawn broke out in the sky, Lunn arrived at the rendezvous site a few miles from the city. Brax's group had beaten him there. He found the big man supervising the deconstruction of their camp while brushing his mustache.

"Lunn, good," Brax said. "Glad to see you did not have trouble getting out of the city."

"Had to take a roundabout route, but we managed," Lunn said.

He motioned to the men taking apart the camp. "How long until we are ready to move?"

"In twenty minutes, no one will ever know we were here. Then we go west, to Rochest."

Lunn nodded. "Lysander will be meeting us there, won't he?"

"Assuming everything went well with his strike at Paulu." Brax chuckled. "The emperor must be scratching his head right now trying to figure out where we will strike next."

"And hopefully will expend his men making a poor guess."

"Here's hoping." Brax sighed and brushed his mustache. "Now is the time for some unpleasantness, I'm afraid. You would be so kind as to handle to headcount?"

Lunn grunted his understanding. *Got to know how many we lost.* He quickly counted up Brax's men and his own. They were three less than when they went into the city.

During the strike, they must have killed or seriously wounded at least forty imperials. Most would consider a loss of three men to forty killed a victory. But The Resistance was running short of men and every loss cut deeply. All together, they numbered just over two hundred now. Conservative estimates put the Empire's forces in the hundreds of thousands. One estimate claimed that between military, navy, guards, and 'special' units, the Empire commanded almost a million men. A loss of forty was negligible.

After reporting the headcount, Lunn took a seat against a tree and dug into his pack. He found a bottle of ale stashed at the bottom. He intended to get good and drunk before they set out. Always made the travel more bearable.

Lucas plopped down next to him. He was smiling his broad, child-like smile. Lunn had to struggle to keep from scowling. He wanted to be left alone to his misery.

"Did you see me out there tonight?" Lucas said brightly. "Those Empire bastards didn't stand a chance. I was cutting them down left and right! Whack! Through the throat! Swing! Chop off an arm! Did you see?"

"You ran too far ahead," Lunn growled. "I lost sight of you. It's dangerous to charge ahead on your own, away from support."

"And yet I was the one who saved you." Lucas chuckled. "But you're right. I could stand to be a little more careful. It's just, when I'm in the midst of the fight, and there are enemies all around, I just lose myself to the excitement of it all. Don't tell me you don't feel the same rush."

"All I feel in the midst of a battle is the desire for it to end." Lunn take a big swig out of his bottle.

"And it seems all you feel after a battle is the desire for ale." Lucas shook his head. "You know, all of us have lost something to the Empire. Friends, family, homelands. But you're not going to find what you lost at the bottom of the bottle."

Now even the kid is lecturing me.

"I'll find what I lost when I'm rejoined with them in eternity. Until then, the ale is a nice distraction."

Lucas shrugged his shoulders. "So what's this all leading up to, anyway?"

Lunn gave Lucas an inquisitive look. "Why, the end of the Empire, world peace, and a new era of peace and prosperity, of course." He gave a bitter laugh.

"Not that. I mean, all these attacks. We're never going to beat the Empire ten men at a time. But Lysander has to know that. All this sneaking around, luring the Empire on a merry chase, spreading rumors about ourselves wherever we go, it all has to be leading up to something."

The kid has some brains after all.

"Lysander has a plan," Lunn said. "It's not my place to spoil it. He'll fill you in on the details when it is time."

"As long as it involves more Empire killing, I'll be happy with it."

Lunn took another swig of ale. "There will be plenty more fighting to be done before we're through."

Konrad Marek read the message again. If the information was accurate, then it was an incredible stroke of luck. Of course, it could be a waste of time from some idiot who thought he could scam some money out of the Empire.

Conners had gotten the bright idea to send out messengers to spread the word that the Empire would pay good money for any information on Beldaken and his companions. Marek hated getting information that way. Most of what turned up was worse than useless. But being stuck at the encampment did not leave him with many options.

Surprisingly, a message arrived in short time. It had details that would be impossible to guess. But the location of Beldaken was strange, to say the least.

A few feet from him Conners was smiling an arrogant 'I told you so' smile. Marek did not want to admit it, but after reading the message over a third time it seemed that Conners's attitude was justified.

"I'll have to leave immediately to follow up on this lead," Marek finally said.

Conners smile died quickly. "You're still the officer in charge here, sir. Maybe you should send someone else. I'd be more than happy to lead a squad after Beldaken."

"Beldaken would have slaughtered your entire squad before I get this place half in order," Marek replied coldly. "No offense, Lieutenant, but I was assigned to hunt this man for a reason. Because officers like you have already tried and failed."

To his credit, Conners's face only gave the slightest hint of annoyance. He knew better than to question orders. But he did have a point. Marek would be unable to pursue Beldaken as long as duty here kept him occupied.

"Conners, I believe you are due a promotion. How would you like to be a Captain?"

Conners was finally caught off guard. The look on his face was almost worth the time Marek had wasted with him.

"Sir? You're only a Captain yourself. Do you have the authority to offer such a promotion?"

Marek smiled. "Not officially, no. But I work directly for the emperor himself. It affords me certain advantages." He reached into his pack and pulled out a small piece of parchment. "This is a letter of recommendation for promotion, made out by me. It is not an official promotion, but its as good as one. No one here will question your authority. A colonel from Mansir should be here in a few days with reinforcements and will take command of the camp. He'll make your promotion official."

Conners still looked like he was in shock, but he was quickly coming around. An arrogant smirk formed on his lips.

"That means I'd be the same rank as you, doesn't it?" Conners said smugly.

"It does." *Technically. But if you ever cross the Empire, that wouldn't stop me from hunting you down.* "Congratulations. You have earned it."

"The camp will be in good hands, sir. Should I arrange an escort for your trip?"

"Shall not be necessary. Send a bird ahead of me telling of my immediate arrival."

"Of course. I'll have the bird sent right now."

Conners rushed from the tent, probably eager to be rid of Marek so he could take command. Marek was only too happy to oblige. He closed his eyes and pictured where he needed to go. He focused hard, felt the familiar pressure behind his eyes. Then he was gone.

Chapter 20

I t was morning, or as close to it as Kester could figure. Avis was preparing a fire to warm up their breakfast as Kester woke the others. At some point over the course of the night Kindra had curled up next to Reis. He felt something close to jealousy but pushed those feelings away. Now was not the time for such trivial thoughts.

They ate a quick meal, then waited while Reis set to work on some alchemical concoction. Pash lent him a hand when he could, boiling water and tending the fire. Reis lectured as he worked, saying something about proper mixing techniques and how to tell when a potion has reached its full potency. Kester was glad to see the two of them working together on friendly terms. There had been tension between them since they set out from the Mankuri fortress. He had been worried that it might have come down to blood before they reached Marjan.

Avis sleepily eyed the forest in front of them. "Think that creature is still out there?"

"Probably," Kester replied. "Pash seems to think so, anyway."

Avis let out a loud yawn. "Hard to sleep, thinking about that thing watching us."

Kester nodded. He had spent much of the night staring at the flowers and trying to take solace in the light they provided.

Their attentions were turned when a sudden light shot out from the fire. It was bright, as if the sun had finally managed to break the canopy. Reis removed a small vial from the fire, the same one that had once contained his healing elixir. Now it filled with a clear liquid that gave off light that was a ten times brighter than the brightest lantern, and yet didn't dazzle the eye against the darkness. It was beautiful and terrible all at once.

Reis bore a satisfied smile. "If that beast is truly afraid of the light, I think we will be safe now."

"And some," Kester said, his fears dissolving in the light. "It will also be nice to be able to see where we're going for once."

"It also makes us a big, glowing target," Pash pointed out. "Anything not afraid of light is going to be drawn to us."

"I would rather face a hundred foes in the light than a single one hidden in the shadows," Kester quoted from the Church's philosophy.

"I'm glad you feel that way, Church-boy." Reis held out the vial. "I was thinking you should be the one to carry it. You are of the Church of True Light, after all. It would only be fitting."

Kester could understand why Reis was eager to hand over the concoction he had worked so hard on. Whoever carried the light would be the first target of anything that might be hunting them. But it did not bother Kester. With the light cast upon him he felt invincible. "I would be honored."

They put out the fire while Kester tied the vial around his neck. Pash took up the lead again as they left the river behind and returned to the deep forest. They moved much more quickly and confidently now that they could make out their surroundings. There was some rustling in the trees, but whatever was there made no move on them. After they had traveled some distance, they were confident that the beast from last night was no longer a threat.

Many strange and exotic animals passed them by, some drawn curiously to the light and others fleeing from it. A troop of monkeys with dark green fur that allowed them to disappear seamlessly into the foliage followed them for a while, making curious glances at the vial of light that hung around Kester's neck and then disappearing again. A magnificent bird with rainbow colored feathers was a bit more bold and dared to circle close to Kester. Pash called it a *Kettibird* and explained that it was a sacred animal the Mankuri. If you encountered one during your trial, it meant that you were destined to be great warrior and leader of the people. Reis muttered something about the alchemical uses of their feathers. Fortunately, Pash did not seem to hear him.

They came upon a path where the trees parted and the plant-life grew low. On either side of the path, the plants and trees towered over them at full height, but here they seemed to refuse to grow. Even the canopy parted slightly overhead, allowing a small trickle of light to fall down upon the path, dim illumination that spread as an eerie haze.

"*The Grave of the Fallen Giant*," Pash said as they walked down the path. "My people tell the story of the Giant whose seed spawned the first Mankuri. The mountains were his home and the forest his hunting grounds. He fought a thousand-thousand great battles in his life and taught his children the warrior's way. His Mankuri children took his lesson to heart and honored their father in the way they knew would please him best: by fighting him to show their strength. They fought back and forth for days, trampling the forest underfoot and forming this path. Finally the great Giant fell, dying with the smile of pride upon his lips. The forest saw and respected the battle so greatly that it left the ground just as it was after the battle, so as to never forget it."

"Another tale of the mountains," Reis said exasperatedly. Pash had told them several Mankuri legends since they had entered the forest. Apparently the Izer was full of landmarks that Pash felt inclined to tell them the tale behind.

"I don't know, I find the stories kind of interesting," Avis said. "They could do with a few more maidens, for sure, but intriguing nonetheless."

Pash raised his arms in the air. "I share lessons of strength and the honor of battle. I share so you can learn. You are little men, and have much to learn if you wish to become warriors worthy of fighting alongside a Mankuri."

Reis snarled at the insult. "You can keep your lessons, savage. I have faith enough in my skills with the blade and I doubt stories about giants are going to do anything to help me improve upon it."

Pash glared at Reis. Kester once again worried that things might turn bloody between them. *Why can't Reis at least pretend at respect for a while?* Reis turned his back to Pash and continued down the path.

Pash shook his head and turned to Kester. "Can this man really be counted on in the heat of battle? He has all the impatience and anger of a boy."

"He might not look like it, but he's quick with the sword, and just as quick of wit. I truly believe he is our best chance for killing Serpentine."

Pash was unconvinced. "We shall see."

Reis walked ahead of the rest of them. The path was simple enough to follow without needing Pash's lead. He was again aware of how much he missed his solitary life. His thoughts drifted to the dream he had last night, where his return to the life he knew was cut short by Kester. There was no doubt that the moment Serpentine fell, their alliance would end. Kester would return to the Church, which would make them enemies. Pash would return to the Mankuri. Avis's contract would be fulfilled, though he wondered if he could afford to keep her on as a retainer. And Kindra...

What would Kindra do? Colby no longer existed, though he doubted that was her hometown to begin with. Where would she go? And why did he care? What happened to her after this was none of his concern.

His train of thought was broken when he a very powerful, sweet scent caught his attention. The smell was sweet as honey but far stronger, like a honeycomb was just inches from his face. He followed the scent and it led him to small, yellow flower. As surprising at it seemed, this small flower no bigger than a rose was the sole provider of this powerful smell. He took a deep sniff and his mouth started to water. He wondered if it tasted as sweet as it smelled.

Of course, in this forest it was likely to be poisonous. Tasting it without knowing its properties would be foolish. He was still curious about it. It wasn't a flower that Thomwood had ever showed him. He wondered what alchemical properties a flower like that might have.

He reached down to pluck it when a strong hand grabbed his arm and stopped him.

"Don't!" Pash commanded.

"I was just planning on examining it," Reis said agitatedly. How stupid did Pash think he was?

Pash pointed into the trees that surrounded the path. Something was moving, hidden by the foliage. Whatever it was moved quietly, but based on the way the tree trembled it must have been huge.

"*Yiver,*" Pash said. "It's a blind hunter, only stalking by smell. Specifically, the smell of this flower. This is *Yiver's Flower.* It gives off a sweet scent that tricks the animals of the forest into eating it. When the flower is plucked the stem gives off a sour scent. This smell lets the yiver knows it is time to strike. Even if the prey tries to flee, the smell of the flower on their breath allows the yiver to find them. When it has finished, the beast buries what remains of the body. The seeds of the flower that the prey consumed grow into a new flower."

"Fascinating," Reis uttered unintentionally. He knew that some animals and plants had symbiotic relationships but never heard of anything like this. He would have to ask Thomwood to hunt a few of these yivers and bring back a sampling of the flowers for him to study.

"Well, thank you, I suppose," Reis said through gritted teeth. "It would have been unfortunate if my life would have ended by being mauled by one of the monsters of this forest."

Pash grinned. "Still plenty of chances of that. You haven't seen half of the dangers the Izer offers."

Kester put a hand on the giant's back. "We trust your expertise in helping us navigate those dangers."

"Though I'll be glad when we're finally free of the forest," Avis added. "So we can be killed by the Empire, instead."

Reis gave the sweet smelling flower one last frown before turning back to Pash. "Lead on."

Chapter 21

Milo Thomwood waited in the heat of the fading sun. In a couple of hours the sun would be gone completely, and a cool wind from the mountains would blow down and drop the temperature sharply. He hoped he would not be waiting that long.

A bird had arrived in the late hours of the morning, just before lunch, that had demanded his immediate presence. Thom was not stupid enough to ignore a summons from the Empire.

He already knew what this was about. He was the one who had originally contacted them, after all. Thom got a bird once a week that brought him news, allowing him to keep up with the important events of world outside the Izer. The last bird brought the news that his longtime business associate, Reis Beldaken, was now a wanted man of the Empire. As if this news was heralding his arrival, Reis himself showed up at his cabin the very next day asking for his help. Thom sent a bird to the nearest Empire outpost as they slept.

He had not expected such a rapid response. The officer must have read his letter immediately and sent his response at once. More surprising was that the response said to expect a full troop of soldiers. That kind of thing should take longer to mobilize. Whatever Reis had done, the Empire was in a huge hurry to get their hands on him.

Thom stood alone in a field just northeast of the Izer, as the letter had instructed. It was an area that was familiar to him. His cabin was nearly inaccessible, flanked by mountains on one side and the Izer on the other. Whenever someone wanted to meet him they usually asked him to come to this field, to save them the trouble of having to go through the Izer to see him. It was a few hours trip through the forest, but as Thom was as comfortable in the Izer as he was in his own home he did not mind.

He did, however, mind being kept waiting. If he was a more foolish man he might be tempted to complain to his Empire visitors. But one thing Thom wasn't, was a fool.

Finally, in the distance he saw the approaching Empire troop. He put on his warmest smile and prepared to greet his new friends.

"I am Captain Konrad Marek, officer of the Emperor Marcus Serpentine," the imperial introduced himself with a soft voice. He motioned to the officer beside him, dressed in blue and sea green instead of the imperial colors. "This is Colonel Sigmund Emerich, of the Passenni Guard."

Thom noticed that Emerich did not object to being introduced second, despite technically holding ranks. It would seem an officer from the capital held higher authority than an officer of one of the Empire's provincial armies.

"Milo Thomwood," he responded with a courteous bow. "I am pleased to be of service."

Marek skipped right past any of formalities. "Tell us everything about Reis Beldaken."

"As you say," Thom responded in a friendly tone. "Reis is an old business associate of mine, and came looking to procure some supplies for a trip across the Izer. He had one of the Mankuri with him, the mountain men who live in this area, so I assume he came over the mountains. He spent a night with me and headed into the Izer the next morning. They're taking a path through the Izer that should take them five days, all things considered. Four days, now."

"How many in his party?" the gruff voice of Emerich asked.

Thom smiled at the provincial officer. He wondered what stroke of poor fate had brought him this far north of his homeland. "Five, including himself and the Mankuri. The others were a woman, a soldier of the Church, and a sellsword. A strange group, but not one to be underestimated if their boasts are even half-true."

Marek eyed the edge of the forest suspiciously. "The path they're taking, you can lead us through it?"

"I can do you one better. I know quicker ways through the forest. With my guidance, we can catch them in no time."

Marek eyed Thom suspiciously. "Is this the point where you tell us what kind of price you will charge for such a service?"

Thom did not let his smile wither. "My good captain, guiding one through the Izer is a rough, dangerous task. Normally for such a thing I would ask for quite the hefty coinpurse. However, I would not think to charge the Empire for my service. I wish nothing more than to show myself as a true friend." Thomwood smiled slyly, glancing at Emerich. "It is my understanding that the Empire takes good care of its friends."

The colonel frowned; the implication not lost on him. The provinces were often called "The Friends of the Empire," meant as a honor by some and an insult by others. They received favor and special treatment that conquered territories didn't have.

"That we do," Marek said with a nod of appreciation. "I assure you that your assistance here today will not go unnoticed."

"Then prepare your men for a tough hike. The Izer is no place for the green and untested. It is likely that if your men miss a single step we will reach Beldaken with less than we set out with. If you feel any of them are not in peak condition, or if any one of them has even a trace of cowardice in his heart, I suggest you leave them here."

Marek turned and examined the force gathered before them, all dressed in the Passenni colors. Marek stood out in his gray and black Serpentine Empire uniform.

"What do you say, Colonel?" Marek asked. "Any cowards among your men?"

Emerich glowered at Marek, his nostrils flaring like a bull ready to charge. Even in his advanced age, Emerich was a physically imposing figure. He towered over both Thom and Marek by at least a foot, with features that might have been chiseled from stone. His face with lined like the crags of a mountain, with his white hair and mustache acting as snow on the peaks.

"Don't mistake the men of Passenni for your Empire whelps," Emerich irritably said. "My men are all seasoned and professional, and there's not a coward among all our people. However, if you are not so convinced, we may take our leave, resume our tour of the Empire holdings, and you can wait until the little boys who make up what you call an army can respond to your summons."

"There's no reason to be so wounded," Marek said passively. "I take you at your word."

It was clear that Emerich did not care for captain, and it seemed the feeling was mutual. Thom found their enmity to be amusing. He wondered if everyone from the provinces was like this, or if Emerich was just an old dog who could not accept the new world order.

In the early days of Serpentine's uprising, when the Empire had proved the might of its military in many battles but had not yet removed many kings from their thrones, the emperor had offered a deal: any kingdom or nation that swore its loyalty to him and put its forces in the Empire's service would be spared the devastation war brings. They would also be granted a small amount of autonomy and would be allowed to keep their customs intact. Five kingdoms accepted Serpentine's deal, Passenni among them. These became the Empire's provinces, territory of the Empire that were not directly under its military command.

The coastal nation of Passenni was a frequent stop for Thom during his trade runs. The traders there did business with the islanders to the south, who were big fans of the exotic items Thom collected. He always made a good profit there, so he had been concerned when the Empire was knocking on Passenni's door. The Passenni Guard had this ridiculous motto, "Honor before Duty, Duty before Justice, Justice before all else." They plastered their motto all over the damn place, hell, it was even inscribed on their damn shields. Thom had been worried their 'honor' would cause them to fight an unwinnable war with the Empire. Passenni lands were just to the south of one of the largest Empire strongholds. They were nestled up against the sea to the south and west, and the lands just east of them had already been securely in the Empire's hands. If they had put up a fight, it would have been very one-sided.

Fortunately, the king had seen reason and accepted Serpentine's deal, although Thom had heard that it had been under great protest from the Passenni Guard. Passenni became part of the Empire without a fight, and Thom's trade there was unaffected. For their part, the Empire seemed to mostly keep its word, at least as far as Thom could tell. Their laws and traditions seemed intact, and their military had been allowed to keep their colors and armor.

It was just another example of why you did not go against the Empire. Thom considered himself a bright man, and he knew that this was just the new way of things. Old men like Emerich might have trouble accepting it, but there was no fighting it. The best thing was to try to get on good terms with the people who mattered, and that was exactly what Thom intended to do.

"Get your men ready at once," Marek ordered. "Mr. Thomwood, if you would be so kind as to describe the path we shall be taking."

"Of course." He bowed courteously. "And please, call me Thom."

Thom led Captain Marek, Colonel Emerich, and twenty-five members of the Passenni Guard into the Izer. To their credit, they were quick and able to follow precise instructions. Thomwood had thought they would lose at least a few of them to the dangers of the forest. Instead they followed close, stepped carefully, stopped when they were told and stayed low when instructed. Emerich had not been lying when he had proclaimed that these were not mere whelps. The darkness and fearsome noises of the Izer were enough to cause most men to lose their courage, and fear causes men to make mistakes. If any of the Passenni felt fear, they didn't show it.

They made their way by torch and lantern light through the thick forest, through a small tunnel that ran under the forest for a few miles, and then over a well traveled path where the overgrowth had recently been cut in front of them. Thom frequently used this path and took care to make sure it was easy to traverse. Being able to get deep into the forest and back out again quickly could mean the difference between life and death.

Taking Thom's route, they reached the river in short time. Thom discovered the pass the river at a ford that was being guarded by some of the creatures of the forest. Sure enough, they were set upon by the small, almost-human natives as they came to the ford.

Emerich barked a few quick orders and his men formed two neat lines, one behind the other. The Passenni were quick with their weapons, raining crossbow bolts down on the tiny savages before drawing their steel. The primitive arrows of the natives could not pierce their shields and their weapons shattered when they clashed with the steel swords of the guardsmen. The confrontation lasted less than a minute before the natives broke into a retreat, leaving behind a pile of their dead. The Guard lost nothing but a handful of crossbow bolts.

After crossing the river at the ford, Thom stopped them and had them double the number of torches that were lit. He warned them that a large beast was stalking the forest ahead. It was afraid of light and would not strike if they remained well lit. They stayed close together and kept themselves in the light of the lanterns and torches. There was some movement in the foliage but nothing came at them. After clearing some distance into the forest Thom told them the threat had passed.

When they came to a path that cut through the forest, splitting the trees and overgrowth to either side, Thom stopped them again. He knelt down and examined the impressions left in the soft grass.

"Looks like they've come onto this path. Perhaps this morning, if not a bit later. If you hurry, you should be able to catch to catch them before they reach its end. It goes on for quite a few miles."

"Then we should make haste," Marek commanded.

"You'll forgive me, my good captain, but I am no soldier. I hunt animals, not men, and I fear I would be most useless in a confrontation with Beldaken and his companions. But the path is clear enough for you to follow without my aid. I will wait here to guide you back after you have apprehended your fugitive."

Marek glared at him. Thom could tell he did not like having one of his orders refused. As much as Thom wanted to be on good terms with the Empire, he did not want to have face Reis in an open confrontation.

"Very well," Marek conceded. "We shall return soon."

Thom gave him and courteous bow and wished them good fortune. Marek did not seem to notice.

"I want Beldaken alive, if possible," Marek was already telling Emerich. "I have no use for his companions; they are all to be killed. I do not want any of them getting away from here. They are all enemies of the Empire. Understand?"

Emerich nodded. He ordered his men into formation and led them into the path, Marek following at the tail end. As Thom watched them go, he thought with some amusement how Reis would react to being so suddenly overwhelmed.

"Wonder who will survive," he chuckled.

It must be well past nightfall by now, Reis thought for the sixth time in the last hour. His legs were burning, his feet were on fire, and his eyes were stinging. It was impossible to tell time in this damned forest, but based on how tired he was it had to be late night. Perhaps even the next morning. Had they been walking all night?

He snapped awake when the kettibird returned, squawking and flapping its rainbow wings in a flurry. They were all compelled to watch the bird as it flew around them in a panic.

"Something has gotten it upset," Kester said.

"The kettibird is sensitive to the calm that precedes a battle," Pash said. "Something may be out there, hunting."

Reis hadn't noticed it before, but there *was* something unusually calm about the forest around them. Besides the squawking of the kettibird there were no other noises. Even the wind seemed to have stopped.

Pash noticed it, too. "There is definitely a battle to be had soon. Be on your guard, and be ready to watch how a warrior of the Mankuri fights."

Chapter 22

Marek followed Emerich and his men for many miles before he noticed that the path ahead was becoming better lit. The path had had a small amount of natural light from the break in the canopy overhead, but here the light was becoming brighter. It was coming from some source up ahead. Whatever it was was certainly brighter than any lantern, or firepit for that matter. What was that?

Emerich's men stopped. Ahead of them was a single man, clad in an old breastplate, standing in the path with his sword and shield drawn. The shield bore the mark of the Church of True Light. Around his neck was the source of the illumination, some kind of bottle that gave off light like the day. It was like nothing Marek had ever seen before.

Beldaken was traveling with a member of the Church, so this was likely this was his companion. But if so, where was Beldaken and all the rest of his comrades?

As if to answer his question, the trees around them trembled and shook. A massive, savage man came bursting out the foliage with a warhammer raised and a terrible cry upon his lips.

Reis heard the approaching of the Empire troops long before they came into sight. There was no mistaking the loud clanging their armor made, a metallic jangle that was completely out of place among the natural sounds of the forest.

"Of all the things to have to worry about here in the Izer."

This was no bold stroke of luck on the part of the Empire. The only way they could have found him here is if they had been pointed this way. Thomwood had sold him out. The idea filled Reis with rage. He had never liked Thomwood, but thought that even he would not stoop so low as to be a dog for the Empire. He mentally added Thomwood to the list of people he needed to kill before this was all over.

"Sounds like there's quite a number of them," Kester said. "We won't stand much of a chance against them all in open combat." His eyes drifted to the thick overgrowth and foliage that surrounded the path. "We can lose them in the deep forest."

Reis spat on the ground. "Unless they've got a half-decent tracker with them. Like Thomwood. We don't have the time to cover our tracks, and even if we did Thomwood would still be able to follow us. Better to take them on our terms than let them surprise us later. Besides, I'd like to make an example of these idiots. Let the Empire know that no matter how many they send against me, all they will get back is bodies."

Pash let out a loud, bellowing laugh. "At last, we agree. A warrior of the Mankuri does not flee from a battle. We will take them all, no matter how many of them there are!"

Avis gave Kester a troubled glance. "I don't suppose there is any reasoning with these two?"

Kester shook his head. "Doesn't seem that way. But if we're going to confront them, let's do it tactically."

They took positions hidden alongside the path. Kindra laid flat on her stomach in an overgrowth of tall weeds where she would be able to see the path well enough to observe the battle without getting caught up in it. Avis covered herself in dead leaves not far down the path. Pash hid his massive frame behind the trunk of a particularly wide tree. As for Reis, he took to a tree, climbing to a low branch where he would have a bird's eye view of the battle. He had his crossbow loaded and pointed at the path. Only Kester remained out in the open, Reis's glowing vial making him a shining beacon in the middle of the dark forest.

The imperials arrived in short order. Reis counted about two dozen of them, or thereabouts. Only one of them was in an imperial uniform, an officer of some importance. The rest wore the colors of Passenni, an Empire province.

The Passenni Guard? What poor luck. This would not be as easy a battle as he might have hoped. It would be up to the element of surprise to even the playing field.

They arrived to find Kester standing alone with his shield and sword drawn. They stood in the path for a moment, as if they were trying to decide how to react. Before they had a chance, Pash exploded out onto the path, shouting a battle-cry and raising his warhammer high in the air. He smashed into the closest guardsman with his hammer. Even from his position atop the tree, Reis could see the guardsman's head burst into bits.

The Passenni responded quickly by trying to surround the

barbarian. He swung his hammer in a wide sweep in front of him. His hammer clashed against the armor of one of the men closest and sent him reeling backwards. The others stayed just out of reach and carefully watched the hammer's movements.

With all their attention diverted by the screaming, hulking brute, they had taken their sights off of Kester. He charged into the fray shield-first. He knocked the first man he ran into to the ground and trampled over him. One of the guardsmen met Kester's shield with his own. Kester managed to hold his ground. He stabbed under the shields, catching the guardsman in a vulnerable point in the midriff.

Avis popped out from her hiding spot among the leaves and took the Passenni from behind. She grabbed the closest one by the arm and stabbed him through the weak point in the armor at the shoulder. The man struggled as the blade pierced him. Avis tore her blade free and shoved the guardsman to the ground.

The advantage of surprise wore off quickly. Reis studied the battlefield and saw how dire the situation had become. These weren't the slow, amateur blades of the Empire that they were accustomed to fighting. These soldiers were quick and their sword-arms were well trained. They fought without hesitation or fear as only soldiers of experience can. Only the chaos of the sudden battle kept them from properly surrounding the group.

Reis picked his targets carefully, watching for one of the soldiers to gain the advantage, move into position to flank, or try for a decisive strike. He picked off one that almost stabbed Avis in the back, a crossbow bolt finding the soldier's neck. As soon as he finished reloading the crossbow he saw Kester struggling with two of the guardsmen coming at him at once. He picked off one and let Kester deal with the other.

Pash had a few close calls. The blades of his enemies came within inches of him. He backed himself against a broad tree to avoid being surrounded and used his superior reach to keep his enemies at bay. With his massive height and the length of of his warhammer's handle, he had twice the reach of the soldiers with their swords. They kept their distance and dodged back out of range whenever he swung his weapon. One daring guard ducked under one of his blows and charged forward with his sword out for the thrust. Pash swung his hammer back around in a crescent arc and caught the guardsman right under the chin. The guardsman's face became a splintcred distortion of what it once was, his body being lifted slightly off the ground and back into his comrades.

Avis was dancing back and forth to dodge many strikes. Every once in the while she brought her sword up to parry a slash or thrust, but mostly kept it low and to her side. Reis appreciated Avis's fighting style. Only necessary movements, conserving energy as opponents exhaust themselves, and then only striking when they show a moment of vulnerability. Those opportunities were few and far between against the polished swordsmanship of the Passenni, but polished or not, their movements were slowed by their armor while Avis was as quick as a panther on her feet, allowing her to sidestep their blows with relative ease.

For a moment it seemed she might get surrounded. Reis steadied his crossbow to support her. Avis whirled around and sprinted into the high foliage. A group of the guardsmen chased after her. Reis lost sight of them.

Reis turned his attention back to the path, scanning the battlefield. The imperial officer was not giving him an opening, keeping low and behind cover. He instead fired a shot at a guardsman near him. The bolt crashed into his shield. The officer turned his attention towards Reis's tree.

Shit. They would be coming for him.

He leaned back into the darkness.

The Passenni had gotten organized enough to form a crossbow line. Kester raised his shield to deflect a barrage of crossbow bolts that came at him. It would take them about ten seconds to reload. He positioned himself in front of group of swordsmen so that they would be placed between him and the crossbowmen. They hopefully would not take a shot with their own in the line of fire. He raised his shield and prepared to charge again but found that he had been beaten to it.

An older soldier bared down on him with great ferocity. His armor was lined with gold around the edges, perhaps the symbol of officer status. Kester was not familiar with Passenni rank. He was wrinkled and grayed, but he moved with remarkable speed.

The officer came at him with a greatsword firmly gripped in both hands. Kester raised his shield to deflect the oncoming blow. The greatsword impacted against his shield with such ferocity that Kester almost lost his grip. There was a spray of sparks as the sword cut deep into shield's face, leaving a deep gash. Kester responded with a slash of his own sword, which the old man easily parried. The two fought back and forth, the greatsword cutting deep into Kester's shield, Kester's sword grinding against the old man's blade, neither of them able to get the advantage. The old soldier left several more gashes in the shield, and Kester began to worry that it might break under this assault. One of Kester's attacks came close to the soldier's face and trimmed off a side of his mustache.

One of the other guardsmen got in close to Kester's side. Kester had to keep his shield between him and the old soldier. As he moved in close, Kester braced himself for the impact of his blade and tried to position himself so the attack would hit the breastplate. The guardsman stopped suddenly in his tracks and then fell. He had a crossbow bolt in the back of his head. *Nice shot, Reis.*

The old soldier's attention was diverted for just a moment as he looked to the source of the bolt. Kester jumped on the opportunity. He pressed against his shield and slammed himself forward with all his weight. There was a loud crash as he caught the old man with his shield. He let out a gasp of breath and a pained grunt. He stumbled backwards a few steps but, to Kester's surprise, kept on his feet.

"Never wanted to have to fight a man of the Church," the old man coughed out. "This is not justice." He shook his head. "Duty before Justice." He raised his sword.

Reis tried to pick off another of the guard but missed. The battle was getting hectic, a chaos of men and blades as they tried to surround Kester and Pash but not quite being able to. It made it tough to get a clear shots. A number of the guard had disappeared off the path to follow Avis. Reis had to trust that Avis knew what she was doing out there. At least it reduced the number of enemies.

Two of the soldiers were gathering close to him now. They had figured out what tree the crossbow bolts were being fired from. It was time for Reis to make his move.

He revealed himself for everyone to see and taunted the guard below by waving his crossbow in the air above his head like a trophy. "Hey idiots! Who are you fighting down there? I thought I was the one you were looking for!"

The crossbow line fired at him but Reis had already leaped from the branch. There was a loud snap as Reis crushed bramble with his landing. He picked himself up and ran.

"What are you gawking at!" the officer yelled. "That was Beldaken! Don't let him get away!"

Half a dozen of the soldiers broke off and followed Reis into the forest. Reis smirked as he watched the soldiers come after him, just as he planned. He hoped he had drawn enough of them away to give the others a chance.

He sprinted at full speed, putting some distance between himself and his pursuers though he stumbled and tripped several times over the roots and low shrubs in his path. He made sure his trail was easy to follow. He did not want his pursuers to give up and return to the battle against the others. When he could no longer see the soldiers behind him, he dived into some tall grass. He breathed in deeply to regain his composure and began to concentrate. It was dark here, the only light coming from the path back in the distance. It was only a faint trickle here, barely enough for him to see a hand in front of his face. He concentrated on the darkness and tried to separate his own shadows from the overwhelming night.

A source of light appeared not to far from him. His pursuers had a torch. He tried not to look at it. His eyes were already adjusted to the darkness and he needed that edge. He extended his shadows till they reached his enemies. In this darkness there was no way they would notice. When he was ready, he had his shadow creep up on the one carrying the torch. He had the darkness engulf the torch and removed their source of light. The soldiers weren't sure what had happened. The one holding the torch passed his hand over it and quickly retracted it when his hand was burned. It was still burning, just not putting off any light.

Reis quietly followed the path of his shadows that led him right to the group of guardsmen. They couldn't even see him coming. He cut down one and then another. Their cries alerted the others. They desperately searched darkness to try and find their attacker, but to no avail. Reis was far more used to fighting in the dark then they were. He hunted them by sound and scent like a beast. Not one of the soldiers ever caught sight of him. He was impressed that they never ran; even the last standing soldier stood his ground without fear before Reis cut him down.

He allowed himself a moment to catch his breath. The strain of using his ability was affecting him now. He tried to shake it off. The fight might not yet be over. He sprinted back towards the light of the path.

Kindra was watching the battle with some fascination. It was terrifying, all the shouting and clashing of steel and the smell of blood, but it was also terribly exciting. It was like a battle out of the old tales, a few valiant defenders facing off against the forces of evil. Pash was a force to be reckoned with. She lost count of how many of the imperials met their end at his hammer. Avis and Reis had both disappeared, with the strangely uniformed imperials following after them.

Kester was trying to put some distance between himself and their enemies. For a while he had been engaged in a fierce battle with an older soldier with a greatsword, until a quick strike with his sword caught the old man in the shoulder and drew blood. Before Kester had been able to make the finishing blow he was set upon by more of the imperials. Their numbers were thinning and Kester was able to prevent himself from being surrounded.

One of the imperials took a long way around, through the overgrowth that surrounded the path. Out of some foul luck he went straight through the weeds that Kindra was concealed in. Kindra had been so fascinated on the battle in front of her she had not noticed him until it was too late. He almost tripped over her. When he noticed it was a person hiding in the grass he gave her a hard kick to knock her into the path.

Pain shot through Kindra's upper body and she couldn't resist when her body started to roll out into the open. She was coughing and hacking when he looked up to see where she was. She looked up right into the harsh face of the old, mustached soldier.

He was clutching his wound with one hand, his sword with the other. His mustache twitched when Kindra rolled out in front of him. "Who in the hells are you?"

Kindra looked around for something to defend herself with. Her eyes fell on the remains of an imperial's sword that had splintered into small, sharp shards. "I'm just a woman. And I'm unarmed. Who are you?"

He looked her over curiously. "Colonel Emerich. Passenni Gaurd." His mustache twitched again as his brow furrowed in thought.

"You stay put. You're going to be taken prisoner when we have finished with the rest of them."

"No." The officer, the only one in an imperial uniform, commanded with a soft voice. "Beldaken is the only one we will take prisoner. His companions all die here. She is with him, she dies."

Kindra focused on the sword shards near her. The familiar pressure behind her eyes began to build. She lifted them slightly off the ground, hoping the colonel didn't notice. If he attacked her, her ability would her only line of defense.

"Captain Marek, with all due respect, she's an unarmed woman," Emerich replied. "She's defenseless. There's no honor in killing the helpless."

"I'm not asking you about your damn honor. I'm giving you an order. Now kill her."

Emerich growled, but raised his greatsword above her, prepared to plunge it down into her heart. Kindra tried to focus on the sword shards. Her breath was heavy and her heart was pounding. Her concentration slipped. She couldn't get the sword shards to move. She looked up helplessly at Emerich, prepared to die.

He lowered his sword. "Honor before Duty. It's the first part of our oath. I can't do it."

Kindra's eyes met with his and she knew what kind of man was behind this harsh face: a man of honor and stern conviction. The next moment his face convulsed and blood spilled out of his mouth. A blade had pierced Emerich in the lower back and out his front. He spat out blood then fall hard to the ground, like a tree that had just been cut down. Captain Marek stood over him, his sword dripping with fresh blood.

"Anyone who disobeys an order is a traitor, and the punishment for treason is death."

He looked at Kindra on the ground, then around to Pash and Kester who were still in combat with the few remaining Passenni. "At this rate, I'm going to have to kill all of you myself," he said exasperatedly. He turned back to Kindra and raised his sword.

Kindra found herself filled with a fury that aided in her focus. The sword shards shot at Marek like tiny arrows. One shard caught him in the face, right below his left eye. Another lodged itself into his neck. The other shards scratched him across his body and arms.

Marek let out a stream of loud curses and grabbed his face.

Kindra tried to use the opportunity to pick herself up and run away but Marek grabbed her and tossed her back to the ground. He put a foot on her chest to keep her from moving. He ripped the sword shard from his face and tossed it to the ground bitterly.

"The bitch isn't as defenseless as she seems, huh? Had that pierced my neck just a few inches over I might be dead right now." He kicked her hard in the chest. She let out an anguished cry that made him smile. He raised his sword once more to make the finishing strike.

A shield collided with him and knocked him away from her at the last moment. Kindra let out a loud shout of surprise and relief. She struggled back to her feet and threw herself off the path. Once she was out of sight she collapsed to the ground and started sobbing.

Those old tales never told of how terrifying facing certain death truly was.

Kester was on the imperial rapidly, attacking him with a flurry of sword blows. Marek caught his footing and parried the the strikes. He sidestepped and backed a few steps away from Kester.

"Those damn Passenni," he growled. "Can't they kill a single one of you?"

Kester raised his shield in front of him and prepared to attack again. Marek attacked first, striking at his shield. Before Kester could respond, Marek skirted aside and struck at the shield again before darting away. He was so quick and his attacks came so fast that it was all Kester could do to keep his shield between them.

Marek sidestepped Kester again, putting himself at Kester's side. He struck at Kester's shield-arm and pierced the skin, leaving a cut dripping with blood and forcing Kester to let go of his shield. Marek grabbed it with his free hand and tore it from its straps. It clattered to the ground.

Kester clutched his sword with both hands and tried to attack back, but Marek easily deflected it. Without the shield to get in his way, Marek unleashed a merciless assault of slashes and thrusts. Kester did everything he could to dodge and parry the attacks, but Marek was far faster than he was. The first of Marek's attacks to land failed to pierce Kester's breastplate and only caused a fresh scratch in the rusted metal. The next thrust cut into his shoulder. It pierced deeply, possibly to the bone. Blood flowed freely from the wound. The arm went limp and

Kester was forced to hold his sword with only one hand.

The next attack cut him at the side of his waist. It was a painful wound that caused Kester to lose his balance and drop to the ground. He managed to roll out of the way of Marek's next thrust and bring himself back to his feet. He held his sword at ready, determined to fight till the end but losing strength fast. His wounds were bleeding badly and the pain was making him dizzy. If it wasn't for the adrenaline pumping through him, he would have just fallen where he stood.

Kester raised his sword for one last desperate assault.

Reis came back to the path just in time to see Kester struggling for his life. He gripped his sword and debated whether or not he should help him. Pash was still locked in combat with four or five of the Passenni and could also use his help, and who knows if Avis had gotten into trouble. Reis couldn't help but remember that in his dream, Kester had been the one to kill him. He could let Kester die here and no one could blame him for it, and it would save him the hassle of having to fight him later.

He still needed Kester, though. He shook his head and rushed in to attack the imperial officer. The officer barely turned in time to deflect the first attack. He pushed forward, moving them away from the injured church-boy. Their blades collided with a series of rapid strikes. The imperial stepped quickly out of Reis' reach, bringing a brief halt to their battle.

"Reis Beldaken. I am glad I got this opportunity to talk to you in person. I am Captain Konrad Marek, loyal officer in service of the great Marcus Serpentine. I have been ordered to bring you in, alive if possible. Drop your weapon and surrender yourself to the custody of the Empire."

Reis bore his teeth. "That's some sense of humor you have there, Empire-dog. Did Serpentine teach you that one while you were kissing his great ass?"

"Your disrespect for the Empire is almost as disgusting as the crimes you have committed against it."

"Don't speak too soon. You have only begun to see the extent of my crimes against the Empire. I think for my next crime I'll cut down an obnoxious imperial Captain."

Kester had dropped to his knees as he struggled with his

wounds. Somewhere down the path Pash was facing off with what remained of the Passenni forces. Avis was nowhere to be seen. Reis could not expect any help from any of them.

Reis leaped at Marek and the two clashed blades. Their exchange was violent and fast. Reis went for vital strikes, trying to use the extra reach of his blade to get a thrust past Marek's sword and pierce him in the gut. Marek stepped close to Reis as he parried the attacks, keeping the distance between them small to remove the advantage of Reis's longer sword. At points, they were so close that there was barely enough room to swing their swords.

Marek was very patient. He waited for opportunities to present themselves while sidestepping and parrying Reis's blows. His attacks didn't need to hit anything vital as long they drew blood. One slash cut Reis across the side of his face, just barely missing his eye. Another stabbed Reis's hand under the guard of his sword's hilt. Reis cursed as blood streamed out of his hand and down his hilt, but refused to release his grip.

Reis put all his strength behind a wild, overhand swing. Marek blocked the attack with his own sword and was forced to brace himself to absorb the impact of the blow. His feet dug into the ground to keep from getting knocked off balance. He was unable to get out of the way of Reis's knee as it impacted against his gut. He lost his breath and almost doubled over, but managed to get his sword up in time to deflect Reis's next strike. Reis lashed out with his free hand and hit Marek across the face. Marek tumbled a few feet away from Reis, clutching his face with one hand and his sword with the other.

Marek's mouth filled with blood. He spat and a piece of one of his teeth came out with it. He glared at Reis with utter contempt. His previously calm demeanor gave way to one of unbridled fury.

Reis was not about to give Marek a moment to recover. He came at him again with another flurry of rapid strikes. Marek deflected blow after blow while carefully maneuvering himself to Reis's side. From this position he was again able to get under Reis's guard, this time stabbing into the soft flesh just above the wrist. Reis involuntarily released his sword and it clattered to the ground between them.

Marek thrust his blade forward for the finishing strike, but Reis managed to leap out of the way. He rolled across the ground and bounded back to his feet with a knife drawn. He was able to use the knife to deflect Marek's next strike and tried to get in close to stab him with it. Marek was too quick, and grabbed Reis's arm as he moved in for the strike. Reis struggled to free himself from Marek's grasp. He grabbed Marek's sword-arm to keep him from being able to strike. They locked in struggle for a few seconds. Marek thrust an elbow into Reis's throat. He put his weight against it and knocked Reis to the ground with himself on top of him.

Reis lost his knife when he hit the ground. It glided across the ground and landed just out of his reach. He struggled to push Marek off of him but he was already putting all of his weight onto his midsection. Marek dug one of his knees into Reis's stomach and held Reis at the throat with his free hand. Reis's legs flailed as he tried to find some purchase in the soft grass to kick himself free but he didn't have any success.

Reis struggled and cursed as Marek brought the sword to his throat.

Chapter 23

Reis reached up to stop the blade. He grabbed the hilt with one hand and the blade with another. The blade cut deep into the palm of his hand as Marek tried to bring the sword down to his throat. Blood dripped down the blade and onto Reis's face. Reis cursed and spit and struggled, but couldn't break Marek's hold on him. Marek's eyes were glazed over in fury. Any notion of taking Reis back alive was tossed aside and replaced by his rage.

He looked around desperately for something to help him. A rock, a branch, a dropped weapon, anything at all he could use to fend Marek off with, but he found nothing. Somewhere down the path he heard Pash yelling amid the sounds of his hammer meeting armor. Even if he saw what was happening, he probably wouldn't be able to help until after the captain had slit his throat.

His eyes darted around desperately for anything he could get his hands on. The blade was hovering mere inches above his throat. That's when he smelled a familiar and sweet scent.

Yiver's Flower. It was the same flower he had previously tried to pick before Pash had lectured him on its danger. He glanced towards the source of the scent and spotted the flower. He only hoped that Pash had not been exaggerating.

He released his grip from the sword's blade and reached for the flowers. His fingers were just barely able to reach. He tore the flower from the ground and was immediately greeted by a potent sour smell.

A confused Marek watched as Reis stuck the flower into the breast of his uniform. The conflicting sour and sweet smells of the flower caused him to scrunch up his face. It must have seemed a strange act for a dying man. The blade was at Reis's throat now, the first trickle of blood forming at the point it made contact, Reis straining against the hilt to keep it away. A few more seconds and he would be dead.

A terrifying roar preceded the massive beast barreling onto the path. It had a body like a brown bear and was just as large. Its head lacked any eyes, instead having a long snout with oversized nostrils. The nostrils were hard at work as the yiver followed the scent that told it that the flower had been plucked. Marek had just enough time to raise his head before the beast was upon him.

A powerful claw knocked Marek away from Reis and opened

his arm like a finely sharpened sword. Marek raised his blade and lashed out at the beast. His sword was barely able to pierce its thick hide. Marek's sword left a small gash on the yiver's arm. The beast picked itself up on its hind legs. It let out a powerful roar. Marek's face went white.

Its fangs came forward and its claws were outstretched as it collided with Marek. Marek screamed and struggled, but was useless against its weight and strength. He slashed his sword widely at it, but for each small gash he left the yiver he received a far deeper and bloodier wound. His uniform became soaked through with his own blood. He made a desperate thrust into the center of the beast. The beast grabbed him with its claws and the two struggled, sword in the beast's stomach and the beast's claws deep in the man's shoulders. During the horrible and bloody struggle, the beast pushed forward and the two went tumbling off the path and disappeared into the overgrowth. The sounds of screaming and roaring went off into the distance as Marek ran and the beast pursued him.

Reis was picking himself up off the ground when a powerful hand reached down to assist him. It was Pash. When Reis was on his feet he took stock of the scene around him. All that remained of the enemy was bodies. That and Marek's quickly fading shouts.

Unfortunately, the victory had not come without cost. Kester was on the ground now, barely conscious. Kindra was over him and doing whatever she could to staunch the bleeding of his wounds. Pash had several cuts across his arms and chest. They didn't look deep, but each cut carried the threat of serious infection out here. Reis's hands were both cut up, one stabbed in the back and near the wrist and the other cut deep along the palm where he had grabbed Marek's blade.

The only one of them who seemed to come out of this completely unmolested was Avis. She returned to the path just as the beast and Marek disappeared from it. Her brow was soaked with sweat and her blade dripped blood, but other than that, she looked unharmed.

"Well, looks like we won," Avis panted. "I just hope it was worth it to teach a lesson to the Empire. From experience, I'd say dead men don't carry lessons well."

"The loss of this many men won't go unnoticed in the Empire," Reis assured him. "When that captain doesn't report back they'll know what fate befell him."

Avis glanced over the field of bodies. "In this forest, there are plenty of sour fates. But no point in debating this now. We should be gone from this place in case there are more on their way."

"We can't move him!" Kindra insisted. She did not taking her eyes off Kester. "He is hurt badly. If we can't treat these wounds soon, I don't know..." Her voice trailed off.

"We all have wounds that need treating," Reis said. "Pash, is there anywhere close we can to recover that would be safe from eyes on the path?"

Pash nodded. "Follow me."

Avis and Reis helped Kester to his feet and they helped him walk. Pash took them off the path and into the deep growth. Reis removed the glowing vial from around Kester's neck and put it into his pack so that they would not be so easily followed. After a short walk they came to a small pond of still but clear water. Pash pulled aside some brambles and revealed a concealed cave. It was dark and warm inside, and comfortably dry. They entered inside and Pash moved the brambles into place after them. He then started a fire so they could properly see.

Reis and Pash's wounds were not hard to treat. Thomwood had supplied them with some medicine for disinfecting wounds, and the cuts were easily enough bandaged. Kester's wounds provided a more serious problem. Avis helped Kindra remove Kester's breastplate and they got a look at just how much blood he had lost. The inside of the breastplate was painted red with his blood, and his clothes were soaked through. They stripped his clothes off him and Avis took the clothes and armor to the pond to soak.

The wound in Kester's shoulder was deep but had already begun to clot, which was a good sign. They treated and bandaged it with little problem. However, Reis feared there might be little they could do for the massive gash in his hip. When they cleaned the wound, they found that the sword had cut right to the bone. The chances of such a wound healing properly on its own were poor. They closed the wound the best they could and bandaged it. In short time the bandage was already soaked through with blood. All they could do was try to keep the wound clean, change the dressing frequently, and hope for the best. Reis gave him something for the pain and Kester drifted off to sleep.

Avis returned and set Kester's things next to the fire to dry. She sat down and leaned against the hard walls of the cave. She looked at Kester with worried eyes.

"Not good," Reis said bluntly. "He's sleeping now, but to be honest I'd be surprised if he ever woke up. Might be more merciful if he didn't."

"He died well," Pash said. "He fought like a Mankuri and died the death of a true warrior."

"He's not dead yet!" Kindra objected. "So don't speak of him like he is!"

"People have recovered from worse," Reis agreed. "But I wouldn't get my hopes up about it."

Pash scratched his beard. "Do not forget, we cannot linger long, even if he does not recover. We have to reach the emperor while it is still possible for us to strike."

Reis nodded. "Kester wouldn't want us to endanger the mission for his sake. He would rather die than be the cause of Serpentine slipping through our fingers."

Avis rummaged through her pack for something to eat. As she stuffed her face she examined the back of her hand. "Reis, what are the odds of you being able to whip up some more of that healing stuff you used on me?"

Reis shook his head. "Very slim. Though a lot of the ingredients grow around here, I would be missing a number of the key components. Also, my capability is limited without a proper alchemy lab. Out in the wild, I couldn't hope to come up with anything with real potency."

"But you could make something?" Kindra asked. "Maybe not something as potent as you are used to, but can you make something that could help with what's available?"

Reis shrugged. "Possibly. I can't say for sure. Depends on what kind of ingredients I am able to find."

Kindra looked at Reis in the eyes, pleading. "You have to at least try. Just a little medicine could mean the difference between life and death for Kester."

Reis sighed and rose. "I suppose I have little else to do while we wait to see what happens with Kester's condition. Pash, come with me, I need your expertise of the forest to help me locate the right components. Avis, you're responsible for keeping watch here while we're gone."

As he and Pash prepared to leave he stopped and turned back to Kindra. "I just want to remind you, don't get your hopes up."

Milo Thomwood crept up on the location of the battle. He whistled lightly as he admired Reis's handiwork. Despite being outnumbered 5-to-1, Reis and his companions had utterly devastated their enemy. The members of the Passenni Guard laid dead, their armors' blue and green speckled with red, while none of Reis's group were anywhere to be found. It seemed his instinct not to join them in battle had been the right one. He had always known Reis was a fierce fighter and had sized up his companions to be just as dangerous. Had he decided to follow the Captain into battle, he would likely have ended up just as dead as the Passenni at his feet. Still, it would have been nice if at least one of the soldiers had survived. Now how was he to get the credit he deserved for aiding them through the forest?

He scoured the bodies for anything of value. With any luck, this expedition wouldn't be completely for naught. A coinpurse, a well crafted weapon, any armor that wasn't too damaged: anything that looked like it was worth carrying back, he stripped from the bodies.

A sound coming from off the path caught his attention. It was a laggardly shuffle, pushing its way through the overgrowth and towards the path. He took hold of his bow and drew an arrow from his quiver. There was a good chance whatever it was making that noise was merely some scavenger drawn by the stench of fresh blood, but it always paid to be cautious in the Izer.

To his surprise it was Captain Marek who stumbled onto the path. It took Thom a moment to recognize him as his face was heavily obscured with blood. His uniform was shredded to pieces, and his body was covered in deep gashes that bled heavily. One arm dangled uselessly as his side and the other clutched his sword. He was unable to walk right and instead was forced to shuffle his legs across the ground in order to move. Thom tried to conceal the items he had been looting from the bodies.

"Captain! I didn't think there was anyone left alive. You're badly wounded, let me help you-"

"Beldaken!" the commander grunted, spitting up blood as he spoke. "Where is Beldaken!"

"There's no sign of them, captain. They must have gone off the path after the confrontation, and all the chaos makes it impossible for me to track them," Thom lied. When only a few people walk away from a battle, finding the path they took should not be difficult, assuming they all went in the same direction. But he was worried the captain might actually try to confront Beldaken in the condition he was in, in which case they would both be dead. "You really need to treat those wounds–"

"Where are they heading!" Marek demanded.

"Based on the path they are taking, I would guess their goal is Rochest. I can lead you myself, when you are well enough to travel, but you won't make it far the way you are now."

"Beldaken, you will not escape from the grasp of the Empire, I promise you this," Marek stammered out.

Thom approached Marek, already fumbling through his pack for first aid supplies. He was not sure how much good it would do. It was astonishing that Marek was standing at all, when by the looks of him he should already be well dead. Before Thom reached him, though, Marek became surrounded by a bright, pure white light. It engulfed him completely until all that remained was a silhouette of his body outlined in white. And then it was gone.

Thom was alone again with the bodies. He looked around but there was no sign of Marek. He had just vanished. It took Thom a few moments to realize he must have just witnessed the ability of a Willer. He had never seen one manifest itself with such force.

When he was convinced that Marek wasn't returning he resumed looting the bodies, smiling the whole time, knowing that Marek would put in a good word for him in his reports.

Chapter 24

Kester and his brother sat on the wall of the Grandium, looking down at the troops marching through the Great Gate on their way to battle with the Serpentine Empire. The armor of the Church gleamed in the early morning sun. Demos would be joining them soon, covering their rear with his own command. Kester would be staying here.

"They've already come as far as Bigasti," Kester said. "It won't be long before they set upon the Grandium."

"Not if they're stopped now," Demos said with absolute confidence. Kester wondered how his brother was always able to do that. No matter how bad things got, what the odds were against him, he never showed any signs of doubt or fear. Listening to him talk, you could honestly believe everything was going to turn out alright, despite all evidence to the contrary.

"Let me go with you!" Kester pleaded, for the fifth time that day. "I'm as skilled a fighter as any, I'd be useful at you side!"

"It's too dangerous," his brother responded, shaking his head. "Especially if you want to remain close to me. You know I go on the most dangerous missions, the ones no one else can do. I take with me only those people I know I can trust."

"And you can't trust me!" Kester yelled, hurt.

"As my brother, yes. As a devout of the Light, yes. But as a soldier, I'm afraid not." Demos turned and looked away from his brother. He had never been so blunt with his brother about his reasons, and it hurt him to say it just as much as it hurt Kester to hear. Kester had persisted and had left him with no option but the plain, hurtful truth.

"You've always been too soft for this job, Kester. I still remember when you were little — that girl half your age pushed you down and took your practice sword, and you came crying to me about it."

"I was a child! You can't judge me now because of it!"

"You were a child, but that was when I first noticed that you were softer than most. And as you grew it was something that stuck with you. You learned how to fight with the sword, you are capable with your shield, you carry your armor well. In training, there are few who can match you one-on-one. But there's more to combat than just skill. It requires you to have a hardness, the ability to put aside doubts and fears and emotions and focus on just the act of survival, on killing or being killed. Nothing else matters at that moment, not your charge, not right or wrong, not even the tenants of the Church. It all need to be lost in that moment."

"How do you know I am not capable of that when I have never been given the chance to prove myself?"

"Because I know you. You are sensitive and feel everything with a big heart. I saw it when the High Cleric died and you could barely hold your sword up in training for weeks. I see it whenever you give out your meals to those who are suffering hunger, despite needing those meals for energy when you train and fight. I see it right now, in the fear in your eyes. And I know that fear is not of the Empire, not of the battle, not even of death. You are afraid of being left alone. You are afraid of me leaving and not returning."

"Is any of that so bad!" Kester demanded, anger flaring. "Caring for your brother? Feeding the hungry? Are these not things that a man of the Church should do!"

"You uphold the tenets of the Church well. You always have. There, your sensitivity is a great asset, and knowing right from wrong comes to you as an instinct. Had you become a cleric, like I had always wanted, you would have excelled. But in the field things are not always so simple. What if we were in a battle, one where we were close to completing our mission, and I become set upon by more enemies than I can fight, but you have the opportunity to slip by and do what is needed to win the battle? Would you be able to leave me behind, your own dear brother, leave me to die to complete the mission? You would not. You would turn back to try and help me, and we would both die and the battle would be lost. This is why softness can not be had on the battlefield. The battlefield is not time for grieving and emotion and empathy, and you are not capable of separating yourself from them."

Kester wanted to object, tell him that he was wrong. But he couldn't. Demos knew him better than anyone else and he couldn't deny the things his brother had seen in him. Instead he just fell quiet, wearing his silence as a shield.

His brother clasped him on the shoulder and looked at him with a warm smile. "You have an important role to play yet. The Grandium needs people to protect it, good people. It is the center of our Church, and many will come here to seek solace and meaning when this war has ended, myself among them. I'm counting on you to make sure its still standing when I return."

"Demos!" a voice called out. Ottone, one of his brother's oldest and most trusted companions, called to him from below. "We're all set to go! Come on, Serpentine is not going to wait for us!"

The brothers exchanged one last farewell. They had said many already and the words seemed to have lost their meaning. Kester watched as his brother departed, not sure when he would return. There were many battles ahead and the Serpentine Empire would not relent easily.

In the distance, clouds began to form. They were dark and unnatural, forming fast and blocking out the light. The marching forces of the Church were covered in darkness, such black and total darkness that Kester could not see them anymore. Demos and his men marched straight forward, undeterred, right into the darkness. Kester tried to call out but it was in vain. His brother was gone.

Kester awoke to a world of heat and pain. He was sweating heavily and his side felt like it was being burned away. It took him a moment to come back to reality and recognize the cave. He remembered the battle and his injuries. He had been dreaming about the last time he had seen his brother. The words his brother spoke were fresh in his mind.

Demos had been right. He was soft. All it took was one look at him now to see that. His brother had left him to protect the Grandium, and now that was gone, burned to the ground. And Demos was dead — he would not be returning to see it.

And now he lay, badly wounded and most likely dying. His brother had seen it coming. In the middle of a battle, when he should have let all emotion go to the wayside, he had seen Kindra in danger and rushed to her aid without thought. Had he thought about it, fought without concern, he could have put himself in a better position before engaging the imperial captain in battle. But instead he rushed right at him and put himself at a disadvantage. He would already be dead if not for Reis.

"You're awake." Kindra hovered over him. "I was worried you might not."

The cave was mostly dark and empty, save for a small fire

burning nearby and Kindra next to him.

"Where is everyone?" His voice was dry and harsh.

"Reis and Pash are out looking for plants to make some medicine for you. Avis is outside standing watch in case we get more company from the Empire. Here, drink."

She helped Kester sit up against the wall of the cave and put a flask of water to his lips. The water was warm, but soothing on his throat.

"How long have I been out?"

"Hard to tell out here, with no sun, but I'd wager just over a day. Are you hungry?"

Kester shook his head. Kindra took a cloth and wiped sweat from his forehead. "You're burning up. Reis told me if you break into a fever you should chew some of these." She gave him a couple of small, blue leaves. "He says they help cool your body."

Kester took one of the leaves and began to chew. It had a pleasantly minty taste. He thought about how ironic it was that he owed his life to a man like Reis Beldaken. Reis Beldaken, who was known as a demon and an enemy to the Church. Reis Beldaken, who was cold, calculating, and pragmatic. Reis Beldaken, who had defeated his brother in combat.

He defeated my brother. For all of Demos's talk about separating yourself from your emotions if you wished to survive a battle, he had lost in combat with Reis, who fought with rage and fury. Reis was almost the opposite of his brother: cold and calm while at peace, but a torrent of emotion and anger when he fought. Perhaps his brother's philosophy was not the final say on combat.

But where did that leave him?

"I need to change your bandages again," Kindra said. As she removed the bandages from his side, Kester saw her try to hide the repulsion at the sight of his wound.

"Just how bad is it?" he asked.

"I've seen worse."

"In someone who survived?"

"No," Kindra admitted hesitatingly. "But I've never had someone like Reis helping me before. He is really capable of some amazing things with these plants."

Kester could smell it now: the smell of death. His wound was rotting. It would not be long before he was dead. He should be upset by it, but he was too tired and weak right now. All he could do now was try to make sure his death meant something.

"Kindra, I need you to do something for me," he said weakly.

Kindra did not look up until she had finished replacing his bandages. "What is it?"

"If I don't make it out of here-"

"There's no reason to suggest such a thing!" she interrupted. "You mustn't give up!"

He didn't want to argue the inevitability of his situation. "Just, in case. Please listen." Kindra set down beside him and listened with all earnestness. "What we are doing, going after Serpentine, it is very important. I feel Reis could really do it. But I fear for his level of dedication. If I'm to die, I want to die knowing that Reis will really go through with it."

"I'm sure Reis will-"

"But I'm not sure. But you, he's concerned about you. He's risked life and limb more than once on your account. Maybe its just because he's really intent on getting in your bed. Maybe there's something more to it, if he is truly capable of feeling something for someone other than himself. I don't know how you truly feel about him, but I think if you asked it of him, he could be convinced to carry out the mission."

Kindra looked at him silently for a while, contemplating his words. Kester felt terrible asking this of her, but he felt he must. "I know it is a terrible thing to ask. To use someone's feelings to manipulate them, even someone like Reis-"

"I don't know if I have as much control over Reis as you think. He definitely desires me, but I fear if he gets what he wants then he will lose interest, and if he doesn't get it he will eventually give up. And even if I do manage to keep his interest, I doubt I could truly control him. He's very impulsive."

"You can if you try. I know you can."

Kindra nodded, but she still looked uncertain. "I promise I will do what I can. If it comes to that."

Kester was satisfied with that and allowed himself to relax. He was so tired.

"I think I'm going to rest for a little longer. Wake me when Reis returns."

Kindra helped him back into a comfortable laying position and soon he drifted back to sleep.

A hideous snake with a yellow head and eyes like rubies hissed a warning at Reis from its position in the deep grass. Pash had warned him that the venom of this snake was enough to paralyze a full grown Mankuri in less than a minute, and kill shortly after. That was exactly what Reis had been hoping for. A small dose of a potent venom made a powerful ingredient in medical salves.

He cursed under his breath as he thought about the risks he was taking to save the life of a man he would one day have to kill. The snake watched him cautiously with its body coiled, ready to strike. Reis hovered over it. In one lightning quick motion, he grabbed for the snake before it had a chance to strike. He kept a powerful grip around its head to keep it from being able to bite. The snakes body coiled tightly around his arm. He brought a cup up to the snake's bared fangs and milked the snake's venom. He only got a few drops, but it would be plenty. When he was done, he uncoiled the snake from his arm and tossed it back into the forest.

"Do you have everything you need now?" Pash asked.

The giant had been leading him through the forest after all the ingredients he needed for Kester's salve. He was incredibly knowledgeable as to where the various plants grew, though they had a little difficulty translating Thornwood's names for the various plants and herbs of the forest. Reis had to describe what he was looking for in some detail before Pash understood. Pash was now carrying a pack filled with leaves, herbs, flowers, and other plants.

The snake venom had been the last thing Reis required. He nodded and they returned to the cave.

Outside the cave, Avis was reclining by the pond. She was clumsily trying her hand at whittling, using a few fallen branches and a dagger.

Reis frowned at her. "Aren't you supposed to be keeping watch?"

"I was bored. Nothing has come this way besides a few small critters who just wanted to drink at the pond. Quietest day I've had since we came into this forest. Hell, quietest day since I signed up with you." She held up the branch he was working on. All of the outer bark had been scraped off and it had begun to take on a rectangular shape.

"Does this look like anything to you?"

"Looks like you should stick to mercenary work."

Kindra rose to her feet when she saw them. She looked exhausted. She hadn't been sleeping since Kester's injury.

"He's getting worse," she said. "His fever's burning out of control."

Reis set down his pack. "Then I should get to work right away. You should get some sleep. There's nothing more you can do for him now."

She shook her head. "I'm fine. I should help."

"I've got Pash to aid me on making the medicine. I will need you later, and I will need you rested."

Pash gave Kindra a serious look. "Even the mightiest warrior still requires sleep."

Kindra looked down at Kester. Even asleep he seemed to be suffering. "Alright, but don't hesitate to wake me if I can be of any help at all."

Kindra laid down next to the fire as Reis and Pash went to work. Pash helped Reis with some of the more basic and repetitive tasks he had been taught. Reis lectured as they worked, teaching Pash about the properties of the plants they were working with and how they worked together when properly prepared. With the pond outside, they had no lack of water and kept some boiling at all times.

Reis took particular care in purifying the snake venom for their use. Prepared correctly, a small amount of venom could help instigate the body's natural healing process. Prepared incorrectly and he could accidentally shorten Kester's life.

They worked for about half a day before they finished the first salve. Reis woke Kindra and explained the procedure.

"We should wake Kester and explain it to him," Reis said. "Otherwise, he'd be in for one rude awakening."

Kindra gently woke Kester as Reis removed the bandages and prepared to apply his salve. The wound underneath stank of death. Even with his medicine it might not be enough.

"I don't have the solvents available to make an effective elixir, not one that could do anything for you, anyway," Reis explained to a half-conscious Kester. "So I made a salve to apply directly on the wound. It works by eating away all the dead tissue and destroying the infection. I'll apply a second salve when it is done that will increase your body's ability to heal the wound, assuming there is enough left to heal." He paused before applying the salve. "Most importantly, this is going to burn like hell, particularly with the condition of the wound. If you're truly as weak as you look right now, its possible the pain alone might be enough to finish you off. And even if you can bear it, its possible that you may be too little too late and you will die anyway."

"I understand," Kester said meekly. "Reis, do you still have that vial of light? If I am to face my end, I would prefer to do so basking in the Light."

Kindra pulled the vial from Reis's bag and placed it in Kester's hand. Kester's eyes glowed with the light's reflection. He smiled. "Such an amazing thing. The clerics of the Church make something similar, much larger and in ornamental glass. They hung them in the Great Hall during times of trouble so the Light could find us more readily. I always wondered how they were made." He was lost in memories for a moment, but the pain of his wound pulled him back out of it. "Go ahead and apply your medicine. I bask in the glory of the Light and fear neither pain nor death."

Reis applied the first salve. The next few hours were a cacophony of Kester's anguished yells. The salve burned deep into the wound and ate away at the dead and infected flesh. Reis had needed to use a similar salve on himself once before and knew that it was no pleasant experience. Your flesh felt like it was melting off your bones, like someone had dipped your body in lava. It felt as if at any moment your skin could suddenly catch on fire. There were few tortures more painful.

Kindra tended to him the best she could. Whenever he stopped yelling and seemed like he was about to die, her eyes welled up with tears. Pash made comments about using the strength of the warrior to overcome his pain, but if anything got through Kester made no sign. Avis came in periodically, updating them on the movements of the animals curiously drawn by Kester's shouts. She would look at Kester with a mix of pity and worry before rushing back out of the cave.

Only Reis's expression remained unchanged. He studied Kester with cold and untroubled eyes. Occasionally he checked the progress of the salve on the wound, but otherwise he remained silent.

Finally, Kester's pain subsided and he quieted. Reis checked the wound. He was pleasantly surprised to see how effective the salve had been. The dead tissue was gone and there was no more sign of infection. A lot of tissue was gone and it left the wound wide open, but hopefully he was on the path to recovery.

He soaked some bandages in the second salve. When they were soaked through, he used them to cover the wound. This salve also served as a mild painkiller and had a gentle, cooling effect. After what Kester had just been through, it would come as a tremendous relief.

"Hopefully, this will cause his wound to heal at an accelerated rate and keep it from getting infected again in the process," Reis explained. "There was a lot of damage, though, so it will take a while. We'll need to apply a fresh coat every few hours."

Pash rose. "We will need more food if we are to wait here. I will go hunting."

Reis grabbed his crossbow. "I'll come with you. I don't like sitting around and waiting. Kindra, I trust you will see to Kester's care and change his bandages."

"Of course."

"Just soak the bandages in the salve for a few minutes before you apply them." He grabbed his quiver of bolts. "Hopefully we'll find birds. It's been a while since I've had some decent fowl."

Outside the cave they found Avis surrounded by her failed attempts at whittling. The unrecognizable, misshapen wood carvings were tossed about her with no regard.

"Kester doing better?" she asked.

"The worst of it's done. With any luck he'll recover in a few days. Me and Pash are going hunting. Keep an eye out."

"Don't worry, if anything scary comes this way you'll hear my screams through all the Izer." She held up her current project, which almost seemed to take the form of a person. "How does my self-portrait look?"

Reis smirked. "You're not that attractive."

"Artistic liberties."

Reis and Pash spent the next few hours looking for game in the forest. There was no shortage of life, but most of the small animals were quick as well as clever. They needed to be, in order to survive the dangerous predators who made the Izer their home. Pash suggested that making noise and making themselves visible would draw out a few of those predatory animals, but Reis preferred not trying to hunt something that was hunting him.

Pash succeeded in jumping upon a wild pig. He wrestled it to the ground and then slit its throat with a knife. Reis fired several bolts at the red feathered birds that watched them curiously from the tree branches, but they were too quick for him. They decided the pig would be sufficient for now, and carried it back to the cave.

They roasted the entire thing over the fire and sat down to the biggest meal any of them had in a while. The meat was tender and flavorful. With their hunger further spicing it, the pig meat became the more delicious than anyone could have hoped. Even Kester joined them. He had regained some of his strength, though he still needed help to move and needed to be ushered to a spot near the fire.

The meal got them all in good spirits and soon they were laughing and talking like old friends. For a small time, they were able to forget their differences and the troubles that surrounded them and just enjoy each others company. Even Reis was talkative, albeit in his characteristic condescending way. They talked of battles won and lost, of old friends and lost loves, of their plans should they return from this mission alive.

The conversation eventually turned back to the mission at hand and where they were now. Their was some concern about how long it would take for Kester to recover. Their window of opportunity to strike at Serpentine was shrinking.

"It's truly a blessing of the Light that you knew of this cave," Kester said. "In this forest, I would be dead without a place to recover."

"I spent time here during my trial," Pash said. "I was in the Izer for several months. I found many little nooks to camp in as I watched to forest and hunted my hawken."

"Months?" Alvis said with astonishment. "I'm surprised anyone could survive that long out here. Are hawken that rare?"

"If you settle for the first one you came across, no," Pash replied. "But the size of the hawken you bring back reflects your strength and determination. Some return from their trial after only a few days, some spend more than a week to hunt one that will bring them respect. I would not be satisfied until I found one larger and stronger than any hawken killed by a Mankuri before."

Reis chuckled. "Have something to prove? Were you picked on as a little barbarian?"

"Reis!" Kindra exclaimed.

Pash nodded solemnly. "It's true enough. I am a *Broduk*, a child of the weak. I never met my father, but learned early on he was a coward. He fled from a losing battle instead of fighting and dying like a warrior. It is thought that those born of weak seed are likely to be weak themselves. Childhood is rough on broduk. No one wished to train with me, or become my brother in arms. My trial was my one chance at redemption.

"So I waited, patiently, living off the forest. I tracked the movements of the beasts, learned where they stalked and hunted and made their dens. I tracked many hawken, but none were large enough for what I needed to prove. I was prepared to give up and settle when I finally came upon the trail of a hawken twice as large as any other. I trailed it for days before I found its lair. I waited for it to go out to hunt and then concealed myself inside.

"Even a small hawken is a fierce thing. It's a feathered creature, like a bird, but does not fly, instead running upon the talons at the end of its long legs. Both its arms end in three long, sharp claws, and they possess the strength to cut clear through bone. And its jaw is long and filled with more teeth than I can count. But the most dangerous thing about them is they are fast. Terribly fast. They can dash across a field, gut you, and rip out your throat in the time it takes to draw a single breath. And the bigger ones are no slower. That's why I needed to catch it off guard.

"When it returned I struck from the shadows. I dug my knife into its belly before it even knew I was there. But the damn beast wasn't going to die easily. It slashed and tore and bit. It got its teeth into my cheek and nearly tore my face off before I stuck out its eye and it released me. We wrestled, the beast was almost as big as I am now. Its claws dug into me as my knife dug into it. I ended up slitting its throat. I was half-dead, but I won, and earned myself a place of respect. No one ever called me broduk again and men clamored to fight alongside me. I proved I am no coward or weakling."

"And now you're next in line to become the leader," Kester said. "Its quite the inspirational tale."

Pash looked solemnly at the ground. "I was. But no longer. Once they realized I was gone I was labeled a traitor, a deserter. I left without permission from the Mankur. I will never be able to return."

"You're going to be outcast?" Kester asked. "I had no idea. After all you've been through to be accepted. I am sorry."

"Nothing for you to apologize for, Church-boy," Reis said. "We didn't ask for his company. He made this decision for himself, full aware of the consequences."

"This is more important than my acceptance, or my chance to be the next Mankur," Pash explained. "The Mankuri can not survive if the Empire does. We will continue to fight, as we always have, but eventually the Empire will wipe us out. I don't want to see that happen. If I am to die, I prefer it to be going after these Empire cowards directly."

"Well there will certainly be no lack of chances to die in our future," Alvis chuckled. "That is, unless our friend Reis perfects his immortality potion sometime soon."

"I wouldn't count on it," Reis snapped.

"A shame. Being immortal would certainly come in handy when raiding an enemy capital with only four people. Well, five, if the lovely Kindra accompanies us that far."

"I wouldn't count on that either," Kindra said, shaking her head. "As soon as we get out of this forest, when we reach town, I should probably go my own way."

Reis frowned at that. That had always been the plan, but somehow he didn't like hearing it out loud.

"Let's just hope the Church-boy recovers soon," Reis said. "I don't know about you, but I'm tired of this fucking forest."

Chapter 25

Kester grew stronger by the day, but he still wasn't strong enough to walk on his own. When it became clear he would survive his wounds, they knew they had to wait on his recovery. The Izer was dangerous enough to cross without an injured man slowing you down. Reis monitored his recovery carefully, making sure his wound didn't show signs of new infection and keeping fresh salve on it. They ran out of the bandages provided by Thornwood, so Reis sterilized leaves in boiling water and used them to keep the wound covered.

He tried not to show it, but Kester's recovery made Reis uncomfortable. He wondered if he had made the right decision saving his life. Had he not run into the battle with Marek, not offered to make medicine, or just made a less effective salve, Kester would have died and no one could have faulted him for it. The dream in which Kester had killed him was still fresh in his mind. He was not one to believe in something foolish like prophetic dreams, but he could not deny that the outcome was possible. He and Kester were not friends, and he doubted that Kester would hesitate to kill him if it came down to it. Once their mutual enemy was gone, they were just a Church-boy and a 'demon.'

He could not think about betrayals without his mind drifting back to his old companion, Sable. Perhaps he had been foolish to trust him so completely. It was folly he almost hadn't lived to regret.

It was the day after they celebrated the successful assassination of the King of Mansir. They possessed jewelry worth a kingdom and needed to move it somewhere safe. They had a hideout east of Leroge where they hid most of the fruits of their labors. They agreed to travel there to split their reward. Even divided, they would each have enough to live out the rest of their lives comfortably.

They did not think it was wise to carry that kind of wealth down the road without some additional protection, so Sable suggested to hire on some sellswords. If Reis had been smart, he would have seen to hiring the sellswords himself. Instead, he let Sable find and hire the mercenaries while he arranged the horses.

Sable hired on twelve sellswords. Typically Reis would not travel with sellswords without first assuring their loyalty himself, but he trusted Sable's instincts and had no reason to doubt the instructions Sable had given them. Together they set off for their hideout. Half the mercenaries rode ahead of them, the others watched their rear.

"I'm quite looking forward to getting out of this game," Sable had said as they road together. "No more fighting, no more almost dying, no more worrying about where the next job would come from, and definitely no more risk of winding up in a jail like that hellhole in Mansir."

"Not an experience I like to dwell on. Although I suppose, in some way, it was fortunate for me. I was arrested trying to escape with trinkets, and now I posses the wealth of the nation."

"Our meeting in that prison was certainly fortuitous," Sable agreed. "We've made a formidable duo."

"We have. It's such a shame that you feel the need to retire. I will have a tough go of it without you."

"I'm wealthier than I ever dreamed possible. A good gambler knows when it's time to take his winnings and leave the table. And I've already gambled more than most. I'm truly surprised you want to continue this sort of life. You already have wealth. What more do you hope to gain?"

"I've got plenty of coin, true. But coin is only a means to an end," Reis explained. "Power is what I desire. I can hire mercenaries, but not loyal swords. I can bribe stewards, but not kings. I can buy land, but not a kingdom."

"King Beldaken," Sable said with a loud laugh. "Is that the kind of power you desire? Cause a title like that is hard to come by."

"I don't care for titles. What I desire is power. When I have that power, people can call me whatever they want."

"Well best of luck to you in acquiring that power. Me, I'll live out the squalor that is the life of an incredibly wealthy man."

For the rest of the day, they reminisced on their adventures together. They talked of the people they killed, the places they robbed, the women who warmed their beds. It was the fond reminisces of two friends about to go their separate ways. Sable never hinted at what he had planned.

Night fell and they decided to set up camp alongside the road. As soon as Reis dismounted his horse, he felt that something was wrong. The sellswords were all looking at him too often, they averted their eyes from his gaze too quickly. They were up to something. If they had somehow gotten a glimpse at the kind of wealth they were carrying, it was possible they decided that they wanted it for themselves.

Before he could let Sable in on his suspicions the mercenaries made their move. They surrounded Reis and drew their swords. Reis would not let them land the first blow. He sprinted towards the closest one, drawing his sword as he ran, and cut him down in one swift motion. The sellswords' surprise was his greatest weapon. He dashed between them, striking down the ones he could, avoiding the strikes of those who tried to counter. He didn't stop to try and fight any one-on-one, pausing meant he might get surrounded again. He needed to be constantly moving. Two fell. Three. Four. There were still eight remaining.

He looked around for Sable. He was nowhere to be seen. Had the sellswords already gotten him?

The sellswords were right on his heels. They were cautious after having seen what Reis was capable of. They kept well grouped together to counter Reis's speed. If Reis stabbed at one, another would be close enough to put a blade through him. Reis could outrun them if he fled, but then he'd be abandoning his wealth to the sellswords. Yet he couldn't win this fight on his own. Where was Sable?

His answer came in the form of a dagger in the back. He had gotten some distance on the mercenaries and stopped to analyze the situation. He glanced back and forth, looking for Sable, looking for a weakness in the mercenaries' formation, looking at how far he was now from the horses that carried their valuable loot. As he faced the oncoming sellswords, he felt the sharp pain shoot down his spine. Before he knew what had happened, his legs buckled under him and he fell flat on his stomach.

He pushed himself on his side and forced himself to look up at his attacker. Sable stood over him, a dagger in hand dripping Reis's blood. Even seeing this it took Reis several moments to realize what had happened. The fact that Sable would betray him was just not possible in his mind.

"Sorry about this, King Beldaken," Sable said with amusement. "You make a good partner for dirty work, but now that part of my life is over and I have no further use for you. I do have use for your half of the loot, however."

"You bastard!" Reis exclaimed as he tried to pull himself to his feet. His legs wouldn't heed him and he fell back to the ground.

"It's nothing personal, Reis. Just business. Next time I pass by a church, I'll toss a few coins at a cleric to say a prayer for your soul." He motioned at the sellswords. "Finish him off."

And then things went dark for Reis. It was only by chance that a traveling medicine man stumbled upon his body, and was able to usher him back from the verge of death.

He had been unprepared for it then. He would not make the same mistake twice. He knew that his companions could not be trusted. Kester, Pash, even Avis — any of them could betray him at any time. But he would be ready for it.

Kester once again awoke to the darkness of the cave, barely illuminated by a low fire. He was stiff and groggy from sleeping so much. At least his pain was subsiding.

"How long have we been here now?" he asked.

"Like I can tell time in this pitch black hell," Reis answered.

"Five days," Pash said definitively.

"Then it's been about six weeks since I first set off on this mission." He forced himself into a sitting position. "I estimated the window of opportunity for our strike to be about two months. After that, the companies sent to engage the last of the Church will be back at the capital. The Willer hunting campaign also can't last forever. If we miss this opportunity, and the palace returns to a full garrison, there will be no chance to reach Serpentine."

Reis rose. "Then we should be moving soon. Can you stand yet?"

Kester struggled to his feet, but once he was standing he was able to walk well enough. He would not be able to bear the weight of his breastplate so Pash volunteered to carry the extra burden. The giant barely seemed to notice the extra weight.

"I worry that I might not be strong enough in time for the attack on Serpentine's palace," Kester said as they packed up the rest of their belongings.

"Don't think you're getting out of it that easy," Reis said. "When we reach Rochest, I will have better ingredients to work with, maybe even a proper alchemist's lab. I'll make you an elixir that will make you feel as healthy as the day you were born."

"I appreciate that."

"It's not a favor. This whole thing was your idea. If I'm going to die in that palace, you're going to die too."

Kester smiled weakly. "I guess that's only fair."

Pash led the way back to the Grave of the Fallen Giant. They followed the path to its end and reached an area of forest spotted with hidden pools of water. Pash stopped to show them one such pool so they would be aware of the danger. It was hidden under the dense leaves of some low-hanging branches. It was a small pool, no more than a yard wide, but it looked deep and there were some nasty-looking fish swimming in it. The creatures were carnivorous and would not hesitate to feast on human flesh, Pash warned them. After that, they were careful to follow closely in Pash's steps to keep from accidentally falling into one.

When they tired, they camped in the high limbs of a wide and sturdy tree. Kester was helped up by Reis and Pash. The limbs were wide enough that there wasn't much risk of them falling off, but they secured themselves with rope, just to be safe. Pash, Reis, and Avis took turns at watch while the others slept. Pash assured them that they were fairly safe from most of the dangers of the forest this high, so they mostly just kept an ear open for the sounds of metal armor, in case more Empire soldiers were around.

The next day, they didn't make much progress. Pash got the sense that there were predators about and figured they were being drawn to the light of Reis's vial. They were forced to walk in almost pitch black darkness to avoid any more unwanted attention from the beasts of the forest, and that meant slow going. They then spent another night in the treetops.

The beasts had moved on by the morning so they dared to light their torches and press on as quickly as they could. They finally stumbled into a stroke of luck and found nothing impeding their progress this day. The next few days seemed to blend together. Darkness, trees, grass up to the waist, biting and stinging insects, little creatures scurrying past. At times, Reis argued that Pash was lost and just refused to admit it. Pash told Reis that he complained too much.

Finally, as they were considering whether they should camp for the night, Pash insisted they were at the last stretch and could camp beneath the stars if they pressed on.

An hour later, they saw that Pash had been telling the truth. The Izer ended as suddenly as it had began, the same unseen force pressing up against it and preventing the forest from spreading any further.

They were now in an open green field. The moon hung high overhead and the stars were out in force. After the darkness of the forest, the light of the moon was as good as the sun. Kester whisperered a quiet prayer to Light.

"Rochest is only a few hours walk from here," Pash said.

"So we can sleep here, or we can have comfortable beds for the first time in far too long," Reis said.

The open sky and brisk smells of the field had a rejuvenating effect and they no longer felt tired, so it was decided that they would press on through the night to reach Rochest.

"You think there's going to be a strong Empire presence in Rochest?" Avis asked. "It is fairly close to the capital."

Reis clutched the sword at his side. "If there is, they will meet the same fate as all the other Empire dogs who have tried to take me on."

Avis sighed. "I know violence seems to be your first instinct for everything from war to lovemaking, but remember, we're down a man. There are other tools available to us."

Reis cocked his head up in interest. "I'm listening."

Chapter 26

D awn was breaking over the city of Rochest. Special permits or proofs of residency were required to enter the capital, Marjan, so the small city had become a major trading hub since the rise of the Empire. Merchants, craftsman, and all manner of skilled labor passed through to trade with citizens and representatives from the capital. Hunters who braved the outskirts of the Izer fetched high prices for rare pelts, meat, and herbs. Fishermen from the northern coast and as far as Passenni in the south traded fish both fresh and smoked, crabs, and shrimp. Farmers from the fertile lands to the south were able to unload wagons full of their crop in the course of a single day.

The city rose early as merchants vied for the best spots to set up their stalls. The city was compact, and always crowded. The tall walls surrounding it prevented expansion and the inns were always full to bursting, so most of the traders stayed in camps outside the city walls or in one of the many inns and boarding houses that had sprung up along the roads into the city. The early morning hours were always filled with the creaking of wagons, the shuffling of feet, and the neighing of horses as the traders poured in through the city gates.

No one paid any mind to the small family of farmers moving along with the crowd entering the city. The guards posted on the city walls barely gave their wagon a bored glance. Two horses pulled a wagon full of freshly harvested vegetables. An old farmer and his wife rode on one horse, a young farmhand on the other. On the back of the wagon a young woman, the farmer's daughter, held hands with her lover. There was nothing about the scene that would draw a second glance.

Once they were past the walls and well into the city, the wagon broke off from the crowd. It took a back path just out of sight of the wall, taking them through the city's residential district. The path would get them to the market square long after all the good spots had been taken, and their own stall would have to be set up in whatever unoccupied corner they could find. It was a sacrifice the farmer had been paid well to make.

When they were certain they were alone the farmer ordered the horses to stop. "Should be as safe a place as any," he called out to his special guests.

Kester was eager to be rid of the uncomfortable garbs of the farmhand. The shirt was so tight around his chest he thought he might suffocate. He walked around to the woman who rode on the horse behind the farmer, a spot that had been held by his late wife until illness took her last season. The large sunhat was pulled down over her face to obscure her features, though if anyone had bothered to look close they would have noticed she was far too youthful to be married to the old farmer. Kester helped Kindra down.

Kester walked around to the back of the wagon where Avis was still making lustful glances at the farmer's daughter. She reluctantly broke away to help Reis and Pash crawl out of the pile of vegetables they had been buried under.

The plan had been Avis's. Once they got into the city, they knew it would be easy enough to get lost amongst the crowds, but there was a risk of being spotted if the Empire had eyes on the wall. Odds were that Serpentine was looking for them all now, especially if Thomwood had truly betrayed them.

They had stopped the farmer as he was heading down the road with his farmhand and daughter. Avis set to work on him with her silver tongue. She talked about just causes and the need of the common man to pitch in in what ways they could. Then she pointed out that Kester was a member of the Church of True Light and was currently in dire need. She had the farmer so convinced, Kester would have bet she could have convinced him that bedding his daughter was also part of the plan. Reis, not taking any chances, offered the farmer what they had left in coin to make up for the trouble.

The farmer provided them all with some spare clothing. Fortunately, Kindra was close in proportions to his daughter and Kester was able to struggle into the farmhand's outfit. Reis's face was too well known and Pash was a large enough man to draw unwanted attention, so they concealed themselves underneath the farmer's crop.

The farmer left them in the alley when they determined that they had successfully evaded notice. His daughter returned a few minutes later as they had agreed, carrying large cloaks they could use to help conceal themselves. She had even managed to find one that fit Pash, barely. It wasn't much of a disguise and close inspection would give them away, but they hoped not to draw any attention in the crowded city.

Kester couldn't help but roll his eyes as Avis bid the farmer's daughter a sad farewell. Then it was time to discuss their next move.

"I don't know about you, but I am not fond of the stink of the forest," Avis said. "My first priority is to find a bath."

"A sharp razor wouldn't hurt, either," Reis agreed as he ran his hand along the starts of a beard.

Kester put his face in his hands. "We're wanted men, on the way to assassinate an emperor, and these are your priorities?"

"Relax." Reis put a hand on his shoulder. "We could all use a day of rest after everything we've been through. We're not going to be much good in a fight against Serpentine if we're all ready to collapse from exhaustion. Give us a day to bathe, eat a quality meal, and sleep in a proper bed. Plus, you're still wounded. I bet I can find a decent lab where I can make an elixir to fix you up properly, but no one is going to let me in their lab while I look and smell like a homeless beggar."

"True enough, I suppose," Kester conceded. "But everything you desire costs coin, which we have little enough of."

Reis smiled wickedly. "Acquiring coin should not be much a problem."

Kester gave him a wary look. "You don't intend to do anything illegal, do you?"

"By whose laws do you mean? The Empire laws, like 'don't assassinate the Emperor?'"

"You know what I mean. Don't steal or kill."

"I'll keep an eye on him," Kindra volunteered.

Kindra found herself the focus of attention. No one had been sure what her plans were once they were safely inside the city.

"Not that I mind the company of one so easy on the eyes," Avis said, "but the path we walk is dangerous, and will grow more dangerous the closer we get to the capital. I had been sure you would separate from us here."

Kindra pulled her cloak tight around herself. "I had every intention. But now that I've had a look at this city, and its walls lined with imperial guards, I can't say I'm very comfortable. If you wouldn't mind, I would travel with you a while longer, until we find a nice, quiet village where I may better live away from prying eyes. I trust there are several on the road to Marjan."

"That there are," Kester said. "You are our responsibility to protect until such time as you are safe. We will not abandon you before then."

Kester was glad to hear she would not be leaving yet. She was a good influence on Reis, and he was growing quite fond of her himself.

"Until that time, I guess you can serve as the Church-boy's eyes to make sure I don't get into any trouble," Reis said. "And Pash, you can keep an eye on the Church-boy. Gods know what the moral code of his Church might tempt him into, and he is not strong enough yet to defend himself."

Pash grunted his acceptance. Kester and Pash found a comfortable spot to keep out sight. They watched as Reis walked towards the market with Avis and Kindra close behind.

"I hope I'm not making a mistake letting them go off on their own," Kester said.

Pash grunted agreement.

"You ever been in a big city like this before?"

Pash grunted as he shook his head.

Well, at least I have good conversation while I wait.

Kester decided to take a knee and go through his prayers. He had a feeling they would need all the help the Light could provide in the coming days.

Reis smiled and laughed as he walked into the bustling market square. *Civilization at last.* He made a solemn vow to himself that he would never allow someone to drag him into the wilderness again.

Avis and Kindra followed close behind him, doing their best to not get separated in the crowds. The market was full to bursting by the time they arrived. There were few enough in imperial uniforms amongst the crowd, but they pulled up the hoods of their cloaks all the same.

Reis put his skills to work in the market. During tougher times, before his lucrative partnership with Sable, he had survived by his ability to appraise, buy, and sell. He managed to sell what remained of his healing salve for a couple of coins to a local doctor. He got much more for the flask of light made of the Caden's Blooms. Kester would be brokenhearted for its loss, he was sure, but he had been able to convince a superstitious trader, who owned a stall full of Church artifacts and treasures, that the flask's light was caused by holy magic. The trader had practically begged for the opportunity to buy it. He gave Reis a small pouch bursting to the brim with coin. Reis imagined he would be very disappointed when the concoction lost its effectiveness over the next few weeks and the light died.

He spent the next few hours going between stalls looking for items worth more than their proprietors realized, and then selling them to traders who overestimated their value. In a short time he had more than doubled their coin. By mid-afternoon, he was satisfied that they had enough to see to all their needs.

Their next stop was the public baths. Avis slyly allowed herself to shed her disguise for a short time and followed Kindra into the female baths. Reis went alone in the male baths. Kester and Pash would have to wait until later for their baths, although whether Pash ever bathed was questionable. The water was pleasantly hot, and Reis allowed himself extra time to enjoy it. The furnace in his mansion had never worked half as well at warming water as whatever they had under the bathhouse. Unfortunately, his time was cut short when several men in Serpentine uniforms came into the baths. They were just patrons, he knew, but it was still a risk if they recognized him. And he had no desire to face them naked. He dressed quickly and left to regroup with the girls.

Avis was back in her man-disguise with a wide smirk on her face. Kindra shook her head and said that she did not want to discuss the embarrassment of being with her in the baths.

They found that a local doctor kept an alchemy lab he experimented with in his spare time. He had little of that lately, as there were far too few doctors in the city to accommodate the wants of the busy market. The lab was little more than a small, cramped cellar, with a handful of instruments lined up on a single shelf as they collected dust, but Reis determined it would do. He laid down a handful of coins to ensure he would have access to the lab as much as he needed and would not be disturbed in his work.

After taking stock of what he had to work with, Reis set off to hunting the market for ingredients. He needed some specific, and rare, ingredients if he intended to make a elixir that would get Kester back in fighting strength in time. They decided to divide their efforts. Reis gave Kindra a list of common chemicals and more than enough coin to acquire it all. For Avis he whispered a simple order, low enough so no one could overhear. Avis chuckled when she heard and promised she would return shortly. Reis himself went from stall to stall, looking over various plants with medicinal qualities.

Most of the stall keepers were useless to him. They couldn't tell the difference between medicinal herbs and poisonous ones. He heard one mention a shop on the outskirts of the market that specialized in herbs and flowers, so he decided to look there.

The walk was further than he had been warned. The market stretched on for miles through twisting alleys, long streets lined with stalls, and aggressive merchants who would grab you by the sleeve and try to drag you towards their wares. On a normal day, Reis would have shoved them on their ass, maybe given one a solid kick as a warning to others. But he couldn't afford to draw any attention to himself, so instead he had to politely shoo them away and idly look over the wares of the most persistent among them.

By the time he reached the outer ends of the market, the sun was low in the sky but the day remained uncomfortably warm. He almost missed the chill of the mountains. It was smoldering in his cloak. He wanted desperately to pull down his hood and let the wind beat his face, but unfortunately, there was a thick crowd of Empire guards about him now. They were in full armor and walking in tight formation as they pushed their way through the crowds. It was easy to tell they were looking for someone. It was entirely possible it was Reis they were looking for, and he was not about to let them find him.

He gambled upon staying close to the guards as he looked for the herb shop. Someone who showed no fear of them was less suspicious than someone who tried to avoid them. Plus, if he was lucky, he might be able to overhear some chatter as to who, or what, they were looking for.

The attack was sudden and fierce. Everything became a blur of chaos and blood. It started with sharp screams of pain and surprise as arrows suddenly sprung out of the armor of the guard's commanding officer. He fell with a sudden thud as his confused guardsmen drew their swords and looked around desperately for a sign of the shooters. Another round of arrows were sent into the guards. Several of them dropped, wounded or dead.

The crowd burst into a panic. People were running and screaming, pushing their way past the guards and trampling over the bodies of the dead. The guards tried to form up defensively, but without their commander to give orders there was no coordination. Many of them hadn't even drawn their weapons yet. With the chaos caused by the fleeing crowd, they couldn't even see where the arrows were being fired from. Another round of arrows sent the guardsmen into a panic.

Reis took cover behind an overturned stall to keep him out of the way of the fleeing shop-goers. When the crowd finally thinned, Reis braved a peek over the stall to watch the rest of the battle unfold.

With the street almost clear now it was possible to make out the shooters. They lined the roof of a long building on the side of the street opposite Reis. There were fewer than a dozen of them. They wore no armor or uniform, just common clothes. They fired arrows nonstop into the guards, barely pausing to take aim. When a quiver emptied, they dropped it and picked up a fresh one. The roof was apparently well stocked with them.

This was a well planned ambush. Reis had to admire the courage it took to assault Empire soldiers in one of their own cities in broad daylight.

The imperials surrounded the building and searched for a way to the roof. They kept close to the building to stay out of the archers' lines of sight. Some had shields and held them up against the arrows as they circled the building.

They were so focused on the archers, they didn't notice the doors opening in the buildings on either side of them. A wave of men, armed and ready for battle, came pouring out and took the guardsmen by surprise. They were dressed in all manner of gear: some wore armor, others were plain-clothed; some wore the symbols of Ryder or Deir or another of the kingdoms to fall to the Empire, others had painted over any markings; some had shields and swords while others wielded axes, maces, hammers, and spears.

The guardsmen had the advantage of numbers, but the rebels had position and surprise on their side. They caught the imperials on both sides and quickly tore into their ranks. The archers on the roof caught any of the guardsmen who tried to move out of the rebel's pin. In just a couple of minutes, the rebels had created a heap of dead imperials while only losing a few of their own.

Reis could tell that most of these rebels were no true soldiers. Many wielded their weapons clumsily, lacking any form or precision. Most had the common look of townsfolk, not the muscular and stern builds of soldiers. A few were old and gray haired, and a few looked so young he wondered if they could even grow beards.

One such boy stood out to Reis, a kid with wild sandy hair who couldn't have been more than sixteen. He wore brown leather and wielded a sword in either hand.   He wielded both swords with impressive speed. He was cutting through the guards so fast that he was getting ahead of the rest of the rebels. Reis was certain the kid was going to get himself surrounded and cut off from help.

A large, flame headed man with a short red beard caught up with the boy. After shoving his axe through the head of the nearest guard, he pulled the boy back to regroup with the others. The boy went with him, though he seemed reluctant. The flame headed man was barking orders to a few others as well, though Reis could not make them out.   He was wearing chainmail armor, dyed red like his hair, and bearing a symbol that Reis was not familiar with. By the way he pointed his axe and shouted, Reis could tell he led this rag-tag group.

The guards broke off and fled. The archers took a few shots at their backs. The men on the ground did not pursue. The flame headed leader barked an order and the rebels dispersed. They ran off in all directions in groups of three and four. The leader stayed just long enough to see the archers come down from the building and go their separate ways, before running off himself.

Reis was tempted to follow him. Anyone actively fighting the Empire this close to capital must know something about how they operate. In the end he decided against it. He needed stay out of sight. Besides, you couldn't trust rebels, even if you shared a common enemy. Instead, Reis continued on towards the herb shop, hurrying to leave the scene of battle before more soldiers showed up and tried to question him.

Still, an interesting story to share with the Church-boy later.

The herb shop was actually a small, one room wooden house. Despite its size, it was most impressive. Beside the small bed behind the counter where the proprietor slept, the shop was filled wall to wall with all manner of potted plants, vines, roots, flowers, fruits, and leaves. Some were exotic species he had never seen before: a tulip-like flower with blue and red petals, a large red fruit composed of two spheres connected into a figure-eight, a delicate yellow leaf that the shopkeeper informed him was incredibly poisonous. It was a veritable treasure trove of alchemical ingredients.

Normally, finding such a shop would put Reis into a scholarly frenzy.   The owner, a wizened old man named Gregir, was knowledgeable and friendly, though not overly talkative. The collection of plants was his own, the proud souvenirs of travels in his younger days.

It was rare for Reis to have someone with his own level of expertise to discuss the properties of plants with. But he just couldn't bring himself to focus.

The battle outside with the rebels dominated his thoughts. It was such a brazen act of defiance, and done so close to the capital. The devastation in the town of Colby had been a clear example of how the Empire handled even a small amount of dissent, and this dissent had not been small. He doubted even Serpentine would wreak that kind of destruction on a city as important to Marjan's stability as Rochest. Still, they were taking a big risk. If the rumors of the torture chambers deep within the Marjan Palace were true, there were fates worse than death awaiting the rebels should they be caught.

What made him more curious was why he had not been aware of this group before. The news he received made it pretty clear that there was no major opposition to the Empire close to Marjan. All the last traces of resistance had supposedly fled over the mountains into Allandane, or gone far east to hide as far away from the bulk of the Empire's force as possible. There was no talk of any significant group of resistance fighters still causing trouble for the Empire this far west.

Yet these rebels were far too organized for this to have been their first attack. They knew when to strike, where, and how to hit for maximum shock value. A group that diverse, made up of a mix of common folk and soldiers from all across Kassia, could only achieve that level of organization through practice and experience. They had been operating here for a while. The fact that Reis had never heard of them before suggested that the Empire was taking measures to keep the news from getting out. And that meant that they considered the rebels a threat.

Reis scowled at the thought. They were an unknown factor. Reis hated unknown factors.

He purchased a selection of familiar herbs and tipped the old man for his expertise. He resisted the urge to ask if he knew anything about the rebels. Gregir could very well be an Empire sympathizer and Reis couldn't afford to take any risks.

The streets were filled with imperials when Reis left the plant shop. They had blocked off the street that Reis had come by. There were squads fanning out in all directions in search of rebels.

He was forced to take a long way around, but eventually Reis was able to reach the alley where Kester and Pash waited. Avis and

Kindra had beaten him there. Kindra was carrying a bag filled with Reis's chemicals. Avis smiled when Reis approached and pulled a small vial from her pocket.

Kindra looked curiously at the crimson liquid in the vial. "Is that blood?"

"Virgin's blood," Avis said, still smiling.

"Reis set you to cut someone?" Kester asked.

Avis chuckled. "That's not how you collect this kind of blood."

Reis shook his head. "I think you can spare us the details. It's not something I relished sending you after, but virgin's blood is useful for amplifying the effects of an elixir."

Kester looked more than a little disturbed. "I don't know if I want to drink an elixir with that in it."

Reis scowled at him. "You will, or we will kill Serpentine without you." He carefully pocketed the vial. "I'll get to work on the elixir tomorrow. It's been a long day. We should find rooms to get some rest. I'll be glad to have a bed under me again."

"Best of luck there," Avis said. "This city is more crowded than a brothel running a special. I doubt there's a room and bed anywhere."

"Then we'll just have to make one free."

Reis led them to an upscale inn he had passed. As expected, the inn had no open rooms. The common room was crowded with affluent looking merchants being waited on by young women in revealing blouses. The innkeeper was a plump man who sat at one end of the room and never rose to do any work, instead shouting orders at the women who worked for him. It was him Reis approached.

"We need two rooms, with five beds between them," Reis said.

"Then you'd best get a hammer and wood and start building them," the innkeeper replied. "Unless you want to wait. I'll have a free room sometime next week."

Reis smiled at the innkeeper. "I think you can find two rooms if you really tried."

The innkeeper eyed him suspiciously. "And what makes you think that?"

"The guards are running around the city, looking for a group of rebels who dared to assault them in broad daylight. What do you think they would do if someone told them that he saw a few of the rebels run in here? Maybe he would even tell them his suspicions that a certain innkeeper was willfully harboring them. How would they react to that,

I wonder?"

The innkeeper scowled and clenched his fists but didn't get up from his seat. "I have two rooms opening up in an hour. I had already promised them to someone else, but I suppose if I'm being blackmailed I don't have much choice but to disappoint them. I hope you at least have the coin to pay for the rooms?"

"Enough. You will be paid upon our departure, as long as we are not disturbed during our stay."

The innkeeper didn't have much choice but to accept Reis's promise of future payment. A short time later they were up in their rooms.

"What was that about rebels?" Kester asked as they settled in.

"Some group of idiots with a death wish. They attacked an Empire patrol earlier, and I got a front row seat. Kicked some imperial ass, too."

He briefly told them about the rebel attack, thinking it an amusing anecdote. To his annoyance, Kester began bothering him for specific details, such as numbers and which symbols they wore.

"You didn't recognize the symbol their leader bore?" Kester asked.

"A lighthouse on a rocky shore beat upon by crimson waves," Reis responded quickly, hoping to end the conversation. "I haven't seen it before."

Kester's eyes went wide when he heard the description. "I have."

Chapter 27

It took Reis three days to produce the elixir he had promised. He preferred to work alone and in quiet. Occasionally, the doctor whose lab he was renting would come down and watch him silently, but otherwise he was undisturbed.

After going through the trouble of renting an inn room, he found that he was not using it often. Kester was convinced that the rebels Reis had seen in action were 'potential allies' despite not knowing anything else about them. Anytime Reis went back to his room, there was a new onslaught of questions waiting for him. He had grown tired of arguing the stupidity of trusting some random group just because Kester recognized a symbol.

The church boy had Avis and Kindra combing the streets for information about them. Reis hoped their searches would be unfruitful. There was too much about the rebels they didn't know.

On the third day, Reis's elixir was complete. It was similar to the one he had fled his mansion with, although not quite as potent. That elixir had been the results of months of experimentation, time which he just didn't have now. This would have to do for their purposes. He managed to fill three glass vials.

One of these vials, he gave to Kester when he returned to their rooms. Kester took it hesitantly, and afterward complained of its vile taste. It had the desired effect, however, and the next morning Kester seemed to be back at full strength.

"Feel as good as I ever did," Kester declared. He examined his body where the wound had been. All that remained now was a nasty scar. Reis decided that when it inevitability became necessary to kill Kester, he would cut him on his other side. For symmetry purposes.

"Then we should get back to the mission," Reis declared, already gathering his things. "We've wasted far too much time."

Kester stared him down. "I still want to make contact with those rebels."

Reis sneered. *We're going to have to have this argument again?* "You've had three days to find them. Chances are, they're not even in the city anymore. And even if they were, I still don't understand your rationale."

"The enemy of my enemy is my friend."

"A stupid adage. If that was true, all wars would be two sided. History is full of wars fought by a multitude of lords all trying to kill one another." They had been through all this before. Reis knew he was fighting a losing battle, but pressed on nonetheless. "Look, it is good that the Empire has other enemies out there. Maybe it will distract them. But we do not know anything about them, or if they could be trusted."

"We know the symbol their leader wears."

Kester had explained that the symbol Reis had described belonged to a group called the Bringers of Light. They were an offshoot that had broken away from the Church of True Light several generations ago. The Church believed in fighting only defensive wars, but there had existed a faction within them that believed the word of the Light should be spread by force if needed in order to finally banish the darkness. These extremists formed their own church and launched a holy crusade in the name of the Light. Supposedly, they had been wiped out years ago by some powerful lord they had been causing trouble for. But groups like that were hard to wipe out in their entirety; there was always a few survivors left behind to spread their beliefs to the new generation.

"If that's who we're dealing with, you really think its smart to approach them?" Reis asked. "You said that your church and theirs didn't exactly see eye-to-eye."

"Ancient history. We both revere the Light. That is enough."

"I hope you're right," Reis said. It was obvious he was not going to win this one.

"If you don't like it, you are free to stay here. I should be the one to make contact, anyway."

Reis had no choice but to accept. "You have one more day, then I'm going on ahead and taking Kindra and Avis with me. You are free to do whatever you want with the barbarian."

"Deal. I believe Avis already has a lead for me. Hopefully I will not take long."

Hopefully you won't be stabbed in the back. He carefully packed away the remaining two vials of his elixir. *The church-boy will not get another, no matter what happens.*

Under Kester's instructions, Avis had staked out the small temple in the city. Multifaith temples such as this one had become a haven for followers of the Light after they lost their churches. Avis had observed the comings and goings of the temple's regulars on Kester's hunch that the rebel would make regular visits.

He was proven correct. Avis spotted a man that matched the description entering the temple at the same time each morning. He took a seat, said a few prayers, and left quietly without speaking to anyone. He would then vanish into the city streets. She told Kester she had tried to follow him once, but lost sight of him.

Kester decided to approach him alone. He arrived at the temple early in the morning when he knew the rebel would be saying his prayers. His flame red hair made him stand out amongst the other worshipers. The rebel had the muscular build of a soldier and walked with the confident gait of a man in command. Kester was sure this this was the man he was looking for.

The flame-headed man was kneeling in front of the fire kept lit for worshipers of the Light. Kester took a spot next to him.

"It's nice to see that some people still have the courage to worship the Light these days," Kester said. "Serpentine has never been a fan of the Church, and many of its followers have suffered for it."

"Serpentine doesn't like the competition," the rebel replied. "He likes the near-godlike image he's built up for himself. The Light threatens to expose him for what he truly is: just another mere mortal who breathes and bleeds like the rest of us."

"Those are dangerous words, should the wrong person overhear them."

"I suppose I'll find out if you're the wrong person soon enough." The man rose and glanced over at the imperials who were supervising the worshipers. "Certainly no shortage of empty spots here. The fact that you came up to me must mean you want something, so why don't you just spit it out?"

"Perhaps it is best if we discussed this elsewhere? The matter on which I would speak to you is most private."

The man nodded. The imperials gave them a suspicious look as they left the temple, but made no move to stop them. Kester followed the rebel down several streets until they reached an alley not far from where Reis had witnessed the attack. The rebel looked back and forth to make sure there was no one looking before leading Kester to the back door of a small building. He motioned for Kester to go in ahead of him. Kester reached for the door handle.

Suddenly he was grabbed from behind and slammed up against the wall. A powerful arm pressed up against the back of his neck and a hand held him by the shoulder. The side of his face ached where it had impacted with the wall.

"Now we talk," the rebel said. "I don't really appreciate being approached in the temple. I have enough eyes on me as it is, I don't need someone drawing even more attention. Are you an Empire spy?"

Kester struggled to get his mouth to form words. "I am a commander in the service of the Church of True Light."

"Right. And I'm the damn High Cleric. Who are you, really?"

The rebel's breath stopped short and his hold on Kester loosened. "I would appreciate it if you let my Church-boy go now," Reis's voice said from behind them.

The rebel released his hold on Kester and backed away from him. Kester turned and saw that Reis had put his sword to the rebel's throat.

"What rock did you crawl out from under?" the rebel asked. "This alley was empty."

"You need to more carefully check the shadows," Reis responded coolly.

"Reis, put your blade down!" Kester commanded as he tried to shake the soreness out of his arms. "This is not the way to make allies."

"So what was the proper method, then?" Reis asked, not lowering his sword or taking his eyes from the rebel. "Yours seemed to be blind trust followed by an ass-kicking. If I hadn't decided to follow you, there is a very good chance you would be dead right now."

"Perhaps we have all gotten off on the wrong foot," the rebel said, his voice still steady despite the situation he was in. "My name is Lysander, although I suspect you may already know that. If you would be so kind as to release me, we can be properly introduced."

"How stupid do you think I am?" Reis snarled. "I see your hand sliding around your waist. As soon as I release you that weapon will be drawn. Perhaps I should let you, that way I can cut you down without Church-boy over there having a reason to be upset with me."

"Still sticking with that story?" Lysander asked. "Tell me, how can he be a commander in the Church? The Church's army is decimated. The High Cleric herself is either dead or captured. There's no way anyone of rank has escaped."

"Delia?" Kester exclaimed in shock. "What happened to her?"

"If your friend here wouldn't mind releasing me, I'll tell you."

Kester repeated his order for Reis to release him. This time Reis complied, although he kept his sword in hand.

"Now tell me what happened to High Cleric Delia," Kester demanded.

"Word has been spreading like wildfire," Lysander said. "Serpentine found where the last of Church's force was holed up and cleaned them out. The High Cleric was among them. The Empire has been quiet as to her fate, which leads many to believe she's dead and Serpentine is trying to avoid the unrest that would cause. The Empire sent so much force, it's impossible for anyone to have escaped. How is that you haven't even heard?"

Kester barely heard the question. The world was starting to spin around him. Reis and Lysander disappeared into a void of white emptiness. His ears filled with a low pitched buzzing. Suddenly he was lurching forward, falling through space. The world was gone. Hope was gone. Everything he had ever worked for, everything he had ever striven to protect, was gone.

He was snapped back into reality by a sharp pain on the side of his face. The world took form in front of him. He had somehow dropped to his knees. Reis was standing above him with a fist raised.

"You back with us?" Reis asked.

Kester nodded weakly and brought himself back to his feet. He didn't want to believe it. The last of the Church, gone. He had known it was a possibility when he set out. That even if he survived the mission, there was a chance that the Delia and the rest of the Church would no longer be there for him to return to. But somehow, he had never expected it to happen. The Church was a constant, a universal truth that would always be there, no matter what else changed in the world. Even when the Grandium had been lost that truth was unchanged. The Church was simply moved, weakened, wounded. But it was still there, as it had always been. And as he thought it always would be.

But now that was no longer true. The Church was gone. The High Cleric was gone. All of his friends and comrades-in-arms were gone. He was all the remained of the once-mighty army sworn to defend the Light.

Him, and the key that Delia had given to him. The key that his brother had wanted him to have. The key that opened the Church's archives buried beneath the ruins of the Grandium. Should he survive this, it would be up to him to use those archives to restore the word of the Light to the world.

But first he needed to survive. He needed to survive, and Marcus Serpentine needed to die.

"You're either a tremendous actor or you sincerely did not know," Lysander said. "I'm willing to gamble on the latter. Still doesn't answer what you want from me."

"We need to work together," Kester said, trying to put strength behind his words.

"Work together to do what?"

"Kill Marcus Serpentine."

Chapter 28

Lysander led Kester down a long, winding stairway. Reis followed carefully behind, hand resting on the hilt of his sword. The stairs seemed to go on forever into the blackness. The small building Kester had been taken to was nothing but a cover. Upon first entering it seemed to be no more than a modest, one-bedroom home. Push aside the bed, however, and a secret stairwell was uncovered.

"I never got your name," Lysander said. He was carrying the only torch between the three of them as he lead them down into the darkness.

"Kester Belisario. My companion is Reis Beldaken."

"Belisario?" Lysander repeated suspiciously. "Like Demos Belisario? If you're going to impersonate a Church commander, you should try for a more inconspicuous name."

"There is no impersonation," Kester said with a tinge of annoyance. "I am a commander in the Church of True Light. And Demos was my brother."

Reis chuckled. Kester imagined he must be wearing a wide, I-told-you-so smile right now.

"I do remember hearing that Demos had a brother. I suppose it's possible that you're him," Lysander conceded. "Though I'm still not entirely convinced you're not an Empire spy."

"If you think I'm a spy, why are you leading me down to your hideout?" Kester asked.

"You won't be leaving here alive if you are," Lysander said.

"You should watch who you threaten," Reis growled from the back. "Or it will be your body tumbling down these stairs."

Lysander laughed loudly at Reis's threat. "Your companion is a violent one. Is he supposed to be with the Church, too?"

"Reis is not with the Church," Kester replied.

"The first thing you said that I can trust."

They finally reached the bottom of the stairs. Kester wondered how many hundreds of feet underground they must be. At the bottom was a short hall with a single door at the end, illuminated by lantern-light. Sitting in a chair in front of the door was a boy with sandy hair. A sword was laid across his lap, another was leaning against his chair.

"Lucas," Lysander addressed the boy cordially.

"Good to see you again, boss," the boy said in a friendly tone. "New friends?"

"We shall see," Lysander said.

Lucas moved his chair aside and opened the door for them. Inside was a massive oval chamber. Lamps and lanterns lined the walls and cast the room in dim light. There was a large table in the center surrounded by chairs, some occupied, some empty. The chamber branched off into several smaller rooms filled with weapons, armor, and training gear. The room was filled with men of all ages and background. Kester had never seen a more diverse group.

"Commander Lysander," a burly man with a big mustache said as they entered. "As expected, the Empire forces are -" He stopped suddenly when he noticed Lysander wasn't alone.

"Please, don't stop on our account," Reis said.

"Welcome to our humble operation," Lysander said. "Before you stands the Resistance, the last defenders of Eastern Kassia against the might and evil of the Empire."

"I thought you would be going under the banner of the Bringers of Light," Kester said. He was looking around at the odd group of fighters who had assembled. Reis had described the seemingly random collection he had seen in action, yet it was still surprising to see it in person. They seemed more like refugees hiding underground than the organized rebels he was expecting.

Lysander chuckled. "That organization is long dead. Wiped out before Marcus Serpentine ever came on the playing field. But my father was a die-hard supporter who passed his beliefs down to me. His beliefs and his armor. I've gotten a lot more use out of the latter lately."

He motioned for Kester and Reis to follow him to the head of the table. The mustached man followed behind them. All eyes in the room were fixed on the newcomers.

"Well if it isn't Demos come again!" a loud, gruff voice called out. There was a great clamor of steel armor as a large man came stomping out of one of the training rooms. "But no, Demos is dead, very dead. And you are too small by half. But other than that, you are a dead ringer for him!"

"He claims to be Demos's brother," Lysander said.

"Ah! Now that explains it!" The large man wore a set of mismatched armor painted white. The breastplate had once had a symbol in the center but it was impossible to make out. The armor itself seemed to be well kept, in stark contrast to the man wearing it. The large man had disheveled brown hair and an ungroomed beard, and he looked as if he had not bathed in weeks. He carried a flask of ale in one hand, and based on how he slurred his speech slightly, it was clear he was already intoxicated. "Yes, the resemblance is unmistakable! He cannot be anything but Demos's brother!"

Kester smiled disarmingly at the rebel's leader. "I hope that is enough proof that I am who I claim, Lysander. Perhaps we can finally get past all this mistrust."

"How positive are you, Lunn?" Lysander asked.

"As positive as I live and breathe," Lunn slurred out. "I had the honor of meeting Demos once, the legend and war-hero himself." He paused for a moment to take a swig from his flask. "Well, not meet, so much as 'get yelled at by.' I was in a unit positioned on the right flank of the Church forces in the Battle of Bigasti. We took heavy losses and some of us broke rank and fled. Later, when the battle was won, Demos collected some of us who fled, called us 'deserters' and blamed us for almost costing them the battle. I was a captain of my squad, so I got a personal talking to. I can remember that day like it was yesterday. Not everyday you get yelled at by a living legend. I guess if you really want to be sure, have him start calling me 'spineless coward.' Then we can see if they sound the same."

"Nothing he said wasn't well deserved," Kester said. "A coward who flees a battle still being fought is a particular kind of despicable, to leave his friends and comrades to their deaths and abandon his cause."

"Ah, yes!" Lunn exclaimed. "You do sound like him, too. Yes, I was a coward. I had this crazy fear. Not of my death, mind you, but of what would become of my wife and children should I no longer be around to care for them." He took a long swig from his flask. "You don't have to worry about that kind of fear being a problem now, though. The Empire saw to that. Now my family are in Eternity. I have nothing left to lose, so I have nothing to fear." He laid the now empty flask down upon the table. "Nice meeting you." He stumbled back in the direction he had come.

"Lunn might drink a bit much but has never given me reason to question his judgment," Lysander said. "I'll take it on his word that you are who you say you are, Kester."

"Oh, isn't that generous of you," Reis said bitterly.

Lysander ignored Reis's comment. "So, you said you're on a

mission to kill Marcus Serpentine. Just the two of you?"

Kester hesitated for a moment before answering. "Well, there are a few others."

Kindra was brought down into the rebel hideout no more than an hour later. She and Avis were met with suspicious stares. Everyone kept their distance from Pash.

"Underground again," Avis sighed. "I was hoping when we left the Mankuri caves that we were finished with the dark, dreary tunnels. I guess you're right at home here, though, aren't you, big guy?"

Pash snorted. "At home, I am surrounded by the strongest warriors in all the world. Here, I am surrounded by green children and farmers."

"Heavily armed children and farmers," Avis corrected. "Doesn't it put you a little more at ease to be surrounded by weapons that aren't pointed at you for once?"

"I know how to deal with weapons that are pointed at me. A weak weapon at my side is far more dangerous."

The rebel leader, Lysander, had taken Kester aside and was speaking with him privately. The rest of them were forced to sit around and wait. Reis muttered angrily about being left out of the loop. Avis and Pash debated how useful the rebels would be in battle. Kindra sat quietly and tried to ignore the looks she got from every young man in the room, and some of the older ones, too. *Guess they don't see many women down here.*

It wasn't surprising. Most women weren't fighters.

Kindra looked over at Avis, who was still locked in debate with Pash. Avis had to dress like a man to be taken seriously, but she was still a woman. Kindra remembered watching her fight in the Izer. How strong she was. While she she fought, Kindra couldn't do anything but hide. She envied Avis's strength.

Kester's meeting finally came to an end and Lysander called a meeting. All the Resistance fighters gathered around the big table. There weren't enough seats, so most had to stand. Kindra forced her way through the press, eager to know what was happening.

"I know you have all been curious about the new faces," Lysander started. "This is Kester Belisario, a commander in the military arm of the Church of True Light. The agitated man in the black is his personal attack dog, Reis Beldaken. If that name rings any bells, its because he's quite the infamous bloodletter. Kester assures me he's on our side at the moment, so I'm taking his word for it."

Reis snarled at being called an 'attack dog.' Kindra thought he wasn't helping his case.

"Kester has been kind enough to share the details of his mission with me. They are going after Marcus Serpentine directly. They have maps of the palace and other details that we had been lacking. Well, great minds think alike. Kester has been kind enough to share his plans with us, so I think it is only fair that we share ours. Brax, if you would."

The burly man with the big mustache rose from his seat. He stroked his mustache as he spoke. "Like you, we are aware of the current vulnerability of Marjan. The bulk of the Empire's army was engaged with the Church and have yet to return. That, combined with the Willer hunts, has left them spread thin. Thin, but still with quite formidable numbers. Numbers seems to be the one thing the Empire never lacks. So we decided to spread them even thinner before we attacked."

A map of the region was unfolded and laid out across the table. Brax ran his fingers across the several towns in the area. "We've got little hideouts like this one in several towns and villages. They are leftovers from the days of the Blood King of Mansir. People would hide their children underground to protect them from being chosen for sacrifice in the King's rituals. Over the years they have been mostly forgotten, lucky for us. We've used them to launch surprise attacks on Empire patrols and guardhouses close to capital. Every time we attack, they are forced to send a unit to search and pursue us."

"And the closest response come from the capital," Reis said.

"Exactly. Every attack we launch diverts more and more of their resources away from defending Marjan."

"But even so, you can't possibly hope to bleed them so thin that a frontal attack is possible," Kester said. "The barracks beneath the palace alone never houses fewer than five-hundred men whose sole duty is defense of the palace. And even with all the diversions you've created, there still has to be more than a thousand between the walls, the towers, the guardhouses, patrols. Marjan is massive, and, as you've said, the Empire has never struggled for numbers."

"Very true," Lysander responded. "The Resistance numbers only about two-hundred, and we count ourselves lucky to have even that many. We could never possibly hope to take Marjan."

"But we could hope to take and hold the inner gate for a short while," Brax said. "Long enough to accomplish something." He laid down another map on top of the other one. This one was a general overview of Marjan. "We had a plan that involved an attack of two parts. Our main force attacks the gate and draws out the palace guard. A second group goes through underground tunnels until they get into the palace. With the maps you've provided, the guesswork there has been greatly reduced. With the palace guards engaged, the infiltration group will face minimum resistance on its way to the throne room."

"Where Marcus Serpentine awaits," Reis said. "He's your target as well."

"The power of the Empire begins and ends with him," Lysander said. "He uses his reputation as a god-like figure to keep his dominance. When he's gone, there's no plan for succession, and no man could possibly fill those shoes. The Empire will begin to collapse in on itself, and a reinvigorated people will retake what was once theirs."

"That's the optimistic outcome, anyway," Reis said. "The other option is that the forces of the Empire become split between power hungry commanders and Kassia becomes encompassed in a civil war so bloody that people will look back on Serpentine's reign fondly."

The room went silent. Reis seemed amused by their reaction. Kindra thought he made a good point. The rebels were so full of self-righteousness they had not considered that their actions could lead to negative consequences.

"If that's your attitude, why are you after Serpentine?" Brax asked.

"Because he came after me."

"Reis has his own reasons for being here," Kester said. "But he wants Serpentine dead as much as anyone."

"His reasons are not important," Lysander said. "We are still not quite ready to put the plan into action. We will have plenty of time to get to know one another before then."

"There is not much time to waste!" Kester protested. "If the Church has truly been defeated for good, than the main body of Serpentine's army will be returning. If we don't strike before they return we miss our chance!"

"Of this we are well aware," Lysander said. "But we ran into a bit of a difficulty."

"Our plans hinges greatly on our ability to take the inner gate," Brax explained. "It's this gate on the map, here. It separates the palace from the city proper. It holds a small garrison, but nothing insurmountable. The gate itself is actually a heavy iron portcullis, strong enough to withstand any battering ram, and can only be opened via a chain mechanism on the palace side. Our plan was the take the gate and then seal it, effectively cutting off the Empire forces in the palace from those in the city."

Lysander sighed and laid his head in his hands. "We had a guard in the city who liked to take our coin. He got himself a post on the gate and was going to arrange a little 'technical trouble' with the chain that would leave the gate raised just enough for us to slip under. Unfortunately, the Empire somehow got wise to him. Last we heard of him he was being dragged down to the torture chambers beneath the palace. Without him, we have a problem. The gate's impenetrability, which we were relying on as our greatest advantage, has now become our greatest obstacle. We can't possibly hope to assault it. Even if we tried to climb over the damn thing, we could never do so before the soldiers in the city muster more than enough force to slaughter us all, not to mention we'd be dealing with arrows and bolts the whole while. Without some way of raising the gate our plan won't work."

"We've been discussing ways of sneaking one or two of our men into the city," Brax said. "But we have yet to determine a way for them to get to the gate, much less the gate's chain mechanism, without being discovered and killed, or worse, captured."

"How much does the portcullis weigh?" Kindra asked, speaking up so she could be heard over the chatter of the men. Many of them looked surprised, like they had forgotten she was down here. She was somewhat surprised herself.

"More than even a team of men could lift, if that's what you're thinking," Brax responded. "More than a thousand pounds. Probably closer to two thousand. Even if we could get enough strong men to try and raise it, the damn thing is smooth. Nowhere to get a grip."

"I might be able to raise it," Kindra said. She tried to sound confident, though she was feeling far from it. "I'm a Willer. My ability manifests as a force which can move or lift objects. It might take me some time to lift an object that heavy, but I should be able to. The longer I focus, the harder I concentrate, the more weight I can lift."

"And here I thought Serpentine got his hands on all the

Willers," Lysander said. "But you really think you can lift that much weight? I've never seen a Willer's power manifest itself with that kind of intensity."

That's a good question. Kindra rose from her seat. She stood silently for a minute, focusing, and then raised her arms. She felt the familiar pressure in the back of her head as she concentrated. The large table began to list from the ground. Some of the men started to snigger, making jokes about the difference between the weight of a table and a gate. They stopped laughing a minute later when their chairs, with them in it, started to be lifted as well. It took her a few minutes but she was successful in adding two dozen men, in their seats, to the table in the air. She then set them down as gently as she could, which was less than gently.

"As I said. I *might* be able to raise it."

Kester noticed Reis was being very quiet as they walked back to the inn. It was not unusual for Reis to be quiet, but this was different. He twice ignored Avis's coaxing and a direct question from Kindra. *Must be in deep thought about the upcoming attack.*

Just abandoning their inn room without warning risked raising some suspicion. They would spend the night and depart early the next morning. There were many roads that led from Rochest to Marjan, each taking about a week's time by horse. The rebels would split up and take different paths to avoid detection. They would regroup a short distance from the capital, at the spot Brax had pointed to on the map.

"I never intended for you to be a part of the fight," Reis muttered as soon as the door to their room was closed. "I thought, bringing you down there, it might be a good place for you to hide until this all blew over. You weren't supposed to ..." He trailed off and started pacing the room. Kester had never seen Reis worked up like this before. He wasn't just angry, he was worried.

"I volunteered," Kindra said defensively. "They never asked me to do anything. This Serpentine and the Empire he's built, they're all scum. I'm happy to play a part in its destruction."

"It's a suicide mission, you know?" Reis barked. "Those rebels, they know they're not coming out of there. They're trapping themselves between a rock and a hard place. On one side, a gate that will be under siege by all the might Marjan can muster. On the other side, the palace guard, who outnumber them almost three-to-one. They're making a sacrifice, and they are aware of that."

"And I can't make a sacrifice?" Kindra responded sharply.

"I never told you that you could."

"I don't need your permission!"

Reis glared at her with such fury that Kester was afraid he might strike her. Avis must have sensed this as well because he got between them. "Hey, come on now," Avis said light-heatedly, trying to break the tension. "We've all only got a week to live, with the odds we are up against. Let's enjoy our last night of relative comfort. I'll go down to the innkeep, get us a couple of bottles of wine or a good, strong ale, and we'll enjoy our night together."

Reis waved his hand in dismissal. "Do what you want. I'm leaving."

"Where are you going?" Kester asked.

"None of your concern. Best of luck on the mission."

Kester watched Reis begin to gather up his things. "Wait, you're abandoning the mission now? You can't possibly be this angry about Kindra's involvement."

"I'm more angry about the rebels' involvement." He turned to face Kester, one hand on his sword like he was considering drawing it. "I should have let you die from your wounds in that damn forest. I could have stuck to the original plan without you. Sneak in, kill Serpentine, sneak out. Involving the rebels has made everything very complicated."

"Their plan has a better chance of succeeding than ours!" Kester objected.

"I'll admit, I think their plan looks a little better on paper as well," Avis added. "At least, as far as my chances not to die go."

"Then by all means, use their plan," Reis spat. "You don't need me for it."

"He's afraid," Pash grunted. "He wants to run and hide like a coward now that the battle looms near. What more can be expected from a man who seeks to avoid death forever?"

"I'm not afraid. I'm practical. I accepted this mission when I thought the chances of success were in our favor. Now things have changed. There are too many moving pieces. There is no way all of those rebels can be trusted. If they could, their contact at the gate would be waiting for them at his post instead of in shackles. And even if they were trustworthy, Serpentine is going to see them coming. There are just too damn many of them to avoid notice."

"Serpentine is going to see us coming," Kester said as he realized Reis's implication. "And he's going to set a trap for us." His brother, Demos, walking in a trap and getting shot full of arrows. His head put on display. It would be dangerous to ignore Reis's instinct.

"Those fools in the 'Resistance' have spoiled our chance," Reis said. "I'll have no part in walking into a trap. You can do what you want. Unfortunately, our dear Kindra is as good as dead. Now that they feel they need her, the rebels will never allow her to back out. They likely have eyes on us now. They won't mind if I leave, they don't feel they need me. But Kindra is stuck."

Pash growled and clenched his fist. Avis's typical easy smile had dissolved. Kindra's face had gone pale. They were all rendered speechless by Reis's warning. But Kester found within himself a sudden fury. Too much relied on this mission for them to give up now. The Church was gone. The High Cleric was dead or captured. Darius had sacrificed himself for this cause. They were so close. It could not end here. He tore Reis's pack from him and tossed it aside. He grabbed Reis by the front of the shirt and forced him close.

"I picked you because you can think like Serpentine. That's why you can sense a trap. And that's why you're going to help us get around it."

"Is that a fact?" Reis responded, his voice eerily calm but his eyes bright with fury. "And why should I do that?"

"Because you came this far. Because you know Serpentine will never stop hunting you unless you hunt him. Because you're not the kind of man who lets a slight go. Thomwood betrayed you, and I don't doubt he will die for it. Serpentine sent men to kill you, and burned down your home, your research. You won't just let him get away with it."

Reis glared at him, his sword-hand twitching over his hilt. Kester didn't flinch. Time passed excruciatingly slowly. Finally, Reis submitted. "No. No I won't."

Kester released him. Kindra and Avis let out a collective sigh. Pash let out a boisterous laugh. "A true man must avenge all slights on his honor. Now you sound like a Mankuri."

"Gods, I hope not."

"Great, so we're all friends again!" Avis said. "I should get those drinks now."

Reis collected his pack from where Kester had tossed it and put it on his bed. "When you were researching me," Reis began, still facing the bed with his back to Kester, "did the name Sable ever come up? Probably not, it was before I made a reputation for myself." He dumped the contents of the pack on his bed. "Allow me to tell you a little story."

He sorted through the items on his bed as he talked. "A long time ago, Sable and I were partners. We did a lot of work as sellswords, thieves, assassins, wherever there was coin to be found, we could be found close behind. And we worked well together. Remarkably well, as a matter of fact. So well that one day, we found ourselves with more wealth than we could have ever dreamed. And on that day, Sable ended our partnership with a blade to the back."

Reis picked a dagger up from the bed. It was one of the blades Thomwood had provided for them. He twirled it in his hand. Kester wondered what was going through his mind.

"It wasn't until several years later that I finally got wind of my old partner again. He had built himself a little inn right on the ocean shore. It was a fine building, I remember, three stories and made of brick. The stables were packed full and there was a crowd bursting from the doors, drinking and enjoying the pleasant company of the girls Sable kept around to warm the beds. It even had its own dock. It was quite the establishment."

Reis tossed the dagger from one hand to the other. "Right when I walked through the front door I saw him. He was in the middle of the common room, a girl on either arm and a crowd gathered round him as he bragged about his adventures. He was using a different name, and the soft life had caused him to pack on the pounds, but I recognized my old partner right away. And he recognized me too. The moment his eyes drifted over to my direction his jaw dropped and he jumped from his seat. I'll never forget that look. Surprise and fear. Seeing that look was almost satisfying enough on its own."

He tossed the dagger suddenly. It stuck into the frame of the bed. "Almost."

Kester could sense where this story was going. "Reis..." he tried to interject, but Reis didn't seem to notice.

"He tried to hide his fear. Act like he was happy to see me. He started trying to talk about old times. I let him ramble on, not responding to anything he said. I savored the moment as he burst into a heavy sweat and stumbled over his words. Finally, when he became tongue tied, I drew my sword. He called in his paid swords. He had four of them working for him. I cut down two without breaking a sweat and the other two fled. His loyal patrons broke into a panic and followed them out. It was just me and him."

Avis and Kindra exchanged uncomfortable glances. Pash had one hand stroking his beard. Kester shifted on his feet. Reis still had his back to them so it was impossible to see his expression, but based on his voice Kester had to imagine he was wearing a wide smile.

"He tried to plead for his life then. He told me he still had my share of our wealth, that he had never touched it. He even offered me everything he owned, all the coin and jewelry and expensive art. I said nothing. He started to break down. He insisted that I owed him, that I was only alive because of him. I said nothing. Then he finally drew his weapon, desperate. If he had been the man I once knew he might have proved a challenge, but he had grown fat and weak and he knew it. He could barely hold his sword still. I lost count of how many times I cut him, I just gave myself to my fury until I was satiated. When I was done, he was so mutilated he was unrecognizable."

Reis picked up one of the vials of elixir from his bed and examined it. "He was the closest thing I ever had to a friend. At one point I trusted him, fought beside him, maybe would have even died for him. But at that moment I killed him, ruthlessly, viciously, without a shred of doubt or remorse. That is because I consider betrayal the worst of all crimes."

He turned and tossed the vial at Kester, who barely reacted in time to catch it. "I saved your life once. But don't ever forget that I would just as quickly take it away. Don't cross me, Kester."

"You think I would?" Kester asked.

"Not if you're smart."

"Well, that story was sufficiently disturbing," Avis said. "But was there was point in telling it now, Reis?"

Reis nodded. "I have an idea on how we can avoid whatever trap Serpentine is setting for the rebels. But the rebels can not learn what I have planned, or it will be spoiled. Kester has been fairly open with their leader, that Lysander, about who we are and what we've planned. So I have to wonder, can he be trusted, or will he go behind my back to warn them of my plans?"

Kester and Reis faced off with stony stares. "If it means defeating Serpentine, I will follow your lead, even if it means keeping secrets from our allies."

"Good. Now, you still have those maps, Church-boy? We have some work to do."

Chapter 29

Konrad Marek was returning from his morning drills with the city guard. As usual, he found absolutely no challenge to the routine. The exercises barely got his blood going, the forms were all easy to maintain, and not one of his fellow recruits could hold his own in a spar long enough for him to get any real practice. Even the officers in charge of the training were useless. Last time the Captain tried his hand at Marek, the officer proved to be no match.

"You'll make officer in record time," they would always tell him. He didn't much like the idea. Leading men, giving orders, it seemed like a job for someone with a big ego and little motivation. He was meant to be in the thick of things, enforcing justice with his own blade.

Justice. Such a powerful word. Short, but was there any word that held more weight to it? More gravity? A sense of justice was what separated a man from a beast. Those that broke the law, who threatened the peace and order of civilization, were little better than animals. In that way, a guard's job wasn't terribly different from that of a hunter.

Marek returned to his home to find the door partly cracked open. He frowned hard at it. He lived in a poor area of the city where crime was an everyday occurrence, but had so far had the good fortune to never be robbed himself. He slowly opened the door with one hand, the other on the hilt of his recruit's blade. It was a shortsword, truly more of a long knife, that would do little good in a real battle but would more than adequately put down any common thug. He stepped quietly into his house, eyes narrowed with focus.

The entry room was empty. He paused in the doorway and let his senses properly take in his surroundings. There was a sound coming from the kitchen. Muffled footsteps. Someone taking great care to move around without being heard. Likely an experienced thief. He had chosen the wrong house this time.

Marek crept carefully towards the kitchen, his hand still gripping the hilt of his blade. He licked his lips in nervous anticipation. Having still not earned a sash on his uniform, Marek had never been allowed to assist in taking down a criminal before. How fortunate that one should come to him. He could barely contain his excitement.

He pressed himself against the wall of his living area next to the kitchen entry. He could hear the thief still inside, his muffled footsteps

right on the other side of the wall. Marek quietly drew his recruit's
blade from its sheath. The light hissing sound it made was like music to
his ears. This time he wasn't drawing his weapon for some pointless
spar against an unqualified opponent. This time his blade would do
justice.

He stepped suddenly around the corner into the kitchen with
his weapon raised. The kitchen came in view and he prepared to cut
down whoever he should find.

A young boy, couldn't be any more than twelve. Marek's sudden
appearance startled him and he fell onto his back. The small bag he had
been carrying fell out of his hands, bread and fruit pouring out.

The boy looked at him with watery, innocent eyes, as if Marek
was the one who was committing the crime. For a moment, Marek was
almost convinced he was. He had to remind himself that this was his
house and this boy was a thief.

"What are you doing here, boy?" he asked.

"I – I'm sorry," the boy said, his eyes fearfully fixed on Marek's
blade. "Is this your house? I'm so sorry."

"Answer the question."

The boy swallowed guiltily. "I was just looking for some food, is
all. My mom and dad both died of the chill. Me and my brothers, we
got nothing to eat and no way to make coin."

"So you admit you're stealing."

The boy's eyes filled with water. "We were just so hungry. I'm
the oldest, I got to care for my brothers, don't I? I couldn't just let them
starve."

Marek raised his sword. The boy's eyes let loose and he began
to sob. "Please. Everything I took is in this bag. Just take it back,
please!"

He looked at the small bag on the floor. The boy hadn't taken
too much. Marek could go to the market and replace everything for a
couple of coins. That did not change what he had to do. The boy was a
criminal, a thief and a trespasser, and he must now face justice.

He brought down the sword and the boy let out a shriek.

Marek awoke to a world of misty haze and pain. The dreams of a day
long past, before he joined the Empire and found his true purpose in
life, slowly began to fade away. As his vision cleared, he tried to make

sense of his surroundings. He was in a bed with sterile white sheets, one of many such beds in a long hall. Most were empty, though a few at the other end were occupied by men with serious wounds, their white sheets stained red. The hall was simple and plain: beds, shelves, and chests. On the wall the banners of the Empire were the only décor.

He realized he was in the hospital beneath the palace. The palace had several clinics, some to serve Marcus Serpentine, the Councilors, and their staff, while others served the Palace Guard. There were no windows in this room, which meant he was underground. The hospital beneath the palace was reserved for the worst cases, those who had little hope of survival.

Slowly memories came back to him. Confronting Beldaken in the Izer. Being on the verge of victory when he was suddenly assaulted by that beast. Barely managing to slay the creature, but not before being mauled near to death.

That hunter, Thomwood, told him where Reis was heading. Marek needed to get word to the capital. He was barely conscious but somehow managed to focus enough to use his ability.

He managed to focus on one his signatures in the palace. He couldn't remember which one; the world had started to blur and he just picked the first one that came to mind. "Beldaken going to Rochest," was all he managed to say before collapsing.

The following days he had been in and out of consciousness. A doctor had forced him to swallow some foul tasting elixir. Nurses came and went to change his bandages. There was the old woman, too. He couldn't remember her name.

He supposed he should. She was the first person he had been ordered personally by Marcus Serpentine to hunt down. She was a Willer whose ability could speed up the body's natural healing process. Serpentine wanted this ability at his command, but the old woman refused on moral ground. "A healer takes no sides in a war and must be ready to heal all," she had said in a haughty tone of righteous indignation. Serpentine had ordered her be brought in unharmed, so taking her by force was not an option. Marek managed to convince her to come willingly when he ordered all her youngest patients be put to death, one by one, until such time as she agreed.

He wondered how many times she had cursed him while she was forced to work on his injuries.

"I see you're finally awake," a voice called out to him.

Marek hadn't even noticed the man sitting at the foot of his bed. With some effort, he was able to sit up. His pain peaked from the exertion. "Lech," he said when he recognized the assassin. His voice was hoarse and dry. Lech pointed to a glass of water on the stand next to his bed and Marek gulped it down gratefully. "What are you doing here?" he asked when he set the glass down.

"I wanted to see it for myself," Lech said. He was idly playing with a dagger in his hand, twirling it between his fingers by the blade. "I could hardly believe it when I heard. Captain Konrad Marek, the emperor's personal fugitive hunter, defeated and almost killed by one of his targets. This is the first time you've ever failed, isn't it? Must be a humbling experience."

"I was defeated by the forest, not the man," Marek responded. "I underestimated the danger of the Izer and paid a terrible price for it."

"Indeed, losing your target must be one of the worst prices a man like you can pay," Lech said with a mocking smile. "I wonder, if it had been some other officer of the Empire who had failed in the way you did, and returned barely alive, what would you have ordered me to do to him?" He stopped playing with the dagger and looked at it as if he was contemplating his own words. "As I recall, I slit the throat of a young lieutenant, on your order, for failing to catch Beldaken. I used this very dagger."

"Are you threatening me?" Marek asked angrily. Infirm as he was, he could put no threat behind the words.

"Just making conversation," Lech said lightly. "Let us not forget, I failed as well. And been left permanently scarred for the trouble." He lifted his shirt to reveal a nasty scar across his side. "He's a dangerous one to underestimate. Shrugged off my poison somehow and nearly cut me in half. That makes two of us who just barely survived our encounters with him."

"Have there been any developments while I've been down?" Marek asked. "Did they send men to Rochest?"

Lech sighed. "If you're asking if anyone has found Beldaken, no."

"So he's still out there," Marek grumbled. "I must warn Emperor Serpentine of his plans."

"You'll get the chance. The emperor put out word that he wanted to speak with you the moment you regained consciousness. One of the nurses just left to inform our friends outside that you're awake."

His words were followed by the raucous sounds of plate armor coming closer. "I believe that would be our escort now."

The imposing figure of Kasimir the Black appeared in the doorway, drawing the attention of everyone in the ward.

"Are you capable of standing?" Kasimir asked. He didn't enter the room fully, just stood by the door and turned his helm in the direction of Marek. Several uniformed soldiers followed behind him.

Marek wasn't sure himself. He slid himself to the side of the bed and put his weight on his feet. When they seemed steady, he forced himself to rise. It took him a few moments to find his balance and the pain in his side flared up even worse, yet he forced himself to bear it.

"Both of you, follow," Kasimir ordered. His voice echoed off the inside of his helm. "The Emperor would see you immediately."

"Summoned by the Emperor himself," Lech said whimsically. "This is a first for me. Quite the honor." He smiled at Marek. "Guess it's nothing new for you, though I'd wager this is your first time being brought to him to him to explain a failure."

"As long as I breathe I have not yet failed," Marek said. "The emperor will know this."

Marek walked with a slight limp and struggled to keep up with Kasimir. Fortunately, the pain in his side subsided to more bearable levels after he took a few steps. He would force himself to remember every ache, every pain, every bit of suffering, so he could use it to fuel his fury next time he met Beldaken.

"Did Emperor Serpentine put someone else in charge of hunting Beldaken while I was recovering?" Marek asked.

"That is not for me to say," Kasimir boomed. "Save your questions for the emperor."

Marek scowled. He was tired of Kasimir's 'silent monster' act. He had to deal with it every time he was summoned to see the Emperor. As commander of the palace guard, Kasimir was responsible for doing most of Serpentine's dirty work. He served Serpentine as a bodyguard, adviser, and executioner. He did this all while never taking off his armor and while hardly saying a word. Even Marek had never seen his face. He sometimes wondered if he slept with his armor on.

The citizens of Marjan feared him, this faceless man in terrifying armor who barely spoke. Marek had heard the rumors that circulated about him. One suggested that he had no face and was actually just a living suit of armor. Another figured that he was a demon summoned by Serpentine to drag the spirits of those that defied him into the Dark. Marek didn't believe any of it. Kasimir was just a man that preferred to let intimidation do the work for him, and having such a reputation helped to that end.

"Near-fatal injury aside, I think I'm starting to like this Beldaken fellow," Lech said as they walked. "He's very bold."

"Don't confuse foolishness with boldness," Marek said.

"Oh, he's a fool, beyond a doubt. And yet we have not been able to stop him. Does that not make us the bigger fools?"

"It makes him lucky."

"Perhaps. But how much of his success can be attributed to luck? Certainly not all of it. Killing one officer, eluding several others, defeating me, nearly killing you. He's obviously got the capability to back up his boldness."

"If you admire him so much, perhaps you should join him," Marek said with some disdain.

"Perhaps in another life in which I was as bold. Unfortunately, I am an assassin, which means at heart, I am a coward. I strike from the shadows instead of confronting a man directly."

"You should not be so proud of cowardice."

"I disagree. A healthy fear of death is an assassin's best tool. It ensures that we think our moves well ahead, makes sure our shots are aimed just right. A bold man may make his move prematurely. A coward only seizes the perfect opportunity."

"A coward knows no loyalty," Marek responded coldly.

"Cowards are loyal to the winning side. Why do you think I have always been such a loyal man to the Empire? They are always the winning side."

Marek had made use of Lech's services several times since his promotion to captain, but they had rarely spoken face to face, preferring to communicate through messengers. Lech had come highly recommended as one of the best assassins the Empire had to offer, and he had never given Marek any reason to doubt his abilities. Marek wondered if he would have put so much confidence in the assassin, had he heard his opinions on cowardice before.

They were led up to the ground floor, through the palace's great hall, up the grand staircase, and then up a second stairway that led directly to the throne room. Two members of the Emperor's personal guard stood in front of the large double doors that bore the Empire's symbol. They were tall, grizzled men, each a distinguished soldier whose deeds in battle caught the attention of the Emperor. They wore only light leather; they were trained to be quick and maneuverable and would be encumbered by heavy armor. They leaned on long halberds with extended spikes past the blade. In case of an attack on the throne room, the angle of the stairway would protect the guards from arrows, and the reach of the halberds would allow them to put a stop to any enemies who tried to rush up the stairs long before they came with sword's reach. In theory, two men could hold this defensible spot against scores of enemies, at least long enough for the Emperor to get to safety. It was a theory that had not yet needed to be put to the test.

The two guardsmen moved aside to let them pass. Marek glimpsed their faces as he walked past and tried to put a name to them, but all the members of Serpentine's personal guard looked the same. They were supposed to. They shaved their head bald, wore the same armor on-duty and clothes when they were off, and were forbidden from growing any kind of facial hair. Any distinguishing blemishes had to be covered up or removed. When you became a member of the Emperor's personal guard you were stripped of your identity. Your family name was taken and you were forced to cut all ties to the outside world. All that remained in your life was your duty to protect the Emperor.

Marek was an Empire man down to his very core, but even he found the prospect of losing his identity to be disturbing. He also didn't think he would be able to stand being cooped up in the palace so much. He preferred to be on the move, taking the fight to the enemies of the Empire.

Kasimir pushed the double doors open and ushered them inside. The throne room was massive, and empty. The ceiling towered overhead a full five stories above, but its dome shape made it appear to be much higher. Balconies ran all along the sides of the room, lined with rows of seats; the balconies alone could seat more than two-hundred. Right now, all the seats were empty.

For the throne room of the most powerful man in the world, it was sparsely decorated and furnished. Only the banners of the Empire broke the plainness of the walls. Lamps were placed throughout to room to keep it brightly lit even at night. Elsewise, the throne room was practically bare.

Emperor Marcus Serpentine was seated in his throne at the far end of the room. The throne was atop a small set of steps which raised it from the rest of the room. At the bottom of the steps stood Serpentine's favored personal guard, Ragnar. Ragnar approached them and met them midway to the throne.

"Only members of the palace guard may carry weapons into the throne room," Ragnar said in his light voice.

Marek was still wearing the simple garb the hospital had dressed him in, which left little room for a concealed weapon, so the comment must have been directed at the assassin. Lech shrugged and began tossing weapons at Ragnar's feet. He produced an astonishing number of daggers and knives. "I believe that's all of them," Lech said as he fumbled around in his cloak to make sure he didn't forget any.

"I have brought the two that were requested," Kasimir boomed. "I shall take my leave."

"No, no, please stay," Serpentine called out from his throne. "I have matters I would discuss with you as well."

"As my emperor commands."

Ragnar led the small procession to the the base of the emperor's throne. Marek did his best to hide his disgust at the sight of the man. Ragnar was the only member of Serpentine's personal guard who didn't look like a twin of all the others, but Marek wasn't sure that was a good thing. He wore the same uniform, but the similarities ended there. He was a deformed, ugly little man. He was shorter than the average man and walked with a forward lean, which made him seem even shorter. His left eye drooped slightly and gave his whole face a lopsided appearance. He was balding, and what little hair he had was thin and the color of straw. Marek couldn't stand the sight of him, but Serpentine trusted him with his life and he was rarely far from the throne. It was not Marek's place to question the emperor's judgment.

"My emperor," Marek said as he went to one knee. "It is an honor to be in your presence."

"And I am glad to see you whole, captain," Serpentine replied warmly. "I was afraid this Reis Beldaken had sent another one of my best officers to their grave. Though I must say, it is most disappointing that so many have failed to bring this one man to justice."

"Perhaps our captain is losing his touch," Ragnar suggested. "Or he stopped moving."

Marek had to hold back a grunt of frustration. Ragnar had a weird way of speaking, always talking about 'moving'. "Never stop moving." That was a phrase that he repeated religiously. Whenever something went wrong, he blamed it on someone who had 'stopped moving,' whatever that meant. And he never stood still. He was always pacing or fidgeting. Even now, he paced uneasily in front of the throne.

Marek could ignore Ragnar. It was his emperor's words that stung. He was disappointed.

He went down to his hands and knees in front of the throne. "If you feel I have failed you, please have my head off immediately," he pleaded. If he had truly disappointed this great man, a thousand deaths would not be enough to make up for it.

"Please note that he does not speak for the both of us," Lech chimed in.

"There's no need for something so dramatic," the emperor said. "You have never failed me before. And I fear I share in the blame here as well. Beldaken killed one of my best officers and in my haste to get revenge, perhaps I did not learn enough about him before issuing my order. He has quite the reputation. A living legend, almost as renowned and feared as our very own Kasimir the Black."

Kasimir did not respond to his name being mentioned. He just stood as silent as ever.

"Had I known what this Beldaken was capable of," Serpentine continued, "I would have put more resources towards overtaking him."

"I had an entire unit of Passenni men with me," Marek said. "They are all dead now. It was not Reis who was underestimated, it was his companions. One of them was a soldier of the Church, a spitting image of Demos, who used to be such a thorn in your side. Possibly his brother, or close cousin. I gave him a nasty wound, not sure if he survived it. Another one of them seemed to be one of those barbarians who are always raiding our encampments in the northern mountains. I'm not sure how he found himself an ally among them. There was another swordsman there, but I didn't get a good look at him. And a woman, another Willer who has so far managed to evade us. The few of them managed to kill the Passenni down to the man. His companions are almost as dangerous as he is."

"That is most disturbing news," Serpentine said. "And it seems he may have made more allies still. Isn't that what you had to report, Mr. Lechin?"

"If it pleases my emperor, you may call me Lech," the assassin responded. "And yes, emperor, that is the report I gave. My eyes on the inside of this group of rebels that calls themselves 'The Resistance' reports that Beldaken and friends just signed on with them."

"Rebels?" Marek exclaimed. "Beldaken was heading here, towards the capital. Last I heard he was on his way to Rochest. There are no active groups of rebels that close to Marjan."

"Oh, is that so?" Lech responded. "I guess we have nothing to worry about then."

Marek was ready to bark at Lech to be serious but Serpentine raised his hand for silence. "There are things that you did not need to know, captain. You were a hunter, sent to track down the targets I decide. I have soldiers for fighting my wars, I have my hunters for hunting."

"Of course," Marek conceded. "I apologize for my arrogance. I am ready to continue being your hunter. Allow me to continue my pursuit of Beldaken. Rebels or no rebels, I will bring him down."

"That might be unnecessary," Serpentine answered. "The rebels are planning to make their move soon. Beldaken will be coming to us."

"They actually plan on attacking Marjan," Lech said with a chuckle. "Can you believe that? Even all the might of the Church couldn't take this city."

"Kasimir, how do the the defenses of Marjan look?" Serpentine asked. "I understand we're a little short-handed these days."

Kasimir the Black took a few moments to consider the question before responding. "The barracks of Marjan proper are less than a quarter full. The main body has not yet returned and several contingents have been called elsewhere. However, the palace guard is still at full strength. Whatever numbers these rebels boast, they will be crushed if they should come after the palace."

"I want the palace guard to supplement our forces at the inner gate," Serpentine commanded. "And I want you to take command there personally. Marjan is too big for us guard everywhere, but if the rebels mean to assault the palace they will have to go through that gate. If they are unable to get through the gate, they will be crushed up against it. Can I count on you to hold it?"

"Yes, my emperor."

"Then get to it. Mr. Lechin, if you would be so kind, Captain Kasimir would benefit from any information you have about the rebels."

"My knowledge is at his disposal," Lech said with a courteous bow.

Kasimir left silently and Lech followed behind. Marek awaited

P.F. Davids

anxiously for his own assignment. Serpentine had grown silent and Marek could do nothing but watch as Ragnar paced around the front of the throne.

Finally, Serpentine spoke. "Marek, you have always been effective and capable. For a while, I had my eye on you for a spot in my personal guard, but I think you would grow bored, and it would be such a terrible waste of such an amazing Willer as you. I promoted you to captain, although you are worthy of much greater titles. Colonel? Maybe even, one day, General? You have the loyalty. You have the skill. You're a natural leader. The only thing that can limit you is your ambition."

"My emperor?" Marek asked, unsure where Serpentine was going with this. He was not in the market for yet another promotion.

"I like to reward those who have served me faithfully, captain. I like to see them get what they desire. So tell me, what is it you desire most, right at this very instant?"

Marek did not hesitate. There was only one thing he wanted right now. "Another opportunity to bring down Reis Beldaken."

Serpentine smiled. "You just might get that chance, captain."

Chapter 30

For the fourth time that night, and the twelfth time since leaving Rochest, Kester inspected the armor the rebels had provided for him. Like Lunn's, it seemed to be cobbled together from an assortment of different armor sets. The cuirass did not quite match the faulds, the helm was a barbute of an old style. The guantlets seemed to be a new model, lighter and with better movement in the fingers than Kester had been accustomed to, while the greaves seemed older than he was. Everything was covered in scratches and dents from hard use, but as far as Kester could tell, everything was still sturdy. Nothing life threatening, anyway.

Still, it didn't hurt to be careful. Especially on the eve of a major battle.

Reis was stretched lazily in front of the fire. He was the only one who seemed completely at ease. Avis was sitting at the edge of the camp, sharpening her sword. She had been working the whetstone across the blade for hours with serious concentration. Kester had never imagined that Avis's face could be serious. Kindra was sitting by herself, pale faced and trembling noticeably. Apparently, whatever had given her the courage to volunteer to be the rebel's secret weapon had worn off. Too late to back out of it now, though. Even Pash seemed nervous, staring solemnly at the fire. Although, telling the difference between nervousness and excitement with him was difficult.

But to look at Reis you would think that tomorrow was just another day, if not a particularly dull one. You would never expect that in just a few hours, they would be regrouping with a bunch of dangerous rebels on a suicide mission against the Empire. Reis actually looked calmer now than Kester had ever seen him, like he found the imminent danger soothing.

Maybe he is just really confident about our chances. This is why Kester sought him out, isn't it? To be the merciless demon who would not wince in the face of the emperor?

He thought back to when he first set off on his impossible task. Back when it had been just him and Darius. So much had happened since then. Darius was gone. In his place was an odd assortment of allies with tenuous reasons for being here. The Church was gone. In its place was the Resistance, who likely would also cease to exist after tomorrow. Where did that leave him?

Kindra was shaking more noticeably now. It looked like she was going to be sick. Kester looked to Reis but he did not seem to notice or care. It would be up to him to make sure Kindra didn't lose her nerve.

He took a seat next to her. She barely seemed to notice.

"Scary, isn't it?" he asked. She nodded. "Nothing to be ashamed of, you know? Everyone gets some jitters before a battle."

"I know," she said softly.

Kester was struggling for something to say. He tried to imagine what Demos would say if he was here. Surely he would have had some kind of rousing speech at a moment's notice that would lift Kindra's spirits and fill her courage. And here Kester was, desperately trying to find two words to put together.

"I think it's time for a fireside chat," Pash chimed in from the other side of the fire.

"What?"

"It's a Mankuri tradition. On a night when a battle is looming, men gather around the fire and share stories. They talk about themselves, the battles they have fought, the trials they have been through. Men who share stories build trust, and fight better together."

Kester frowned across the fire. He wasn't sure stories were going to do anyone any good.

"I'll lead," Pash said firmly, making it clear this was not a matter open to discussion. "I will share the tale of my first battle. Might be it'll help you find some courage." He looked away from the fire with a look of concentration on his face. To Kester's surprise both Reis and Avis were looking at the big man with some interest. *Seems everyone could use a good distraction.*

"Back before the Empire started raiding our homes, the Mankuri were just one of many clans who called the mountains home," Pash started. He spoke in the slow, clear tone of an experienced storyteller. "The strongest, of course, but that didn't stop the other clans from trying to prove otherwise. There was one clan especially that had it out for us, the Hakuri. Our clans were rivals for generations. Fought tooth and nail for every inch of worthless rock between us. And it so happens my first battle was over one of those rocks."

His eyes drifted and his face broke out in a smile. *Fond memories?* Kester couldn't imagine smiling about his first battle. All he could remember of it was the paralyzing fear.

"It was right after I completed my trial, hunted my hawken. They put a weapon in my hand, a battleaxe half as big as I was at the time, and sent me alongside a few of our seasoned men to fight for a path that did not really mean much for us, but the Hakuri held it so we wanted it. The night before we had a fireside chat, just like this. I got to hear the tales of our veteran warriors, the battles they won, the enemies they defeated, the odds they overcame. Really got my blood going. By the end of it I was so excited I couldn't sleep at all. All I could think of was proving myself on the battlefield and all the glory I was going to win. I was ready to take on the whole Hakuri clan myself."

He looked back towards the fire, his smile slowly fading. "We got to the path early the next morning. The Hakuri looked fierce, but we were fiercer. They outnumbered us, but I felt no fear. I was eager to wet my axe with their blood. I picked the biggest one of them out, a nasty looking bastard with a mace big around as my head. I raised my axe and charged ahead, loudest war cry I could muster on my lips."

"And let me guess," Reis ventured. "You killed him, charged through the enemy lines, and won glory and honor and all that crap."

Pash laughed. "Hardly. I barely got within a few strides of the bastard when he smacked me across the side of the head with that mace. Nearly burst my head right open." He dug his fingers through his beard and tried to part some of it aside to show his face beneath it. Kester could barely make out a nasty looking scar. "Put me down good. Gave me a new respect for a good blunt weapon. Why I decided to pick up the hammer." He motioned to his weapon.

"Inspiring," Reis muttered.

"Well, that's not the point of the story. There I was, on the ground, sense knocked out of me. Nasty looking bastard standing over me, mace raised, ready to crush my head into pulp. Next thing I know one of our men is over me, clashing mace with axe. Another one grabbed me by the legs and pulled me to safety. I blacked out shortly after. By the time I came to the battle was over, we had won, and I was missing a few of my teeth. But I was alive."

"Still not seeing the point," Reis said.

"The point is this. In the end, in a battle, it doesn't matter much if you go in with experience or without it, eager or afraid. What matters most is who you go into battle with. You can survive anything with the right men around you." He nodded to Kester, then to Reis, and even to Avis. "Some tough ones around this fire. I think we just might manage to survive."

"I sure as hell don't intend to die tomorrow," Reis added.

"I doubt Serpentine is planning on it, either," Avis said. "Funny how plans change."

Despite himself, Kester felt reassured by Pash's story. Demos had often talked about how important his companions were in his adventures, how he counted on them to watch his back.

Until they all died, anyway.

Kindra also seemed to be feeling a bit better. She had stopped shaking so much and was glancing at Kester. *Relying on me to keep her safe.*

"Your turn," Pash grunted, pulling Kester away from Kindra's gaze.

"What?"

"We each got to share a story," Pash stated, as if it was an obvious fact.

"Come on, Church-boy, surely you have plenty of tales of valor to please us with," Reis said with a smug smile.

Kester didn't want to admit that his brother had kept him from battle for much of his career, and there was little valor in his battles since.

"Afraid no tales jump to mind. Maybe someone else should go," Kester pleaded.

"Don't have to be about a battle," Pash said. Apparently there was no getting out of it. "Just something to let the others around the fire get a sense of your worth."

"How about how you joined the Church?" Kindra suggested.

Boring a story as any, but I guess I have to say something.

"My brother, Demos, and I were orphans. I was too young at the time to remember what happened to our parents, but I remember Demos taking me to a local Church for shelter. We ended up being raised by clerics and joining the Church itself when we were old enough. Demos was large and athletic and he was immediately asked to join the Church's military arm. I was smaller and more sickly, so they started to educate me as a priest."

"I guess priesthood didn't stick," Avis said. "Kind of glad it didn't. You're preachy enough already."

"I took to the lessons well enough, but I always wanted to be with my brother in the military. I trained on my own every day, trying to prove them wrong. Against the protests of my brothers, I was finally permitted to be trained as a soldier. Unfortunately, Demos was always several steps ahead. By the time I finished my training, my brother was already making a name for himself as a great hero of the Church. I've spent most of my life trying to catch him."

"Yeah, well now he's dead and you're not," Reis said bluntly. "Kill Serpentine tomorrow and all of Demos's accomplishments will seem trivial in comparison."

Kester winced at this blunt reminder. He remembered his brother smiling confidently before he set off on a mission. Before he set to shutting down Reis's alchemic operations in Mordoven. Before he went to retrieve High Cleric Delia from radicals who had taken her hostage. Before the Battle of Bigasti when his reputation as a hero would be cemented. Every time Kester would watch him go, he would count the number of heroic acts he would have to accomplish in order to catch up. Maybe then Demos would allow him to join his adventurers.

Now here he was, on the precipice of accomplishing something great, and Demos was dead. He could catch him, surpass him even, but he would never get that recognition from him.

"Afraid the story is not much more interesting than that," Kester said, desperate to change the topic. "I think someone else should go."

Avis jumped on the invitation. "This seems like the perfect time to share the tale of my path to becoming a sellsword. I must warn you, it is an epic tale, filled with excitement and sorrow. Don't be alarmed if you feel it right here." She put one hand over her heart.

"Sounds like a good time to take a piss," Reis said, feigning like he was going to get up.

"All right, all right. I'll just tell the short version." Avis shook her head. "No sense for the dramatic. Anyway, my tale begins in the Westernlands, in the city of Capua. If you haven't heard of it, Capua is a city of the arts. Music, theatre, sculpting statues and painting murals, they ate that crap up. And there is no art they love more than the art of combat. The grand coliseum of Capua, capable of seating thousands and always packed full, where men test their martial skill against great beasts and one another." She motioned with her hands through the air as she described the coliseum, like she was trying to paint a picture.

"Is all of this leading up to you telling us you were a coliseum fighter?" Reis asked.

Avis shot him a nasty glare. "It was a little more complicated that."

"You shouldn't interrupt," Pash grunted. "You'll get your turn. Avis, go on."

"Thank you, Pash. I had the notion that somewhere underneath all the hair was a proper gentleman." Pash scratched at his beard like the notion confused him. "As I was saying, the coliseum produced no shortage of large names, not least among them was my father, Seraph the Striker. I have five brothers, each trying to follow our father's footsteps. As you have all discovered to my embarrassment, there is a woman underneath this hardened exterior, and women are not allowed to take part in the coliseum, so I could not join them. I thought it was terribly unfair — after all, I could easily defeat any of my brothers when we trained together. So I first took up the disguise of a man so I could compete."

She rose to her feet and drew her sword. She flourished it quickly and showed off some quick jabs. "I quickly rose through the ranks and defeated all my brothers, even my father, in fair combat. The crowd was going wild. Naive as I was, I thought that a good time to reveal myself. How proud my father will be, I thought. How the crowd will be shocked but accepting, I thought. Perhaps they will even change the rules, I impressed them so." She shook her head. "Of course, quite the opposite happened. The crowd went into an uproar. My opponents claimed they had been defeated through deceit and dishonorable tactics. My own father denounced me, and none of my brothers would stand for me. I ended up having to flee the city in the middle of the night to save myself from prosecution."

Her easy smile had dissolved. For a moment she looked weak and vulnerable. She looked away, and when she looked back her smile had returned. Kester wondered how she always managed that.

"I never learned any other trade, so I had to find a way to live by my sword. I could not join in the army, so that meant banditry or mercenary work. I was strongly considering the former when I had the luck to fall in with the captain of the Company of the Red Hand. He is the one who taught me the ins and outs of mercenary work and advised me to maintain the persona of a man. I'm proud to say I built quite the reputation with the company, and became one of the most famous sellswords in all of Westlands."

"And yet here you are in the east," Reis said.

Avis shrugged. "I've made a lot of poor decisions in my life, some of which forced me to come seek my fortune on the other side of the world. But those are stories for another day." She sighed. "I promised myself I would not make the same mistakes here, that I would be more careful of who I made my enemy. And yet I find myself now making an enemy of the greatest military power in all the world. So much for that promise."

"Regretting taking the job?" Kester asked.

"I'm not much for regrets," Avis said, smile beaming. "Things are what they are. And at least it's not boring."

"Unlike your story," Reis said dully.

Avis just smiled back at him. "Well, perhaps yours will be more entertaining. I believe it is your turn."

"Oh, fun," Reis said, suddenly perking up with interest. "I wonder what story I should tell? Perhaps one my exploits slaughtering the men of the Church?" Kester grimaced but refused to rise to Reis's bait. "No, they never put up enough of a fight to make a good story. The time I single handedly turned a mercenary company? No, I already told Kester that one. How about a more recent one, when I killed an Empire colonel who thought he could press me into Serpentine's service?"

A thought came to Kester's mind of a topic Reis had been carefully avoiding since they met. Making Reis feel a little uncomfortable might be gratifying.

"We've all been sharing the stories that made us what we are," Kester said. "Pash's first battle. My joining the Church. Avis becoming a mercenary. Why don't you tell us what made you, well, you?"

Reis frowned. "I don't know what you mean."

"I think he means this whole 'angry loner who doesn't care about anyone but himself' act you have going on," Avis said.

Reis somehow frowned even harder. "I've just always been like this."

Avis prodded further. "Oh, come now. Surely something happened that turned that little heart of yours to stone. What was it? Get jilted by a lover? Robbed of your inheritance? Oh, no, something more romantic! You're a prince, exiled from your rightful homeland, hardened by a tough life on the run!"

Reis raised one eyebrow. Pash looked concernedly at Reis like he was really considering the possibly.

"No," Reis said.

Avis sighed. "Is it so much to ask that I meet just one exile prince in my travels?"

"I'm more interested in how Reis acquired his skills than his personality," Kindra chimed in. "Master swordsman, alchemist, Willer in control of his abilities. Each pursuit could take a lifetime of practice and study, yet you've mastered them so young."

"Young?" Reis smiled. "How old do you think I am?"

Something about the way Reis said it made Kester uneasy. For how long the tales about Reis Beldaken had been around, Reis had to be even older than Demos. But where Demos's face had begun to show signs of age, with its lines and lightening hair, Reis's face was smooth and unblemished. Kester had just assumed that Reis had one those faces that never seemed to age, but the way Reis was smiling now, Kester had to wonder if perhaps he was closer to his dreams of immortality than he had let on.

Kindra smiled back at Reis. "I never imagined you'd be so shy. The fearless Reis Beldaken, embarrassed to talk about his own past."

Reis sighed, defeated. "I don't understand why you care so much, but fine." He sighed again and grimaced like thinking about his past was physically painful. "My father was a soldier and my mother was a school teacher. During the day my mother had me in my books, drilling history, geography, and numbers into my head. Then in the evening, when my father was back from his duties, he would have me training with the sword till I could barely lift my arms. Quite an obnoxious schedule, though I suppose I owe them for my current versatility."

"Your mother taught you alchemy?" Kindra asked.

"No, I picked that up later. But she did teach me how to control my ability. She was a Willer herself, and had the notion that the power might run in the blood. When I started to show signs of possessing an ability, she added a couple of hours of control training. I hated it even more than my sword lessons. It would make my head feel like it was ready to explode. At the time, I could barely extend my shadow a few inches. It seemed so pointless." He paused. "My ability has gotten me out of many tough spots. Guess it was worth it, in the end."

"Getting nostalgic for your parents, Reis?" Avis said. "It is nice to get an image of you as a 'caring son' as opposed to 'demon spawned from the pits of the Dark.'"

"If it matters to my image at all, I killed my father," Reis said, in a manner-of-fact tone.

Patricide. Once again, Reis revealed a new low.

For some reason, Avis was chuckling. "Now that sounds more like you."

"Why would you do that?" Kindra asked. "You must have had a good reason."

Reis smiled. "Oh, a brilliant one. But you were interested in how I acquired my skill-set, and that is unrelated." He stretched out in front of the fire. "I'm tired of talking about myself, though. Kindra can take her turn. Why don't you tell us how you learned to have such a control of your ability?"

"You're just going to try and change the topic like that?" Kindra asked.

"You have a couple hundred lives depending on your ability tomorrow," Reis said. "Something you volunteered for, by the way. Which topic seems more relevant?"

Kindra jumped to her feet. She kicked some dirt at Reis then walked hurriedly away from the campfire.

Reis shrugged. "Guess that means we aren't getting a story from her."

Avis craned her head to watch Kindra walk away. "I think you made her angry."

"What tipped you off?"

"I think it was the part where she kicked dirt on you."

Pash scratched his beard. "Women are hard to figure wherever you go."

Kester doubted it would do any good, but he thought he should try to reason with Reis. "Maybe you should go after her. Apologize."

"I'm not in the mood to act the sweet boy. I don't know if you recall, Church-boy, but we're trying to assassinate the most powerful man in the world tomorrow. I have to stay in the right mindset."

"Fine, I'll go." Kester quickly got to his feet and turned his back on Reis before he had to deal with any more of his condescension. He found Kindra seated against a tree just out of earshot of the camp.

"I'm fine," she said when she saw him approach. "I just wanted a moment alone."

"Alone or away from Reis?" He took a seat next to her.

"I know I owe him my life, and I know you're relying on me to keep him motivated. But he's just so…" She trailed off, but Kester got the point.

"I understand. He saved my life, too. He's not a man its easy to be in debt to."

She looked him in the eyes. "Do you think he is an evil man?"

Kester looked away, unable to hold her gaze. "I've been trying to figure that out since I met him. He is selfish, arrogant, and violent. But evil? There does seem to be some good buried within him. The fact that we are still alive is proof of that."

"Or he saved us for his own reasons. He needs you and he wants me. Perhaps there is nothing redeeming about him."

Kester shrugged. "Perhaps."

"It seems to be the kind of man I attract." Kindra looked at him at him with eyes wide and full of despair. She always appeared to be so strong, it surprised him to see her look so vulnerable.

"After tomorrow, you can go wherever you want. You never have to see Reis again if you don't want to." *Assuming we survive tomorrow.*

"Go where? I have no home to return to, no family. I'll be trying to start over in a new, strange place, with strange people and no coin."

Kester put a reassuring hand on her shoulder. "I promise I'll do whatever I can to make sure you're comfortable before we part."

Kindra put a hand over his. "What if I don't want us to part?"

She looked him in the eyes and time seemed to slow. He knew this look. He had seen it hundreds of times when Delia was around his brother. His heart began to speed up like in the moments before a battle. Despite the dirt and grime built up from the last week on the road, she was still beautiful. Even moreso, with an earthy charm. Her hand was warm against his. His face grew unbearably flush.

He forced himself to his feet suddenly. "I should get back to the camp. I still have preparations to make for tomorrow."

She looked disappointed but made no move to stop him. As he walked back towards the campfire he forced himself to remember what was important. The upcoming battle. The death of Serpentine and the end of the Empire. He could not allow himself any distractions. *I must remain focused.*

He glanced back over his shoulder. Kindra was lost in the darkness. *At whatever cost.*

Chapter 31

"We already have some of our men inside the city," Lysander was saying with great enthusiasm. Reis got the impression he was enjoying his moment of triumph a little too much, considering the real battle was just about to take place. "They snuck across the walls in the dark of night. In an hour's time they will begin causing a diversion by starting fires and generally making a mess of things. This should draw the majority of the city guard and leave us fairly uncontested as we make our way through the city's main gate and towards the inner gate." He waved his arm in the direction of the city. "We expect minimum resistance at the inner gate. We shall fight them off while Kindra gets the gate open. If we're quick about it, we shall be through the inner gate before the city's forces are organized against us. With the gate closed behind us, they shall be cut off from the palace."

Reis feigned at attention while wishing the pompous bastard would get on with it. They had already been over the plan more than enough times.

"The palace guard will be forced to come out and engage us, leaving the palace undefended. Meanwhile, Brax will lead two dozen of our best through the underground tunnels and into the palace. They will strike quickly for the throne room and assassinate Serpentine." He made a chopping motion with his hand. "Afterwards, we scatter and try to make our own ways out of the city and regroup here."

'If anyone is still alive' was implied.

"I'm with Brax's group," Reis demanded. "I didn't come this far not to get the satisfaction of killing Serpentine myself. Church-boy, you go into the assault. Stay close to Kindra, try to get her out of this alive."

Kester glanced over at Kindra and nodded. She looked away. Those two had been acting strange around each other all morning, but Reis did not have the luxury to worry about it.

Lysander also nodded, as if he had a say in the matter and his disapproval would mean a change in plan. "I'm also putting Lunn on her defense."

That warranted a grimace from Kester. "That drunk?"

"Not that drunk when it matters," the disheveled man said as he approached. Lunn did seem a bit more sober than the last time they met. He was able to speak without slurring his words and walked steadily and confidently, though Reis could still smell alcohol on his breath.

Lysander looked more offended than Lunn was. "Lunn is one of my best swords and has more combat experience than any other of my men."

"One more defender can't hurt," Kindra said.

"I'll be joining 'em," Pash grunted. "Mankuri warriors belong in the fight, not sneaking around."

Avis looked like she was carefully considering her options. "Guess I'll join you in the tunnels, Reis. You are my 'employer', after all."

Brax stood just to the side of Lysander, yanking at his bushy mustache like he intended to pull it right from his face. "I suppose it's alright. As long as you both can be quiet. Don't want Serpentine to hear us coming."

Like he doesn't already know.

Reis forced a smile. "Don't worry, you won't even know I'm there."

Brax yanked at his mustache one more time. "Alright. We should be off now. We have some ground to cover before we get into the tunnels."

Kester stepped forward and extended his hand. "Good luck to you, Reis."

For some reason, Reis could not help but think back to his dream. Kester killing him right after Serpentine fell. He felt the urge to smack his hand away.

Instead he grabbed it. It was likely one or both of them wouldn't live through the day, and they had been through enough together that he warranted that much. "And to you, Church-boy."

The vial of elixir was secured inside his shirt. It was not the same quality as the elixir he had left Alleways with, but in a pinch, it could mean the difference between life and death. He had left the other vial with Kester, for however much good it would do in the middle of a heated battle. Knowing Kester's chivalry, he would sooner use it to save Kindra's life than his own. In fact, Reis was counting on it.

"Looks like the descent into hell, doesn't it?" Avis peered down

down the steep staircase they had assembled in front of. "A real homecoming for you, eh?"

It certainly was an intimidating approach. A small, crumbling archway marked the start of the stairs, black stone covered in mold and overgrown in a with blood red ivy. Over the arch some words had once been carved, but they had faded so severely that they were now nothing more than indecipherable runes. The steps were uneven and descended sharply. One wrong step, and there would be nothing to stop you from tumbling down into the darkness. The walls of the stairway were lined with the same black stone as the archway.

The boy, Lucas, squinted against the darkness. "What do you think this path was used for?"

"Couldn't tell you," Brax said. "But it connects to the Marjan sewers, that is all that matters." He pulled at the corner of his mustache. "Well, in we go."

Brax took the lead himself. He carefully picked his way down the steps with a lantern held out against the darkness. His two dozen men followed after in pairs, with torches passed between them. As they had discussed the previous night, Reis and Avis lingered in the back, leaving a small gap between them and the rebels.

"What do you think Serpentine is like?" Avis pondered.

"What do you mean?"

"My experience in the Westlands is that kings love themselves and love their image. You can hardly go into any city without finding statues and portraits by the score. This one shows the king as a great warrior and leader of men at the front of a charge he was never a part of. This one shows him as caregiver, feeding the poor and downtrodden."

"A bunch of bullshit."

Avis chuckled. "Being a king seems to have a way of going to your head. I think they might actually believe half the shit in their portrayals. Point is, I've seen none of the kind from Serpentine. Not a single statue, or portrait, or banner featuring a crude likeness. For a man as ambitious as Serpentine you'd expect to him everywhere, but I actually don't have a clue what he looks like."

Reis had never considered it before. Now that he did, the thought was somewhat unsettling. He had always had a vision of what Serpentine looked like and now realized that he had nothing to base that image on.

"Serpentine likes to maintain a god-like image." To Reis's

surprise, Lucas had dropped back from the rebels to let them catch up. "At least, that's what Lysander told me when I asked him that same question. He never made an actual claim at godhood, but he works to make his followers think of him as something greater than human. Portraits would only serve to put a human face on him. It's the reason he has such a problem with the Church, the religion detracts from his image."

"Lysander is just full of insight, isn't he?" Reis said. "He didn't also tell you what Serpentine looks like, did he?"

The boy smiled knowingly. "He did. Golden blond hair, blood red eyes, death's smile upon his lips. He carries himself like a tiger that one day got up and put on a king's robes, regal but always ready to pounce."

Avis looked disappointed. "Huh. Not what I was expecting."

Reis was afraid to ask. "What were you expecting, exactly?"

"Honestly? Your twin."

Lucas rested his hands on the sheaths on his sides. "Well, at the end of the day he's going to look gutted at the end of my sword."

A lot of confidence in this kid.

"Lucas!" Brax called from the front. "Stay in position. Don't fall behind."

Lucas quickly rushed back to the front of the rebels, falling in a few steps behind his commander. The swords sheathed on either side of him clamored as he ran. Reis vaguely remembered seeing him in the rebel attack at Rochest, fighting with both swords at once. It took a special combination of arrogance and skill to fight like that, and based on what Reis could gleam of the kid's personality, he figured arrogance played the bigger role.

Reis gestured towards Lucas. "Keep an eye on that boy. I have a feeling he will let us know when it's time to make our move."

Avis didn't speak, just nodded her recognition.

The stairs were coming to an end. The stink of the sewers greeted them.

Soon, Marcus Serpentine. You will pay for what you did to my home and my research. All that familiar anger began to bubble up within him, and he allowed himself a moment to enjoy it. *Soon.*

P.F. Davids

Smoke was rising from somewhere within Marjan. Kester raised his hand to shield his eyes from the afternoon sun. He tried to get an idea of where the smoke was coming from, but Marjan was huge. The descriptions he had heard of it hardly did it justice. Buildings five or six stories high were packed tightly together and loomed threateningly overhead. They were occasionally broken up by towers of all sizes and shapes, some of which were taller than the highest spire in the Grandium. Even at this distance, the sounds of bustling populace filled the air.

In the far distance, past seemingly endless rows of imposing concrete buildings, the massive Palace of Marjan overshadowed it all. Its golden framework glistened in the sunlight like something out of Eternity. Kester had never been closer to Serpentine, but looking at that palace, he still felt impossibly far away.

Kester had been taught that the famous explorer Marjan had crossed the mountains that now bore his name, on a journey to found the greatest city in all of Kassia. Looking up at the great walls that surrounded the city, it seemed he had succeeded. It was not hard to imagine why Serpentine had made the city the capital of his Empire. Just the notion of assaulting such a city was ludicrous. And yet here Kester was, accompanying a hilariously tiny force marching towards those walls.

Lysander pointed up at a second pillar of smoke rising from somewhere within the city. "Our advance teams are starting fires within the city. The city guard should be nice and distracted dealing with them."

It would not be smart for nearly two hundred armed men to just walk up Marjan's walls. Most of them were cramped tight into covered wagons. The wagons approached the city as any trade caravan would. The rest followed close behind on foot, using the wagons to block them from the view of anyone atop the walls. If they were spotted too soon their whole plan would be in danger.

They were getting close to the wall now. Any second now it would come to swords with whoever was guarding the outer gate. Kester did his best to maintain a look of ease and confidence despite the fact that he felt sick to his stomach. Many of those around him looked similarly nervous. Except Pash. If he felt anything about the impending danger his stony face did not show it. He still refused to wear any armor, but he had at least been convinced to carry a shield to guard against arrows and bolts. The round shield seemed tiny compared to his massive frame.

Lunn raised his own shield to his face and tipped it back. It took Kester a moment to realize he was drinking from a flask strapped to the shield's back.

"You're getting drunk now?" Kester snapped.

Lunn just gave a passive shrug. "Might be my last chance. Want a swig?"

Kester wanted to shout "No!" instinctively. All of his training screamed that he needed to be focused absolutely on his duty, that he should offended at the mere suggestion. "Actually, yes. Pass that here."

Lunn grinned, at least Kester thought it was a grin behind that mesh of greasy hair, and tossed his shield over at Kester. Kester couldn't remember the last time he had allowed himself a drink. Whatever Lunn was drinking was strong, and burned going down. Kester only allowed himself a tiny swallow for courage before passing the shield back to Lunn.

Lunn fussed with the shield's straps for a while as he put it back on his arm. "Nothing worse than a loose strap on your shield. When I die, it won't be because my shield fails me."

"Don't worry. Plenty of other things to kill you ahead." Still, Kester decided to double check his own shield's straps.

Kindra followed close behind. Lunn and Pash flanked her on either side. Her protectors. She looked nervous but determined, a far cry from her shakiness last night. Kester remembered when Delia became High Cleric right at the outset of the war with the Empire. She had had the same look then.

He winced as memories of Delia came to him. Her warm face when she congratulated him after his promotion. Her confidence when she preached to the troops on the righteousness of their cause. Seeing her and Demos together, trying to hide their burgeoning romance from the other members of the clergy.

Demos and Delia. Both dead now. And in all likeliness, he would be joining them by the end of the day.

Lysander motioned forward. "We're at the gate now. Be ready."

The first of their wagons was stopped by a bored looking guard. The wagon would not withstand much scrutiny, but the guards did not seem like they would be giving it much. They were completely at ease.

After all, who would be stupid enough to cause trouble in the capital of the Empire?

"Big merchant caravan," the guard with the largest star on his uniform said to the driver of the lead wagon.

"A lot of money to be made in Marjan," the driver replied. He did not look directly at the guard as he spoke, just continued looking forward with an unfocused gaze.

The guard glanced around at the wagons. Kester held his breath, certain that he would see the mass of rebels hiding behind them.

"You need a permit to trade here. Everyone else is being instructed to bring their trade to Rochest."

The driver still didn't turn to face the guard. "Oh, the permit. Yes, I have one of those."

The guard frowned. "Well why didn't you say so sooner? We both would have saved time. Come on, produce your permit. Don't have all day."

The driver reached slowly into a satchel on the seat next to him. There was a flash of metal and suddenly the guard had a dagger buried in face. The driver pushed the body away from him as he reached under his seat for a sword.

The other guards stood dumbstruck. One was staring stupidly down at the body of his former commanding officer. Another was looking wide-eyed at the driver. One had the good sense to go for his sword, but was fumbling with the sheath.

The rebels came pouring out at them from the wagons all at once. A collective shout went out as they bore down on the guard with swords and axes. Before Kester could have even reached the gate, the battle was over. The guards lay dead in front of him. Only one of them seemed to have managed to draw his sword. One was cut down from behind as he tried to run.

Atop the gate, an alarm was sounding. The watchmen were scrambling for their bolts. The rebels would be well out of sight before they organized.

"Forward!" Lysander shouted. "To the inner-gate!"

And with that, two hundred rebels invaded the capital of the Empire. Kester swallowed hard as he passed under the wall.

Light guide me.

During his days as a thief, Reis had made his way through a variety of sewers. He could not remember one that ever smelled this bad. *What is Serpentine feeding his people?*

Avis walked alongside him with her usual smirk plastered on her face, as if she didn't even know she was surrounded by human waste. The rebels ahead of them were far less stoic. One young man suddenly stepped out of position to vomit, making a mess of his short beard. Another had painstakingly wrapped an old flag of some northern nationaround his head in a symbol of defiance. It was now in his hands, held up against his mouth to try to block out the stench.

Brax still led the group. To his credit, the conditions did nothing to slow him. Lucas was only a step behind him. The kid had slowed down a bit when they first entered the sewers as he choked and gagged. Reis imagined the sewers were nothing like the kid's dream life of the rebel hero. He had recovered well and now walked eagerly near the front. If he continued like this, he would outpace Brax soon. Reis was watching him carefully.

The sewers were full of twists and turns, paths used for the waste to flow and paths for those who maintained the tunnels. Reis had taken the time to memorize the whole layout. The path the rebels had chosen would take them into the palace through an old maintenance corridor. Reis suspected they wouldn't get that far, which is why he had committed to memory three other paths into the palace.

They came to another fork. Brax motioned to the left and the rebels began to follow. Reis peered to the right. He knew that direction would put him on another path. He needed to be ready to find an alternate route at any time.

Lucas made the next turn a step ahead of Brax. There was an eager spring in his step.

"We're close now!" he declared excitedly.

Brax did not share his enthusiasm. "Slow down, Lucas. Back to your place."

Lucas wasn't listening. He was already several strides ahead and showed no signs of slowing.

They were coming up on a sharp right turn. Reis slowed down and motioned for Avis to do the same. He didn't like not being able to see around the corner.

Lucas did not pay the turn any mind. He made for it, practically sprinting.

"Lucas!" Brax called out.

Reis took two steps back as he sensed what was coming next. Lucas turned the corner without even peeking around it. Just a second later several bolts sprouted from his chest. He stood there for a few seconds like he hadn't even noticed he had been shot. Then he dropped suddenly on his face.

The fate of heroes.

The rebels were already drawing their weapons. Brax at the front was barking orders but Reis couldn't make them out. He was too busy retracing their steps as fast as he could. Avis was right beside him, her smirk entirely gone.

Behind them was the sounds of a confrontation. As Reis had expected, the imperials had gotten word of the rebel's plans and laid an ambush for them. Lucas had spoiled their element of surprise. Now they would have to engage the rebels directly. Maybe Lucas's sacrifice would allow Brax and his men to take a few of the imperials down with them.

They reached the fork they had passed earlier and went down the path to the right. Reis mapped in his head the path to the palace they would now take. They had not gone far before the sounds of fighting petered out, then stopped completely. Brax and his men were dead.

Neither Reis or Avis said anything. They didn't need to. This had been the plan.

The imperials would believe the rebel plan had been successfully thwarted. Still, they needed to hurry in case the imperials decided to sweep the rest of the sewers. The sooner they were in the palace the better.

Now it was up to the Church-boy to keep up his end of things. Otherwise they would be walking into a palace filled with guards. And to their deaths.

Chapter 32

Kasimir could not understand why, with all the innovations in modern armor, they could not make a set that wasn't hot as an oven. This morning, when he opened his window, he had been greeted by a cool breeze that marked the start of a nice day. But in this armor, he might as well be in the middle of the desert.

A soldier on horseback came riding up at full speed. His horse skidded to a stop and the rider jumped off. He snapped off a quick salute.

"Report," Kasimir commanded.

"Sir, the rebels have breached the wall. They are heading this way."

Kasimir nodded, then remembered that the nod would be nearly imperceptible with his helm.

Seems our information was accurate. Insanity, attacking here.

"What are the numbers?"

The scout fidgeted nervously. The fearsome reputation that came with being Kasimir the Black had its advantages, but watching soldiers nearly wet themselves while they carefully picked their words was not one of them. It slowed the whole process down.

Finally, the scout found his voice. "It is a bit of chaos, sir, getting an accurate number is difficult. They came through the gate en masse but have not stuck together in the city. We are getting conflicting reports from different lookout points, but we're estimating just over one-hundred men."

As expected.

"Keep an eye on them. If you see any variance in their path or behavior, I expect to be notified immediately."

"Sir!" The scout nearly stumbled over himself getting back on the horse, eager to be away.

Kasimir turned his attention to his own men. Two hundred members of the city guard, hand-picked for the job by the guard captain himself, though that wasn't saying much. The city guard had rarely had a chance to be tested in a large scale battle. How well any of them would do in a one on one confrontation with a desperate, battle hardened rebel was questionable. Fortunately, Kasimir had the numbers.

Greater numbers would have been better, but for the ambush to be successful, they had to remain undetected until the last possible moment. Any more men, and the rebels might spot them and scatter like roaches. They had to remain concealed until the rebels reached the gate. Then, as the rebels struggled to get the gate open, they would take them from behind. Backed up against the gate they would have nowhere to run and would be truly crushed, once and for all.

One less problem, though I'm sure the emperor will have another for me tomorrow.

He remembered back when he used to have lofty dreams of a comfortable life made possible by the spoils of war. Now his dreams amounted to being allowed to sleep in once in a while.

One problem at a time.

The gate itself was only manned by a dozen soldiers, none of whom had any idea what was coming. They would be relying on the weight and strength of the gate to slow the rebels.

Kasimir faced his troops and raised his hand for attention. He did not need to say anything; everyone was silent immediately. "The Resistance is on its way right now to seize this gate. We will be ready for them." His voice boomed in his helmet and expressed a level of confidence he didn't feel. "No one makes a move until I give the say-so. Anyone who gives away our position won't have to wait for the enemy to kill them." He could see on their faces that the threat had hit home. Facing the enemy was a serious and frightening prospect, but disobeying Kasimir was a thousand times worse. "When I give the signal, we hit them all at once. Accept no surrender and let none get away. Understood?"

"Yes, sir!" his men replied in unison.

"Good. Positions!"

Back when Serpentine first took the city, a good portion of the area around the gate had been undeveloped, allowing the men on the gate to see for a greater distance. Marjan's population grew rapidly since becoming the capital of the Empire, and the quick development saw buildings being constructed closer and closer to the gate. A foolish decision from a military standpoint, but at the moment it would serve to help conceal a waiting ambush. They had cleared some lower apartments and now waited for their chance to strike.

Kasimir watched for the enemy while envisioning a nice, cool bath back in his apartments in the palace. He had been sweating in his armor for so long, he didn't doubt that he smelled as fearsome as he looked.

One problem at a time.

In his time in training, Kester's instructors had made him run five miles every morning in the weight of armor. That experience did not properly prepare him for the task of marching through an enemy capital accompanied by a rebel horde into what he had been assured was a trap. He could feel his heart pounding in his throat; he couldn't tell how much was from the physical exertion and how much was from the fear of inevitable death. The sun was not helping matters.

The rebels had split up into five separate groups shortly after passing through the gates, in order to confuse and distract any pursuing troops. Kester's unit's path took them directly through the heart of the city. As they marched down the main street, the city's civilians desperately parted to get out of the way of this sudden swarm. Others stood by the side and stared dumbstruck at this sudden breach of their daily lives. More appeared from the windows of the tall buildings that surrounded them on every side. Hundreds of eyes watched them everywhere they went, all with that same look of mixed curiosity and fear. Who were these heavily armed men? Why were they here? Was a battle about to break out in the streets?

Kester found himself constantly scanning the crowds for a sign of a threat. He didn't fail to appreciate that they were massively outnumbered at any given moment by the throngs of civilians. Even if there wasn't a soldier hiding behind one of those windows with a crossbow, ready to take pot shots at the rebels, all it took was one brave soul to lead the citizens in the defense of their city. It had happened many times during history, civilians grabbing whatever kind of weapon they could get their hands on to try and repel the invading forces. By all accounts, Marjan had flourished as Serpentine's capital, and it would not surprise Kester if its citizens did not wish imperials removed. But so far, they just seemed to be watching.

They came upon a market square. Merchants struggled to gather their wares before fleeing, stall-keepers knocked over their small booths as they tried to scramble for cover, shoppers dropped their bundles where they stood before sprinting for safety. If this were a proper raid, the market would be a treasure trove of valuables and resources that would be picked clean. The rebels had another target.

At the other side of the market, a group of imperial guards had finally gotten their act together enough to create a barricade. A baker's dozen of them stood behind a pile of overturned wagons and stalls that clogged the road. Somewhere ahead of Kester orders were shouted; he couldn't tell from which side. He reacted by instinct. He raised his shield out in front of him just as he heard the strum of crossbow bolts being let loose. Nothing impacted his shield, but he could hear the bolts find homes in the shields and armor of those around him. Somewhere to his right, a rebel dropped dropped to the ground with a fresh bolt in his face.

Kester worriedly looked over his shoulder for Kindra. She was fine, keeping pace with the others despite the danger. A step in front of her was Lunn. He had imposed his body in front of her to protect her and had splinters of bolt fragments stuck in his shield. *Perhaps he is not so much a coward as he seems.*

More orders were shouted, though the rebels already knew what they had to do. They could not afford to lose pace for even a moment, or risk being overwhelmed by imperial reinforcements. Kester sprinted towards the makeshift barricade. Many of the rebels were already ahead of him. Behind the barricade, the imperials were struggling to reload their crossbows. It was a complicated procedure when the stress was on. The rebels reached the barricade and started trying to break it down, shifting its components out of the way. A couple of the imperials got onto the top of the barricade and jabbed down with their swords at the rebels. One leaned over too far and got jabbed with a rebel sword instead.

Kester grabbed hold of the wheel of an overturned wagon. Pash grabbed the other side of it with his massive hands. Pash nodded and the two of them pulled. Slowly the wagon came out of place. Around them, the other rebels were succeeding in shifting other parts of the barricade. Exposed to superior numbers, the guards wasted no time in fleeing from the scene. An officer lingered for a moment, as if he was considering taking on the entire rebel force single-handedly, before turning and escaping himself.

The rebels poured through the barricade and further into the city. The buildings were newer here and packed even more tightly together. The curiosity of the citizenry seemed to have faded at the sound of conflict, and now they did all they could to get themselves indoors and out of the way. Windows were closed and doors were slammed shut. Soon the streets were emptied and a silence fell over the city.

Kester could not see the inner gate over the rows of buildings, but he knew they were getting close. Reis had been sure that whatever trap Serpentine had set would be sprung when they reached it. He had warned Kester not to let the rebels know a trap awaited them until the last possible moment, just in case the traitor amongst them still had a way of informing the imperials. Now seemed to be as good a time as any.

He caught Pash's eye. "Keep an eye on Kindra." He pushed himself to sprint to the front of the crowd. Lysander was there, leading his men from the front. A foolish choice, in Kester's opinion. Lysander's leadership was needed here, he shouldn't be taking such unnecessary risks.

"Lysander! I need a moment!"

Lysander motioned for him to follow alongside him. "Talk on the move. We can't afford a pause."

"The empire's going to be waiting for us at the gate."

Lysander didn't so much as blink. "Of course they are. But the gate is never too well defended. It's deep within the city, after all. Have some faith, we've caught the Empire with its pants down. By the time they rally the city's defense, we will have control of the gate."

"No, listen. The Empire set a trap and we're about to walk right into it. They will be waiting for us at the gate!"

"Getting cold feet, Belisario?"

"No." Kester struggled to find the right words. Lysander had a poor opinion of Reis; he doubted he would listen if he said "Reis has a hunch."

Lysander narrowed his eyes on Kester. "Why are you just telling me this now?"

"Does it matter? We need to form up a strong rear-guard should the imperials try to press us against the gate."

"If we take our focus away from the front it will take us longer to take the gate. We might give the imperials time to organize. What if you're wrong?"

"If I'm wrong we can shift our focus back to the gate. But if I'm right and we do nothing it will be slaughter."

Lysander looked like he was contemplating pushing Kester to

the ground and continuing on. "One result or another, we need to have a long talk about this once this is all over. But I can't ignore the possible threat, either. Get back in line, I'll make sure word gets out. Nothing sneaks up on us."

His fears somewhat alleviated, Kester fell back to his place beside Kindra.

"Everything alright up there?" Lunn asked.

"Fine. Just be on alert. The Empire may be planning a surprise for us."

"Nice to know they are thinking of us."

The gate was coming into view now. It wouldn't be long.

Light protect us.

Kasimir could hear the rebels coming long before he could see them. They came all at once, a cacophony of clanking armor, anxious yells, and drawn steel. Atop the gate, the small garrison scrambled for weapons they had never imagined they would need. By the time they had begun firing into the mass of rebels, the rebels were already responding with bolt and arrow. It was clear they were getting the best of the exchange.

He had to wait for the right moment to signal his men. If they attacked too soon the rebels who had not yet reached the gate might turn and scatter, and if they waited too long the gate might fall. It was a delicate balancing act. At least the numbers seemed to be as expected...

Another wave of rebels burst onto the scene, just as large as the first. They moved more cautiously and did not go straight for the gate. Instead, they kept some distance, forming a line facing away from the gate. Facing the direction in which Kasimir and his men were laying in wait.

A rearguard.

Kasimir had to keep himself from cursing out loud. A slip like that could allow his men to know he was having doubts, and Kasimir the Black never had doubts. The situation was bad, though. Not only were there twice as many rebels as he had expected, the rearguard meant that there would be no element of surprise. Even if his men could win the battle, something which was a far cry from certain, the gate might still fall. If he lost that gate to the rebels, Serpentine would have someone else wearing this armor by tomorrow.

The rest of the city's defenses must have been mounting for a counterattack by now, though there was no way to tell when they would finally arrive. If Kasimir could just keep the rebels at the gate until then, they would be finished.

According to Lech, the rebel strategy relied on a woman's Willer ability to raise the gate. If she fell, the rebels would have no way to raise the gate. They would be stuck. She would be the target.

The remaining members of the gate's garrison were taking cover from the rebel fire. They would be moving the Willer into place now. It was now or never.

He turned to face the men closest to him. "When I say go, you will follow me. While everyone is fighting, we will hit them straight down the center. There will be a woman near the gate. She must die." The guards seemed less than enthusiastic about the idea of going right into the thick of the rebel force. "Fall on rebel blade, or fall on mine. Your choice." A murmur of consent. They weren't happy, but they would follow.

He drew his sword and pointed it towards the rebels. "Attack!"

Lysander was waving his axe with dramatic motions, as if he could somehow draw the imperials out of hiding by cutting the air. What remained of the gate's garrison had taken to hiding, only popping their heads out to take pot shots at the rebels. They were still dangerous, but were at the moment unreachable.

"They're holed up in there good," Lysander said as he finally lowered his sword. "We need to get this gate open now. Bring Kindra forward. Keep her covered, I don't want one of these bastards getting a lucky shot."

Kester turned to Kindra and put a hand on her shoulder. "You ready?"

Kindra gave a quiet nod. Her eyes were confident. Kester thought finally having the task in front of her allowed her allowed her to focus and momentarily forget her worries.

"Alright, get as close to the gate as you need. We'll make sure-"

A sudden roar sounded the arrival of the imperial guard. Hundreds of them came pouring out of the surrounding buildings, a wave of gray uniforms and armor that washed over the pavement. The first of them lined up and let loose a well-coordinated volley of crossbow bolts. The rearguard was on alert, but even so, not all of them were quick enough on the defense. The bolts pierced the armor of many in the first row. Some fell silently, dead instantly, others let out a cry and staggered around.

Then the imperials were suddenly on them. They mixed with the rebel's rearguard and both sides became lost in the struggle. The lines of men rapidly dissolved into heaps of violent fury, writhing anger, and desperation.

Lysander stood with his mouth gaping open like a fish suddenly plucked from the water. His men stood by, waiting for him to give an order.

It was Lunn who finally started giving orders. "Don't just stand there gawking! You, take your squad and support the center! Lead yours to the right side, don't let them spill over! Form a line of archers! Anything gets through the melee gets shot down!"

Lunn's voice seemed to snap Lysander back into focus. He turned his attention to Kindra. "We need this gate open, now!"

Kindra was brought directly up to the gate. Shields were raised around her to protect her from crossbow fire. She raised her arms and her eyes narrowed in concentration.

"It's heavy," she said. "It might take me a few minutes to build up the right amount of force,"

Lysander looked nervously behind him. "Just do it."

Pash nudged Kester and pointed towards the center of the melee. "Trouble's coming."

It took Kester a moment to spot what Pash was referring to. A group of imperials were pushing hard near the center. The rebel line there was bulging to the point of breaking. Kester couldn't make out exactly what was happening through the chaos, but it was clear the imperials were taking heavy casualties. Yet something was driving them forward.

Kindra. They were coming for her.

Lunn saw it, too. "Get ready!"

The imperials broke through the line. A group of them came pouring through, led by a big bastard in terrifying black armor. He wielded a greatsword with a single hand and did not even bother with a shield. Even at this distance Kester could recognize Serpentine's famed champion, Kasimir the Black.

The archers let loose. Imperials hit with arrows dropped to the ground. Their comrades did not even slow, merely stepping around or running right over the fallen. The arrows did not seem to so much as scratch Kasimir's armor. The archers dropped their bows and drew their steel as the imperials set upon them. Again, the imperials did not even slow. The archers lasted moments against the imperial charge. One poor man was cut right in two by Kasimir's greatsword.

Kester drew his sword as the others around him hesitantly grabbed their weapons. Kasimir's legend was feared by all enemies of the Empire, and the man himself was even more frightening. Kester was worried the rebels might break and run any moment. He half felt like running himself.

"Protect the Willer at all costs!" Lysander yelled, his axe in hand. "Scary bastard he might be, Kasimir is just a man! Put a blade in him and he will die!"

Kester was bracing himself for the imperials when he was distracted by a scraping sound behind him. He glanced behind him to see the gate shaking. At the bottom he could see light from the other side. *The gate is rising.*

He turned back to find an imperial bearing right down on him. The guard's sword was poised to strike. Kester would have paid for his distraction, but Pash's hammer saved him. He struck the imperial under the chest with such force that he was actually lifted off the ground. Before he had a chance to thank Pash for the rescue, another imperial was on him. He raised his shield and deflected a sword blow, then pushed back against the shield to knock his foe off-balance. He cut under the imperial's shield and caught him in the gut. The imperial squealed, turned like he intended to run, then fell.

Kester looked around for another enemy and saw only chaos. Somewhere near him, Pash was grappling with a guard, the imperial's sword stuck between them. A rebel with a slashed open face bumped into him, screaming, before dropping to his knees. An imperial jumped headfirst into the fray only to stumble on a body and fall right into a waiting sword. Lysander was standing close to Kindra, waving his axe around in long sweeps to keep the imperials at bay. His back was to the gate. Kester saw movement atop the gate.

"Lysander!" he shouted, but it was too late. There was the sound of a bolt tearing through the air and suddenly Lysander was stumbling across the ground. A bolt had pierced right through his pauldrons and deep into his shoulder, near his neck. Kester made to help him when he was overshadowed by the imposing figure of Kasimir.

Kasimir was no more than a few strides from him. He swung his greatsword around as if it weighed no more than a dagger as he cut his way through one of their defenders. His sights were now set on Kester, the last remaining obstacle between him and Kindra. Kester instinctively raised his shield and braced himself for the blow.

He could have never been prepared for the amount of force which impacted his shield. One moment he was standing firm, the next his shield was crushing into his shoulder and his feet were no longer on the ground. He found himself on his back, dazed and disoriented. He looked over at his shield which had landed on the ground beside him. There was a massive gash in the steel face and the metal was bent in the center.

Kasimir was walking past him. Finishing Kester was not the priority, killing Kindra was. Kester grabbed his sword, forced himself to one knee and lunged. His sword struck Kasimir in the back, but did not even leave a scratch on his armor. Kasimir turned and, almost casually, caught Kester in his face with the back of his gauntleted hand. Kester could hear the bones in his nose crunch and his mouth was filled with the metallic taste of blood. The world spun around him, then disappeared into flashes of color.

When the world finally came back into focus, he found that he was face down in the dirt. There was something wet against his skin, underneath his armor. For a moment he thought that he had been stabbed without realizing it, but the liquid was cold. He realized the vial of elixir Reis had trusted him with must have shattered when he hit the ground. *So much for survival.*

He forced himself up on his elbows and looked towards the gate. Kindra had it lifted almost a foot off the ground now. In a few moments it would be open enough for the rebels to pass under, but she did not seem to have a few moments left. Just behind her was Kasimir, his sword raised. Lysander was on the ground nearby, clutching at the bolt that had pierced him. There was no one left to protect her.

Suddenly Pash came bursting forward, yelling at the top of his lungs and bringing his warhammer around to strike. Kasimir turned just in time to take the warhammer square in the chest. The impacted resounded like thunder. Kasimir stumbled back. Despite being hit with a force strong enough to crush in that black armor of his, somehow he remained standing.

Pash brought his hammer up and swung down at Kasimir's

head, but this time Kasimir grabbed his arm mid-strike. He slammed Pash's face with the butt of his sword. Pash's head snapped back but he refused to be moved. He threw his shoulder against Kasimir and the two of them stumbled around, each clutching at the other's weapon. Kasimir let go of the hammer and grabbed Pash by the throat. It was surreal seeing a man of Pash's size lifted off the ground by one hand.

Kester could only yell out in despair as Kasimir ran his sword straight through Pash's stomach and out his back. Pash struggled for a moment, never wanting to give up, and then went still. Kasimir removed his blade from him and then tossed his body aside like a child's doll.

Still reeling, Kester struggled to his feet. A wave of dizziness rushed over him and he felt like he might vomit. He glanced around him but couldn't figure out where his sword had landed. He stumbled forward, not sure exactly what he could do but determined to do something. He reached out for Kasimir.

Between Kasimir and Kindra, there was Lunn. The man who Kester had once called a coward was now standing stalwart against the most terrifying of Serpentine's minions. He gestured at the gate, now a few feet off the ground.

"Get everyone through the gate!" Lunn shouted. "I'll hold this bastard off!"

Kester was in no position to argue. He turned towards the rebel line to give the order to fall back through the gate, unsure how long the gate would even be open. How long could Lunn hold out against a monster like Kasimir? And how long did Kindra have to live once he fell?

If he had known this morning that he would be facing off, one-on-one, with Kasimir the Black, Lunn might have opted to stay in bed. Or at the very least had more to drink for courage. As it stood, he was far too sober.

He forced himself to inch towards Kasimir, trying to put a little distance between him and Kindra. She was the only thing keeping the gate up right now; he couldn't afford to let one of Kasimir's swings with that monstrous sword get near her. Kasimir didn't move. He just stood there with his sword at ready, perfectly still. If Lunn had not seen him tearing through the rebel lines just moments before, he might have been convinced that he was facing off against a statue.

Kasimir suddenly stepped forward and brought his sword down hard. After seeing how that sword decimated Kester's shield, Lunn knew that simply blocking it was not an option. He jumped to the side while shrugging his shield towards the sword. The sword scratched across its surface. Lunn swung his sword at Kasimir's side. It scratched off his arm-guard but failed to find a weak point. Kasimir swung again. Lunn jumped back and let the point graze against his breastplate.

He noticed Kasimir was favoring his right side and understood why he had been acting less aggressively. The barbarian's attack must have hurt him more than it originally seemed. Broken ribs, maybe. His armor was certainly crushed in enough. Lunn darted to Kasimir's left. As he expected, Kasimir struggled to keep up with him. He swung his sword only to again be repelled by Kasimir's armor. Kasimir brought his greatsword around but Lunn was easily able to step out of its way. It seemed as long as he kept to Kasimir's left side, he would be fine.

Kasimir surprised him with a powerful left hook. In hit Lunn square in the chest. His breastplate absorbed the bulk of the blow, but it still left Lunn reeling. He caught the flash of Kasimir's sword coming down on him. He brought his sword up to parry. Kasimir's sword shattered Lunn's into three different pieces. Lunn shielded his eyes, certain that one of the shards was about to fly right into his face. He felt it graze past his cheek.

Kasimir brought his sword down again. All Lunn could do was raise his shield. He heard metal clash on metal and his shield-arm snapped back with painful force, forcing him to let go. Lunn couldn't help but be brought to his knees from the impact. He was left at Kasimir's mercy, the hilt of his shattered sword clutched tightly in one hand, and in the other ...

His shield. He had let go of the handle, yet the strap had held strong and kept it attached to his arm. Kasimir was bringing his sword around for a killing blow but he was swinging from the left and was slow. Lunn rose while he gripped his shield's handle and slammed it upwards with every bit of his strength. He slammed into the bottom of Kasimir's helmet so hard that the straps of his helm snapped and the whole thing went flying off his head.

To his surprise there was no kind of devil under the helmet, just a shocked old man. Blood dribbled from his mouth where the helmet had smashed into his face. Tired, worn out eyes looked at Lunn in a mix of bewilderment and resignation. Lunn quickly jabbed the edge of his broken sword into the old man's face. He buried it up to its hilt. Kasimir brought one of his arms up and grabbed Lunn's arm. His eyes drifted to the ground, his grip went limp, and then he was still.

In spite of everything, Lunn couldn't help but respect the old man for dying on his feet.

He quickly scanned the battlefield. The melee had broken up as the rebels poured through the gate, now open to a man's height. Kester was urging the men through as the imperials were bearing down on them. They had to seal the gate quickly.

Lunn grabbed the first sword he could find on the ground, then rushed to Kindra. "Thirty seconds, then we go in and close it, whether everyone is through or not."

He saw Lysander on the ground, bleeding badly from his bolt wound. He lowered himself down, put one of Lysander's arms around him, and helped him up.

"I can't believe you killed that son-of-a-bitch," Lysander muttered. "Bet Serpentine is shitting himself right about now."

He looked back into the crowd. Not all of the rebels were through but the imperials were just behind. They could not afford to wait another moment.

"We're going through. Close it now!"

Kindra relaxed her ams and the gate began to close. He rushed through, pulling Lysander with him. Kindra got through just as the gate slammed shut.

He set Lysander carefully down. "Lysander's been hit! Whose got a field kit?"

One of Lysander's lieutenants ran up to him. "Sir!" It took Lunn a moment to realize that he was addressing him. *With Lysander down, and Brax in the sewers, I guess they look to me for leadership.*

"We stormed the stairs and took the top of the gate. The surviving imperials up there surrendered. Orders?"

Lunn frowned. He wanted nothing more but to take another swig from his flask, but that hardly seemed the *leaderly* thing to do. "Toss 'em over the gate. We don't have the men to hold prisoners. Maybe they'll survive the fall, best mercy we can do them right now."

The lieutenant snapped to his task. Lunn surveyed the situation, trying to figure out what else to do. If Lysander did not pull through, it would fall to him to lead what remained of the rebels against the palace guard. He looked back to the gate which they had sacrificed so much for.

We've taken the gate. Now how long can we hold it?

Chapter 33

Another mess of palace guards came rushing past. That was the third unit in the past five minutes. The moved with the unmistakable urgency of men on the way to battle. Reis slowly closed the door he had been peeking out of.

"Looks like Kester and the others successfully stirred up the hornet's nest," Avis said. She paused thoughtfully. "Serpent's nest?" She shook her head. "No, I'm not proud of that."

"Too many coming this way." Reis tried to imagine the palace's map in his mind to plan another way around. The map was outdated, and many of the paths it showed no longer existed or had been blocked off. To make matters worse, Serpentine had guards posted everywhere. Even with the bulk of them running upstairs to join the battle, getting around without being detected was difficult. *It's almost as if he doesn't want assassins sneaking around his palace. How rude.* "This way."

"Right behind you, boss."

They doubled back through dark halls that it seemed Serpentine had been neglecting for years. Every step brought up a new cloud of dust, and more than once Reis had to brush cobwebs off his clothes. *Once this over, no more forests, no more camping outside, no more wading through sewers and sneaking through dusty hallways. Just hot baths and long nights at the alchemy table.*

A low moan from up ahead caused Avis to perk up. "I hope that's a good sign."

"We should be getting close the hospital. My guess is an imperial is being less than stoic about his injuries."

Avis smiled knowingly. "You're thinking Serpentine's guard will be light there."

"If it exists at all. Serpentine is only concerned about himself. He has personal doctors to take care of him, and his men are of no use to him while they are recovering. He would have no reason to post a guard there."

There was another moan, a little louder than the last. Avis stifled a chuckle. "Poor guy, no idea his day is about to get even worse."

As Reis expected, the halls around the hospital were nearly empty. They found one doctor walking alone, whom Avis blindsided with the flat of her sword. They left him unconscious on the ground, confident that it would be a while before anyone stumbled on him.

They followed the hall to a large, bare hospital room, packed tight with beds. The beds were mostly empty, save for a few imperials either fast asleep or dead, and one moaning as he clutched a crossbow bolt dug into his leg. A single woman in white robes shuffled around at a table with some sharp-looking surgery tools. At the other side of the room was the passage they wanted. Reis and Avis strode quietly across the room. Reis kept one hand on his sword, ready to pounce should the doctor turn around.

"You're never going to get up that way, you know," the doctor said in old, leathery voice. "You'll be heading right up the central stairs. Very well guarded."

Reis tried to conceal his surprise as the doctor turned around to face him. She was as old a woman as he had ever seen, almost grotesquely so. Her entire face was nothing but a mass of wrinkles and loose flesh, her hair was white and sparse, her eyes had a pallid color that matched her pale skin. She looked more like a corpse than a living person.

Somehow she twisted those fleshy features into a look of annoyance. "What? You think I'm deaf and stupid? I hear the palace guard running around like chickens with their heads cut off, I know there is something going on outside. Then my assistant up and disappears. Not hard to figure out that you are on your way up here."

Avis made a grab for his sword but Reis stopped him. "You know who we are?" Reis asked.

"Rebels of some variety, I assume. Or thieves with very particular timing."

"And yet you haven't called for the guard yet."

"I don't bear any love for the empire. I'd be more inclined to help you, truth be told. I could get you upstairs."

Avis wasn't convinced. She kept her hand hovering around her sword. "Oh, how convenient, that we'd run into a sympathetic supporter down here. I suppose we should just let our guards down and let you lead us into definitely-not-an-imperial-trap."

The doctor was unconcerned about Avis's suspicions. She merely shrugged and returned to examining the tools on the table. "You don't have to take my help, I won't force it on you. But if you decide you want it, you'll have to give me just a moment to finish up with my patient."

She went to work removing the bolt from the imperial's leg. Her patient was barely conscious between the pain and the blood loss and seemed completely unaware of what was going on around him. She was remarkably efficient about her work, within a minute she had the bolt out and was closing up the wound.

Avis bounced on the heels of her feet impatiently. "We should go. Who knows how long we have."

Reis could recognize something in the old woman's eyes as she worked on the imperial. It was an expression he was familiar with. *Hatred.*

"I think we'll take your help after all."

Avis frowned but didn't argue. Not that she had any say in the matter. Reis knew a thing or two about hatred and its motivating power. Soon they would be at Serpentine's throne room to face the man himself.

He just hoped Kester and the others could hold out that long.

Lysander did not seem like he would last much longer. His face had lost most of its color and his eyes kept drifting shut for longer and longer periods. The crossbow bolt had been removed and the wound bound, but he had lost a lot of blood and the bolt had dug deep into his neck. Kester knew a dead man when he saw one.

He had to swallow a wave of guilt. What if he had warned Lysander about the trap sooner? What if he hadn't listened to Reis and trusted Lysander to keep the secret from his men? What if he had spotted the archer a few seconds sooner?

"Archers, ready!" Lunn called out. A chorus of bowstrings being strung responded. "Volley!"

The sky filled with arrows. In the distance the imperial palace guard scrambled for cover. At this distance, very few of the arrows even reached them and most went far wide, but the volley succeeded in causing chaos in the ranks. Each volley delayed the imperial counter-attack by a couple of minutes, and right now the rebels needed every second they could get.

One of the rebels watched the palace guard through a spyglass. "They're bringing out their horses."

"Might be they're getting tired of waiting for their ranks to get organized and getting ready for a cavalry charge," Lunn said with some grit. With Lysander down, Lunn had taken command of the rebels. Kester was impressed with how well he had taken to the role.

Kester tried to predict the imperial's actions the way Reis would. "They wouldn't risk expending their cavalry too early. The imperials are nothing if not patient. They will hit us with their cavalry only when their ranks are ready to take advantage of it."

"Best we stay ready, just in case." Lunn commanded the small number of men they still had to form a line. They had a few spears amongst them, but the line was utterly ill-suited to withstand a full cavalry charge. They would be relying on the archers and crossbowmen behind them to take out many of the horses.

Kester had seen, and been a part of, enough calvary charges to know exactly how things would unfold. The line would break and the rebels would be thrown into chaos, and the imperial ranks would sweep them up easily. And there was not a thing anyone could do about it.

Just have to stall. Just have to buy Reis as much time as possible.

"Kester! Lunn!" Kindra's voice.

Kindra was crouched over Lysander. Kester had wanted to hide her somewhere safe after they had passed through the gate, but she had refused and insisted on helping the rebels with their wounded. She was covered in blood and sweat. It reminded Kester of when they had first met, in the ruins of Colby.

Lysander's eyes were no longer open. Kindra shook her head sadly. *That's that, then. Lysander is dead.*

Lunn let out a loud, guttural cry. Then he brought himself quickly back into focus. "Distribute his equipment, put his body with the others. No time for sentimentality." He turned his back and returned to the line.

Kindra lingered over the body. She looked on the verge of tears. "You alright?" Kester asked.

"Pash is dead. Lysander is dead. So many others ... I've never seen so many people killed in front of me before."

For some reason, Kester felt agitated. "You volunteered to be here. This is war. People die. I don't know what you were expecting."

Kindra got up and glared at him before storming off to help someone else. Kester sighed. He didn't know why he had snapped at her. Maybe it was because this whole time he had been comparing her to Delia, and Delia would never be shaken by something like this. It wasn't that he didn't feel the losses as deeply as she did. Pash, who would have been leader of his people if he hadn't come with them. Lysander, who had dared to lead an open rebellion against Serpentine. Demos, Delia, Andreas, Darius, everyone he had ever cared about from the Church. All dead.

Kester needed to get his mind off the fallen and focus on what he could do now. He climbed the steps to the top of the gate and peered over. A seemingly endless ocean of imperials had poured into the area around them. Kester was grateful that a strong gate kept them at bay.

Atop the gate, the rebels were scavenging supplies from the imperial stockpile. They found weapons, arrows and bolts, rations, bandages, lamps and oil, and boxes filled with uniforms. There was also one box set aside from the others. It seemed the garrison here had been desperately digging for something in their last moments. Kester searched into the box and found what they had been looking for at the bottom.

Firesticks. Alchemically treated wood that would spark easily and burn fast, often used to light signal fires. The guard must have been trying to call for help. Kester carefully wrapped two of the firesticks in uniform shirts soaked in lamp oil, and secured them to his pack. *Never know when fire will come in handy in a battle.*

"All men to the lines!" he heard Lunn bellow from below.

In the distance, the palace guard had finally gotten its act together and was slowly progressing forward. Hundreds of heavily armed imperials marched in time towards the gate. Kester's hand instinctively went towards his sword, then he remembered he lost it fighting Kasimir. He was carrying an imperial blade he had scavenged. Its weight was strange compared the sword he had been used to, like it was off-balance somehow. *When you have to equip hundreds of thousands of soldiers, I guess quality is not a concern.* He still had his own shield, scratched and dented but still functional.

Kester took the steps two at a time and rejoined the rebels. He looked around for Kindra, but couldn't find her. He hoped she had gotten somewhere safe. He took a spot in the front line next to Lunn and waited for the imperials. Waited for his death.

They followed the old doctor, who still had not given them her name, up through the higher floors of the palace. They passed a few servants and guards who gave them suspicious glances, but did not stop them. Whoever the doctor was, she seemed to have fairly free roam of the place.

Most of the halls were empty or near to it. The palace guard was heavily engaged outside, and it seemed a majority of the servants had taken shelter downstairs in the small chance that the rebels were able to storm the palace. Inside the palace was ghostly quiet. Outside, the sounds of soldiers on the move resonated like a thunderstorm.

"That's the central staircase up ahead," the old woman said. "Keep your mouths shut and follow my lead."

The grand staircase was at least five men wide, with gold trim carpet and ornate railings. It was oddly lavish compared to the sparse efficiency of the rest of the palace. As the doctor had claimed, it was still well guarded. Three men stood at the base of the stairs, with two more on either side of them. At the top of the staircase, another half dozen guards were armed with crossbows, ready to shoot down anyone stupid enough to try and storm the stairs.

"I don't like this," Avis said. "They're never going to let us just walk up the stairs. This old bat is going to get us killed."

Reis was unmoved. "You have any better ideas?"

"Fleeing for our lives sounds pretty good right about now."

The doctor did not slow her pace as they approached the staircase. The guards on the staircase spotted them. It was too late to change their minds now. Reis just hoped the old woman knew what she doing.

"Hold on, where are you going?" one of the guards asked as they approached the stairs. He wore an officer's sash despite looking like he had barely reached an age to grow facial hair.

"Upstairs, where do you think?" the old woman croaked in reply.

" All right, why are you going upstairs?" the young officer asked patiently.

"I'm ill-supplied to deal with the amount of patients I will receive from the battle going on outside. I'm going upstairs to the clinic to borrow more."

"Who are these two?"

"My escorts."

"They're armed."

"There's a battle going on, if you hadn't noticed."

The officer scratched at his stubbly excuse for a beard. "I guess that's fine. You have access to the clinic. But your escorts over there will have to wait down here."

The old woman looked and spoke as if she was dealing with a child. "Do I look like I can carry heavy boxes all the way downstairs by myself? I wouldn't have brought them if I didn't need them."

The officer twitched nervously like a boy who had been caught misbehaving. "The top floor is off limits to anyone -"

"Perhaps you want to abandon your post to help me?"

"Well, no-"

"Maybe you don't care about your fellows in the palace guard, who were not so lucky as to be stationed here on the stairs on the day of the attack? Maybe you don't care if your comrades all die of infection or blood loss because I'm not equipped to help them?"

"Of course that's not true!" the boy objected. He glanced at the guards to either side of him than looked back to the doctor. "Alright, fine. Make it quick, though. I don't want to get in trouble here."

"Last thing I'd want to do is cause you trouble."

Reis had to suppress a smile as the guards stepped aside to let them pass. *You'd best hope I succeed. Who knows what kind of trouble you get in for allowing assassins past your post.*

As soon as they were up the stairs and out of sight the old woman stopped. "That hall will take you right to Serpentine's throne room. I'm afraid I won't be much use there, I'm not allowed down that way."

"Guess we'll have to just deal with whatever we find, then," Reis said. The map of the palace unfolded in his head. They were close now. Very close.

"Do try not to get yourselves killed," the doctor said. "I'm going to be in very big trouble one way or another, but I'd like to die thinking I accomplished something."

"Oh come now," Avis said. "We're just going to storm the throne of the most powerful man in the world. What could possibly go wrong?"

The rebel line had been completely destroyed by repeated cavalry charges, and any form of order had completely disintegrated. Now there was just desperate chaos, an everyone-for-themselves brawl as the rebels struggled just to survive one more moment. Kester thought he could hear Lunn shouting orders somewhere, but he couldn't make them out. He doubted anyone could, or cared to.

An imperial on Kester's right swung at him. Kester positioned himself so it would hit him where his armor was thick. When he felt the impact, he drove his sword forward through the softer metal on the guard's neck. On his left, he saw a flash of steel and just barely got his shield up in time to deflect it. He shoved his shield back hard, felt it push against the attacker he couldn't even see. The pressure released as his assailant was knocked back. In front of him, another imperial leaped over the body of Kester's last victim and came at him with his sword high. Kester swung low, taking the guard's legs out from under him, then cut across his midsection with the backswing.

He was in the middle of the chaos, surrounded by enemies on all sides. His only allies had their own concerns for survival. He had lost track of how many imperials he had cut down, how many attacks he had shrugged off, had many near misses that could have ended his life. He should have felt tired, afraid, broken. In battles in the past he'd had to struggle to keep himself together. All he felt right now was anger.

Demos had said that emotion in the middle of a battlefield could cost you your life, that survival depended on keeping a cool head in the most desperate of situations. Kester had tried to live up to his brother's example all his life. All that was tossed aside now. His rage fueled him, made him forget his pains, gave him energy, gave him focus.

Darius. A strong man, loyal, willing to give up everything in the name of the Church. Killed by the Empire. Kester used the anger to stab his sword into the face of the nearest imperial. As the body was falling limp, he kicked it towards another one of his assailants to knock him off balance.

Andreas. A man who had been a father figure to him and his brother. He'd never see him again. He smashed his shield into the face of an imperial officer. He did it again and heard a satisfying crunch.

Pash. The strongest of the Mankuri. He'd only known him for a short time, but felt like he had lost a close comrade. A guard on horseback came riding by. Kester brought his sword around and cut the beast across its side. The horse toppled suddenly over, its rider bouncing across the ground.

Delia. The High Cleric. Paragon of his faith, blessed of the

Light. The strongest, most resilient, most beautiful woman he had ever met. The woman he loved, though she had only had eyes for his brother. Who knew what terrible fate she had befallen at the hands of Serpentine's thugs? He barreled forward, his shield in front of him, pushing himself right into a mass of soldiers. He knocked an imperial to the ground and ran right over him, crushing his face beneath a heavy boot.

Demos. His brother. His friend. His mentor. His rival. The man he had spent his life trying to catch. To surpass. And the Empire had robbed him of that chance. He lashed out, left, right, forward, swinging in wide, wild arcs, his defense forgotten. Blood was flowing from him somewhere, but he felt no pain.

He heard the sounds of hoofbeats bearing down on him. He instinctively dove to the ground as a sword passed by overhead. By some miracle of the Light, he managed to avoid getting trampled. The horseman came around to make another pass at him. Kester got to his feet and darted away, managing to shrug the imperial's sword off his shield. He reached out and grabbed the imperial by the leg and, through a strength that he didn't even know he had, tore him from his saddle. His leg got caught in its stirrup and for a moment the horse dragged him along the ground. His leg twisted unnaturally and finally came free.

The confused horse finally stopped. Its eyes darted around at the chaos of the battle around it, unsure whether it should flee or wait for its rider to return. Kester wondered if the horse was properly trained to only allow specific riders. *Only one way to find out.* Kester ran up to the horse, ignoring all the danger around him, put one foot in the stirrup and climbed onto the horse's back. The horse looked back at him but didn't resist. Kester dug his heels into the horse's sides and they were moving.

On all sides of him, confused imperials darted to get out of his way. He trampled over one, swung his sword to the side and cut down another. One made a grab for him and tried to pull him from the horse. Kester urged the horse forward into a full sprint and gripped the reins tight. The imperial lost his grip and went tumbling to the ground.

And suddenly Kester was free of the chaos. The horse broke out, and Kester found that the melee was behind him. He brought the horse around and was prepared to charge right back into the fray when he realized the palace, now barely defended, was just a short ride away.

With just the faintest glimmer of a plan in mind he kicked the horse into action and bolted towards the palace.

He heard hoofbeats behind him as imperial horsemen tried to chase him down. Ahead, a line of the imperial cavalry was waiting to chase down any rebels who tried to run. Kester had to bring his horse around and found himself himself being pursued on both sides. Didn't matter, he just needed to get a little bit closer. He dashed to the right, trying to keep just outside the reach of his pursuers, then back towards the palace. He played a deadly game of cat and mouse, absolutely surrounded but determined to press forward.

A sword flashed by, missing him by just a hair. The next one didn't. It scratched him across his side, piercing his armor through the sheer force of the strike. The jolt of the impact nearly knocked him from the saddle, he had to grip the reins with all his might in order to steady himself. He felt the sharp, terrible pain and immediately knew the wound was bad. He grit his teeth and focused on his anger.

He reached for one of the firesticks. Wrapped in oil-soaked cloth, it would create a powerful flame. The palace came up in front of him. He struck the back of the firestick against his shield and it immediately burst into flames. He rode up in front of the palace as guards and curious servants scrambled to avoid getting trampled. He chucked the firestick as he passed by the entrance.

The firestick burned futilely on the ground, catching nothing. *Damn.* The imperials were all around him, he couldn't stop moving. He bolted around in a wide arc, then commanded the horse straight forward at the palace. The imperials were breathing down his neck as he brought his last firestick to his shield and sparked a flame. He got close and chucked it, not even daring to aim.

The flaming stick got caught up on one of Empire's large, proud banners. One moment it was proudly displaying Serpentine's insignia, a sword floating on a blood red ocean. Then in an instant it was in flames, bright as anything man had ever been blessed with by the Light.

Kester just had time to see the flames spreading to the palace's walls before something hard impacted against his back. Next thing he knew the ground was coming up to meet him. Then everything went dark.

One last hall. That was it. If Reis's memory of the map was correct, this hall would lead them into a large chamber, at the end of which would be Serpentine's throne room. They were close now, so close, and hopefully still undetected.

Avis bounced expectantly on her heels as she walked. The closer they got, the more excited she seemed. *Least she's not losing her nerve.*

Reis felt his senses heighten as his own nerves were tested. He heard every breath and every step. He saw every detail of the tapestries on the wall. He thought he smelled smoke, though he couldn't imagine from where. It was because of his awareness that he detected the guards ahead before they were spotted. A lot of them, based on the amount of footsteps he heard. He stopped Avis.

"When we get in there, charge straight through anything in our path," he whispered barely audibly. "There's a small staircase to the throne room on the other side. Go right up it."

Avis nodded her understanding. The pair silently slid their weapons out of their sheaths. Reis took a moment to steady himself. In tandem, the two of them stormed down the hall.

Two guards at the front of the chamber spotted them and drew their swords with an expression of utter confusion. Reis slashed up and under, cutting the guard on the left across his gut. On his right Avis feinted an upper slash. As the guard made to parry, Avis jabbed instead, piercing the imperial through his chest. They pushed through into the chamber before the bodies even touched the ground.

There were more imperials here, all drawing steel. A dozen, maybe more, Reis didn't stop to count. Reis parried a blow to his midsection and lashed out with his fist. He connected with the imperial's face and almost certainly loosened some teeth. Avis put a foot out in front of her and tripped another guard who thought it wise to charge them head on. The others were coming on them from all sides, but Reis and Avis were already at the foot of the stairs. The double doors of the throne room were right ahead.

They were halfway up the stairs when Avis turned and thrust her sword back at their pursuers. The imperials nearly tumbled over one another in an attempt to get out of the way.

"A fairly defensible position," Avis said, confident smile beaming. "Go do what what we came here for. I'll make sure we don't get stabbed in the back for the trouble."

There was no time to argue. Reis bounded the last few steps, pushed the double doors open, and burst into the throne room.

He was greeted by the sounds of arrows being nocked. All along the balconies above him were archers, just waiting for the word to loose. The doors closed shut behind him. No way to turn and open them quick enough to not take an arrow in the back. Ahead of him was the throne of his enemy, but it was empty. Instead a man stood just before him. An imperial officer he had left for dead in the Izer.

"Captain Marek, isn't it?" Reis said. The words tasted like venom.

Marek smiled a wickedly. "Reis Beldaken. It has been too long."

Chapter 34

Reis shifted between being infuriated that he was about to die to being impressed that Serpentine was able to trap him like this. He had thought that keeping the rebels in the dark would blind the Emperor from his true intentions. Marek's presence here meant Serpentine not only expected another assassin, he knew exactly who it would be.

"You've caused me quite a bit of pain, Beldaken," Marek said. His voice was triumphant, cocky. Reis hoped he could goad him into making a mistake.

"Wasn't you I was trying to pain," Reis said. He kept his voice steady and calm. He was a man with a trump card he had yet to play, or at least so he wanted to appear. "Get your coward of a boss out here and I'll show you what I mean."

"I'm afraid the Emperor is not available at the moment. Pressing matters elsewhere, you understand? He didn't want to appear rude, so he left me to entertain his guests in the Resistance."

Reis's eyes darted around the room, desperate for anything he could use to his advantage. The throne room of Marcus Serpentine was surprisingly sparse. The balconies rested on slender, unadorned pillars. Some strange symbols, a script he had never seen before, had been painted on the walls recently. There were barely any furnishings, and nothing nearby for him to duck behind.

Got to keep him talking.

"So, what's the plan, Marek? You going to arrest me, parade me down the city streets for a public execution? You going to order your men here to do the dirty work and just kill me where I stand? Or perhaps you want a rematch of our battle in the Izer, you and me, one on one?"

Marek licked his lips. The idea appealed to him, though it was likely against his orders. Reis shuffled forward, slightly and slowly, hoping his movement wouldn't be noticed. He had only one plan in mind and a very short window to do it.

Marek sighed. "As tempting as it is, the Emperor was quite specific. He considers you very dangerous. If you are willing to drop your weapon, I can make this painless. Otherwise -"

His eyes shifted just an inch towards the archers. It was all the opportunity Reis was going to get. He burst into a full sprint. His focus was on clearing the space between him and the imperial captain. Above him, a handful of archers with quicker reflexes let loose. An arrow thudded into the ground ahead of him, another soared by his ear so close he could hear it piercing the air. A searing pain in his leg signaled an arrow finding his flesh. He grit his teeth and pushed down the pain.

Marek's eyes were wide with surprise but his sword was already half-drawn. Reis grabbed his sword arm with his free hand. Marek locked Reis's elbow with his other arm, preventing Reis from being able to maneuver his sword. Reis brought Marek closer to him until they were embracing as close as lovers. He hoped the archers wouldn't risk taking a shot at him with their superior in the way.

They danced an awkward shuffle around Serpentine's throne. Marek struggled to get his sword out of its sheath while Reis tried to position himself away from the bulk of the archers. Marek's men looked on uncertainly. Reis's leg throbbed and bled, threatening to come out from under him at any moment. Marek's lips tugged at the corner of his mouth, like he was trying to suppress a smile. *Was he enjoying this?*

Marek kicked him in his injured leg. The shaft of the arrow broke off as Marek's foot pushed the arrowhead deeper. Reis let out a howl of pain and frustration as his leg buckled. Marek gave him a hard shove and Reis tumbled to the ground. His sword clattered and slid away from him. The captain's sword sang as he finally succeeded in unsheathing it. Reis spat a stream of curses as he rolled to his feet. For a split second he considered going after his sword, but it was too far out in the open. The moment there was distance between him and Marek, those archers would make short work of him. He instead kept himself right where he was, right within Marek's reach.

Marek swung at him. Reis danced out of his reach and the sword cut against the front of his shirt. Marek stepped forward and tried to get Reis with the backswing. Reis tried to get around it but the pain in his leg slowed him and the blade cut him just under his ribs. He clutched the wound with one hand while lashing out with the other. Marek was easily able to avoid the clumsy excuse for a punch. He backed off just enough for Reis to make a dive for the nearest pillar. He rolled and got behind the pillar just as arrows impacted it behind him.

"Come on!" Marek called out to him. "You're making this far

tougher on yourself than it needs to be. Be a man and come face the Emperor's justice!"

Reis struggled to clear his mind and think. The pain in his leg was excruciating and he was losing a lot of blood from the wound in his chest. He tried taking some deep breaths and wound up in a coughing fit. *Smoke again?*

"All of you are the same," Marek proclaimed as he approached. "Criminals. You know well what the inevitable consequences of your actions will bring, and yet you can't resist. Like a moth drawn to the flame, you fly to your demise." He came up to the pillar and stopped to crane his neck towards the spot where Reis was taking cover. "It's not your fault, of course. It's in your blood. It's tainted. No matter what path you may wish your life to take, you will always be a criminal. Just as the blood of justice flows through me. There was never a chance for me to be anything else, to do anything else, to be anywhere but right here at this moment. Only when I am acting as a servant of order does my blood truly flow."

Reis reached into his shirt and pulled out his vial of elixir. By some miracle, Marek's blade had missed it. He popped open the lid and greedily swallowed its contents. The elixir was slow acting, but hopefully it would at least numb his pain enough for him to fight.

The captain came around the side of the pillar, sword first. He was no longer trying to contain his smile. "It is just the way of things."

Reis slowly came around the opposite side of the pillar, back into plain view and the sight of the archers. He feinted left and then darted right as arrows flew past him. Fewer arrows than before, he noted. His eyes were watering. The smoke was getting worse. Where was it coming from?

He found where his sword had come to rest. He made a grab for it and turned, just in time to block Marek's blade. He could only barely keep up as Marek swung and jabbed with no hesitation and no mercy. Reis's wounds made him sluggish and he couldn't find a single opening in Marek's form. Marek's blade came closer and closer to finding its mark.

And then suddenly there was fire. The walls burst into flames like a great dragon had suddenly awoken. Marek couldn't help but stop and stare in awe and horror. Reis took the advantage and jabbed at Marek's sword hand. The captain silently watched as his sword dropped in front of him. He ducked away from Reis and ran. Not fast enough.

Reis was right behind him, ready to stab him through his back.

A flash of bright light and then he was suddenly gone. *A Willer?* Reis realized he was alone in the middle of the room. He looked up at the balconies but they were obscured by the thick smoke. If any of the archers were still up there he couldn't see them.

He saw the flash of the blade just out of the corner of his eye. He ducked back too slow and the sword cut across the side of his face. Marek had reappeared, sword in hand, and was coming at him hard with a flurry of rapid cuts. Reis parried what he could but he still found himself getting pressed back. He could feel the intense heat of the flames at his back. A few more steps back and he'd become charcoal. Reis brought his sword up close and the two blades locked together at their hilts.

Marek pressed his weight against him and his blade edged close to Reis's face. Reis's lungs burned, his injured leg had gone completely numb, the hair on the back of his head was getting singed by the flames. He growled and twisted his blade violently and their swords came free. As Reis expected, Marek made for another quick jab. Reis brought the strike wide with his own sword while he lashed out with his fist. His punch landed right in the captain's gut and knocked the wind out of him. Marek tried to bring his sword up for a slash. Reis punched again, this time right into his face. Marek stumbled back and spat blood.

"Very fucking clever!" Marek spat. "I am Konrad Marek, Captain of the Empire, enforcer of the law of Marcus Serpentine! The blood of justice flows through me! You will not humiliate me!"

Reis ignored his words. He ignored his pain. He ignored the heat of the fire and the stinging of the smoke. He focused hard, and felt a familiar pressure behind his eyes.

"Just fucking die already!" Marek yelled as he charged. In his rush he didn't notice that Reis had edged a few steps to the right. He also didn't spot that Reis's shadow seemed unaffected by the light of the flames around him. He ran right over the shadow that concealed a burning patch of rug. He yelled out in pain as his leg caught on fire. Then he fell silent as Reis plunged his sword through his stomach. He looked Reis in the eye, an expression more of disbelief than fear or anger, before he slid off the blade and into the fire.

Reis looked at his sword, coated in the captain's blood. *Strange. The blood of justice looks no different than mine.*

Reis made for the doors but he was all out of strength. The

room was filled with smoke and he couldn't breathe. His wounded leg refused to move and the wound in his chest burned like it was aflame. He tried to will himself a few more steps, but his body would not respond. He collapsed to one knee. He was too exhausted to even curse fate. *Is this how I die? Burned within Serpentine's palace?*

His vision went blurry. He forced himself to steady and found Avis standing over him. "Come on, boss! We got to get out of here!" Then he was being lifted by one arm and dragged from the flames of the throne room.

I guess I live one more day after all. That thought was immediately soured by the next. *As does Serpentine.*

Chapter 35

Kester was in a land where only darkness and pain existed. No wait, there were voices, too. He couldn't make out what they were saying. Yelling. He didn't care. Everything hurt. His head in particular felt it had been repeatedly bashed against a brick wall. And he was cold. So cold.

Suddenly there was brightness. The voices around him were in a panic. What was that they were shouting over and over? "Water?" The cold gave way to heat. Glorious heat, grandest of the gifts of the Light. It washed over him. Consumed him.

I've died. I've died and I'm joining Eternity. I will finally become one with the Light.

But if I'm dead, why am I still in so much pain?

He was being jolted around, first gently and then more violently. Each jolt sent his sent a fresh wave of pain wracking through his spine and up his neck. There were more voices now, different from the one before. One of them sounded familiar. Female. *Delia?*

Then he returned to the silence.

When he finally awoke, the tall buildings of Marjan had been replaced with tall, ancient trees, and the sun had gone down from the sky. A cool wind blew against his face and brought his senses back to him. He could hear the sounds of boots rustling through overgrowth and people talking in hushed tones.

He recognized one voice. Lunn. "We'll wait one more hour."

Another voice, one he didn't know, responded. "Sir, I don't think anyone else got out of there. If they did, they would have met us here already. The longer we wait, the greater the chance the imperials discovering us."

"One more hour." The tone of Lunn's voice made it clear this was not a matter that was open for discussion.

Kester struggled to pick himself up onto his elbows. A gentle but strong hand grabbed him and helped him sit up.

"Kester, thank the Light," Kindra said. "You haven't moved in hours. You had me worried."

He focused and Kindra's face became clear. She was scratched up and one of her eyes was purple and swollen. "What happened?" he asked, his voice coming out as little more than a murmur.

"You saved our asses is what happened," Lunn said. He bent over and put a hand on Kester's shoulder. "You are a crazy bastard.". I don't know what was going through your mind when you decided to charge the palace by yourself. But you pulled it off. After the palace was in flames, the imperials all scattered like ants. Too bad you weren't conscious for it, but it was quite a sight, the palace burning on one end and a score of panicking imperials on the other. We were able to get away in the confusion. After we rescued our hero from the flames, of course."

The Light shielded me. "And Serpentine? Was he ..."

"He got away." The curt voice of Reis. With some effort Kester glanced over. Reis looked like he had been through hell. His face and arms were burned, his hair was singed, he had a nasty cut running down one cheek, and he was sporting bandages across his chest and leg that were bled through. "Afraid this was all for nothing."

"Ever the optimist, boss," Avis said. She stood close to Reis looking somewhat ruffled, but otherwise no worse for wear.

"I'd like to hear a positive spin on it," Reis snapped. He waved his arms around at the poor showing of the survivors of The Resistance. Less than two dozen men. "The rebels are nearly all dead, we got beaten half to death ourselves, and worse of all, Serpentine got away. And he knows we came for him. We'll never be able to catch him with his guard down now."

Avis shrugged and looked away. Kester looked down at himself. He had burns all over his hands, arms, and legs. His head was ringing. He must have hurt it when he fell from the horse. *All of this for nothing.*

"I'll tell you what the bright side is," Lunn said. He pointed off in the far distance where even by moonlight a pillar of smoke was clear. "That. With a few men and a lot of balls we stormed the Empire's capital and put Serpentine's palace to the torch. Our casualties might have been heavy, and the man himself might have gotten away, but I'm still counting this as a victory. Everyone will hear about this and realize that the Empire is not all-powerful. That when men with courage stand against Serpentine, he can be beaten. The sacrifices our men made today will not be in vain when our numbers are replenished ten-fold. Serpentine will have a new war on his hands."

Reis scoffed. "Well, you can have your war. I'm no damn soldier."

"Coward," Kester said, surprising even himself. It took him a moment to even realize it was him who said it.

Reis glared at him. "What did you call me?"

Kester chuckled. It hurt his chest to do so, but he just couldn't help it. "Serpentine beats you once and you're ready to give up. Are you really the same Reis Beldaken who terrorized the Church for years? I would have thought your commitment to revenge to be greater."

"I'm not about to fight a damn war."

"Who said you had to? The Resistance has their tactic, but we've always had only one goal. To kill Marcus Serpentine. A man of his arrogance can't possibly protect himself at all times. He'll get careless. And that's when we'll strike. It may take some patience, but the opportunity will come." Kester didn't have to feign confidence. He knew it was true. "And next time, he won't get away."

Reis thought about it for a few moments. With the calm of his expression, he could have been contemplating a grocery list. "I suppose if I ever want any peace in my research, I will need to make sure the Empire is no longer after me. Only one way to guarantee that."

Kester smiled. "Only one way."

Avis sighed. "I believe my contract was fairly specific in regards to 'killing Serpentine.' As long as he's alive, it seems I am still bound to you."

"If you get bored playing assassin, you could always sign up with us, Alvis," Lunn said. "We could use a man like you."

"There are no men like me." Avis smiled at Lunn's confusion.

Kindra was changing the bandages on Reis's leg. She looked over at Kester. Their eyes met.

"I'm worried about your injuries," she said. "I think I should stick around, until you are both back in fighting form."

Reis winced when the new bandages were applied. "Might be a bit longer than that. The imperials knew about you. It's possible they know what you look like. Might just have to stick with us for a while."

"For you safety," Kester added.

Kindra smirked. "Is that the only reason?"

"Also, never hurts to have a looker around," Avis said. " Especially one that can lift two thousand pounds with her mind."

Kindra leaned over to Avis and gave her a kiss on the cheek.

"At least someone around here is honest." Avis beamed.

They all enjoyed a good laugh. It was strange to be laughing now, after all that had happened. But it felt good nonetheless.

Kester looked up at the moon, wondering what more he would have to endure before this was all over. Knowing Reis, only some of it would be at the hands of the Empire.

"We can get through this, can't we?" he asked. "You and me, Reis? We can get through this without killing each other?"

Reis shrugged. "Probably. Just don't ever cross me."

"Don't ever make me."

"We'll see."

There was nothing left to say. The four of them sat together amongst the remains on The Resistance, watching the rising smoke of the Marjan palace.

Epilogue

Lech moved quietly through the shadows of the laboratory. He passed by all manner of strange instruments he couldn't even begin to guess the purposes of. Vials filled with fluid of all colors of the rainbow, some black charcoal-like substance that was giving off smoke in a rectangular bowl, strips of thin red paper that looked melted at one end, as well as a wide variety of sharp objects that looked more like the tools of a torturer than the instruments of a scientist.

This time I'll do it. This time I'll sneak up on the bastard.

"What do you want, Lech?"

Damn.

Seated in his usual spot overlooking the laboratory proper, Gerad was looking right at him. He was a short man, but even in the poor lighting of the lab, no one would mistake him as being anything less than dangerous. It looked as if someone had sculpted him out of pure muscle, and his face was more scars than not. His eyes were narrow and strikingly green, like a cat's eyes.

Lech held up his hands and walked out of the shadows. It seems he would not be getting the best of the watchman this time, either.

"One of these days, Gerad, I am going to find a way of getting past those eyes of yours."

Gerad shook his head. "Must we play this game every time you visit?"

"I believe we must."

Gerad grunted his annoyance. Lech wondered if there was ever a time in Gerad's life when he wasn't annoyed.

"What do you want, Lech?"

Lech removed a scroll from his robes and presented it to the watchman. "From the emperor himself, for your boss."

Gerad examined the scroll but did not open it. "The Emperor really doesn't trust birds, does he?"

"Not for matters of this import."

The watchman sighed. "The boss is not going to be happy to be interrupted again."

He rose from his seat and leaned over the railing. Downstairs, the doctor was working on his latest subject, a young man. The man was sobbing, but the gag over his mouth blocked out most of the noise. Strapped to the board as he was, all he could do was watch with fearful eyes as the doctor poked and prodded him with his instruments.

"Hey doc!" Gerad called out. "You got a message!"

Doctor Ludwig turned away from his work and looked up towards his watchman. As usual, his thick spectacles leaned forward on his nose as if they threatened to fall off. His graying brown hair was in disarray and his white coat was stained with blood and some other unidentifiable fluid. He always seemed to be a bit more plump each time Lech saw him; right now he straddled the line between tubby and fat.

Ludwig adjusted his spectacles. "Ah, Mr. Lechin. Yes, I will be right there."

He waddled his way up the stairs. When he reached Lech he was noticeably out of breath.

"Doctor, it is good to see you again." He glanced over the railing to the poor test subject, momentarily given a breather from Ludwig's experiments. "How goes the research?"

"Good!" Ludwig responded with enthusiasm. "Great, even! With all the test subjects the emperor has given me, I am able to make great strides!" His spectacles slipped down his nose again and he adjusted them. "Tell me, Mr. Lechin, should I be concerned that the emperor chooses to communicate with me through an assassin? Is he sending me a message? Because if he is, I would like you to assure him I am moving with all haste."

It was hard to imagine the plump little man moving with haste.

"Who knows why the emperor does what he does. I only met the man in person for the first time a short while ago. He's still a mystery to me. I just do what he says. Seems to be the smart thing."

"Brilliant advice," the doctor replied.

Gerad handed the doctor the scroll. Ludwig broke the seal and unraveled it. He frowned as soon as his eyes hit the paper.

"He's always so wordy. Don't suppose you could summarize it for me, so I could get back to work?"

Lech shrugged. "Long story short, we need the stuff to produce a new Kasimir."

Ludwig's eyes went wide. "Really? He executed the old man? I really liked him."

"Fell in battle, actually."

Ludwig let out something close to a gasp. He ran a hand through his graying hair. "That's never happened before, has it?"

"Nope."

"I assure you, this one was just as good -"

Lech cut him off before he started babbling. "No one's blaming you, doctor. His helmet came off and he got stabbed in the face. These things happen."

"Oh." He looked at the ground. "Such a shame." He looked up with a sudden realization. "Wait, were there witnesses? Cause if there were, how are you going to explain -"

Once again, Lech cut him off. "Don't worry about it. We already have the rumor mill working. Fortunately, the old man had the good sense to die on his feet. Only those standing close to him could have known he was dead, and they are being paid very well to forget it. Anyone else would have seen him still standing. Any rumors of his death are going to be shot down as rebel lies."

Ludwig nodded. "Yes, of course. Brilliant." He fumbled in his pockets for something. "Guess we should just get this over with, so I can get back to work." He pulled out a small key. He hurried over to a small box not far from where they were standing and used to key to unlock it. When he opened it, a wave of cool air blew out. He removed a flask filled with a purple liquid.

"Remember, this must be kept cold, after one day at normal temperature it loses its effect," Ludwig reminded him.

"I know, doctor. Don't worry, I have an ice box outside ready."

Lech took the flask and, after making sure the seal was properly secured, stored it in one of his pockets.

"Will that be all, Mr. Lechin?"

Lech smiled. "For now, doctor. You best get back to work. Next time I could be coming as an emissary, or as an assassin."

The doctor's face went white. Lech doubted the doctor's life was in any danger, but it was fun to mess with him.

Ludwig hurried back downstairs to resume his work. The boy strapped to the board moaned weakly upon his return. Lech watched curiously for a moment.

He wondered what all this research on Willers was leading up to. What was the emperor's end goal?

None of my concern. I just need to keep doing as I am told.

That was what would lead him closer to Serpentine. That was

what would gain him Serpentine's trust. And once he had it, that was what would give him the opportunity to stick a dagger in him.

Lech was nothing if not patient.

He turned and strode out of the laboratory, smiling about the prospects of a new day.

45436958R00181

Made in the USA
Lexington, KY
27 September 2015